KT-466-684

Award-winning author **Robin Perini**'s love of heart-stopping suspense and poignant romance, coupled with her adoration of high-tech weaponry and covert ops, encouraged her secret inner commando to take on the challenge of writing romantic suspense novels. Her mission's motto: "When danger and romance collide, no heart is safe."

Devoted to giving her readers fast-paced, high-stakes adventures with a love story sure to melt their hearts, Robin won a prestigious Romance Writers of America Golden Heart Award in 2011. Robin loves to interact with readers. You can catch her on her website, www.robinperini.com, and on several major social-networking sites, or write to her at PO Box 50472, Albuquerque, NM 87181-0472.

Though born in Chicago and raised in L.A., *USA TODAY* bestselling author **Cassie Miles** has lived in Colorado long enough to be considered a semi-native. The first home she owned was a log cabin in the mountains overlooking Elk Creek, with a thirty-mile commute to her work at the *Denver Post*.

After raising two daughters and cooking tons of macaroni and cheese for her family, Cassie is trying to be more adventurous in her culinary efforts. Ceviche, anyone? She's discovered that almost anything tastes better with wine. When she's not plotting Mills & Boon Heroes books, Cassie likes to hang out at the Denver Botanical Gardens near her high-rise home.

A Golden Heart Award winner for Best Paranormal Romance in 2004, **Elle James** started writing when her sister issued a Y2K challenge to write a romance novel. She has managed a full-time job and raised three wonderful children, and she and her husband even tried their hands at ranching exotic birds (ostriches, emus and rheas) in the Texas Hill Country. After leaving her successful career in information technology management, Elle is now pursuing her writing full-time. Elle loves ... nes@ earth

3011780342690 3

Her Christmas Hero

ROBIN PERINI
CASSIE MILES
ELLE JAMES

MILLS & BOON

First Published in Great Britain 2018
by Mills & Boon, an imprint of HarperCollins*Publishers*
1 London Bridge Street, London, SE1 9GF

HER CHRISTMAS HERO © 2018 Harlequin Books S. A.

Christmas Justice © 2014 Robin L. Perini
Snow Blind © 2014 Kay Bergstrom
Christmas At Thunder Horse Ranch © 2014 Mary Jernigan

ISBN: 978-0-263-27467-7

1218

CHRISTMAS JUSTICE

ROBIN PERINI

With love to my aunts, Gayle, Earlene, Sissy (Lynn) and Barbara. I'm blessed to know you are always there. No matter what.

Prologue

Today was no ordinary day.

Normally Laurel McCallister would have adored spending an evening with her niece Molly, playing princesses, throwing jacks and just being a kid again, but tonight was anything but typical. Laurel let the wind-driven ice bite into her cheeks. She stood just inside the warm entry of her sister's Virginia home, staring out into the weather to see the family off to the local Christmas pageant. Her fist clutched the charm bracelet Ivy had forced into Laurel's hand.

A gift from their missing father.

He'd been incommunicado for over two months. Then suddenly the silver jewelry had arrived in Ivy's mailbox earlier that day. No note, only her father's shaky handwriting on the address label, and postmarked Washington, D.C. Laurel squeezed the chain, quelling the shiver of foreboding that hadn't left her since Ivy had shown her the package. Her sister had told her they needed to talk about it. Tonight. The news couldn't be good, but it would have to wait.

Bracing against the cold, she met her sister's solemn gaze, then picked up her five-year-old niece. Laurel snuggled Molly closer. At the end of a bout of strep throat, the girl had insisted on waving goodbye to her mother. Ivy returned the farewell wave from across the driveway, apprehension evident in her eyes. And not typical mom-concern-for-her-youngest-daughter's-health worry.

Laurel scanned the rural setting surrounding Ivy's house. With the nearest neighbors out of shouting distance, it should be quiet. And safe. Laurel might only be a CIA analyst, but she'd completed the same training as a field operative. She knew what to look for.

Nothing seemed off, and yet, she couldn't stop the tension knotting every muscle, settling low in her belly. For now, her sister and brother-in-law refused to let the trepidation destroy Christmas for the kids, but Laurel had recognized the strain in her sister's eyes, the worry on her brother-in-law's brow. Too many bad vibes filtered beneath the surface of every look her sister had given her.

Laurel touched the silky blond hair of her youngest niece.

Molly stared after her mother, father, brother and sister, her baby blues filled with tears. "It's not fair. I want to go to the pageant. I'm supposed to be an angel."

The forlorn voice hung on Laurel's heart. She placed her hand on the little girl's hot forehead. "Sorry, Molly Magoo. Not with that fever."

Ivy bundled Molly's older brother and sister into the backseat of the car. Laurel sent her sister a confident nod, even though her stomach still twisted. She recognized the same lie in her sister's eyes. They were so alike.

One of the kids—it must have been Michaela—tossed a stuffed giraffe through the open car door. Ivy shook her head and walked a few paces away to pick up the wayward animal.

Laurel started to close the door. "Don't worry, Molly. They'll be back s—"

A loud explosion rocketed the night, and a blast of hot air buffeted Laurel. She staggered back. The driver's side of the SUV erupted into flames. Fire and smoke engulfed the car in a hellish conflagration. Angry black plumes erupted into the sky.

God, no! Laurel's knees trembled; she shook her head. This couldn't be happening. Horror squeezed her throat. She wrenched Molly toward her, turning the little girl away from the sight, but Laurel couldn't protect Molly. Her niece had seen too much. Molly's earsplitting screams ripped the air.

No sounds came from the car. Not a shout, not a yell.

Laurel had to do *something*.

"Stay here!" She scrambled through the door, racing across the frozen yard. She glanced back; Molly had fallen to the floor in tears. Laurel squeezed her eyes shut against the heart-wrenching cries, then snagged her phone from her pocket and dialed 9-1-1. "Help! There's been an explosion."

Blazing heat seared Laurel's skin. It wasn't a typical car fire. It burned too hot, too fast. Laurel choked back the truth. This wasn't just any bomb. This was a professional hit. A hit like she'd read about in dossiers as part of her job with the CIA.

Unable to look away, she stared in horror at the interior of the car. In a few minutes, nothing would be left. Just ash. They wouldn't even be able to tell how many people had been in the car.

The phone slipped from her fingers.

Ivy's family was gone. No one could have survived. Frantically, Laurel searched for her sister. Her heart shattered when she saw the smoking body lying several feet away from the car. She ran to Ivy and knelt next to her sister's body, the right side blackened and burned beyond recognition, the left blistered and smoldering.

"Laur—" the raspy voice croaked.

"Don't talk, Ivy." Laurel couldn't stop her tears. She could hear her niece's wails from inside the house, but Ivy. God. Her clothes had melted into her skin.

Ivy shifted, then cried out in agony. "Stupid," she rasped. "Not c-c-careful enough. Can't…trust…"

"Shh…" Laurel had no idea how to help. She reached out a hand, but there wasn't a spot on Ivy not burned. She was afraid to touch her sister. Where was the ambulance?

Ivy coughed and Laurel bent down. "Don't give up. Help is coming."

"Too late. F-find Garrett Galloway. Sheriff. Tell him… he was right." Ivy blinked her one good eye and glanced at the fire-consumed vehicle. A lone tear pooled. "Please. Save. Molly." The single tear cut through the soot, and then her eyes widened. "Gun!"

Laurel's training took over. She plastered herself flat to the ground. A shot hit the tree behind her. With a quick roll, she cursed. Her weapon was locked up in the gun safe inside the house. A loud thwack hit the ground inches from her ear. The assault had come from the hedges.

"Traitor!" Ivy's raspy voice shouted a weak curse.

Another shot rang out.

The bullet struck true, hitting Ivy right in the temple.

Horrified, Laurel scampered a few feet, using the fire as a shield between her and the gunman. She panted, ignoring the pain ripping through her heart. She would grieve later. She had one job: protect Molly.

Sirens roared through the night sky. A curse rang out followed by at least two sets of footsteps, the sound diminishing.

Thank God they'd run. Laurel had one chance. She flung open the door and grabbed a sobbing Molly in her arms. She hugged her tight, then kicked the door closed.

Through the break in the curtains, she watched. A squad car tore into the driveway. No way. That cop had gotten here way too fast. Laurel pressed Molly against her, then locked the dead bolt.

She sagged against the wall. "Oh, Ivy."

"Aunt Laurel?" Molly's small voice choked through her sobs. "I want Mommy and Daddy."

"Me, too, pumpkin."

Laurel squeezed her niece tighter. She had two choices: trust the cop outside or follow her sister's advice.

After the past two months… She slipped the bracelet from her father into her pocket, then snagged a photo from the wall. Her sister and family, all smiles. She had no choice. The high-tech bomb, the cop's quick arrival. It smelled of setup.

Laurel raced through the house and grabbed Molly's antibiotics and the weapon from the gun safe, half expecting the cop to bang on the door. When he didn't, Laurel knew she was right. She peeked through the curtains. Her sister's body was gone. And so was the police car.

The flames sparked higher and Laurel nearly doubled over in pain.

The sound of a fire engine penetrated the house. No time left. She snagged the envelope her father had sent and stuffed it into a canvas bag along with a blanket and Molly's favorite stuffed lion.

She bundled Molly into her coat, lifted her niece into her arms and ran out the back door. Laurel's feet slapped on the pavement. She sprinted down an alley. Shouts rained down on her. Smoke and fire painted the night sky in a vision of horror. One she would never forget.

She paused, catching her breath, the cold seeping through her jacket.

"Aunt Laurel? Stop. Mommy won't know where to find us." Molly's fingers dug into Laurel's neck.

Oh, God. Poor Molly. Laurel hugged her niece closer. How could she explain to a five-year-old about bad people who killed families?

Laurel leaned against the concrete wall, her lungs burning with effort. She wished *she* didn't understand. She wished she could be like Molly. But this wasn't a child's cartoon where everyone survived even the most horrendous attacks. Reality meant no one had a second chance.

Laurel had to get away from the men who had shot at her, who had killed her sister and her family.

But Laurel didn't know what to believe. Except her sister's final words.

Which left her with one option. One man to trust.

Garrett Galloway.

Now all she had to do was find him.

Chapter One

Normally Trouble, Texas, wasn't much trouble, and that was the way Sheriff Garrett Galloway liked it. No problems to speak of, save the town drunk, a few rambunctious kids and a mayor who drove too nice a car with no obvious supplemental income.

Garrett adjusted his Stetson and shoved his hands into the pockets of his bomber jacket to ward off the December chill. He'd hidden out in Trouble too long. When he'd arrived a year ago, body broken and soul bleeding, he'd trusted that the tiny West Texas town would be the perfect place to get lost and stay lost for a few months. After all, the world thought he was dead. And Garrett needed it to stay that way.

Just until he could identify who had destroyed everyone he loved and make them pay. He'd *never* imagined he'd stay this long.

But the latest status call he'd counted on hadn't occurred. Not to mention his last conversation with his mentor and ex-partner, James McCallister, had been much too…optimistic. That, combined with a missed contact, usually meant the operation had gone to hell.

Garrett's right shoulder blade hiked, settling under the feel of his holster. He never left home without his weapon or his badge. He liked to know he had a gun within reach. Always. The townsfolk liked to know their sheriff walked the streets.

He eyed the garland- and tinsel-laden but otherwise empty Main Street and stepped onto the pavement, his boots silent, no sound echoing, no warning to anyone that he might be making his nightly nine o'clock rounds.

James McCallister's disappearance had thrown Garrett. His mentor had spent the past few months using every connection he'd made over his nearly thirty-year career, trying to ferret out the traitor.

Big risks, but after a year of nothing, a few intel tidbits had fallen their way: some compromised top secret documents identifying overseas operatives and operations, some missing state-of-the-art weapons. The door had cracked open, but not enough to step through.

Garrett didn't like the radio silence. Either James was breaking open the case or he was dead. Neither option boded well. If it was the first, Garrett contacting him would blow the whole mission; if the second, Garrett was on his own and would have to come back from the dead.

Or he could end up in federal prison, where his life wouldn't be worth a spare .22 bullet.

With his no-win options circling his mind, Garrett strode past another block. After a few more houses, he spied an unfamiliar dark car slowly making its way down the street.

No one drove that slowly. Not in Texas. Not unless they were up to no good. And no one visited Trouble without good reason. It wasn't a town folks passed through by chance.

His instincts firing warning signals, Garrett turned the corner and disappeared behind a hedge.

The car slowed, then drove past. Interesting.

Could be a relative from out of town, but Garrett didn't like changes. Or the unexpected. He headed across a dead-end street, his entire body poised and tense, watching for the car. He reached the edge of town and peered through the deserted night.

Nearby, he heard a small crack, as if a piece of wood snapped.

No one should be out this way, not at this time of night. Could be a coyote—human, not the animal variety. Garrett hadn't made friends with either one during the past year.

He slid his Beretta 92 from his shoulder holster and gripped the butt of the gun. Making a show of a cowboy searching the stars, he gazed up at the black expanse of the night sky and pushed his Stetson back.

Out of the corner of his eye, he caught sight of a cloaked figure ducking behind a fence: average height, slight, but the movements careful, strategic, trained. Someone he might have faced in his previous life. Definitely. Not your average coyote or even criminal up to no good. James McCallister was the only person who knew Garrett was in Trouble, and James was AWOL.

The night went still.

Garrett kicked the dirt and dusted off his hat.

His muscles twitchy, he kept his gun at the ready, not wanting to use it. This could be unrelated to his past, but he needed information, not a dead body on the outskirts of his town. What happened in Trouble stayed in Trouble, unless the body count started climbing. Then he wouldn't be able to keep the state or the feds out.

He didn't need the attention.

He could feel someone watching him, studying him.

He veered off his route, heading slightly toward the hidden figure. His plan? Saunter past the guy hiding in the shadows and then take him out.

He hit his mark and, with a quick turn on his heel, shifted, launching himself into a tackle. A few quick moves and Garrett pushed the guy to the ground, slid the SIG P229 out of reach and forced his forearm against the vulnerable section of throat.

"What do you want?" he growled, shoving aside his pinned assailant's hood.

The grunts coming from his victim weren't what he'd expected. With years of experience subduing the worst human element, he wrestled free his flashlight and clicked it on.

Blue eyes full of fear peered up at him. A woman. He pressed harder. A woman could kill just as dead. Could play the victim, all the while coldheartedly planning his demise. He wasn't about to let go.

The light hit her face. He blinked back his surprise. He knew those eyes. Knew that nose.

Oh, hell.

"Laurel McCallister," he said. His gut sank. Only one thing would bring her to Trouble.

His past had found him. And that meant one thing. James McCallister was six feet under, and the men who wanted Garrett dead wouldn't be far behind.

THE PAVEMENT DUG into Laurel's back, but she didn't move, not with two hundred pounds holding her down. He'd taken her SIG too easily, and the man lying on top of her knew how to kill. The pressure against her throat proved it.

Worse than that, the sheriff—badge and all—knew her name. So much for using surprise as an advantage.

She lay still and silent, her body jarred from his attack. She could feel every inch of skin and muscle that had struck the ground. She'd be bruised later.

Laurel had thought watching him for a while would be a good idea. Maybe not so much. Ivy might have told her to trust Garrett Galloway, Sheriff of Trouble, Texas, but Laurel had to be cautious.

The car door opened and the thud of tiny feet pounded to them. "Let her go!" Molly pummeled Garrett's back, her raised voice screeching through the night in that high-pitched kid squeal that raked across Laurel's nerves.

He winced and turned to the girl.

Now!

Laurel kicked out, her foot coming in contact with his shin. He grunted, but didn't budge. She squirmed underneath the heavy body and pushed at his shoulders.

"Molly, get back!"

The little girl hesitated, sending a shiver of fear through Laurel. Why couldn't her niece have stayed asleep in the car, buckled into her car seat? Ever since that horrific night four days ago, she couldn't handle Laurel being out of sight, knew instinctively when she wasn't near.

Suddenly, Garrett rolled off her body, slipped her gun into his hand and rose to his feet with cougarlike grace. "Don't worry. I'm not going to hurt either of you." He tucked her weapon into his pants and stared her down.

She sucked in a wary breath before her five-year-old niece dived into her arms. "Are you okay, Aunt Laurel?"

She wound her arms around her niece and stared up at Garrett, body tense. "You're my hero, Molly." She forced her voice to remain calm. At least the little girl hadn't lost the fire in her belly. It was the first spark Laurel had seen from her since the explosion.

Molly clutched at Laurel but glared at Garrett.

He struggled to keep a straight face and a kindness laced his eyes as he looked at Molly.

For the first time in days, the muscles at the base of Laurel's neck relaxed. Maybe she'd made the right decision after all.

Not that she'd had a choice. There'd been nothing on the national news about her family. No mention of gunfire or Ivy being killed by a bullet to the head. There had been a small piece about an SUV burning, but they'd blamed a downed power line. That was the second Laurel had known she was truly on her own.

Until now.

She hated counting on anyone but herself. She and her sister had been schooled in that lesson after their mother had died. With their father gone, Ivy and Laurel had been pretty much in charge of each other.

But Laurel was out of her league. She knew it. She didn't have to like it.

She held Molly closer and studied Garrett Galloway. Something about him invited trust, but could she trust her instincts? Would this man whose expression displayed an intent to kill one moment and compassion the next help her? She prayed her sister had been right, that he was one of the good guys.

Garrett tilted back his Stetson. "I could have…" He glanced at Molly, his meaning clear.

Laurel got it. She and Molly would be dead…if he'd wanted them dead.

"…already finished the job," he said harshly. "I'm not going to."

"How did you know my name?"

He raised a brow and slipped his Beretta into the shoulder holster and returned her weapon. "I know your father. Your picture is on his desk at…work."

His expression spoke volumes. She got it. Garrett had worked with her father in an OGA. While the CIA had a name and a reputation, her father's Other Government Agency had none. Classified funding, classified missions, classified results. And the same agency where Ivy had worked. Alarm bells rang in Laurel's head. Her sister had sent Laurel to a man working with the same people who might be behind the bomb blast. And yet, who better to help?

Garrett held out his hand to her. "You look like you've been on the road awhile," he said. "How about something to eat? Then we can talk."

Laurel hesitated, but what was she supposed to do? She'd come to this small West Texas town for one reason, and one reason only. To find Garrett Galloway.

She didn't know what she'd expected. He could have stepped off the set of a hit television show in his khaki shirt, badge, dark brown hat and leather jacket. Piercing brown eyes that saw right through her.

If she'd imagined wanting to ride off into the sunset with someone, it would be Garrett Galloway. But now that she'd found him, what *was* she going to do with him?

He didn't pull back his hand. He waited. He knew. With a sigh, she placed her hand in his. He pulled her to her feet. Molly scrambled up and hid behind Laurel, peering up at Garrett.

He cocked his head at the little girl. Laurel sucked in

a slow breath. Molly's face held that fearful expression that hadn't left her since they'd run from Virginia, as if any second she might cry. But then her eyes widened. She stared at Garrett, so tall and strong in his dark pants and cowboy boots, a star on his chest.

He was a protector. Laurel could tell and so, evidently, could Molly.

Garrett met her gaze and she recognized the understanding on his face. "Come with me," he said quietly.

"I have my car—"

He shook his head. "Grab your things and leave it. If anyone followed, I don't want them to know who you came to see."

"I was careful. I spent an entire extra day to get here due to all the detours."

"If you'd recognized you had a tail, you'd already be dead." His flat words spoke the truth of the danger they were in. He walked over to the vehicle and pulled out the large tote she used as a suitcase, slinging it on his shoulder opposite his gun hand. All their belongings were in the bag. "Until I'm certain, we act like you have one."

Laurel stiffened. In normal circumstances she could take care of herself and Molly. As if sensing her vulnerability, Garrett stepped closer.

"*You* came to *me*," Garrett said. "You may have blown my cover. You need to listen."

He was on assignment. She should have known.

She prided herself on her self-reliance, her ability to handle most any situation, but his expression had gone intense and wary, and that worried her. Ivy had been a skilled operative. She had always been careful, and she was dead. Laurel had to face reality. She'd jumped into the deep end of the pool her first day on the run and Garrett Galloway was the lifeguard.

She swallowed away the distaste of having to rely on him, nodded and lifted Molly into her arms. "How far?"

"Across town," he said, his gaze scanning the perimeter yet again.

"A few blocks, then?" Laurel said with an arch of her brow.

Garrett cocked his head and one side of his mouth tilted in a small smile. His eyes lightened when he didn't frown.

"Let's go."

One block under their feet had Laurel's entire body pulsing with nerves. She'd never seen anyone with the deadly focus that Garrett possessed. He walked silently, even in boots, and seemed aware of each shadow and movement.

Suddenly he stopped. He shoved her and Molly back against the fence, pulling his gun out. Then she heard it. The purr of an engine. It grew louder, then softer. He relaxed and tilted his head, looking from Laurel to Molly. "Let's move."

Molly gazed up at him, her eyes wide. She looked ready to cry. He tilted the Stetson on his head. "You ready for something to eat, sugar?" He gifted her with a confident smile.

Just his strong presence soothed Molly. For Laurel, his nearness had the opposite effect. She wanted to pull away, because the draw she felt—the odd urge to let herself move into his arms—well, that was something she hadn't felt before. She'd never allowed herself to be this vulnerable. Not ever.

He could snap her neck or take her life, but he might

also do worse. This man could take over and she might lose herself.

A dog's howl broke through the night, followed by more barking. As Garrett led them through the town in silence, Molly clung to Laurel. Her eyes grew heavy and her body lax. The poor thing was exhausted, just like her aunt.

Garrett matched his steps with hers. "Whatever brought you here, it was bad, wasn't it?" He bent toward Laurel, his breath near her ear, the words soft.

She couldn't stop the burning well of tears behind her eyes. She had no reserves left. She wanted nothing more than to lean closer and have him put his arm around her. She couldn't. She recognized her weakness. Her emotions hovered just beneath the surface, and she'd be damned if she'd let them show.

In self-preservation, she tilted her head forward, expecting her long hair to curtain her face, to hide her feelings, but nothing happened. She ran a hand through the chopped locks. Gone was her unique titian hair, and in its place, she'd dyed it a nondescript brown that stopped at her chin. She had to blend in.

"I understand," he said, his voice gruff. "Better than you know."

Before Laurel could ponder his statement, he picked up the pace. "My house is ten minutes away. Across Main and around a corner two blocks."

With each step they took, the blinking lights and garlands, then the tinsel, came into full effect. He paused and shifted them behind a tree, studying the street.

Molly peered around him, her small mouth forming a stunned O. "Aunt Laurel, lookie. It's Christmas here." The little girl swallowed and bowed her head until it rested on Laurel's shoulder. "Our Christmas is far away."

Laurel patted her niece's back. "Christmas will follow us, Molly Magoo. It might be different this year, but it will still happen."

Molly looked at her, then at the decorations lining the town, her gaze hopeful. "Will Mommy and Daddy come back by then?"

"We'll talk about it later," Laurel whispered. She didn't know what to say. Even though Molly had seen the explosion, she still hadn't processed the reality that her mother, father, brother and sister were never coming back.

She gritted her teeth. As a grown woman, she didn't know how long it would take her to accept her family's death. That she was alone in the world. Except for Molly.

"We need to move fast." Garrett held out his arm. Main Street through Trouble wasn't much. Two lanes, a single stoplight. "Go." They were halfway to the other side when an engine roared to life. Tires squealed; the vehicle thundered directly at them.

Garrett pushed them behind a cinder-block wall, dumped the tote, then rolled to the ground, leaving himself vulnerable.

A spray of gunfire ratcheted above Laurel's head as she hit the ground. Molly cried out. Laurel covered the little girl's trembling body and pulled her weapon. She lifted her head, scooting forward. To get a clean shot, she'd have to leave Molly. Bullets thwacked; concrete chips rained down. Laurel tucked Molly closer, gripping the butt of her gun.

A series of shots roared from behind the wall.

Skidding tires took off.

At the sound, Laurel eased forward, weapon raised. She half expected the worst, but Garrett lay on the ground, still alive, his gun aimed at the retreating SUV. He squeezed off two more rounds, then let out a low curse.

She couldn't catch her breath. They'd found her.

"What's going on out there?" An old man's voice called out, and the unmistakable sound of a pump-action shotgun seared through the dark.

"I'm handling it, Mr. McCreary," Garrett called out. "It's Sheriff Galloway. Get back inside."

A door slammed.

Garrett held his weapon at the ready for several more seconds, then picked up his phone. "Shots fired just off Oak and First, Keller," he said to his deputy. "Activate the emergency system and order everyone to stay inside. I'll get back to you when it's clear."

He shoved the phone in his pocket and ran to Laurel. "Everybody safe?"

Molly sobbed in Laurel's arms. She clutched the girl tighter. Laurel didn't know how much more her niece could take.

"Come on." Tension lining his face, he scooped up Molly. His boots thudded on the ground; Laurel carried their belongings and her footsteps pounded closely behind. He led them down an alley to the rear of a row of houses. Then, when he reached the back of one house, he pulled a set of keys from his pocket. "We've got to get out of sight. Plus, I have supplies to gather. Then we need a safe place to hole up."

"I'm sorry," she said quietly. "I brought this to you."

He gave a curt nod. "Who knew you were coming to Texas?"

"No—no one."

"Who told you about me? Your father?" Garrett said.

"My...my sister."

"Ivy?" Garrett's brow furrowed. "She worked for the agency, but we never tackled an op together."

Laurel bit her lip. "My sister said your name with her dying breath. She said to tell you that you were right."

THE SUV THUNDERED down the highway and out of Trouble. Mike Strickland slammed his foot on the accelerator and veered onto an old dirt road leading into the hellish West Texas desert. When he finally brought the vehicle to a halt, he slammed it into Park and pounded the steering wheel with his fist. "Son of a bitch. Who was that guy?"

"The law," his partner, Don Krauss, said, his tone dry. "You see the badge?"

Krauss could pass for everyman. He was great to have on the job because he excelled at blending into the background. His medium brown hair, medium eyes, medium height and nothing-special face got lost in a crowd.

Strickland had a tougher time. A scar from his marine stint and his short hair pegged him as ex-military. He could live with that. He tended to work the less subtle jobs anyway. But Krauss came in handy for gathering intel.

"No sheriff has reflexes like that," Strickland said. "She should be dead. They both should be."

"The girl avoided us for four days, and she's just an analyst, even if she does work for the CIA. She's smart. Switched vehicles twice and never turned on her cell phone." Krauss tapped the high-tech portable triangulation unit.

All this equipment and a girl in a beat-up Chevy had driven over halfway across the country and avoided them. "She got lucky." Strickland frowned.

Krauss let out a snort. "No, we got lucky when she used her ATM for cash. The only stupid move she made, but she cleaned out her account. We won't be lucky again. And now she's got help." He hitched his foot on the dash. "If Ivy talked—"

"I know, I know." Strickland scratched his palm in a nervous movement. In four days the skin had peeled, leaving it red, angry and telling. Not much made him nervous, but his boss… He forced his hand still and gripped the steering wheel, clenching and unclenching his fists against the vinyl. "We can fix this. Forensics will be sifting through what's left of that car for weeks. I made sure it burned hot, and I've got friends in the local coroner's office. If they stall long enough for us to provide two more burned bodies, no one will ever know. Everyone will believe the woman and girl died that night along with the rest of her family."

"You blew her head off," Krauss said. "Cops had to notice."

"It hasn't been on the news, has it?" Strickland said with a small smile.

Krauss shook his head. "I figured they were holding back details as part of the investigation."

"Hell, no. First guy there threw her into the fire. Everyone else is keeping mum. They think it's *national security*."

"Lots of loose ends, Strickland."

"I got enough on my contacts' extracurricular activities. They won't be talking anytime soon. They know the rules." Strickland slid a glance at his partner. "You read the paper? Remember last year, that dead medical investigator? I had no choice. He was a loose end. Like the boss says, loose ends make for bad business."

Krauss tugged a toothpick from his pocket. "Guess the boss was right in choosing you for this one, because we have two very big loose ends." He turned in the seat, his normally sardonic expression solemn. "You ever wonder how we ended up working for that psycho? 'Cause I'm starting to regret every job we do."

"For the greater good—" Strickland started, his entire back tensing. He cricked his neck to the side.

"Yeah, I might have believed that once," Krauss said.

"Don't." Strickland cut him off. "Don't say something I'll have to report."

"Says the man who's hiding his screwup."

"I don't plan to be on the receiving end of a lesson," Strickland said. "You talk and we're dead. Hell, we're dead if we don't fix this."

"I know," Krauss said, his voice flat. "I got a family to protect. Let's get it done fast, clean up and get the hell out of this town. I already hate Trouble, Texas."

"No witnesses. Agreed?" Strickland turned the motor on.

"The sheriff, too? Could cause some publicity."

"This close to the border, this isolated, there's lots of ways to die."

Chapter Two

"*I was right.* Great, just great," Garrett said under his breath, cradling a sobbing Molly in his arms.

He rocked her slightly. She tucked her head against his shoulder and gripped his neck, her little fingers digging into his hair. He held her tighter while his narrowed gaze scrutinized the alley behind his house. A chill bit through the night, and Molly shivered in his arms. He needed to get them both inside and warm, but not in the place he'd never called home.

Another thirty seconds passed. No movement. The shooter probably didn't have an accomplice, but he couldn't assume anything. Assumptions got people dead.

A quick in and out. That was all he needed.

He led Laurel into the backyard of the house James McCallister had purchased on Garrett's behalf and closed the gate. He wouldn't be returning anytime soon. His time in Trouble had ended the moment he'd tackled Laurel to the ground.

But he needed his go-bag and a few supplies. On his own, it wouldn't have mattered. He shifted Molly's weight in his arms. These two needed more shelter than to camp out in the West Texas desert in December.

Molly clung to him tightly. He rubbed her back and

his heart shifted in his chest. God, so familiar. The memories of his daughter, Ella, flooded back. Along with the pain. He couldn't let the past overcome him. Not with these two needing him. He led them to the wood stack.

"Give me a minute," he whispered. "Stay out of sight, and I'll be right back."

He tried to pass Molly to Laurel, but the little girl whimpered and gripped him even tighter.

"It's okay, sugar. Your aunt Laurel will take good care of you."

With one last pat, he handed Molly to Laurel, his arms feeling strangely empty without the girl's weight. Laurel settled her niece in her arms, her expression pained. He understood. "She's just afraid," he said.

"I know, and I haven't protected her." Laurel hunkered down behind the woodpile. She pulled out her pistol. "I won't fail again."

Laurel McCallister had grit, that was for sure. He liked that about her. "I'll be back soon."

He sped across the backyard, slipped the key into the lock and did a quick sweep of the house, eyeing any telling details. He couldn't leave a trace behind. Nothing to lead any unwelcome visitors to his small cattle ranch in the Guadalupes or to his stashed money and vehicle.

Garrett pressed a familiar number on his phone.

"Sheriff? What happened? Practically the whole town is calling me." Deputy Keller's voice shook a bit.

"Old man McCreary's not putting a posse together, right?" Garrett had a few old-timers in this town who thought they lived in the 1800s. This part of Texas could still be wild, but not *that* wild.

"I talked his poker buddies out of encouraging him,"

Keller said. "It's weird ordering my old high school principal around."

Garrett pocketed a notebook and a receipt or two, then headed straight for his bedroom. "Look, Keller, I'll be incommunicado tracking this guy. I don't want to shoot anyone by mistake. Keep them indoors."

"You need me, Sheriff?"

"Man the phones and keep your eyes out for strangers, Deputy. Don't go after them, Keller. Just call me."

"Yes, sir."

Garrett ended the call. If the men following Laurel and Molly had a mission, his town was safe. Assassins tended to have singular focus. He probably wasn't the target, except as an opportunity. Still, Ivy had known his name. She'd said he was right. He couldn't be certain how much of his identity had been compromised.

If anyone had associated Derek Bradley with Garrett Galloway before today, he'd already be dead. He *might* still have surprise on his side, but he couldn't count on it. And if he'd been right…well, that was all fine. It didn't make him feel any better. There was a traitor in the agency, and he didn't know who. Ivy's message hadn't identified the perp.

Garrett grabbed his go-bag from the closet, then opened a drawer in his thrift-store dresser. He eased out an old, faded photo from beneath the drawer liner.

"It'll be over soon." He glanced at the images he'd stared at for a good two hours after his shift earlier. Hell, it was almost Christmas.

Tomboy that she'd been, his daughter, Ella, would have been after him about a new football or a basketball hoop, while Lisa would've rolled her eyes and wondered when her daughter might want the princess dress—or any dress, for that matter. His throat tightened. He'd never know what kind of woman Ella would have become. Her life had ended before it had begun.

Garrett missed them so much. Every single day. He'd survived the injuries from the explosion for one reason—to make whoever had murdered his family pay. He wouldn't stop until he'd achieved his goal. He'd promised them. He'd promised himself.

He ground his teeth and stuffed the photo into the pocket of his bag. The perps should already be dead. He and James had failed for eighteen months and now... what the hell had happened? Now James's daughter Ivy had paid the ultimate price. And Laurel was on the run.

James was... Who knew where his mentor was?

The squeak of the screen door ricocheted through the house. He'd been inside only a few minutes. He slipped his gun from his shoulder holster and rounded into the hall, weapon ready.

Laurel stilled, Molly in her arms. "She has to go to the bathroom," she said with a grimace.

"Hurry," Garrett muttered, pointing toward his bedroom. "We can't stay. I wore my uniform and badge tonight. If they saw it, they'll find this place all too easily."

Laurel scurried into his room and Garrett headed to the kitchen. By the time they returned, he'd stuffed a few groceries into a sack. "Let's go."

Gripping his weapon, he led them outside. The door's creak intruded on the night, clashing with the winter quiet. Pale light bathed the yard in shadows. A gust of December wind bit against Garrett's cheeks. A tree limb shuddered.

He scanned the hiding places, but saw no movement, save the wind.

Still, he couldn't guarantee their safety.

"Where are we going?" Laurel asked, her voice low.

Garrett glanced at her, then Molly. "I have an untraceable vehicle lined up. We'll hole up for the night. You need rest. Then after I do a bit of digging, we'll see."

Laurel had brought his past to Trouble. No closing it away again. If his innocent visitors weren't in so much danger, Garrett would have welcomed the excuse to wait it out. His trigger finger itched to face the men responsible for killing his wife and daughter. Except a bullet was too good for them. They needed to die slowly and painfully.

Garrett might have failed to protect his family once, but he wouldn't allow their killer to escape again. He didn't particularly care whether he left the confrontation alive, as long as the traitor ended up in a pine box.

He just prayed he could get these two to safety before the final battle went down.

LAUREL STOOD ALONE just behind a hedge at the end of the alley, out of sight, squeezing the butt of her weapon in one hand, balancing Molly against her with the other. Garrett had risked crossing those streets to retrieve his vehicle, putting himself in the crosshairs in case the shooters came back.

Every choice he'd made focused on protecting them, not himself. She shivered, but it wasn't the winter chill. She'd made a choice eighteen hundred miles ago to come here. Garrett's immediate response to their arrival had frozen her soul. Now instinct screamed at her to run, to disappear, to try to forget the past and somehow start over.

Maybe she should. He knew what they were up against.

He was worried. Maybe vanishing would be easier. She didn't see Garrett Galloway as a man who would give up easily. But sometimes accepting the reality and moving on was the only way to survive.

A dark SUV pulled into the alley, lights off. Garrett stepped out. "Laurel?" he whispered, searching the hedges with his gaze.

She almost stayed hidden, frozen for a moment. She had some cash. People lived off the grid all the time. So could she.

She could feel his penetrating gaze, compelling her to trust him. What was it about him...?

With a deep, determined breath, she stepped out from behind the hedge. Beads of sap still stuck to her pants from hiding in the firewood pile. The scent of pine flashed her back to memories of camping and fishing and running wild without a care in the world. Her heart broke for Molly. Could Laurel help her niece find that joy after everything that had happened?

Laurel was so far out of her element. She'd taken a leap of faith coming to Trouble and to Garrett, trusting her sister's final words. Her sister had known she was dying; she wouldn't have steered Laurel into danger. Laurel could only pray she had understood Ivy correctly.

She carried Molly to the vehicle. Garrett didn't say anything, but his dark and knowing eyes made Laurel tremble. Did he know she'd almost taken off?

"You decided not to run," he said, opening the door. "I pegged it at a fifty-fifty chance."

He could see right through her. She didn't like it. "I almost did," she admitted. "But I can't let them get away with what they've done." She pushed back a lock of Molly's hair and lifted her gaze to meet his. "Our lives have been turned upside down. Can you help us?"

She didn't usually lay her vulnerabilities out so easily, but this was life and death. She needed his help. They both knew it.

He gave her a sharp nod. "I'll do what I can."

She placed Molly in the backseat and buckled her up. Laurel climbed in beside her. She tucked the little girl against her side. "Where to?"

"I contacted a friend. We need food for a few days. He runs the local motel and does some cooking on the side." Garrett paused. "I don't know how long we'll be on the road. His sister is about your size. I noticed that Molly has a change of clothes, but not you."

Laurel could feel the heat climb up her face at the idea he'd studied her body to determine her size. But he was right. They'd left so quickly, she hadn't had time to do more than purchase a few pairs of underwear at a convenience store. How many men would even think about that?

Garrett didn't turn on the SUV's lights. He drove the backstreets, then pulled up to the side of the Copper Mine Motel behind a huge pine tree, making certain the dark vehicle was out of sight from the road. A huge, barrel-chested man with a sling on one arm eased out of the side door. His wild hair and lip piercing seemed at odds with his neatly trimmed beard, but clearly he'd been on the lookout for them.

Garrett rolled down the passenger-door window. "Thanks, Hondo."

The man stuck his head inside and scanned Laurel and Molly. The little girl's eyes widened when she stared at his arm. "Who drew on you?" she asked.

Hondo chuckled. "A very expensive old geezer, little lady," he said. He placed a large sack on the seat, then a small tote. "You're right, Sheriff. She's about Lucy's size. These clothes are brand-new. Just jeans and some shirts and a few unmentionables." His cheeks flushed a bit.

Laurel scrambled into her pocket and pulled out some bills. "Thank—"

Hondo held up his hand. "No can do." He looked at the sheriff. "If you want them to stay here—"

"After what happened last time, Hondo, I won't let you risk it. Thanks, though." Garrett handed Hondo his badge. "When folks start asking, give this to the mayor."

"Sheriff—"

Laurel clutched the back of the seat, her fingers digging into the leather. She wanted to stop him from giving up his life, but she'd brought trouble to his town. She'd left him with no choice.

"We all have a past, Hondo. Mine just happened to ride in tonight. Something I have to deal with."

Hondo nodded, and Laurel recognized the communication between the two men. The silent words made her heart sink with trepidation.

"Keep an eye on Deputy Keller. He's young and eager, and he needs guidance." Garrett drummed his fingers on the steering wheel. "Come to think of it, you'd make a good sheriff, Hondo. You've got the skills."

"Nah." Hondo's expression turned grim. "I won't fire a gun anymore, and I couldn't put up with the mayor. He's a—" Hondo glanced at Molly "—letch and a thief."

"And willing to take a payoff. I should know. It's how I became sheriff."

Hondo's eyebrow shot up. "You still did a good job. Best since I've lived here."

Garrett shrugged and shifted the truck into Drive. "Goodbye, Hondo."

A small woman with wild gray hair shuffled out of the motel, a bandage on her head. "Hondo?" her shaky voice whispered. "Cookies."

Hondo's expression changed from fierce to utter tenderness in seconds. "Now, sis, you're not supposed to be out of bed. You're just out of the hospital." He sent Garrett an apologetic grimace.

"But you said you wanted to give them cookies," she said, holding a bag and giving Hondo a bright smile.

Laurel studied the woman. She seemed so innocent for her age, almost childlike.

The older woman's gaze moved to Garrett and she smiled, a wide, naive grin. "Hi, Sheriff. Hondo made chocolate chip today."

"We can't say no to Hondo's famous cookies, Lucy."

Garrett's smile tensed, and his gaze skirted the streets. Did he see something? Laurel peered through the tinted windows. The roads appeared deserted.

Lucy passed the bag to Hondo. An amazing smell permeated the car through the open window.

Molly pressed forward against her seat belt. "Can I have one, Sheriff Garrett?"

Hondo glanced at Laurel, his gaze seeking permission. She nodded and Hondo pulled a cookie from the bag. "Here you go, little lady."

With eager hands, Molly took the treat. She breathed in deeply, then stuffed almost the entire cookie into her mouth.

Lucy giggled. "She's hungry."

Hondo placed a protective arm around his sister. "They've got to leave, Lucy. Let's go in."

She waved. "'Bye." Hondo led her back into the house, treating her as if she were spun of fragile glass.

Garrett rolled up the window, lights still off. He turned down the street. "She was shot in the head a couple months ago. We didn't think she'd make it."

Laurel wiped several globs of chocolate from Molly's mouth. "You've made a place for yourself in this town." She resettled the sleepy girl against her body. "I'm sorry." What else could she say?

"They'll find someone else. Things will continue just as they did before I came to Trouble."

The muscle at the base of his jaw tensed, but Laurel couldn't tell if he really didn't mind leaving or if something about this small town had worked its way under his skin. She didn't know him well enough to ask, so she kept quiet and studied the route he took. Just in case.

He headed west down one of the side streets almost the entire distance of town.

Laurel couldn't stand the silence any longer. "Where are we going?"

Garrett met her gaze in the mirror. "I'm taking the long way to the preacher's house. The church auxiliary keeps it ready, hoping they can convince a minister to come to Trouble. It's been empty for almost a year."

"We're just hiding across town?"

"Sometimes the best place to hide is in plain sight," Garrett said. "Besides, I want to do a little searching online. See what I can discover about your sister."

"There was never a news report on the car bomb," Laurel said quietly. On the way here, she'd searched frantically at any internet café or library she could. She kept expecting some news story on an investigation, but she'd seen nothing except a clipping about a tragic accident. In fact, they'd simply stated the entire family had perished in a vehicle fire.

She hugged Molly closer.

They'd lied.

"That tells us a lot." Garrett stopped in the driveway of a dark house, jumped out and hit a code on a small keypad. The garage door rose.

"Small towns," he said with a smile when he slid back behind the wheel. "I check the house weekly."

"Is it safe?"

"The men who took the shot will assume we're leaving town. I would. And I don't want to be predictable."

He pulled the SUV into the garage. The automatic door whirred down behind them, closing them in. Laurel let out a long breath. She hadn't even realized she'd been holding it.

"We're safe?"

"For the moment," Garrett said, turning in his seat. "We need to talk." His gaze slashed to Molly, leaving the rest of the sentence unsaid. *Alone.*

"I know." Laurel bit her lip. She didn't know much. She'd hoped Garrett would somehow have all the answers, that he could just make this entire situation okay.

It wouldn't be that simple. She clutched Molly closer. Laurel had no idea how they would get out of this situation alive.

THE INKY BLACK of the night sky cloaked Mike Strickland's vehicle. Stars shimmered, but it was the only light save a few streetlights off in the distance. Trouble, Texas, was indeed trouble.

"They couldn't have just vanished." Strickland slammed his fist onto the dash of the pickup he'd commandeered.

He'd switched license plates and idled on the outskirts of town, lights off, in silence. He tapped a number into his cell.

"They come your way?" he barked.

"Nothing," Don Krauss said through the receiver, his voice tense. "There are only two roads into town."

"But a lot of desert surrounding it," Strickland muttered in response to his partner's bad news. "We need satellite eyes."

Krauss let out a low whistle. "You request it, the boss'll wonder why."

Strickland activated his tablet computer. The eerie glow lit the cab. "You see the history on this sheriff? Garrett Galloway?"

"Yeah," Krauss said. "So?"

"It's perfect."

"What do you mean?"

"I mean, his backstory is perfect. He grew up in Texas. Went to school at Texas A&M. Joined the corps there. Got a few speeding tickets. Headed to a small town, ran for sheriff."

"Like a thousand other Texas sheriffs."

"Everybody's got something. No late taxes, no real trouble. It feels wrong," Strickland said quietly.

Silence permeated the phone. "What are you thinking?"

"You saw his moves. He didn't learn those in college. Maybe Laurel McCallister didn't get here by chance. Who comes this close to nowhere on a whim?" Strickland glanced around. "And we're at the frickin' end of the earth."

"Still doesn't help to explain if the boss asks about using the satellite."

"I'll say it's a hunch."

Strickland could almost see his partner's indecision. "You gotta learn to take risks, Krauss. If we don't get rid of those two, we're dead. But if my hunch is right, and Garrett Galloway isn't just some hick sheriff, we might be able to feed the boss something new."

"And save our skin. I like it."

"Keep digging on Galloway. Even the best slip up sometimes."

"I'm on it. What do we do until then?"

"I'm contacting headquarters. I want to see a sweep of this part of Texas from the time we arrived until now. This place is dead at night. I want to know who's been moving around and which way they went."

"This could go to hell real fast, Mike."

Strickland scratched his palm. "We just need one break, Krauss. One opening, and our targets won't live long enough to disappear again."

A DIM LIGHT illuminated the preacher's garage. A plethora of boxes provided too many invisible corners and a variety of spooky shadows along the walls. Laurel shivered, but slid out of the car anyway. She bundled Molly into her arms before following Garrett into the preacher's house. He carted in the supplies while she scanned the kitchen, studying each corner, each potential hiding place, each possible weapon. One thing she'd learned in her job: details mattered.

Laurel stepped into the living room. A front door and a sliding glass back door. Not exactly secure. And, of course, doilies everywhere.

The muscles in her shoulders bunched and she cocked her hip. Molly grew heavier and heavier with each movement. She walked back into the kitchen. The decor erupted with grapes and ivy.

So very different from Garrett's house. She'd seen enough of the place to know it hadn't been a home to him, just a way station.

With a sigh, she sat down at the table, shuffling Molly in her lap. She and Garrett needed to talk, but not with Miss Big Ears listening to every word. Molly let out a small yawn. The girl had to be exhausted, but she wouldn't be easy to put down. Even then, the nightmares came all too easily. "Do you have any milk?"

"Warm?" he asked, searching through a couple of cabinets. He pulled out a small saucepan before Laurel could answer.

She nodded. Molly sat up and rubbed her eyes, a stubborn pout on her lip. "I don't want milk. This isn't home. I want my mommy and daddy. I want Matthew and Michaela."

Laurel froze. Molly hadn't mentioned her brother's and sister's names since they'd left Arlington. She blinked quickly and cleared her throat. "I want them, too, honey. But we have to hide. Like a game."

"I don't like this game. You're mean."

The girl's lower lip stuck out even farther and her countenance went from stubborn to mutinous. She crossed her arms, and all Laurel could see in her niece's face was an enraged Ivy. Some might think she could wait Molly out, but her niece could be as tenacious as…well, as Laurel herself.

"It's late, Molly." Her tone dropped, words firm and short. She didn't want to have another drawn-out adventure getting the little girl to bed. Before the car bombing, it had taken some cajoling, at least two stories and two tiny glasses of water before she could get the child to close her eyes. Now…Molly didn't fall asleep until her poor body simply rebelled. "It's time for bed."

"Then why aren't you having hot milk, too?" Molly scrunched her face and crossed her arms.

Garrett turned around. "We're *all* having warm milk, and I made you a *very* special recipe," he said, adding a dash of sugar and a little vanilla and nutmeg to the cups he held.

He set a plastic cup in front of Molly and a glass mug in front of Laurel, then brought over a plate of vanilla wafers. The aroma mingled in the air around them, and Laurel sighed inside. It smelled like home and family. She swallowed briefly, her eyes burning at the corners.

Garrett took a seat, the oak chair creaking under his weight. His large hands rounded the cup. He raised it to his lips, sipped and stared at Molly. She glared back, but when he licked his lips, dunked a vanilla wafer into his cup and bit down, she leaned forward and took a small sip from her cup.

Molly's eyes widened a bit and she tasted more. "Wow. That's yummy. But I want chocolate chip."

"Glad you think so." He slid one of Hondo's cookies toward the little girl and she gifted Garrett with an impish smile.

He winked at Molly, who downed another gulp. Laurel couldn't resist, even though she detested the drink. She chanced a taste. The nutmeg and vanilla hit her tongue with soothing flavors. "Mmm. How'd you come up with this recipe?"

"My wife invented it, actually. Put our daughter to sleep." A shadow crossed his face, then vanished just as quickly. "They're gone now."

"My mommy and daddy and brother and sister are gone, too," Molly said with a small yawn. "I hope they come back soon."

Laurel bit her lip to keep the sob from rising in her throat. "Is there someplace I can settle her down?"

Molly's body sagged against Laurel. A few more minutes and the little girl wouldn't be able to fight sleep any longer.

"Pick a room," Garrett said. "I'll check the perimeter and secure the house."

He strode toward the door.

"Garrett," she said, her voice barely above a whisper. "Thank you. For everything."

"Don't thank me yet, Laurel. Thank me when this is over. Until then, I may just be the worst person you could have come to for help."

GARRETT STOOD SILENTLY in the kitchen doorway as Laurel padded into the living room.

"She asleep?"

Laurel whirled around. Then her head bowed as if it were too heavy for her shoulders. He could see the fatigue in her eyes, the utter exhaustion in every step.

"She was bushed. It's been a rough few days. She just downed the last of her medicine, so hopefully the strep throat is gone."

He tilted his head toward the sofa. "You look ready to collapse. Have a seat. My deputy's been busy tonight calming the town. He received a report of an SUV speeding out of town early tonight. I told him to keep out of sight but watch for it. If they're smart, they'll dump the vehicle."

"But they won't give up," Laurel said.

"I doubt it."

Laurel lowered herself to one end of the sofa, twisting her hands on her lap. "You work for the agency? With my father?"

Garrett sat in the chair opposite her. "In a way." No need to volunteer that he was off the roll. If the agency didn't think he was dead, he'd probably be awaiting execution for treason.

Just one of many reasons he shouldn't allow himself to get too close to Laurel.

But even as he faced her, he felt the pull, the draw. And not because she was gorgeous, which she was, even with that horrible haircut and dye job. Beauty could make him take notice just like any man, but that didn't turn him on half as much as how she'd fallen on top of Molly to protect her.

She was a fighter—a very good thing. She'd have to be for them to get out of this mess alive.

Which put her off-limits. That and the fact that she was James's daughter.

"Your father trained me," Garrett said, trying not to let himself get lost in his attraction for her. "He saved my life, actually."

Laurel tucked her legs beneath her. "I thought it had to be something like that. I used to watch Dad train in the basement when I was a kid. I recognized that move when you dived to the ground." She rubbed her arms as if to ward off a chill. "Ivy worked every night to perfect it. In spite of Dad."

"I heard about the destruction to his office. I don't think James wanted her to join up."

"He was furious, but Ivy has…*had,*" she corrected herself, "a mind of her own." Her voice caught and her hands gripped her pants, clawing at the material. "Dad raised us to be independent. She wanted more than anything to follow in Dad's footsteps. She wanted to make the world safe."

Laurel's knuckles whitened and she averted her gaze from his. Every movement screamed at him not to push. Garrett could tell she was barely holding it together, and if she'd given him the slightest indication he would have crossed the room and pulled her into his arms and held her. Instead, he leaned forward, his elbows on his knees, studying her closely. He hated to ask more but he needed information. He had to know. She might not even be aware of the information she possessed. "Where's James, Laurel?"

Her breath shuddered and she cleared her throat. "I don't know. He stopped calling or emailing two months ago. Then out of nowhere a package arrived this week. He sent a charm bracelet to Ivy."

This week. So if James had really sent the package, he'd been alive a week ago. Garrett's shoulders tensed. "Did you bring it?"

Laurel pulled a silver bracelet from her pocket. She touched the small charms and the emotions welled in her eyes. Reluctantly she handed it to him. "Ivy shoved it into my hand as she was leaving that night…" Her voice broke. "She said it was important."

He studied the silver charms. Nothing extraordinary. A wave of disappointment settled over him. Surely there was *something* here. He studied each silver figure, looking for a clue, a message from James. A horse, a dog. A seashell. Several more. Nothing that Garrett understood, but he'd bet Laurel had a story to tell about each one.

The question was, did any of those stories have a hidden message? He handed her back the treasure.

"Tell me about the figures."

She walked through a series of memories. A trip to the ocean with the family right before her mother passed away. Their first dog and his predilection for bounding after fish in freezing mountain streams just to shake off and soak everyone. A horse ride that ended in a chase through a meadow. Her voice shook more with each memory, but the hurt didn't provide anything new. Garrett couldn't see a connection.

He let out a long, slow breath. He had to ask. "How did Ivy die?"

Laurel stared down at the floor. He knew exactly how she felt. Sometimes even looking at another human being could let loose the tears. After Lisa and Ella, he hadn't allowed himself to give in to his emotions. He'd shoved the agony away, buried it in that corner of his mind where it wouldn't bring him to his knees. Garrett had focused on revenge instead. He'd had to in order to survive.

But since Laurel had landed underneath him on the streets of Trouble, the pain he'd hidden had begun scraping at him, digging itself out.

She didn't look up. She simply twisted the denim fabric in her fists. "The explosion burned Ivy almost beyond recognition. She lived. She gave me your name. Then they shot her in the head."

Her voice strangely dispassionate, she went through every detail. When she told him about the single cop's arrival, Garrett closed his eyes. At least one law-enforcement officer on the take. Probably more.

Asking for help was out of the question. And with

James AWOL, they were on their own. She knew it. So did Garrett.

Laurel lifted her lashes and silent tears fell down her cheeks. She wouldn't be facing this alone. In a heartbeat, Garrett knelt at her feet. He pulled her into his arms and just hugged her close.

She clung to him with a desperation he understood. Her fingers dug into his arms. The tiny tremors racing through her tore at his heart. Laurel's heart was broken, and she had a little girl who needed her to be strong.

Laurel needed him, but his body shook as the memories assaulted him. How many nights had he dreamed of his wife and daughter calling out to him, begging for him to save them? But Laurel's pleas were real, in every look, in every touch as she clung to him.

The similarities between Ivy's death and his wife's and daughter's couldn't be denied. He'd find the culprits this time. They wouldn't get an opportunity to hurt anyone else.

Garrett stroked Laurel's back slowly, but she didn't let him go. Her grip tightened.

His pocket vibrated. With one arm still holding Laurel close, he tilted his phone's screen so he could see it. He blinked once at the number. The country code was too familiar. Afghanistan.

"Hello?" He made his greeting cautious, unidentifiable. This was Sheriff Garrett Galloway's phone and number. No one from Afghanistan should know it. That was a life he'd hidden away.

"Garrett?" A weak voice whispered into his ear. A voice he knew.

"James?"

Laurel froze in his arms.

"Garrett, listen to me. The operation has been compromised. Go to Virginia. Get my daughters to safety. They're in danger."

"James, Laurel is with me. What's going on? Where have you been?"

"Oh, God," James cursed. "Ivy knows too much. You have to get her out of there."

Garrett nearly cracked. He didn't want to tell his old friend the worst news a man could receive. Garrett knew the pain of losing a child. Your heart never recovered.

Laurel snagged the phone away from Garrett. "Daddy?" she shouted.

"Laurel, baby. Don't believe what anyone tells you," James said, his voice hoarse. "Promise."

Shouts in Arabic reverberated through the phone. "Find him!"

"Laurel," James panted. "Remember. Ivy's favorite toy."

A spray of gunfire exploded through the speaker.

The phone went silent.

Chapter Three

The phone slipped from Laurel's hand. Her father couldn't be gone. "Daddy?" Her knees gave way and she slid to the floor. She looked up to Garrett. "Get my father back, please."

Garrett scooped up the phone and pocketed it. "I'm sorry. I can't."

He slid his arms beneath her and lifted her. Laurel grasped at him. Her mind had gone numb. She couldn't feel a thing.

With silent steps he carried her to the sofa and sat down on the smooth leather, anchoring her beside him. "Laurel." He used a finger to force her to meet his gaze. "Stay with me, honey."

Her body shuddered, and she couldn't stop the trembling. This couldn't be happening. She wanted to bury herself in Garrett's arms and just forget everything. Pretend the past few days hadn't happened. But she couldn't.

Molly. Molly needed her.

She fisted the material of her jeans, fighting to calm the quake that threatened to overtake her. She had to know. Slowly she lifted her gaze to meet his. "My father? H-he's dead, isn't he?"

Laurel hated the words coming out of her mouth. The

last bit of childish hope, that her father would rescue her and Molly, disintegrated into a million tiny pieces.

Garrett's face resembled a stone statue. He gave nothing away from his expression. He didn't have to say anything.

A burning crept behind her eyes and she pressed the heels of her hands against them, trying to curtain the emotions. "God."

James McCallister had always been invincible. But after the past few months, when she and Ivy had been braced for the worst, for a few brief moments tonight Laurel had gotten her father back.

Now she'd lost him again. Maybe for good this time.

"So many bullets flying," she said, her voice hushed. "How could he possibly survive?"

He hugged her close. "James is smart. And resourceful. If anyone can survive out there, your father can. Right now, I'm more worried about you."

Garrett pulled a small leather case from his pocket and unzipped it before grabbing a small screwdriver. He pulled his cell from his pocket and opened the phone. Quickly, he popped the battery and a small chip from the device and tossed it onto the coffee table before tucking his kit back in his jacket.

"You removed the GPS." The truth hit her with the force of a fist to the chest. "If they're tracing his calls, they know our location. That's what I do for the CIA. Track locations from cell towers and satellites."

"Then you know we can't stay here." Garrett stood.

Laurel swiped at the few tears that had escaped. "How long do we have?" She wasn't stupid. She made her living analyzing data. A price came with being connected at all times. Cell phones, computers, tablets, internet—everyone left a trail. She rose from the couch, her body slightly chilled once she left the warmth of his. She shouldn't get used to it. She knew better. "I'll get Molly."

At her turn, Garrett touched her arm, stopping her. "I'll see you through this."

Laurel paused. "I've driven clear across the country, and a phone call from Afghanistan is bringing whoever killed my family down on top of us...and you. How can it ever be all right? How can I ever keep Molly safe?"

The question repeated over and over in her mind. She knew better than most people how easy it was to track virtually anyone down. Biting her lip, she hurried into the bedroom and wrapped the blankets around Molly. There was no telling where they'd end up.

Molly squirmed a bit. "Aunt Laurel?" she whispered.

"Go back to sleep, Molly Magoo."

"I had a bad, bad dream," she said.

"I've got you," Laurel whispered. "I won't let you go." She hugged Molly tight, humming a few bars of "Hush, Little Baby." Thankfully, Molly snuggled closer, yawned and settled back to sleep.

Laurel exited the bedroom, hurrying to the garage door. It squeaked and she paused, praying Molly wouldn't wake up.

Her niece didn't budge. The dim garage light shone down. Garrett shoved a few last boxes into the back of his SUV and opened the back door, a tender expression when he looked at the sleeping girl in Laurel's arms pushing aside the intensity of just a moment ago. "You better do it. Better if she sleeps."

Laurel gently settled Molly onto the backseat, snapping the seat belt around her.

Garrett closed the door, his movements almost too quiet to hear. "Watch her. I'm going to wipe the house down."

Laurel gave him a quick nod and he disappeared into the house. When he returned, he stuffed a microfiber cloth into his jacket pocket, hit the garage-door opener and slid into the SUV beside her. "Fingerprints would make it too easy for them," he said. "You're on file with the FBI because of your clearance, and so am I."

With a quick turn of the key in the truck, the engine purred to life. He quickly doused the automatic lights and pulled out slowly.

After pressing the outside code, the garage door slid down. The house appeared vacant again.

Laurel looked through the windshield, right, then left, then behind. Tension shivered between them.

Garrett maneuvered onto the deserted street, still without headlights. Trouble had gone to sleep. He didn't plan on anyone waking up as they left town.

He didn't need lights to see anyway. The church auxiliary had gone and wrapped every lamppost and streetlight with garland and twinkle lights, ribbon and tinsel. With each gust of wind the decorations clattered against metal, leaving his neck tense and his hair standing on end.

He gripped the steering wheel, his knuckles whitening. God, he hated Christmas. Hated the memories it evoked. But at least the bulbs lit their way through Trouble.

"Where are we going?" Laurel asked, still alert and searching the surrounding landscape for anything out of the ordinary.

"The middle of nowhere," Garrett said. "Even though some consider Trouble just this side of nowhere."

The vehicle left the city limits, only a black expanse in front of them. This part of West Texas could seem like the end of the world at night, the only light the moon and stars above.

"They'll keep looking for us," Laurel said. "They want us dead."

"No question." Garrett watched the rearview mirror, but no lights pierced the black Texas night. So far, so good.

Laurel shifted in her seat beside him, peering out the front windshield. "It's so—"

"Dark?" Garrett finished.

She glanced over at him, her face barely visible from the light of the dashboard dials. "I've never seen the sky so black."

"When I first moved here from the East Coast, I couldn't get over how bright the stars shone or how dark the countryside could be."

"You didn't grow up around here?"

Garrett quirked a smile. "I was an army brat. I'm from everywhere, but we were never stationed in Texas."

Laurel's eyebrow quirked up. "I'd have taken you for a Texas cowboy."

"I was for a while."

But not anymore.

Garrett focused on the white lines of the road reflecting in the moonlight. No lights for miles around. The tension in his back eased a bit. They were alone.

"It's spooky," Laurel said, her voice barely a whisper. "No sign of civilization."

"You lived on the East Coast all your life?" he asked.

"Dad's job has always been headquartered in D.C. He'd leave town…" Her voice choked. "Someone has to know where he was," she said.

Garrett had been mulling that over. James had been his sole contact since Garrett's attack. He had no backup. No one he could trust.

"What about Fiona?" Laurel's voice broke through the night.

"You know about her?"

"I'm not supposed to. Dad tried to keep his personal life separate, but a few years ago, we caught them at a restaurant. They looked really happy. I'm surprised he hasn't married her. From what we figured out, he's dated her for at least five years."

"More like six," Garrett said. "Though I'm surprised he took her out into public. They work together. That was a huge risk." He drummed his fingers on the steering wheel. "Fiona might be the only person we can trust. She could get at his travel records."

"She could get him backup." Laurel flipped open a cell phone. "He needs help."

"What are you doing?"

"It's prepaid," she said. "I'm not stupid."

Garrett snatched the phone from her. "Not from here. I have equipment we can use to call her. It's more secure. For both of us. We don't want to place her in danger either."

"Dad needs help now."

"James either made it out of that situation alive and is hiding, or there's nothing we can do to help him."

A small gasp escaped from her. Garrett cursed himself, lowering his voice. "Look, I don't mean to be callous, but your dad wanted you safe. That meant more to him than his life or he wouldn't have called. We have to be careful, Laurel. We're alone in this right now, and we have to choose our allies carefully. One slipup…" He let the words go unsaid.

One mistake and they'd finish the job on him and Laurel and Molly would vanish without a trace.

"I understand," she said finally, her voice thick with emotion. "I don't have to like it." She twisted in her seat. "So, this place we're going… How'd you get a secure system?"

"Your dad set it up while I was…incapacitated."

Almost dead.

A small dirt road loomed at the right. Garrett passed it by, drove another ten miles, then pulled off onto a county road heading toward a mine.

"Are we getting close?"

"As close as things get in West Texas," Garrett said. He turned off the lights and the motor. The residual heat would keep them warm for a while.

"We're stopping? We're not that far from town."

Garrett leaned back in his seat and turned his head. "We're waiting. If your tail followed, they should show up soon enough."

Thirty minutes later, the air in the vehicle had chilled. Molly whined in the backseat, wrapping the blanket tighter around her. Garrett cast one last look down the desolate road, then turned the key, and the engine purred to life. He pulled onto the highway, heading back in the direction they'd come.

"You're cautious," Laurel said.

"I'm alive when I shouldn't be." Words more true than he could ever articulate.

"*Who* are you? Really." She shifted and moonlight

illuminated her suspicious expression. "Why did Ivy send me to you?"

The tires vibrated over the blacktop. Garrett refused to let the question distract him. The men following her were good, and he couldn't risk them being seen. Besides, he couldn't tell her. He knew James wouldn't have mentioned his new identity, and if Garrett revealed his previous name, she'd recognize it. As a traitor and a spy.

James had given testimony about Garrett's many infractions. The world had believed the agency's statements. Congress and the covert community trusted James McCallister. Without fail. He might not be a man the public would ever recognize, but in the intelligence community, James McCallister was a legend. The man's lies had saved Garrett's life. And made it so he could never go back. Not unless he wanted a target on his back.

Laurel would have every right to run once she learned the truth, but he couldn't allow that. James's call had done more than warn them. James had risked Garrett's life—and his own—to save the McCallister family. Garrett wouldn't let him down. He owed James too much. He owed the men who had killed his wife and daughter, Laurel's sister and her family—and maybe James—justice. Not courtroom justice, though. The kind that couldn't be bought or bargained for.

"Let's call me a friend and leave it at that," Garrett finally said. "A friend who will try to keep you safe."

"A friend," Laurel mused. "Why doesn't your comment engender me with faith?"

Garrett gripped the steering wheel tight.

"You came to me, Laurel."

"And if I had a choice, I wouldn't be putting our lives in the hands of someone I don't know if I can trust to keep us alive. I like to have all the facts, all the data. You don't add up, Sheriff Garrett Galloway. And that makes me nervous."

What could he say? Her words thrust a sword into his heart. He hadn't been good enough to protect his family. He hadn't seen the true risks when he'd followed up on a small leak at the agency. That one thread had led to their deaths.

Within minutes, the small dirt road appeared. He veered the SUV onto it, the narrow lanes barely visible. The farther they drove in, the bumpier it got. And the more the tension in his chest eased.

Soon they'd started a climb into the Guadalupe Mountains. Leafless branches scraped the sides of the vehicle. Before too long an outcropping of rock blocked their way.

Relieved that the county hadn't seen fit to clear the debris off the glorified cow path, Garrett backed the vehicle into a small clearing. Branches closed over the windshield, barricading them in.

With a sigh he shoved the gear into Park.

"Waiting again?" Laurel asked. "I can't imagine anyone would follow us here."

"The rest of the way to the cattle ranch is on foot. I didn't want the place to be too easy to find."

"I'm known for my sense of direction and I studied the terrain, but even I'm not sure I could find my way here."

"That was the point of buying it," Garrett said. He pressed a button on his watch and the face lit up. "Several hours until daylight. To dangerous to go by foot. One wrong move and we step into nothing and down a two-hundred-foot drop." He reached behind his seat and pulled out a blanket and pillow, thrusting them at her. "Get some rest. When the sun comes up, we'll hike the rest of the way."

"We'll start the search for my father tomorrow?" she pressed, taking the pillow and holding it close to her chest. "I can help. I have my own contacts."

He nodded, but he had his doubts. Laurel might be a gifted analyst, but the moment they ran a few searches, whoever was behind this would start backtracking. Garrett might not know the names of the traitors, but he knew a few dollar amounts. It was in the billions. Too much money was involved for them not to be tracking. Loyalty shouldn't be for sale, but it was.

Which was why Ivy was dead.

Damn it. Garrett should have come out of hiding sooner. He shouldn't have listened to James. He'd wanted to believe his old mentor was close. He'd wanted to believe justice was in their grasp.

"Try to sleep," he said. "Light will come soon."

Laurel snuggled down under the blanket. Garrett shifted his seat back a bit. He'd slept in far worse places.

His hand reached for his weapon. He had to find a way to end this thing. Not only for his family, but before Laurel and Molly paid the price their family had.

The question was how.

James had obviously slipped up.

Garrett couldn't afford to.

A small sigh of sleep escaped from the woman beside him. He tilted his head toward Laurel.

Her blue eyes blinked at him.

"Are we going to get out of this alive?" she whispered. "Truth."

"I don't know."

THE CHRISTMAS LIGHTS decorating every damn corner in Trouble, Texas, twinkled with irritating randomness. Strickland's eye twitched. He leaned forward toward the steering wheel as far as he could and still maneuver the vehicle.

He passed by the sheriff's house for the fifteenth time. Still dark, still deserted.

Headlights illuminated a house ahead.

Strickland whipped the steering wheel and turned down a side street to avoid the deputy crawling all over town. He plowed through a mailbox. With a curse he righted the car.

"Face it," Krauss said, propping his leather work shoe against the dash. "We lost them."

"We can't," Strickland muttered. "She has to die. Her and the kid."

He made his way to Main and pressed the gas pedal. Trouble was a dead end. The SUV shot ahead. The deserted streets of the small town slipped past. They headed into the eerie pitch blackness of the desert without headlights to light the way.

"We have to tell the boss that the McCallister woman is alive, Mike. There's no way we can keep it a secret."

"We still have another day or two," Strickland argued, a bead of sweat forming on his brow. Just the thought made his chest hurt. His pulse picked up speed. He knew what the boss would do. What had been done to others.

"Too risky. If we come clean—"

"We're dead."

Strickland's phone rang.

He yanked the steering wheel and nearly drove off the road. Cursing, he straightened the vehicle.

The glowing screen on the phone turned into a beacon in the night.

Krauss shoved it at Strickland. "It's the boss."

"How—?" He pressed the call button. "Strickland." He forced his voice to sound confident, arrogant.

"The car made the papers," his boss said. "The coroner believes the family died. Well done."

"Thank you." A shiver tickled the back of his neck, as if a black-widow spider had crawled up the base of his skull.

"I have another job for you. It's important."

A string of curses flooded through Strickland's brain. Another job. He had to finish this one first. He couldn't leave it undone. "Of course."

"Two years ago. Another car bomb. Another family. You were in charge."

Strickland remembered it well. No mistakes that time. He'd earned the boss's trust on that job.

"Our target is alive."

Strickland slammed the brakes. The car skidded to a halt. "What?"

"You told me he was dead."

"He wasn't breathing. No way he could have survived those burns." Strickland pulled at his hair. God, a mistake. No. He jumped out of the SUV and paced the pavement. His hand shook as he gripped the phone. Mistakes weren't tolerated. Ever.

"Well, he did. I'm taking care of that loose end. I want you to finish the job. Make certain this time."

Strickland turned on his heel and glared at the twinkling lights of Trouble. He was so screwed. "I'll find him. You can count on me."

"We'll see."

His heart thudded against his chest; his stomach rolled. Bile burned his throat.

"I'll search for him. He can't hide."

"He's not living under his real name."

Krauss rounded the vehicle. Maybe they could split up. It was the only way either man would make it off this assignment alive.

"How do I find him?"

"Your target is Sheriff Garrett Galloway. Trouble, Texas. Kill him this time, Strickland. Be very sure he's dead."

Strickland met Krauss's wide-eyed gaze. He'd heard the words. His partner shook his head in disbelief.

"Oh, and, Strickland? This is your last chance. One more less-than-adequate performance and you'll pray your life will end well before I allow it."

A SLIVER OF SUN peeked over the horizon, the light pricking Laurel awake. She blinked. The muted blue of the winter sky through the windshield brightened with each passing moment. Her cheek pressed against the leather seat. Awareness of the past week washed over her, drowning her in grief.

Ivy, her family. Her father.

Molly.

She jerked her head to one side, then the other, her gaze finally resting on Molly's sweet face.

"She's hasn't stirred," Garrett whispered, his voice low and husky.

Laurel longed to reach out and cuddle her niece, to touch her, to be certain. Molly's pink cheeks were just visible at the edge of the blanket; a small frown tugged at her mouth.

"No nightmares?" Laurel asked, shifting in her seat, combing her hair back from her face with her fingers.

"A few whimpers in the middle of the night. She's obviously exhausted."

"She can't wrap her mind around what happened." Laurel avoided Garrett's sympathetic gaze. She pretended to study the rugged bark of the piñon branches rapping gently against the window. "I can't understand most of the time."

He said nothing, and for that she was thankful. What could he say?

She sent him a sidelong glance. She'd avoided thinking about him as a man, but now, in the close proximity, she couldn't deny her heart stuttered a bit when she looked at him. He was handsome, but that wasn't what drew her. The hard line of his jaw, the determination in his eyes. And his gentleness with Molly. He was the kind of man she could fall for.

Smart, driven and deadly, but with a kind soul. And a heart.

She wanted to reach out and touch him. Just once. She blinked, staring at him. His gaze had narrowed, an awareness in his eyes.

He felt it, too.

The next moment, she wondered if she'd imagined the spark between them. He blinked; the heat doused.

Garrett pulled her SIG from below the seat. "You have extra ammo?"

"Of course," she said. "In my duffel. Dad trained me to go everywhere prepared."

"Not to mention the agency."

"They weren't as tough as my father."

A small grin tugged at the edge of Garrett's mouth.

"So true. I'm going to check out the ranch house. If I'm not back in one hour, I want you to leave." He handed her the keys and a slip of paper. "Contact Daniel Adams. He's the only other person I know who can get you the kind of help you need."

She pocketed the number and clutched the butt of the SIG.

"I'll be back," he said, opening the door.

"Be careful."

He tipped the brim of his Stetson before closing the door softly.

His catlike moves revealed more training than Laurel had. He disappeared around a pile of rocks. She caught a glimpse of his hat for a moment, but within minutes he'd vanished.

She clutched the keys in her hand. She had a full tank of gas, Molly in the backseat. She could run, just disappear.

Forget the past?

The fiery inferno of her sister's car burned the backs of her eyelids. Where was the justice in disappearing?

Her sister never would have let it go. Laurel dug into her pocket and pulled out the prepaid cell. No signal. If anything did happen, how would she find help? Her father wouldn't appreciate it if she put Fiona at risk.

Who could Laurel ask?

There was a reason she'd traveled all the way across the country. She had no choice but to trust Garrett. Him and his secrets.

Her father had called Ivy the judge and jury and Laurel a lie detector. Perhaps it was true. If she had enough information, Laurel could usually figure out the truth. It was what made her good at her job.

As long as the information was solid.

And with Garrett, she had nothing.

Laurel wrapped her arms around her knees, the gun heavy in her hand, comforting in its power. The chill of the winter air outside seeped into the car. She tugged the blanket closer and glanced at the clock. Thirty minutes. And he wasn't back.

A gust hit the tree, scraping the side of the truck. She tensed, gripping the butt of her SIG even tighter.

Forty-five minutes.

Laurel eyed the keys she'd placed on the dash. Fifteen minutes left.

A loud yawn sounded from the backseat. "Where are we?" Molly sat up. "Cars aren't for sleeping." She looked outside, and her eyes widened. "We're in the woods."

Laurel twisted in her seat and faced her niece with a forced smile on her face. "Like the three bears."

Molly gave her aunt a skeptical, you-can't-be-serious expression.

"Look!" Molly squealed, pointing out the window.

Laurel brought the gun to the ready and aimed at the window.

Garrett paused in his tracks and raised his hands with an arched brow.

Molly giggled. "Sheriff Garrett is a good guy. You can't shoot him."

Laurel dropped the weapon and stuffed it into her jacket.

With a forced smile on his face, he opened the back door. "And how is Sleeping Beauty this morning?"

"Hungry," Molly said, rubbing her eyes.

"I think we can take care of that. But first we're going

for a little walk." Garrett met Laurel's gaze and gave her a slight nod. "All clear."

She slipped out of the seat and headed to the back of the truck.

"Don't carry too much," Garrett said. "The terrain is rocky. I'll come back for the rest later." He turned to Molly. "Want to wear my hat?" he asked, holding it out to the small child.

Molly gazed up at him, her blue eyes huge. She nodded and Garrett tipped the hat on her head. It fell over Molly's eyes and she giggled. "It's too big."

"Are you saying I have a big head, young lady?" Garrett asked with a smile, his eyes twinkling.

Molly's grin widened and for the first time in days she lost that haunted look in her eyes. "Bigger than mine," she said. "You're funny. I like you, Sheriff Garrett."

"I like you, too, sugar."

The endearment made Molly smile again, but a swallow caught in Laurel's throat, because the normalcy wouldn't last. It couldn't.

Garrett led them through the jagged mountains, so unlike the woods in Virginia. Craggy rocks, the evergreen of piñon trees, lower to the ground, searching for water. Dry and harsh. Laurel stumbled and fell against a rock, scraping her hand.

Garrett was right beside her in an instant, helping her to her feet, his arm firm around her waist. His touch lingered for a moment, as did the concern in his brown eyes. "You okay? It's not much farther."

Molly stood, holding her lion against her chest. The little scamp hopped from one rock to the next.

"Fine," Laurel said, but her belly had started to ache. It always did when the nerves were uncontrollable. Every moment buried the truth further. They were truly out in the middle of nowhere. Without communication, without anyone but Garrett. How long could it last? How long would they be here?

How could they help her father from here? Much less themselves?

The questions whirled through her mind until a small stone-and-wood structure jutted from an incline.

The ranch house, with a porch surrounding it, wasn't large. Off to the side a small corral appeared more abandoned than anything. She couldn't see any sign of livestock.

"Here we are," he said, climbing up the steps and opening the door. He opened a panel and entered a code. Laurel raised an eyebrow.

"Sensors around the perimeter."

She nodded just as Molly raced in. The little girl's vibrating energy circled the room. She ran from the couch to a nightstand, finally bending down to poke at the fireplace screen. Rocks climbed ceiling to floor, the structure dominating the small living room.

Garrett set a bag in the simple kitchen on one wall.

"Put your things in here." He pushed into a small room with a double bed, chest of drawers and nightstand. No photos, no pictures on the wall. Plain, simple and utilitarian.

"The bathroom is through there," he added. "Just a shower and toilet."

"Is this your bed?" Laurel set down her duffel. "It's fine, but where will you sleep?"

Garrett hesitated. He glanced down at Molly. "Which side of the bed do you want, sugar?"

Molly grinned. "*I'm* gonna sleep in that big bed?" She

ran over and bounced on the side. "When my brother
and sister get here, all three of us can fit."

Laurel averted her gaze from Molly, landing on Garrett. A glimmer of sympathy laced his expression.

"I'm going to show your aunt Laurel something.
Okay?"

Molly nodded, hugged her lion and started a conversation with the beast.

Laurel took one last look at Molly and followed Garrett into the great room. "I don't know how to explain
it to her."

He rubbed the stubble on his chin. "It won't be easy,
but she has you. Molly will be okay, eventually. There's
going to be a fall when she recognizes that her family is
gone. Believe me, I know."

Laurel stilled and took in Garrett's features. Strain
lined his eyes and a darkness had settled over his face.
She reached out her hand and touched his arm. "I can
see that."

He looked down at her hand touching him. "I'll show
you my setup here. You may need it."

A step away had her clutching at air. He'd fled her
touch. She didn't know why she'd reached out to him, but
something in his expression called to her, made her want
to comfort him, even as her own heart was breaking.

He unlocked the door leading into the second room
in the cabin. She gasped. High-tech equipment she recognized from her job at the CIA lined two walls. Moni-
toring equipment—a secure phone and a very top secret
computer system. A world map hung on one wall. Several pegs dotted some of the more sensitive countries.
Below the map, a cot with a pillow and a rumpled blanket seemed to speak volumes.

The bedroom he'd given to her and Molly wasn't where he slept. When he visited this ranch house, he slept here.

"And I was worried I didn't have cell service," she said. "You could contact anyone anywhere in the world from here."

"Hand me your phone," Garrett said.

"It's powered off." She handed it to him.

"Good. They shouldn't be able to trace it to you since it's prepaid, but we can't afford to take chances. It still pings a cell tower." He removed the battery and GPS chip. "Pop in the battery if you have to use it," he said, tossing the GPS in the trash.

"You could track my father with this equipment," Laurel said, moving into the room.

"Maybe." Garrett sat down in one of the chairs and nodded his head at Laurel to take the other seat. "You have to understand, I promised James I'd stay out of the investigation. I have. For his sake."

"But—"

Garrett raised his hand to interrupt her argument. "I get it. Things have changed. We're taking a huge risk, though. I could make his situation worse. You have to understand that, Laurel."

How much worse could it get?

Laurel couldn't sit still. She paced back and forth. Her father could already be dead. But if he wasn't, what if this decision caused him to lose his life? Her mind whirled with confusion. The analytical part of her brain didn't like the missing data.

She lifted her gaze to him before taking her seat again. "If your father were missing, what would you do?"

"If my father were still alive, I'd do whatever it took to find him."

"And live with the consequences?"

"In this situation, yes. The alternative is worse," Garrett said. "Your father has made a lot of enemies over the years, but more than that, if we don't discover who is behind your sister's murder, you and Molly will never be safe. Those men will never stop coming after you."

"Oh, a big kitty! Come here, kitty, kitty." Molly's voice rang out from outside the cabin.

Laurel jumped to her feet at the same time as Garrett. "What kind of cats—?"

"Not domestic."

Chapter Four

Garrett pulled the Beretta from its holster and slammed through the front door of the ranch house. Laurel's footsteps thundered behind him.

"Oh, God," she whispered.

Molly stood about ten feet from the porch, across a clearing. Her hand reached out toward a large cougar, its long, thick tail swinging to and fro.

"Good kitty," Molly sang out, stepping forward.

The cat crouched, hissing.

"Molly," Garrett said, his tone firm with what his daughter had called his *mean voice.*

The little girl froze. "I didn't do anything wrong."

He guessed the *mean voice* still worked, but the memory also returned that horrible helplessness that he never experienced when facing his own death—or even the death of another agent.

Only a child's death could evoke the fear that seeped through his very soul.

Without hesitation, Garrett aimed his weapon at the animal, cursing inside for the animal to stop moving. As it was, it was going to be an impossible shot.

"Molly." Garrett forced his voice to remain calm.

"That's not a kitty cat. I need you to stay very, very still, sugar. Don't move. I'm going to shoot a gun."

"Too loud," Molly whimpered, shaking her head back and forth, clasping her ears with her hands and squatting down.

Damn it. She'd made herself a target. The cat hunched down on its front paws, clearly preparing to pounce. Garrett couldn't wait. What he wouldn't give for his father's old Remington. He could take out the animal with one shot. A rifle was so much more accurate than a handgun at this distance.

The cat growled, opening its mouth in a show of aggression.

Molly squealed and tumbled backward, becoming a perfect target for the predator.

Garrett ran at Molly, shouting. He had to get closer. Startled, the animal shifted its focus, turning away from Molly. Garrett took four shots at the mountain lion. The big cat yowled once and bounded away, disappearing into the cover of the trees. He'd aimed the shots wide on purpose. Injuring the animal could have done more harm than good, especially if he hadn't been able to take it down. A wounded cat could tear out Molly's throat in seconds.

He'd played the odds.

Thankfully, the animal hadn't gone against its nature. Garrett kept his weapon on hold, searching beyond the shrubs and piñons for the cougar. Cats were normally reclusive, avoiding humans, but they were curious as well.

"Get her," he called to Laurel.

Behind him, she scooped Molly into her arms. The little girl sobbed. Laurel hugged her niece close. "It's okay. You're safe."

Garrett backed toward them, scanning the perimeter,

but there was no movement beyond the tree line. He kept the Beretta in his hand and headed to the house.

"I—I want my mommy." Molly hiccuped from Laurel's arms. *"Mommy!"*

"It's gone," he said.

No need to take chances, though. Within seconds, he'd escorted them inside. Once they were safe, he shut and locked the door. The little escape artist had figured out the dead bolt. He'd have to secure the door another way. It had been a long time since he'd childproofed anything.

His knees shook slightly, and he grabbed the doorjamb for support. Garrett could face down at AK-47 or an Uzi without increasing his heart rate by a beat or two.

A milk-faced Laurel sank into the sofa, rocking Molly in her arms. The little girl's cries tugged at his heart. Laurel rubbed her niece's back, and she turned her head to Garrett.

Thank you, she mouthed.

He'd brought them here, though. He'd put Molly in danger. He should have anticipated. He knew better. Whoever said girls didn't get into as much trouble as boys hadn't lived with his Ella. Or Molly.

"I just wanted to play with the kitty," she said through hiccups. "He's the same color as my lion."

Now that they were safe, Garrett's breathing slowed from a quick pant. He crouched next to the sofa. "I know, Molly, but that kind of kitty doesn't play. He's a wild animal. No more going outside alone. Okay?"

"I want your promise, Molly," Laurel said, her voice stern. "You can't go outside without me or Sheriff Garrett."

The little girl squirmed in Laurel's arms. "Okay."

Laurel allowed her niece to slide to the ground, but Garrett didn't trust that look. His daughter had played the game before. He held Molly firmly by the shoulders, looking her squarely in the eyes. "Listen to me, Molly. Outside is dangerous. We're in the woods and you could get lost. We might not find you. I want a real promise."

Her lower lip jutted out.

"Molly."

She let out a huge sigh. "I promise. Cross my heart, stick a nail in my eye, even if I don't want to."

Garrett held on to a chuckle at the little girl's mutilation of the saying. He stuck out his hand. "Deal."

She straightened up and placed her small hand in his. "Deal. Can I have something to eat? I'm hungry."

Kids. Hopefully she'd been scared enough to mind him. Mulling over how he could keep Molly in the cabin, Garrett walked over to the bag of food on the table.

"Play with your stuffed lion, Molly. We'll let you know when breakfast is ready."

"His name is Hairy Houdini. Daddy named him after me 'cause I always disappear." She ran off to the other room, swinging the lion in the air as if he were flying.

Laurel staggered to the kitchen table and slumped in the chair. She held her head in her hands. "Oh, God."

"You okay?" Garrett asked after pulling a skillet from a cabinet and setting it on the stove.

"My niece was almost a midmorning snack for a mountain lion. Not really."

"She's something else."

Laurel looked at the bedroom door. The little girl had an animated discussion going on with her toy. "Like nothing happened. Is that normal?"

"Kids are more resilient than we are," Garrett said before he could stop himself.

"You've had experience." Laurel folded her hands together. Quiet settled in the room, with only Molly's chatter breaking through.

Garrett's teeth gritted together. He wasn't having this conversation. She didn't need to know how he'd failed to protect his own wife and daughter. Not when he needed her to trust him.

So why did silence feel like a lie? "I'll be back in a few minutes," he said. "I need to get the rest of our supplies." He hurried out the door without giving her time to quiz him.

Idiot. The winter chill bit through his bomber jacket. He scrambled over the rocks and made it to the SUV in record time. He was giving too much away. What was it about her that made Laurel feel so…comfortable? He couldn't afford to like her. Emotions had no place in his world right now. Not when he was fighting an enemy that held all the cards.

He had to get back on track.

By the time he returned to the house with the last of the supplies, the crackle of bacon and a heavenly aroma filled the room.

"I found the bacon in the freezer," she said.

Garrett's stomach rumbled. He hadn't eaten since last night. Without saying a word, he set the groceries on the table and started putting them away. They worked side by side, together. Too comfortably. He sliced a couple of loaves of Hondo's homemade bread. Laurel slid one out of his hands, her touch lingering for a moment. She slathered the toast with butter and popped the slices in the broiler.

"After Molly eats, why don't you distract her?" Garrett said, clearing his throat. "I'll do some looking into your father."

Laurel put down a knife and turned slowly toward him. "How long have you been out of the game?" she asked.

"What makes you think—?"

"At first glance I didn't notice," she said, "but I checked out the equipment a second time while you were gone. Most of it is a couple years old. You haven't upgraded. If you were active, you'd have the latest."

"Molly, time to eat," Garrett called out.

He heard the slap of shoes as she raced into the room. She squealed and sat at the table. "Hairy and I are starving to death." She dug into the bacon and toast, munching down.

"Not a topic for conversation. I get it," Laurel said. "So, you have a favorite football team, Garrett?"

He looked over his shoulder and sighed. "Between your job and your father's career, you have to know sharing information is a bad idea."

"Not much choice. My father is in trouble. So am I. You may be able to help us, but you need me. I have contacts. People I trust. If we're careful they won't be able to trace us back here."

"Really? Even on my *outdated* equipment? Did Ivy trust them, too?"

Laurel hissed at the barb, but Garrett didn't waver.

"I won't apologize. Right now it's all about finding your father. And that means finishing the job your sister started. On our own."

MIKE STRICKLAND SAT in the SUV a block down from the sheriff's office. They'd gotten nowhere searching the man's house. The damn town hadn't had one 9-1-1 call the entire night.

He stroked his stubble-lined jaw. He'd been awake all night, knowing if he fell asleep and missed his chance, his life would be worth nothing.

Strickland couldn't believe Garrett Galloway was actually acknowledged traitor Derek Bradley.

Wasn't his fault the man had decided to take his family somewhere that day. Strickland shoved aside the prickle of regret. He'd gained the boss's confidence with that job. And he'd stayed alive.

He'd also attached himself to the organization the boss had created. Selling guns and secrets to the highest bidder: governments, terrorist organizations, corporations—it didn't matter.

Nothing mattered but the dollars. Loyalty didn't mean squat, and the boss didn't suffer fools. The stakes in the game were too high to risk compromise.

Unless Strickland killed Bradley—make that Galloway—before he saw the boss again, he'd be the next example.

A beat-up truck trundled in front of the sheriff's office. A young deputy jumped out of his truck. He turned the doorknob, then paused.

So, the sheriff was usually in before now.

The deputy dug his keys from his pocket, inserted one into the lock and pushed the door open.

Strickland's phone vibrated. "Tell me you have something," he bit out to Krauss.

"Nothing. Checked out the abandoned house where we triangulated the sheriff's cell signal. Evidence of someone there, but gone. No prints."

"His place?"

"Nothing."

"We're out of options," Strickland said. "I'm going to have a chat with the young deputy." He ended the call, tucked his unidentifiable Glock in his holster, waited for a couple of cars to pass by and stepped out of the vehicle.

He crossed the street and slipped into the sheriff's office.

"Deputy?"

"Can I help you, sir?"

The young man poked his head out from the back room. Strickland could take him out now and no one would have a lead to follow. He ran his hand over the weapon. "Looking for the sheriff."

The deputy sighed. "You and me both. He's not here yet."

"When do you expect him back?"

The kid stiffened, finally recognizing Strickland could very well be dangerous. "I told you I don't know. How can I help you?"

The kid shifted his stance, subtly showing his side-arm.

Strickland flashed his identification badge. "Federal business," he commented. "Contact him."

The deputy's face paled. "Of course." He stumbled to the desk and dialed a number. After thirty seconds his face fell. "Sheriff, a federal agent is here. He needs to see you—"

Strickland grabbed the phone. He lifted the receiver and punched in the erase code. "I didn't tell you to leave a message. Can't risk it."

The deputy stood up, his gaze narrowed, suspicious. "Why are you here?"

"Your sheriff might not be who he says he is, Deputy. I'm here to find out exactly who Garrett Galloway is."

"With all due respect, no way, sir. Sheriff Galloway is the real deal."

"You think so, do you? He ever talk about his past? He ever tell you anything about where he came from?"

"Well, no, but still, he's a good sheriff. Everyone says so."

"Maybe now. My agency has reason to believe he's behind a lot of crimes. Under his *real* name. You recognize the name Derek Bradley?"

The kid gasped. "He's a traitor. Sold secrets to terrorists. Caused a lot of men to get killed overseas. He got himself blown up a couple years ago."

"So the public was led to believe."

The deputy shook his head. "Not Sheriff Galloway."

Strickland leaned in. "Does he trust you?"

The kid nodded. "Yeah."

"He wouldn't leave town without letting you know, would he?"

"No, sir."

Strickland patted the kid's cheek. "Okay, then, here's what I want you to do. If he contacts you, I want you to keep your phone on. Don't end the call." He squeezed the deputy's shoulder. "What's your name?"

"Deputy Lance Keller, sir."

"Well, Lance, are you a patriot?"

The kid sprang to attention. "Yes, sir."

"Okay, then. You do this, and your country will thank you."

The deputy met his gaze. "I think you're wrong about the sheriff, sir."

"Could be. If he's innocent, nothing will happen, will it? And you'll have helped clear him."

Keller smiled. "Yes, sir."

"If he's guilty, you've saved a lot of lives."

Strickland turned and opened the front door. "I'm counting on you, Keller."

He walked back to his truck and picked up his phone. "Kid's clueless."

"You kill him?"

"Came a second away from pulling the trigger, but not yet. Galloway's a straight-as-an-arrow spy. It's what got him into trouble in the first place. He might contact the deputy. And if he does, we'll have him." Strickland paused. "*Then* I kill him."

GARRETT PEEKED INTO the living room. Laurel and Molly were playing hide-and-seek, with Hairy Houdini the key player. He smiled softly. It had been so long since he'd heard that kind of joy.

So many lost memories.

And Laurel. She had his heart beating again. He didn't know if he liked feeling again. A cold heart made it easier to focus on revenge.

She let out a laugh and tackled Molly in a gentle hold. Those two had melted the ice encasing his heart. And Laurel had lit a fire.

He wanted to scoop her into his arms, touch her and hold her until she trembled against him. They could both forget the past and lose themselves in each other. He'd recognized the heat, the awareness in her eyes.

She wouldn't say no.

Problem was, Laurel was a forever kind of woman. And Garrett had stopped believing he had a forever.

The reality made this decision easier. He planted himself in his office chair and picked up the secure line. For a moment he hesitated. Daniel Adams had been through hell, but the man had connections…and he was one of the good guys. These days, men who lived by a code of honor were few and far between. Many talked the talk. Few walked the walk.

He punched in the number Daniel had given him.

"Adams." Daniel's voice held suspicion.

Garrett was silent for a few moments. Daniel said nothing either, obviously unwilling to give anything away.

"It's Garrett Galloway," he finally said.

"If you're calling on this line, it must be serious, and not to request an invitation to Christmas dinner."

"You said to call if I needed a favor. I might. And it's a big one. Just how covert can your *friends* be?"

"Very. What's the situation?" Daniel's voice went soft. A few loud squeals sounded in the background before the snick of a door closing muffled the noise.

"My past is raising a dangerous head, complete with teeth. A woman and her niece are in the cross fire. If I fail, they need new identities and a new life. Untraceable, undetectable."

Daniel let out a low whistle. "I always wondered about you, Garrett."

"Look, Daniel, don't run a search on me. Eyes are everywhere. The minute you pull strings, those eyes will come back on you and your friends. You get me?"

"I played the game," Daniel said. "Do your friends know what they're in for if they disappear?"

"I'll make sure they understand. We're not far from

that gorge you hid out in. How long will it take you to get here?"

"I can have a chopper there in less than an hour."

"I think we'll have to talk about that." Behind him Laurel stood in the doorway, foot tapping. "You're palming us off? Where's that idea of working together, *Sheriff*? I'm not ready to give up on having my life back yet."

Daniel chuckled at the other end of the phone. "She reminds me of my wife. Doesn't take any prisoners. You need me, call this number. I'll have the helicopter on standby."

"No details. To anyone."

"None needed. They know me. You had my back once, Garrett. I've got yours."

Garrett hung up the secure phone and turned around in his chair. He'd know very soon which direction this operation would be taking.

He had a feeling he knew. And that Laurel wasn't going to like it.

NOON HAD COME and gone. Laurel kissed Molly's forehead and quietly closed the door to the bedroom. The little girl had fallen asleep before her usual nap time, but she was exhausted. Even though the weather was brisk, the sun had shone. They'd explored outside, careful to make enough noise to startle any other predators from coming too close. They'd collected pinecones. The moment Laurel had crossed the baseball-sized tracks of the big cat, she and Molly had scurried back to the house. She didn't want to come face-to-face with it again, even with her SIG.

She hovered over the sleeping girl for a few minutes. Molly hadn't mentioned her brother or sister all morning. Laurel couldn't help but worry. When the truth hit, it would hit hard.

She left a small crack between the door and the jamb so she could hear Molly if she woke.

Quietly she exited into the living room. Garrett must still be in his office. She padded across the wood floor and stuck her head through the door.

He sat in front of the wall of electronics, bent over, studying the monitor intently. He typed in a few keystrokes. The screen turned red.

He cursed and quickly pressed a button.

"No luck?"

The chair whirled around. He'd removed his hat and his hair stood up, as if he'd run his fingers through it dozens of times.

"They've closed off most of the loopholes I knew about. Not surprised, just irritated. I let James…" His voice trailed off.

She eased through the doorway. "What about my father?"

For a moment it looked as if he wouldn't tell her. Finally he met her gaze. "I kept a low profile. It was the wrong decision."

"I can help," she said. "Let me do my job. What are you looking for?"

He glanced at the cracked-open door. "Molly?"

"Asleep. Her afternoon naps are usually an hour or so, if her visits with me hold."

"Front door locked?" he asked with a raised brow.

"Dead bolted and chained at the top," Laurel said with a shake of her head. "Ivy said Molly started finding ways out of her crib at just a year old. Once she caught her climbing over the side rail and then just hanging there by her fingertips before jumping down and going after her lion."

"Maybe she'll be a gymnast." Garrett chuckled. "Or a spy." His face turned serious. "I'm trying to identify James's last *official* location, but I haven't found a record of travel, much less any files. His data is locked down tight."

He faced the screen and Laurel bent over him. She rested her hand on his shoulder and leaned in. "I monitor data coming from Afghan tribal leaders," Laurel said. "I might have access to some locations or at least chatter."

"Can you get in from the outside?"

"Are you on a classified network?"

"Secure, not classified," Garrett said. "No way I could pull that off for this long without someone noticing."

"I could get at some information." She gnawed at her lip. "I could end up leading them here, Garrett."

"I know."

He rose from his chair and paced the room. "James said the operation had been compromised. That probably means they'll be looking for my signature."

"He also mentioned Ivy's research."

Garrett tapped his temple with his forefinger. "You know your sister. You know how she thinks. Maybe we can get to her files through you, instead of me or James."

"There's still the problem of leading them here. If I use her name or any identifying information, they'll know it's me. Us."

"You're right." He patted the console. "We do much more here and it'll be the last bit of info they need to come after us."

At the look on Garrett's face, Laurel stepped back,

understanding flooding through her. Garrett *had* learned from her father. Classic James McCallister M.O. "You *want* them to catch you?" She grabbed his shirt collar. "You saw what they did to Ivy. You can't do that."

"You're too damned observant." Garrett scowled at her. "And yeah, I know *exactly* what they might do to me. On the other hand, they won't be expecting me to be ready for them. I'm going to let them think they're getting the drop on me. Surprise is worth a lot."

"It's crazy."

"You think I love this plan, Laurel? If I were planning this op, this would be option Z. But that's where we're at. It's the *only* option. We don't have the insider to help us. We don't know who the traitor is. Your father hasn't contacted us again. We have no choice."

"What about Molly?" Laurel whispered.

"I called a friend while I was retrieving the groceries. He's someone I can trust. Maybe the only person I can trust. He has friends who can hide you and Molly while I go after James."

She could see he'd made up his mind, but there had to be another way. She sat across from him and grabbed his hands, squeezing them tight. "Let me try? We can cut off communication if it's taking too long or if I detect someone tracing us." She met his gaze. "I'm good at what I do, Garrett. Let me try."

"I watch every move. The moment there's feedback, we turn it off and go with my plan. Agreed?"

She was silent for a moment.

"Those are my conditions, Laurel."

"Agreed."

She took a seat and stared at the keyboard. She prayed her abilities wouldn't fail her now.

A LOUD SCREAM yanked James McCallister awake. For a split second he didn't know where he was. Then the pain overwhelmed him. He fought not to cry out.

He shifted his legs, trying to ease the tension in his shoulders. His jailer had shoved him into this dirt-walled prison, clamped a manacle over each wrist and whipped him until he lost consciousness.

James had said nothing.

Footsteps walked down the hallway. James looked up; his eyes widened with shock, and then nausea rose up his throat.

He couldn't believe it.

And yet the proof stood before him.

"I…I wouldn't have guessed," he said through dry lips. "You fooled me."

"Of course I did, but you cost me nearly a billion dollars this month, James. I'm not happy. You know I get cranky when I'm not happy."

A knife sliced down his chest, drawing blood. He hissed, pulling away, but the movement only caused droplets to fall to the floor.

"And Garrett Galloway."

James struggled to keep his heart from racing.

"Oh, yes. I know he's alive. You hid him well. I just wanted you to know that I'm smarter than you are." His captor lifted out a small device.

James nearly groaned. Impossible. No one should have discovered his secret.

"That's right. I can track Garrett Galloway anywhere. He's dead, James. And it's all your fault."

Chapter Five

Laurel leaned forward in the chair, staring at the screen. The disappointment nearly suffocated her.

"It's okay," Garrett said softly. His hand rubbed her back.

"I can't find him." She shrank away from his touch. She didn't want comfort. She'd failed. She'd been so certain. She shoved away from the console.

"Don't do this to yourself." He stood beside her and turned her into his arms. He looked down at her. The expression on his face held too much sympathy.

"I failed my father. I failed Ivy. I failed you." She tried to push away, but he refused to let her go. She shook her head. "I failed Molly."

Laurel couldn't stop the tears from rolling down her face. She'd thought she could do this. She'd believed if she were in her element she could save them all. What a fool she'd been.

"Listen to me. These people are good. I wasn't able to catch them. Neither was Ivy. Or your father. You didn't let anyone down."

He pressed her into his chest. She clung to his shirt, gripping him tight. His warmth seeped through her as the sobs racked her body.

"Shh," he muttered. "It's okay."

Laurel couldn't stop the flood of emotions: the guilt, the pain, the grief. Everything overwhelmed her. She didn't know how long she stood in Garrett's embrace, but when she came up for air, her body was spent.

He rubbed her back awhile longer, whispering soft words of comfort—lies, really. Because nothing would be all right. It couldn't be.

Finally she pushed against his chest and tried to hide her face from him. He tilted her chin up. "You don't have to hide. You just did what I wanted to do from the moment I came to Trouble."

With a swipe of her tears, she cleared her throat. "Doesn't do any good. Now I'm exhausted and fuzzy headed."

"And less likely to crumble under the pressure. Molly will need that strength from you."

"You're going to lay down a trail of bread crumbs, aren't you?"

"Yeah."

"Without backup? You can't."

Garrett brushed aside the chopped hair that didn't feel like hers. "I can't let them use you and Molly as leverage. Not against James. Or me." He closed in on her, his large frame looming. His presence sucked the air from the room. He took her hand in his. "You can trust Daniel, and he has connections. If I fail, they can give you a new life."

She gripped his fingers. "Dad will kick my butt if I let you sacrifice yourself without a fight."

"He'd understand," Garrett said, his face certain, frozen like stone.

"Convince me," Laurel said, placing her hand on his chest. "They could end up using you anyway."

Garrett whirled away from her, stalked across the room and shoved his hands through his hair. "You are the most stubborn woman I have ever had the misfortune of meeting. And that's saying a lot given the work I do. Why can't you just agree?"

"Because I can't let you go on a suicide mission." She followed him, reaching up to his shoulders. Something more was going on with him. She could feel it.

She tugged at his arm, trying to see his face, look into his eyes. When he finally faced her, she gasped at the pain in his expression.

"Why are you doing this, really?" she whispered, leaning into him.

"It's not important." Garrett cleared his throat and then his hand trembled. He cupped her cheek. "You and Molly need to be safe. I can't let anything happen to you."

The air grew thick between them.

"Because of your loyalty to my father?"

His thumb stroked her skin. She closed her eyes. Something had been simmering between them since they'd met.

"Because I can't let anyone else I care about get hurt."

With a groan he lowered his mouth to hers. She clung to him, holding his face between her hands while he explored her lips.

He tasted of coffee, a hint of cinnamon and something uniquely Garrett. With each caress of his mouth, a tingle built low in her belly as if he had a direct line to her soul. A low rumble built within his chest and he scooped her against him, flattening her breasts against his chest.

This wasn't like any first kiss she'd ever experienced. He took her mouth as if he owned her, and she met him more than halfway. When he tried to raise his head she tugged him back down.

"More," she whispered. "Make me feel."

She wanted to lose herself in his touch. She tugged his shirt from his pants and let her fingers explore the skin of his belly, then up to the hair on his chest.

"You're playing with fire," he muttered.

"Then let me burn."

A squeaking door erupted between them. Laurel's eyes grew wide.

"Molly."

"AUNT LAUREL, I'M BORED. There aren't any toys here." Molly shoved into the office, her little arms crossed. Laurel sprang out of Garrett's arms, her face flushed.

"What are you doing?"

Garrett cleared his throat and tried to order his body under control. He glanced down at Laurel. She didn't appear any less flushed. Her cheeks went red and she pulled her hands from beneath his shirt. He regretted the loss, but in some ways Molly had saved them both. He smiled at the little girl. "So, sugar, it's almost lunchtime. How would you like to go on a picnic?"

Laurel stepped back, her expression stunned. "I don't think—"

"What about the big kitty?" Molly asked, her voice tentative.

"Well, I'll be there, and cats usually stay away from people. We'll be fine."

"Absolutely not." Laurel shook her head. "It's December."

"December in West Texas isn't the same as anywhere else," Garrett said. "All she needs is a jacket. And we both need to run off some energy, take in a bit of brisk air." He sent her a pointed glance.

"Oh, please, Aunt Laurel," Molly said, tugging on her shirt. "I wanna have lunch outside and go 'sploring with Sheriff Garrett."

Laurel's face softened, and Garrett could see her indecision. Laurel loved her niece. He liked her fierce protectiveness. Laurel McCallister had a lot of her dad in her. Courage that started with a spine of steel. Courage that made her way too attractive for his peace of mind.

Besides, if they stayed in this cabin, Garrett didn't know how much longer he could resist her. James would take him to the torture chamber if Garrett put the moves on his little girl.

"I need to take a look around and set a few pieces of equipment." Laurel sent him a meaningful gaze. So she'd decided to work with him.

One surprise after another, this woman.

"Yay!" Molly twirled around and around. "We're going on a picnic. We're going on a picnic," she repeated over and over again in a singsong voice.

She skipped around the small cabin.

"Are you sure about this?"

"Do you want to try to keep her inside all day and then get her to sleep tonight?" Garrett arched a brow.

Laurel's gaze fell to Molly's movements, and then she sighed. "I thought she'd grieve more," she said. "I thought she'd be sad." She reached into the box of staples Garrett had brought and pulled out the homemade bread, then grabbed the sandwich fixings Hondo had provided out of the small refrigerator.

"She will be. She'll have a moment when she falls, but right now, something isn't letting her process what happened."

Laurel spread mustard over a piece of bread, then bent over the sink, clutching the porcelain. Her shoulders sagged. For a moment or two she fought the emotion. Everything inside Garrett made him want to hold her, comfort her, but he also knew sometimes grief needed space.

When her shoulders quivered, then shook, Garrett couldn't stay away. He crossed the small kitchen in two steps and placed his hands on her shoulders. He bent to her ear. "It's okay," he whispered.

Molly entertained herself across the room. He turned Laurel in his arms. Tears streamed down her face. She buried her head against his shoulder to hide them.

"I miss Ivy. I miss my family." Her voice had thickened with grief. Garrett rubbed her back, holding her close.

After he'd woken from the coma, alone in a hospital, with a new name, he hadn't had time to cry. God, he'd wanted to, but there was no one left to comfort him or hold him. His family was gone.

He could hold Laurel, though. His arms wrapped tighter around her. He kept his gaze locked on Molly, who'd found an afghan and a small cardboard box and was creating a fort under a beat-up end table.

"Can she see me?" Laurel whispered, her voice thick with tears.

"She's playing," Garrett said.

Laurel trembled against him. Then a calmness flowed through her. She stood in his arms, soft, welcoming.

Comfort shifted to something more, something else.

Something simmering beneath the surface. She cleared her throat and straightened, swiping at her wet cheeks. Through her lowered lashes, she looked up at him. "I'm okay now."

He stroked a tear from her cheek. "You don't have to be."

She glanced over at Molly. "Yeah, I do." Laurel pasted a smile on her face and strode over to Molly, hunkering down. "Whatcha doin', Molly Magoo? Can I come in your fort?"

Garrett turned back to the half-made picnic lunch, thankful Laurel had crossed the room. She and Molly had reawakened his emotions, emotions he couldn't afford to have.

He'd gone against his best instincts when he'd fallen in love with Lisa seven years ago. James had warned him, had told him that there would be secrets he could never tell his wife, lies he'd be forced to live. He'd even said there was a remote chance of danger from the enemy.

The enemy wasn't who'd gotten him… He'd been framed by one of his own. Of that he was certain.

He snagged some bottled water and a juice box from the refrigerator, completing their lunch. "Ready, ladies?" he called out.

Molly scooted from under the blanket and ran across the room. She peered into the makeshift picnic basket Garrett had created using a box. "Cookies?" She blinked up at him, those baby blues innocent and hopeful.

"What's a picnic without Hondo's cookies?" Garrett said. "Can you take this?" he asked Laurel. She grasped the box and he strode into his room. He unlocked the closet and entered a combination into a hidden safe. Quickly, he pulled out his dad's Remington.

He walked over to her. She tugged the box closer. "I'll take this. I like your hands free. In case the big kitty shows up again."

They walked out of the ranch house. The midday sun shone through a bright blue sky. Laurel gazed up. "I've never seen a color like that before."

"Welcome to the desert," Garrett said. "A little different from the East Coast, huh?"

"Considering they started today getting doused in snow, I'd say yes."

Molly bent over and picked up a pinecone. "Ooh. Sticky," she said, dropping it. She skipped around Garrett and Laurel, then ran a bit ahead.

"Molly," Garrett said with a warning tone.

She stopped and turned. "Sorry." She bowed her head and kicked a small rock.

"Just let me go first when we come to a thicket of trees," he said.

"What's a thicket?"

"A big group. Like right here."

Garrett stepped into a small grove. He bent down. "See where the winter grass is bent over? An animal slept here sometime last night or this morning."

He looked around and knelt beside a few tracks, two teardrops side by side. "Deer, probably mule deer in these parts."

Molly crouched beside him. "You can tell that?"

"Everything and everyone makes its mark." He shot her a sidelong glance. "Most everything can be traced or tracked. No one is invisible."

"My job was to analyze data from sources no one can imagine," Laurel said. "I know it's difficult to hide. But not impossible."

"Fair." Garrett stood. "But if it were easy to hide, Ivy would never have found me at all."

The admission didn't come easy, but Laurel needed to understand how difficult her life was about to become.

"There's a small pool nearby. We've had some rain this year, so it might be full."

They climbed over some more craggy rocks to a granite outcropping. The sun had warmed the rock, and below, a large pool of water glistened in the light.

"Just the place for our picnic."

He looked at the surroundings. Safe, and it was clear enough that he had a view where he could see anyone coming.

"Not exactly rolling hills," Laurel said, sitting down with the small box holding their lunch.

"I want to sit by here," Molly said, pointing at a small, flat rock.

"Just your size," Garrett said.

"Nothing rolling or quaint about West Texas," Garrett offered, pulling the sandwiches from the bag.

"It's dramatic," she admitted. "You can see forever."

"I like this spot. I come here sometimes. To think. Nothing small about this land. About seventy-six miles that way is the border with Mexico. North fifty miles and you're in New Mexico. On a clear day like today, you can see one hundred and fifty miles. Can't do that on the coast." He handed Molly a juice box.

"You miss D.C.?"

Garrett bit into his sandwich, swallowing past the lump in his throat, and considered his answer. "I miss the life I had." He missed his family. Every day. He no longer wanted to die along with them. The need for revenge made a body fight. Just to make the guilty pay.

Laurel's gaze fell to Molly. "I understand that. Going back will never be the same, will it?"

"Nothing is ever the same."

Molly crossed her legs and gazed into the water. "Can I touch it?"

"It's cold," Garrett warned.

Molly tiptoed to the edge of the pool, squatted in front of it and dipped her hand into the water. She snatched it back with a yelp.

"I'm not swimming in there." She raced back to Laurel and hugged her legs. "Too cold."

"Molly, do you see this rock?" Garrett picked up a piece of dark granite.

"It sparkles."

Molly's eyes widened as the stone glittered in the sunlight. "Can I keep it to show my mommy when she comes back?"

"You can have it," Garrett said, then lifted a familiar bag from the box.

Molly grinned. "Cookies?"

He set the treat aside. "Of course."

Molly popped a cookie in her mouth. When she finished it off, her leg swung on the side of the rock. "Can I go 'sploring?"

Laurel started to shake her head, but Garrett interrupted, "We've made too much noise not to drive the animals away." He turned to Molly. "Stay in sight. If you leave the clearing, we'll have to go back to the house."

"Cross my heart, hope to die, stick a nail in my eye," Molly said, making a motion across her chest.

A chuckle escaped Garrett. She was so like his Ella.

But so different, too. Molly jumped from the rock. She scampered to the edge of the clearing.

He folded Laurel's hand in his. "She'll be okay. I promise we're making too much noise for the cougar to be interested," he said.

"Bears?"

"Not here. Not enough vegetation and large animals."

Laurel dropped her half-eaten sandwich in the box and stood. She watched Molly. "I'm scared for her."

Garrett rose from the rock. "She's a strong girl. She's got a great aunt. You'll both make it through this."

"What if whoever killed Ivy gets away with it?"

Garrett couldn't stop his teeth from grinding together. No way would he let that happen. Not while he still lived. But he couldn't promise anything. The people after him had no morals, no conscience. If anyone got in their way, they killed them. And they didn't care about the innocent ones who got hurt in the process.

He turned Laurel in his arms and stared into her eyes. "However this goes, I'll make sure you and Molly find a way to be safe."

Laurel lowered her lids. "They might get away with it."

Garrett couldn't deny the truth of her words. Instead, he tilted her chin up with his finger. His heart stuttered at her pain-filled gaze. She'd lost her sister, her brother-in-law, one niece and nephew, and she might have lost her father. She'd lost the life she once had. He wanted to make everything go away, but he might not be able to. "I won't stop until I find them, Laurel."

She shivered in his arms. He tugged her a bit closer, his gaze falling on Molly. The little girl had hunkered down, stacking pinecones. He wrapped Laurel in his arms, pulling her close, and rested his cheek against her hair. Her warmth seeped into his skin, even as the sun shone down on his face.

For one moment he could comfort her. She sighed, leaning against him. "I wish we could stay here forever and the rest of the world would stop," she said.

Garrett closed his eyes, breathing in the fragrance of her hair. He turned and kissed her temple. Her arms tightened around his body. The comfort shifted into something more. Laurel tilted her head, her gaze stopping at his mouth. Garrett stilled, unable to stop the desire flaring just beneath the surface.

"I found a track, Sheriff Garrett," Molly shouted.

Laurel stiffened in his arms. He sighed and touched his finger to her lips. "Sometime soon," he promised. "When we can't be interrupted."

A pang of conscience needled the back of his neck. They were in danger and no one knew what was going to happen, but he couldn't deny the pull between him and Laurel. He'd been so alone for so long. Having her in his arms made him...made him feel hope again.

She squeezed his hand, her gaze warm, her cobalt eyes flaring with a hidden fire. With a sigh of regret, he walked across the small clearing where Molly hunkered down just at the edge.

"What have you found, sugar?"

She pointed a few feet past the row of pines. Garrett stilled. The track was human.

He peered past the trees into a clearing. The remains of a campfire had been hastily shoved aside, but the ash and rocks used to surround the small flames couldn't be mistaken.

Garrett's hand hovered over his weapon. His voice soft and low, he reached out a hand. "Come on, Molly."

"But I found a track."

"And you did well, but we need to go." He scooped her into his arms and strode away from the edge of the trees, one hand still inches from his weapon.

"What'd I do?" Molly whispered. "I didn't do anything wrong."

Laurel met him and he handed over the little girl. "What's wrong?" Laurel pulled the girl to her. "Shh, Molly."

"Company," he said, his voice calm.

Her eyes widened and a line of tension drew her mouth.

Molly squirmed in her arms. "I'm scared."

"Go back the way we came," Garrett said. He tugged the Beretta from beneath his jacket. "You have your SIG?"

She nodded.

"Be ready."

She shuffled Molly in her arms.

"Fire in the air if you see anything or anyone and then head back toward the ranch. I'll catch you. Can you find it?"

She nodded, placing herself at the edge of the clearing, ready to bolt, her hand gripping the weapon.

Garrett pushed through the pines and studied the ground. There were at least two sets of shoes. He sifted the dirt. The fire's remains were cold. They hadn't been watching. The tension in his chest eased a bit.

He glanced over at Laurel. She stood alert, watching everything. She would protect Molly with her life. He didn't like leaving them alone, but he needed to discover who these two people were. He followed the trail. The ground told many truths. One person fell, then scrambled to his feet. Garrett hit some granite rock and the trail vanished, but he picked it back up again on the other side.

Kneeling down, he studied the prints. "Who are you?"

Then he caught sight of a small impression. A kid's sneaker.

Aah. Quietly, he topped a hill. Below, a man hurried his wife and son across the terrain. The guy looked at him, and Garrett knew he recognized the sheriff's uniform, even without the star.

His face erupted in terror, but he didn't pull a weapon. He shoved his wife and son behind him and stared up at Garrett.

Not a great place to cross the border. Especially with a family. Was a coyote nearby? Most of the men who made a living illegally bringing people across the border made Garrett's stomach turn. They charged thousands of dollars to cross into the United States, and if their "customers" were lucky, the coyote got them to civilization. The unlucky ones ended up dead of thirst in the desert.

Garrett scanned the horizon, searching for signs of a coyote, but he didn't see anyone.

With a quick nod to the man, he turned and hurried back toward the clearing. He had to get Laurel and Molly to safety.

They might end up much like that man and his family. Living under the radar.

Unless Garrett succeeded where he and James had failed for the past eighteen months.

Garrett shoved his Stetson on his head. Now, though,

he had to succeed for more than just revenge—he had to succeed to protect two innocent lives.

He wouldn't lose. He couldn't.

LAUREL CARRIED MOLLY back into the cabin. Her niece was way too quiet. The little girl toyed with the collar Ivy had placed around the neck of her lion.

Garrett followed her in. "I'm canvassing the area once more. Lock the door behind me. I'll knock three times when I get back. And keep the gun handy."

"Shoot if someone else tries to get in," Laurel said. "Got it."

"Not if it's me." Garrett shut the door, putting the box of food on the floor.

Molly wiggled from Laurel's arms. "I want to go into my fort," she muttered. "I want Mr. Hairy Houdini to come with me."

"Want me to play with you?"

The little girl whispered into her stuffed animal's ear and shook her head, disappearing beneath the afghan.

Laurel sighed and put away the groceries, keeping a close eye on Molly.

Within a few minutes, the little girl was rubbing her eyes and yawning. It had been a tough few days. Not to mention just getting over strep throat.

Massaging her temple, Laurel scanned the room. They couldn't stay here forever. The only way out was to find who was behind Ivy's murder. And her father's disappearance. And stop them.

Garrett knew more than he was revealing. She believed that, and she didn't know who he was, really. That uneasy feeling at the base of her neck increased the urgency. She needed to *do* something. To protect Molly and herself. Not just for the moment, but for the future.

Laurel checked once more on her niece, but the little girl had zonked out.

Careful not to make any noise, she opened Garrett's office door and walked inside. She propped the door open so she could hear Molly or anyone outside and turned the machines on.

She'd had an idea. Maybe, just maybe, it would work.

Growing up with her father's ability to discover what his daughters were doing, Laurel had become adept at hiding her tracks. She'd joined the computer club at school. Yeah, it had helped her get into college, but more important, it had taught her a few tricks. Tricks that came in handy at her job, and that might come in even handier now.

She risked a lot doing this without Garrett here, but she had to try. It was her last chance or they'd have to go with Garrett's plan.

She navigated to a portal leading into some of the intelligence organization's unclassified databases.

When the log-in came up, she tapped her finger on the keyboard.

If she entered her information, she was starting a ticking clock. Eventually they would know she'd entered the system; they'd know what she discovered.

Garrett still hadn't returned.

She took a deep breath. She had to take the chance.

Her finger trembled typing in the password.

She was in.

Glancing at the time on the computer screen, she quickly

navigated to the travel database. Relatively low priority. She entered her father's name.

Access denied.

Interesting. She backed out, this time searching for Ivy's name, then hers. Finally, with her own name, she received a different screen.

Clicking on a link pulled up her personal data.

Status: Missing, presumed dead.

"What the hell do you think you're doing?"

Chapter Six

Strickland cursed. "Waiting around in this godforsaken town is getting us nowhere." The December Texas sun heated up the SUV and sweat trickled down his neck. He wiped his arm on his forehead. "Garrett Galloway isn't coming back."

"Do you think he knows the boss has found him?" Krauss asked, rolling down the window enough to allow a small crack. A soft, cool breeze flowed in. "I sure wouldn't stick around."

"Could be he ran. Or maybe he's hiding the woman and the girl."

"We're screwed either way, you know." Krauss's tone held nothing but resignation. "The boss'll find out we lost him, and we'll be dead. We're expendable and you know it. We both know it."

Krauss was right. But there had to be a way out. Maybe that deputy… Derek Bradley, aka Garrett Galloway, had lived in this town awhile. Strickland had discovered the people liked him. The waitress at the diner, the deputy, the local motel owner—they all thought the guy walked on water. Though that motel guy had shown Strickland the door too fast when his loopy sister had shown up and started yammering.

Maybe the tattooed freak knew more than he let on.

Strickland drummed his fingers on the steering wheel. "So, Krauss. You think Galloway would come back if real trouble visited Trouble, Texas?"

Krauss slowly nodded his head, a glimmer of hope reaching his eyes. "After what we know about both his identities, yeah. He's just enough of a hero to take the risk…if the bait is right."

"And I think I know exactly who—" Strickland's phone sounded. One glance at the number appearing on the screen and he could feel the blood drain from his face.

"It's the boss, isn't it?" Krauss said, a string of curses escaping from him. "What are you going to say?"

"I don't know." Strickland rubbed the back of his neck and tapped the phone. "Strickland."

"Imagine my surprise when I discovered your current location. Why didn't you tell me you were already in Trouble, Texas?"

At the biting tone of his boss's voice, he shivered, then gulped. He didn't have a good answer.

"Don't bother lying. There aren't a thousand people in that town. You come clean, Strickland, I might let you live…minus a body part or two."

Strickland met Krauss's gaze. The man's expression looked as if he'd scarfed down a large helping of bad fish. He'd seen the boss's handiwork. Missing fingers, missing toes, missing eyes…and worse.

"I—I saw a note Ivy Deerfield wrote when we went to set up the bomb." Strickland couldn't prevent the squeak in his voice as he lied. "She wrote down this sheriff's name. I just wanted to make sure she hadn't given anything—"

"How did you discover the connection between the McCallisters and Galloway?" his boss asked sharply.

"I didn't know about a link. I just had a bad feeling." More truth in those words. Strickland swallowed again. "You ordered us to follow up on loose ends. And to get rid of them."

"Which you enjoy a little too much," his boss muttered. "Okay, Strickland, I'll let you fix your little problem, but if I find out you're keeping something from me—"

"I've worked for you too long, boss," he said. Yeah, long enough to know that if he told her the truth of how he'd had them and lost them, she wouldn't just take a body part—she'd make him suffer and want to die.

Krauss just shook his head.

"Perhaps." The boss paused for a moment. "Well, Strickland, this may be your lucky day. I have Garrett Galloway's location for you. A gift from…a good friend."

The boss gave him a frequency. Krauss entered the number into the small tracking device. A red dot appeared on the screen. "He's in the mountains not far from here," Krauss said. "Rough country."

"Are you sure it's him? Or could this be his laptop or something?" Strickland asked.

A chuckle filtered through the phone. "It's inside him. You track that frequency, you'll have your target."

Strickland scratched at a surgical scar from a rotator-cuff repair a year or so ago. "That's not possible."

"Really? You have an inside track on the latest research and development of the agency, do you?"

Strickland gulped at the disdain in his boss's voice. "Of course not."

"You better be glad the chip isn't widely available. If I'd had one inserted inside you, I have a very good feeling you'd already be paying the price for some extracurricular activities."

The muscles in Strickland's back tensed. The only way out of this mess was clean it up and beg…or find out something he could bargain with.

"Find him, Strickland. And kill him. No mistakes." The phone call ended.

He grabbed the map from Krauss's hand and smiled for the first time since he'd realized the McCallister woman had escaped the bomb. "We have a pointer to Galloway. Which means we have McCallister and the kid, too. They're out in the middle of nowhere."

"Easy to dispose of bodies out there. No one will ever find them."

"Yeah." Strickland stared down at his phone. Now if he could only find a way that he wouldn't disappear either.

AT GARRETT'S BITING WORDS, Laurel's hands froze above the computer keyboard. She winced and whirled her chair around. If she'd thought he might be glad she'd taken the initiative to use her skills, that notion vanished the moment she took in his tight jaw and narrowed gaze.

"I had an idea," she protested. The niggling doubts that had skittered up her spine when she turned on the machine gnawed through her nerves. But what choice did they have?

"You've started the ticking clock." His cheek muscles pulsed.

That she had an answer for. "The clock would have

started anyway. We both know that. I just happened to control the start."

"Explain."

"I set up the signal to bounce all over the world. We're on a ticking clock—like you wanted, but thirty-six hours from now. Maybe forty-eight."

"How certain are you?"

"I wouldn't play with Molly's life like that. Or yours."

He studied her expression, then finally nodded his head. "Then sit down in the damn chair and get us some information. You started this. Let's see what your stint at the CIA can do for us."

Garrett snagged a kitchen chair from the other room and flipped it around, sitting astride the hard wood. She let out a long, slow breath. She knew her business, but her nerves crackled at his constant stare. Leaning forward, she focused on the monitor.

Soon she lost herself in the task, following path after path. She didn't know how long she'd been beating her head up against dead ends when a folder suddenly appeared.

Laurel stilled. "Look. The directory belongs to Ivy, but it's not official."

Garrett straightened in his chair. "Unauthorized?"

She nodded and clicked on the folder. It contained only one file. "It could be a trap."

"You've been at this awhile. What's your gut say?"

"To open it."

"Then do it."

She held her breath and double-clicked the file.

A password box came up.

"You know it?" Garrett asked.

"Maybe," Laurel said. She typed in her sister's anniversary.

Access denied.

Her children's names.

Access denied.

Her birthday.

Access denied.

"One more shot and I'm locked out. I'll have to start over," Laurel said, rubbing her eyes. "I may not even get access to the file again."

A long, slow breath escaped from Garrett. "You know your sister. Most of these passwords require at least one capital letter, one symbol and one number. And once you encrypt a file, if you forget the password, you're screwed. She'd have to be able to remember it."

Laurel drummed her fingers on the desk and sat back in the chair. She closed her eyes. "Ivy, what did you do?"

The room grew quiet, just the fan of the equipment breaking the silence.

Garrett didn't chatter, didn't interrupt her thoughts. She liked that about him. So many people didn't know when to simply be quiet.

"I may have it." She turned her head, meeting his gaze. "Ivy was older than me. She'd just started to date when Mom died. They had this special code. Even while Mom was in the hospital, she made Ivy promise to let her know if she was okay at nine o'clock. If there was trouble, there was a special message she'd leave on the pager."

"What was the code?"

"Mom's name, then nine-one-one, then an exclamation point. But if I'm wrong…"

"What do your instincts say?"

"That Ivy knew she was in danger and that she would pick something I knew." Laurel kneaded the back of her neck, her eyes burning. "She knew there was trouble."

"Do it."

Laurel swerved around and placed her hands on the keyboard. She couldn't make her fingers type in the password. What if she was wrong?

"Trust your gut." Garrett placed his hand on her shoulder. "Do it."

Laurel picked the keys out one at a time, taking extra care. Finally, she bit down on her lip and hit the enter key.

The machine whirred. The screen went blank.

"Please, no." She half expected a message with red flashing lights and alarms to appear stating the file had been destroyed.

A few clicks sounded and the word-processing program sprang to life.

Ivy's file opened. Laurel blinked. Then blinked again.

At the top of the file in bold letters were just a few words.

Derek Bradley is alive.
Alias: Sheriff Garrett Galloway.

THE WORDS SCREAMED from the page. Garrett groaned and gripped the wooden slats of the chair until his fingers cramped. Ivy had found out about him. This couldn't be happening. If she knew…others knew as well.

James's plan had failed. And God knew who he could trust.

Laurel launched out of her chair and faced him. "*You* are Derek Bradley? The traitor?" She backed away, shaking her head.

"Laurel—"

"You caused the deaths of dozens of agents. My father told me. He said you finally got paid back. You died with your wife…and daughter." Her hand slapped against her mouth, and her eyes widened. "It was a car bomb."

"I should have died. My wife and daughter *did* die," Garrett said, his voice holding a bitterness that burned his throat. How many times had he begged to die only to have first James, then the doctors, fight to save him? How many weeks had he lain in his hospital bed planning revenge when he discovered who had taken them from him?

Laurel's eyes were wide with horror. "Like Ivy."

Garrett gave a stiff nod. "I was running late on my way home from the office. I'd promised my wife I'd get home early, but I'd been hell-bent on tracking down an insider. I'd discovered a few hints, nothing concrete, but enough to keep me asking questions, pursuing leads in areas where I had limited need to know." He could barely look at the knowledge in her eyes. She knew what was coming, but he had to get it out. She had to understand. "I was running late, tying my tie. Lisa took my daughter and put her in the c-car." He cleared his throat. "I'd just walked out the door, dropped my keys. Lisa was tired of waiting. She turned on the engine and it blew. I had my back to the car or else the explosion would have taken me out."

"But why doesn't everyone know you're alive?"

Garrett shoved his hands back through his hair. "Your father. I don't know how, but he knew something was wrong at the agency. He'd seen some questionable information cross his desk. I was being framed. He came by right after the bomb went off. Just lucky, I guess, because he fixed it." Garrett raised his chin and met Laurel's gaze. "Derek Bradley died that night with his family."

Laurel's entire body shook. "My father called you a traitor."

"Your father didn't know if I would survive. He knew I wouldn't if whoever set the bomb realized their mistake. So he created a new identity and took me to a hospital in Texas, and I recuperated there. By the time I came out of the coma, I was dead and buried, and Garrett Galloway was born."

"How could no one find out?"

"I was in a coma for months, under another name. James tried to identify the leak, but there were no leads. By the time I woke up the case was closed. I had several months of physical therapy."

"If you're telling the truth, why didn't he warn Ivy?" Laurel's pleading gaze tugged at Garrett. She paced back and forth, her movements jerky, uncoordinated. She swiped at her eyes. "Why didn't my father protect Ivy? He could have told her to quit. She might still be alive."

"I don't know." Garrett stepped in front of her and took her shoulders, tilting his head to force her to look him in the eyes. "I know your father. James McCallister loved his family more than anything. If you want to blame anyone, blame me. I shouldn't have stayed Garrett

Galloway this long. I let your father convince me he was closing in on the traitor, that if they thought I was still dead they'd eventually get complacent. I agreed to let him continue the search."

"Dad could convince someone in North Dakota to buy ice in the winter," Laurel said, shaking her head. "He always thought he knew the best for everyone else."

"He believed I'd take too many risks. He was right." Garrett had to face the truth. "I'm sorry, Laurel. So sorry. If I'd come back, maybe I could have forced the traitor's hand."

She scrubbed her hands over her face and stepped out of his embrace. "This doesn't make sense. Ivy knew about you and your case. She said you were right. You have to know *something.*"

"I discovered there was a mole in the organization, but I never figured out who."

"Maybe Ivy did." Laurel's expression turned eager. She plopped into the computer chair and scrolled down her sister's file. Garrett leaned over her shoulder. She'd taken his identity in stride. The more time he spent with James's daughter, the more Garrett recognized the similarities. Smart, tenacious, optimistic. Traits he admired in his mentor. Qualities he liked in Laurel. A little too much.

He shifted closer, aware of the pulse throbbing at her throat, the slight increase in her breathing. He wanted to squeeze her shoulder, offer her encouragement, but he didn't want to distract her either. He backed away, forcing himself to focus on the file. Lists of operations, lots of questions, brainstorming. Ivy had been smart, curious and methodical. And her quest had gotten her killed.

As Laurel scrolled, an uneasy tingle settled at the

nape of Garrett's neck. Every operation involved James somehow. Several involved Garrett; some didn't.

"Slow down," he said softly, his voice tense.

"Ivy had more questions than answers." Laurel shot him a sidelong glance then stilled her hand. "What's wrong?"

That she read him meant he was out of practice. He guarded his expression. "Probably nothing."

"I can see it in your eyes." She snapped the words in challenge. "You've already lied about your identity, Derek. Don't lie about anything else. I deserve the truth. So does Ivy. And Molly."

"I'm Garrett now." He stiffened, but knew she was right. If something happened to him, she couldn't be in the dark. She had to be cautious. Around everyone. "James was involved in all the cases Ivy investigated."

Laurel's back straightened and her expression hardened. "My father is not a traitor. Who else was involved?"

"I didn't say he was—"

"You were thinking it. Tell me."

He couldn't deny the thought had crossed his mind.

"I was involved," he said.

"You know, Garrett, sometimes you have to have faith in the people you love. Even when the whole world seems screwed up, there are people who live by honor out there." She looked over her shoulder at him. "You're proof of that. My father trusted you with his family when he was in trouble. So have I. My father deserves the same consideration. Unless you really are a traitor."

Man, Laurel McCallister went right for the jugular with a few well-placed words.

"Then why aren't you afraid of me? Are you afraid that I might betray you?"

"You would have killed us already. Instead, you saved us. You sacrificed your hideaway. You put yourself at risk. Face it, Garrett, you're a hero. Just like my dad believed." Laurel scrolled to the end of the file. "There's a link here."

She clicked it. Another password. She tried the same one.

Access denied.

After three more attempts, Laurel shoved back from the keyboard with a frustrated curse. "I'm out of ideas."

Laurel shook her head, and he could see the fatigue and disappointment on her face. He kneaded her shoulders. "You're good with that machine. Is there another way to figure out the password? Are you a code breaker?"

"It's not my area, but…" She drummed her fingers on the table. "Maybe I can do one better." She chewed on her lip. "I developed a code-breaking computer program with some friends when I was in college." She winced. "We nearly got kicked out of the computer-science department when our adviser found out. I could run it from here, but it will take a while."

"As in we'll be connected to the network for a long time?"

Laurel nodded, and then her eyes brightened. "Unless I download the file."

At this point, it was worth the risk. "Do it."

Laurel clicked through options so quickly Garrett's eyes nearly crossed. "You never hesitate."

"My dad and Ivy have the gift of thinking on their feet. I do better with zeros and ones."

"Mommy!" Molly screamed at the top of her lungs. "Daddy!"

The terrorized cries pierced the air. The sound speared Garrett's heart. He didn't hesitate, throwing open the door to the living room.

At the same time, Laurel exploded from her chair, racing to her niece.

Molly sat straight on the sofa, her cheeks red, sweat dripping down her face, her eyes screwed up tight.

Laurel sat beside Molly and wrapped the little girl in her arms. "Shh, Molly Magoo. I've got you."

Laurel rocked her back and forth, but Molly refused to open her eyes, shaking her head so hard her hair whipped around, sticking to her tearstained face. She clutched at Laurel.

"Is she still asleep?"

"She's clinging to you. She knows you're here."

Laurel hugged Molly closer. "What do I do? This has never happened before."

Molly's sobs gutted Garrett's heart. Ella hadn't had a lot of nightmares, but she'd watched part of *Jurassic Park* at a friend's house and that evening the night terrors had stalked her. Only one thing had calmed her.

Molly struggled against Laurel. "You took me away," she whimpered.

Laurel's face went pale. The agony in her expression made Garrett hurt for her. "Give her to me," he said.

Laurel hesitated.

"I know what to do," he whispered.

Reluctantly, she handed the twisting little girl to Garrett. He sat down in a large overstuffed chair and held

Molly close to his chest. "It's okay, sugar," he said, making his voice soft and deep and hypnotic. He snagged a blanket and wrapped her like a burrito inside it, one arm tight around her.

He rocked her slowly and started singing in an almost whisper. "The ants go marching one by one, hurrah, hurrah. The ants go marching one by one, hurrah, hurray. The ants go ma-ar-ching one by one, the last one stops to look at the sun, and they all go marching down, in the ground, to get out of the rain."

The melodic, low tone of the song echoed in the room. He rubbed her back in circles. Her sobs quieted a bit.

Garrett sang the second verse, all the while rocking her, rubbing her back, holding her close.

Molly's cries turned to hiccups and finally softened. His chest eased a bit. Just like Ella. He looked up. Laurel's face had turned soft and gentle, and awed.

She hitched her hip on the arm of the chair and fingered Molly's locks. The little girl's eyes blinked. She opened her baby blues, looking up at Garrett, then at Laurel.

"Mommy?" she asked. "Daddy?"

"They aren't here, sugar," Garrett said. "But your aunt Laurel is. She won't let anything happen to you. Neither will I."

Molly bit down on her lip. "There was a 'splosion. Daddy's car burned like in the fireplace."

A tear trickled down Laurel's face. "Yes, honey, it did."

"Are Mommy and Daddy coming back?" she asked, her voice small, fearful.

Laurel glanced at Garrett. He warred with what to do, what to say. He simply nodded. It was time.

He tightened his hold on Molly. Laurel cleared her throat. "Honey, they aren't coming back, but they're watching over you. They're in heaven."

Tears welled in Molly's eyes. "Even Matthew and Michaela?"

"Even them, sweetie." Laurel handed her Mr. Houdini. Molly hugged the lion close.

Tears rolled down her face. "I want them back."

Laurel sank closer to Garrett. He shifted and she nestled next to him. Her arm wrapped around Molly, her cheek resting on the little girl's head. "So do I, Molly Magoo. So do I."

Molly clutched her stuffed animal. She didn't scream, as if the pain was too much for that. She laid her head on Garrett's chest. Fat tears rolled down her cheeks.

"Sing to me," she pleaded. "My heart hurts."

"The ants go marching…" Garrett fought against the emotions closing his throat. Memories too horrible and too deep slammed into him. Nights lying in the hospital bed after he'd awakened, reaching out his hand for Lisa's or for Ella's and no one had been there.

Just anonymous nurse after nurse—or no one at all.

Laurel leaned against him, her shoulders silently shaking. He knew she was crying. She buried her face in his neck.

Garrett held on to them, the children's tune now a mere murmur. Soon Molly went still in his arms.

He fell silent.

Sunlight streamed into the window, but he could tell from the angle it was low in the sky. Late afternoon.

He looked over at Laurel. Her eyes were red. "It breaks my heart," she whispered.

His own emotions raw and on the surface, he gave

a quiet nod. "I should put her in bed. She'll wake up at some point, but she needs the rest."

Laurel shifted away from him and he rose, taking the precious bundle into his bedroom. He pulled off her shoes and tucked her under the covers. He kissed her forehead. "Sweet dreams, sugar."

His arms felt empty. His throat tightened as the past overtook him. His own little girl, afraid. His Ella hadn't known a nightmare would come. Neither had Molly.

He turned and Laurel stood in the doorway watching him, her face ravaged with grief. His own festered just beneath the surface. Part of him wanted to escape the claustrophobia of his bedroom, to run to the top of a mountain and shout his fury. Instead, he walked toward her and she backed up. He stepped into the living room and closed the door softly behind him. The latch clicked.

She said nothing, and he didn't know what to say. Molly's tears had torn away the defensive emotional wall he'd worked so diligently to build over the past eighteen months.

She simply walked into his arms, and he could do nothing but enfold her, cling to her and struggle to contain the dam of feelings that threatened to break free.

Laurel stood there silently for several minutes. Her warmth seeped through his shirt. How long since he'd just let himself be this close to someone?

Much too long.

"Thank you," she said. She eased back and touched his cheek with her hand, her whispering caress soft and tender.

"You handled her well. She'll cry more. It won't be over today, but she'll make it. So will you."

He kissed her forehead and she wrapped her arms

around his waist, hugging him tight. He knew she just needed someone to cling to, but he couldn't ignore the slight pickup of his heartbeat. She was too vulnerable. And so was he. Laurel and Molly's presence reminded him of a pain he'd barely endured. Now somehow he had to find the strength to help them survive.

A small whimpering filtered from his bedroom.

"Go to her." Garrett stepped away. "She needs family."

Laurel gripped his hand and kissed his cheek. "You're a good man, Garrett Galloway." She disappeared behind the door and he heard her softly speaking to Molly.

Once he was certain the little girl was calm, he grabbed his Beretta from atop the refrigerator, where he'd stashed it, and strode onto the porch. The sun had turned red as it set on the western side of the ranch. The face of the mountain had turned light red and purple. Garrett sucked in a deep breath of mountain air. He exhaled, shuddering, and gripped the wooden rail until his knuckles whitened.

He blinked quickly, shoving back the overwhelming emotions that threatened to escape.

Molly and Laurel could rip what was left of his heart to shreds. When he'd come to and realized Lisa and Ella had paid the ultimate price for his job, only the need for revenge had kept him alive those first few months during therapy. He'd buried the grief deep in a hole where his heart had once resided.

Garrett scrubbed his face with his hands. Molly had reminded him of what it was like to protect someone who was truly innocent. And Laurel. God, that woman made him want what he couldn't have. He couldn't even let himself think about her that way. Not until whoever had killed his family—and hers—was no longer a threat.

A rustle in the trees made Garrett still. He focused on the movement. For several seconds he watched. Another slight shift of the pine needles, a scrape. Not the wind.

Someone, or something, was out there.

He gripped his weapon and moved behind the stone pillar at the corner of the house. If a weapon had a bead on him, he needed cover.

Once he decided to move, he'd have only a split second.

A shadow shifted in the fading sunlight. Two eyes peered at him from between the pines.

Garrett stepped off the porch. "So, you're back."

Chapter Seven

Laurel snuggled Molly next to her. The little girl twisted the flannel of her Christmas nightgown. It had been a present from Ivy when she'd realized Molly wouldn't be able to attend the pageant that fateful night.

When Laurel had followed Molly into the cabin's bedroom, her niece had pulled her mother's gift from the duffel and silently handed it to Laurel.

"You can wear my T-shirt, Molly Magoo," Laurel had said, barely able to speak.

"Mommy said Santa would know where to find me if I wore my special nightgown. He'd know I was being a good girl even if I couldn't be an angel." Molly had looked up at her. "Santa can find me here, can't he?"

"Of course he can. He knows you've been a very good girl this year."

Laurel stroked Molly's hair. "I'll have to find Christmas for you, Molly," she said under her breath. "Somehow."

The little girl hugged her lion close, her face buried in its mane. Her breathing slowed, growing even. She sighed and tucked her tiny hand under her cheek. Laurel held her breath, but Molly simply snuggled down under the covers.

Hopefully sleep would bring peace. For a while.

Minutes ticked by. Laurel's heart ached with an emptiness she'd never imagined. She wanted Ivy to walk through the door, tell her it was all a mistake. Tell her this had all been a bad dream, a setup. One of their father's elaborate plans.

A small part of her still hoped that were true, but she knew it wasn't. She'd heard her father's voice on the phone. This had nothing to do with the intelligence game he played. Every moment was real.

Her father was probably dead as well.

She and Molly were alone.

Laurel dug her fingernails into her palm, savoring the bite of pain. She wasn't dreaming—even though she was in the midst of her own nightmare.

Her niece's blond hair fell over her forehead. At least Laurel had Molly. The little girl gave Laurel a reason to not curl up in a ball and disappear. She'd never imagined her heart could feel so empty. That loneliness could suffocate her as if she were drowning.

Garrett had lost his wife and daughter. Laurel couldn't imagine the agony he'd gone through. How had he survived? Alone, with his entire past erased, how had this not destroyed him?

Laurel glanced at the door. She could stay in this room for the evening. Every muscle in her body ached with exhaustion and fatigue. Each time she blinked, grit scraped her eyes, but for the first time in days, she felt safe. At least for the next twenty-four hours.

She should sleep, but Garrett was out there. Alone.

Her father had told her Derek Bradley was a traitor, but the more she recalled the conversations, the more she recognized the inconsistencies. Her father was an excellent liar, no doubt, but he'd been cagey about Bradley. He'd set up the doubts, so she would be able to trust him.

"Derek took too many risks," James McCallister had said last Thanksgiving. *"He paid the price. So did his family. Traitors always get what's coming to them. Eventually."*

Her father had never called Derek Bradley a traitor.

Something from around Laurel's heart eased, and she realized that somewhere deep inside she'd still had doubts. They were gone now. Besides, her image of a man who would sell out his country for money didn't mesh with the man who could sing Molly into calmness from hysteria.

As she'd said to Garrett, at some point you had to let faith lead you. Careful not to jostle Molly, Laurel rose from the bed and padded across the room. The little girl didn't stir. Laurel pressed her hand against the door and slowly turned the knob. She opened it and eased out of the bedroom.

The living room was empty.

She peeked into his workroom, but he wasn't there. The encryption program still ran.

Finally she looked out the front window. He stood on the porch, his back to her, staring out at the sunset. His entire body screamed tension. As if he wanted to be left alone.

Laurel hesitated. She could return to the bedroom for the night, plant herself in front of the computer and wait, hoping the program would find the password, or she could go to Garrett. Except she knew what would happen the moment she touched him. They were both vulnerable. They both needed something only the other could provide.

She opened the front door. The cold gust of wind made her shiver. The last rays of light disappeared behind a mountain and deep purplish-blue painted the sky, rimmed at the horizon with a splash of pink and red. "Garrett?"

He didn't turn around. She glanced down. He held his gun at the ready. She froze.

"In the trees," he said softly.

She followed his gaze. Two piercing blue eyes peered at them, intent and calm.

The cougar.

"He's back," Laurel whispered.

"Cats are curious, but cautious. He won't come closer."

Garrett walked down the steps and picked up a large stone, tossing it toward the animal. The cat scampered off into the trees. "We need to keep Molly inside," he said. "That cat's learned people are a source of food. Probably eating after some of the border crossers left provisions behind."

He shoved his gun into the back of his jeans and escorted her inside the house. "How's Molly?"

"I'd guess out for the night, though she'll probably be up before dawn."

"Which reminds me." Garrett flicked the dead bolt in place, then shoved a chair underneath the doorknob before activating the sensors.

"You think that will stop her?"

"She'll make a lot of noise trying to get that chair out. I'll hear the little Houdini."

Laurel couldn't help but smile. "She's just like Ivy. When we were kids—"

"I would imagine she got you into a lot of trouble."

"Dad would get so furious at us. I tried to take the fall

a time or two, but Ivy wouldn't let me. She was so much fun. I would have never had all those adventures if not for her." Laurel sighed. "I'll always miss her, won't I?"

Garrett double-checked the chair then faced her, his expression solemn. "I won't tell you it gets better. The scab may get a little tougher."

She chanced a glance at him under her lashes. His stance was a bit awkward, as if he didn't know what to say either. Maybe she'd been wrong. She should have just turned in with Molly.

"We'd better check on the computer—" he started.

"I guess I'll turn in—" she said at the same time.

She shifted from one foot to the other. "I just looked at the program's status," Laurel said. "Still running. No answers."

"I see. Then I guess it's good-night."

Something solemn and painful had settled behind his eyes. And vulnerable. She didn't want to leave him. She didn't want to be alone tonight. She crossed to him, her heart rate escalating with each step. She knew exactly what she was inviting. So did he.

She stopped inches away from him, still staring into his eyes. They darkened into a deep mahogany flaring with want, maybe with need.

"What are you doing, Laurel?" His voice had grown deep, husky.

Her touch tentative, she placed her hand on his chest. She needed him. "We're safe for a while," she said. "Aren't we?"

"That's debatable," he said softly.

He covered the hand resting on his chest with his and lifted her palm to his lips. He nipped at the pad then threaded his fingers through hers. "You know this is a mistake," he said, his voice barely audible. "You don't know me. Not really."

A shiver skated down her spine at his words, but the naked longing in his eyes shoved aside her doubts.

She knew him.

"I've watched you. You gave up your safe existence to help me and Molly. You calmed her fears tonight. I know everything I need to know."

"Even though the world thinks I'm a traitor."

"I know the truth." She shook her head, leaning closer, wanting more than anything for him to stop talking and kiss her.

"What if you're wrong, Laurel?" He cupped her cheek and held her gaze captive. Her heart fluttered in response. His thumb grazed her cheek. "What if I'm a man who would do anything to get what he wants? I'm good at keeping secrets. And I'm *very* good at telling lies."

She couldn't stop staring at his lips. "I can tell when you're lying, Garrett. Your eyes grow dark, and the right corner of your mouth tightens just a bit."

Would his mouth be hard or soft, passionate or gentle against hers when they kissed?

"I don't want you," he said softly, his breath whispering against her cheek as he moved closer to her lips.

"You're bluffing."

"You're too trusting." He lowered his mouth to her ear. "But I don't have the strength to pull away."

She smiled. "Now you're telling the truth."

With a groan he fastened his lips to hers and wrapped his arms around her. She didn't hesitate. She clung to him and let his mouth drive away the memories of the past week. For this wonderful moment all she could think about was his touch, his mouth exploring hers, the taste of him.

He lifted his head. "Be very sure, because I won't let you go all night long."

She didn't answer, just pulled his mouth to hers once more. He groaned and swept her into his arms. With a long stride he carried her into the smaller bedroom, closing the door behind them. She didn't notice the Spartan furniture; her only focus was on Garrett. She used the name of the sheriff she'd come to know, not the name of the man he used to be.

"I don't know what the future holds, but I know what I want right now," Laurel said. "I need you, Garrett."

"Not more than I need you." Gently he laid her on the bed, following her down, covering her with his weight.

She didn't resist, but relished the feel of him on top of her. With a groan, he buried his lips against her neck, exploring the pulse points at the base of her throat. Laurel threaded her hands through his hair. Every kiss made her belly tingle with need. She wanted more.

"Please," she whispered. "Kiss me."

"I am," he said softly, nipping at the delicate skin just below her ear.

"Garrett." She couldn't stop the frustration from lacing her voice.

"How about here?" He nibbled the lobe of her ear. "Or here?" He worked his way down, shifting her shirt aside, and tasted the skin just above her collarbone.

Laurel stirred beneath him until finally he raised his head. He tugged at her lower lip. "Or how about here?"

His mouth swooped down and captured hers. He pressed her lips open and she moaned in relief that she could finally taste him. She returned his kiss for kiss.

Her hands seemed to have a mind of their own, exploring the strength of his back through his shirt. She hated the barrier between them. She wanted to touch him, skin to skin. She wedged her hands between them, unbuttoning his shirt and shoving the material off his shoulders.

He stilled above her, looking at her, his gaze intense, hesitant, full of warning. Her fingertips paused when she encountered roughened skin.

Burns. The car bomb.

He let out a slow sigh then moved off of her, lying on his back. "I should have warned you." His shirt fell open and she pulled away. His chest was mostly unmarred, except for a long surgical scar down his midline.

"You think what happened changes anything? It makes me want you even more." She didn't hesitate, but straddled his hips and traced the scar.

He looked up at her and caught her fingertip. "My entire back was turned when the car exploded. There was a lot of damage. I had several rounds of skin grafts. During surgery my heart stopped. I died on the operating table and they cracked me open." His voice was detached, his jaw tight, holding back emotion. "It's not pretty," he said. "It will never be pretty."

"And if I could have Ivy back, you think the scars would make me love her less? You earned these badges of courage." Laurel moved her hands up to his shoulders, venturing a tentative touch on the puckered skin. "Does it hurt?"

"I can't always feel when you touch me. And in some places the nerve endings go a little haywire, but mostly no. It's healed as much as it's going to."

He didn't move, didn't try to pull her to him, didn't try

to kiss her. He simply lay there gazing up at her. "You don't have to do this."

"Neither do you, but you're the bravest man I know and I don't think you'll chicken out now," she said and leaned forward, gently, tenderly pressing her lips to his. "I want this. Now. With you. Tell me if I hurt you."

She lifted her shirt over her head and removed her bra. His eyes hooded as he cupped her breast in his hand and drew his thumb across her nipple. It beaded in response and a sharp tingle lit in her belly. A small whimper escaped her and she gripped his shirt.

He smiled, the defensive expression in his eyes darkening to desire once again. "I can't believe you want me." Garrett tugged her down to him, his palm against the small of her back, rocking her hips against his, his desire evident.

"Can you feel me now?" she whispered, shifting her body, evoking a groan from him.

"Definitely." He flipped her over and threw his shirt off the side of the bed. "You're an amazing woman, Laurel McCallister."

She wrapped her arms around him, blinking back the hurt for him when she encountered the mottling of scars down his back and a few strips of unblemished skin. She yanked him down closer and wrapped her legs around his hips. "Show me how amazing you think I am. I don't want to wait another second."

THEY WERE IN the middle of nowhere. Still.

Strickland peered out the front window. The SUV's headlights broke through the early evening, but a cluster of trees and an avalanche of rocks blocked the path. They'd reached the end of the road.

"Damn it." He hit the steering wheel. "How far is Bradley from here?"

Krauss studied the screen. The red dot was immobile. "Couple of miles, according to this. He's not moving."

Strickland rubbed the stubble on his chin. "Give me the city any day of the week. I hate the West. Too much godforsaken territory to cover."

"We going back to Trouble?"

"Not a chance. Get your canteen," Strickland ordered. "We're going after him. He won't expect us to track him out here."

"We're really heading out at night?"

"You want to tell the boss we're taking the evening off?" Strickland asked.

Krauss muttered to himself as he grabbed the water and his weapon. "This is a mistake. Weren't you a Cub Scout or something? We don't know the country. Anything could be out there. It's easy to get turned around in the darkness."

Strickland tapped the glowing red light on Krauss's monitor. "We've got a beacon to light the way. Besides, we don't have a choice. Now come on."

They exited the SUV and Strickland grabbed an M16, slinging it over his shoulder. "I'll tell you one thing, though. I'm not hauling those bodies down this mountain. Once we kill them, we leave them to rot."

GARRETT COULDN'T BELIEVE Laurel was here, in his bed, beneath him, with her long, lean legs wrapped around him. His body surged in response to her arch.

She grasped his shoulders and her hands moved to his back.

He couldn't believe she hadn't politely said good-night and walked away. Garrett didn't think about the scars on his back that often. Just when he'd rub against something the wrong way and the nerves fired, as if a thousand pins were stabbing him.

Laurel nipped at his ear. "I want you," she whispered. "Now."

No more than he wanted her.

He rubbed his chest against her, reveling in the feeling of their skin touching. With each caress of his chest against her budded nipples, she let out a low moan, shivering against him. He moved again, and this time, she hugged him close, tilting her pelvis into his hardness. God, she was so responsive. She didn't hold anything back. He'd never been with a woman who was so honest about what she wanted.

Her hands worked their way between them to the waist of his pants, tugging at his stubborn belt in frustration.

He lifted away, forcing her legs to release him. He hated she no longer held him captive, but he wanted her wild for him. He wanted to drive them both so crazy that the past and the past week would vanish…at least for a moment.

With a quick flick, he removed the leather belt and threw it to the side of the bed before unbuttoning the waist. She shoved at his hand, but he gripped her fingers. "Not yet."

He lifted her hands above her head, pinning them down with one of his own. He gazed at the rise and fall of her chest. Her breathing quickened beneath his gaze, her blue eyes transformed into cobalt pools. That she trusted him enough to give him control caused his body to throb in response. He let his fingers stroke her cheek and drew her lip down. Her tongue snaked out to taste his finger. He smiled at her and let her suckle for a moment before taking his hand around her jawline, down her throat, where the pulse raced.

Her legs shifted but he trapped her beneath him. With a butterfly-light touch he teased her breasts, circling one nipple, then the other. Her chest flushed; her back arched. He followed a trail, teasing her, relishing in the soft sounds of pleasure coming from her lips.

"Garrett," she finally pleaded. She didn't tug her hands away, though. She wanted more. And he wanted to give her more than she'd dreamed of.

Ever so slowly he explored each delectable inch of skin, first with his fingertips, then with his lips and finally with his tongue. When he reached her waist, tasting the sweetness just above her belly button, she sucked in her stomach. He flicked open the button of her jeans.

Prolonging her pleasure, and his painful desire, he slid down the zipper and eased her pants over her hips. Simple white bikini panties hid her from his gaze.

Garrett tugged at the elastic, swallowing. He throbbed against his zipper. He was going to lose control. He'd been determined to drive her mad, but he was losing his mind.

And his heart.

He rose to his knees and tugged at the elastic waist.

She wrenched her hands from his grip and sat up. "I can't take it anymore," she said. She shoved her jeans and the small scrap of cloth down her legs, leaving her bare to his view.

God, she was beautiful.

Without hesitation she pushed against his zipper. His body surged.

"I'm too close," he said, his voice tight.

"So am I," she countered. "Make love to me, Garrett."

He gritted against the sensitivity of his body as he shucked off the rest of his clothes. He reached into the bedside table and grabbed a condom.

Her legs parted for him and she pulled him to her. She didn't play coy or hesitate. "Make love to me, Garrett. Now."

Unable to resist, with one thrust, he sank deep inside her.

She was ready for him, welcoming, hot and needy. He lost himself in her. The past disappeared, the uncertainty.

She cocooned him in her warmth. With each stroke, she sighed, and then the rhythm built, slowly at first, then stronger, faster, more intense.

His heart raced; his body trembled. He wanted to feel her fall apart in his arms. She tightened around him and he couldn't hold off. He thrust against her and his body pulsed in release. He sagged on top of her, the rhythmic quivering of her body gripping him.

She'd fallen over the edge with him.

For a moment he couldn't move, letting his heart slow, feeling her heartbeat calm.

"Wow," she mumbled, stroking his hair.

He moved off of her, disposed of the condom and spooned her. She felt so good, so right lying against him. He kissed her temple, wrapping one leg around hers, unwilling to let her escape from his embrace.

"Yeah. *Wow* about covers it."

She wiggled her back end against him before settling down. She gripped one of his hands between hers.

"I feel like a boneless jellyfish," she said. "I never want to move from here."

He didn't either. He stared at the wall, just listening to her breathe. In and out, soft and steady. He hadn't planned this. But he couldn't find it inside him to regret.

That in itself made him wince. What had he done?

He toyed with a small curl of hair against her cheek. She was so soft and yet so strong. And so smart. Her fingers had flown across that keyboard and he had seen her analyzing the problem, creating a solution and acting on it.

More than that, she was brave. She hadn't hesitated to protect Molly.

"I can feel you thinking," she said softly. She turned in his arms and looked at him. "What about? Regrets?"

A hesitant expression had settled on her face. He kissed her nose. "No regrets, even though—"

"Don't," she pleaded. "I don't want to think about what's happening. Not yet. Can't we just be, with nothing between us? Just for a few minutes."

"Of course." He wrapped his leg over her hip, pulling her against him, saying nothing.

She played with the smattering of hair on his chest for a moment, then sighed. "But it won't go away. They're coming."

Her hands slowed then stilled. "Do you think Dad is okay?"

"Do you want lies or truth?"

"Truth."

He twirled a strand of her hair. "I don't know. I'd have hoped he'd get word to me by now. Somehow."

"You're worried."

"James has kept himself alive a long time."

"Are you trying to convince me or yourself?" Laurel asked, her voice laced with sadness.

"Both, maybe."

She huddled into him and he wrapped his arms around her. She went quiet for several minutes, and Garrett wondered if she'd fallen asleep. He hoped so. She could use the rest.

"How do we catch them, Garrett?" Her breath kissed his bare chest. "They haven't made a mistake."

The despair in her words touched his very soul. More because he couldn't guarantee anything. Not even her safety. All he knew was he'd do his damnedest to keep her and Molly alive.

His arms gripped her tighter. "Actually, they have made a mistake. Your sister was killed because she identified evidence. Which means—"

"They left a trail," Laurel finished.

"Once you find a way into that file, we could have the answer." Garrett closed his eyes and stroked her hair. An answer to the revenge that had eaten away at his gut since he'd woken up from that coma with his life changed forever.

Lisa and Ella might finally be able to rest in peace. Maybe he would, too. He moved away from Laurel. He unwrapped himself from her and sat on the side of the bed, his head in his hands.

Laurel sucked in a breath from behind him. He'd forgotten about his back. He grabbed for his shirt. "I'm sorry."

"Don't," she whispered.

The bed shifted and she moved behind him. She rubbed the base of his neck. He groaned, feeling the tension that had been sitting there for so long dissipate. Her hands drifted down, in and out of his ability to feel.

Her touch caressed his lower back. "Can you feel me?" she asked.

"Mmm-hmm."

She nipped at the back of his neck with her teeth. "How about now?"

"Oh, yes." He let his head fall forward while she explored.

Her touch danced just beneath his shoulder blade. A sharp prick raced through him and he tensed.

"Did I hurt you?" She yanked her hands away.

"Don't," he said. "Just the nerves going crazy."

"How many surgeries did you have, Garrett?"

"More than I can count. Skin grafts, shrapnel got embedded into my back. I was a mess."

Her fingers returned to his shoulder blade. "I guess that's what happened here. There's evidence of sutures. It's strange—"

A loud beeping sounded from Garrett's phone. He jumped to his feet. "Get dressed. Someone's broken the perimeter."

Chapter Eight

Laurel rolled off the bed and yanked on her jeans, slipping on her shirt as she raced after Garrett. She followed him out of the bedroom and into his office. He flipped on a switch on one of the consoles. A map flickered to life on the screen. Two green dots headed directly to the center.

"They're getting close to the cameras," he said, turning on another switch. Three monitors buzzed on, the infrared images fuzzy.

A few trees, but nothing more.

Laurel slipped on her shoes and glanced down at the computer monitor where she'd been running the decryption program. "We don't have the password yet," she rushed out. "It hasn't finished. What are we going to do?"

Garrett stared at the monitors. Slowly a figure came into view. She squinted, then recognized a man pushing through the trees, his movements jerky, holding a weapon. A second person followed behind him.

He let out a loud curse. "How did they find us so fast?"

"Who are they?"

"*Not* the family I saw earlier today. There were three of them. And no one was carrying an M16. I could recognize the outline anywhere." Garrett scanned the room and grabbed a duffel from the corner, tossing it toward her. "Pack up what you and Molly need. Only the bare necessities. There's not much time."

At Garrett's grim expression, Laurel's stomach twisted in fear. She raced from the room and quietly opened the door to the bedroom where Molly slept. Using the shard of light piercing through the slit, she fumbled for a few sets of clothes and toiletries. And Ivy's family's picture. Everything else was luxury. Except Mr. Hairy Houdini.

She slipped out of the bedroom and back into the office. "Done."

Garrett sat at one of his monitors. "I'm wiping the entire system. It will disable everything and leave no trace."

"Are they close?"

"They're making a beeline for the cabin, but they're still a half mile away. In the dark in the woods. Idiots."

"Do you recognize them?"

Garrett grabbed a control stick and zoomed in. "No. How about you?"

She squinted at the grainy green image. "I can't tell."

The computer next to her sounded her college fight song. Garrett's eyes widened, and she flushed. "We were…enthusiastic."

She plopped onto the chair. "I've got the password." She typed it in. "I can download it."

Garrett typed in a few commands on his screen. "Copy it. We're out of time."

Two figures appeared on the second screen. This time she could see the second man's gun. Another automatic weapon.

"Military-issue weapons," she said.

"Good eye. They've found us. No telling how many are out there. I'm getting you out of here."

"We should have had another twenty-four hours at least," Laurel said. She looked over at Garrett. "This is my fault."

"Our opponent is better than we both thought."

"Do you have a thumb drive?" Laurel asked.

He opened the drawer and handed her the small device. She stuck the drive into the system, copied the file, then ejected it.

"We're out of time." He grabbed the Remington from a closet, slung the strap over his shoulder and hit a button. The computers started whirring.

"Is it going to explode?" she asked.

"Nothing so *Mission: Impossible,*" Garrett said. "Just wiped clean and its components melted down. Can you carry this?" He lifted up a small backpack.

She took it from him and stuffed it into a duffel, zipping it up. She took her SIG and placed it in the back of her pants. She wished she had a holster. Next time she went on the run, she'd remember to bring one.

"I'll carry Molly." He hurried into the spare bedroom. The little girl had sprawled on her back, clutching her stuffed animal. He slid his hands under her body and lifted her up over his shoulder, settling her on one arm and hip.

"Let's go," he whispered, unclipping a narrow flashlight from his belt. "This has a red filter so it doesn't kill the night vision. I'll lead the way. Keep your weapon handy."

He quietly closed and locked the door behind him. Laurel balanced the duffel on her shoulder. They stepped into the darkness. Only the moon lit their way. He pointed the beam of light at the ground in front of him. "Don't veer off this path. You could walk off a cliff."

Taking it slow but steady, they picked their way through the trees, around a series of rugged rocks, careful not to make any noise. Garrett jostled Molly once and she whimpered. He froze. Laurel held her breath. If Molly started crying she could give their location away.

They started off again.

A burst of gunfire in the distance peppered the night.

Laurel hit the ground. Garrett knelt, covering Molly. She yelped in fear. He placed his hand on her mouth. "Molly, listen to me."

Laurel crawled over to Garrett. "I'm here with you, Molly Magoo. We have to be quiet, even if those noises are scary. Can you do that?"

She nodded her head.

Slowly, Garrett pulled his hand away. Molly slapped her hand on her mouth. "Good girl," he said. "You're very brave."

"Will Santa know?" she asked.

"He's definitely watching."

"Do Mommy and Daddy know?" Molly asked, her voice muffled through her fingertips.

"They're very proud of you, Molly Magoo."

"Lay your head on my shoulder, sugar. We're getting out of here."

Laurel could tell, even in the moonlight, that Molly squeezed her eyes shut.

Another bevy of gunfire erupted.

Garrett didn't slow. "It's at the cabin. Keep moving."

A loud curse pierced the night.

"He said a bad word," Molly muttered. "Santa won't visit his house."

"Definitely not," Garrett said. "Hush now."

They trudged forward. It seemed so much farther back to the SUV than it had hiking up to the ranch house. Laurel focused on the ground in front of her. All she needed was to fall.

She stepped on a twig and the dry wood cracked beneath her weight. Garrett stilled. She stopped, her heart quickening. He motioned her forward.

Laurel didn't know how long they walked before she finally recognized the outcropping of rocks ahead. Garrett paused. Laurel stopped as well, listening to the sounds of the night.

In December, not many animals sounded their call. But neither did the men following.

A twig snapped not that far behind them.

"Go!" he shouted. Placing the keys in her hand, he pushed her through a gap in the rocks. The SUV was just feet away.

"Take her." Garrett shoved Molly into Laurel's arms and took off running in the opposite direction.

GARRETT RACED AWAY from Laurel and Molly. How the hell had these guys found them? He slammed through the pine trees, making as much noise as possible. A gunshot echoed in the night, the bullet hitting a pine tree just above his ear. They had night vision. Great.

Garrett took his flashlight and turned the powerful miniature beam on high, then flipped off the filter, shining the bright light in the direction of the fired shot.

A curse of pain sounded toward him. The guy would be blinded for a few seconds. Garrett veered in the direction of the house. Anything to keep them away from Laurel and Molly. He prayed she'd gotten away, that no one else had intercepted them.

"This way!" one of the men shouted. Footsteps pounded at him. They weren't even trying to be quiet. He took a ninety-degree turn away from the ranch, toward some of the cliffs. He had to keep his bearings. A rock outcropping should be coming up to his right.

Sure enough, the strange formation loomed from the ground.

The men following him kept coming.

The sound of a stumble, then a loud curse, filtered through the night. He hadn't lost them. Garrett rounded the rock formation and paused. Fifteen feet away was the edge of a steep hill, its base jagged rocks. Dangerous, deadly and convenient.

He flipped off his flashlight and raced toward the hill. Those guys trailed after him as though they had radar on him.

Was he carrying a GPS? His phone shouldn't be traceable. How did they have a bead on him? He couldn't hear anything above him; a chopper would be crazy to fly at night in these mountains.

No time to figure it out.

He still couldn't be sure if he wasn't walking into a trap, if someone was waiting for him.

"Laurel, I hope you got away."

He stopped in front of the drop-off. They shouldn't have been able to find him, but the two men barreled into the clearing just in front of him.

The red-filtered flashlight one of them carried crossed his body, and they stopped.

A smile gleamed in the moonlight. "Two years late," the man said, lifting his gun.

Garrett dived to the side just as the man charged. The guy tried to skid to a halt, but momentum carried him over the side. He shouted out and disappeared down the hill.

"Strickland!" the second man shouted. Garrett launched himself at the guy and pinned him. "Who are you?"

The man shook his head.

Garrett shoved the barrel of his Beretta beneath the guy's chin. "I'm not playing games."

"Yeah, well, neither is my boss. I'm dead if I say anything."

The man's eyes were resigned. A bad sign.

"How about we make a deal?" Garrett said, easing the gun just a bit. "You tell me your boss's name. I let you go. You disappear out here. You're a few hours from the border."

A flare of hope flashed on the guy's face before a gunshot sounded. A sharp burning slammed into Garrett's back. His gun dropped from his hand. He rolled off the guy and behind a rock, his back screaming in pain. He sucked in a breath and blinked.

His Beretta lay in the open.

Strickland heaved himself up over the edge of the hill and lifted his M16. "Get out of there, Krauss, or so help me, I'll shoot you, too."

Krauss scrambled away. Staggering toward Garrett, Strickland peppered the rock. Dust and shrapnel flew into the air.

If it had been daylight, Garrett would be dead.

Another blast of firepower and he was running out of time.

"You're dying this time, Bradley. Damn you. Your wife and kid weren't even part of the deal."

The words slammed into Garrett's pain-riddled brain. This son of a bitch had killed his family.

"Yeah, that's right. I set the bomb. You want to come out and face me?"

Garrett rolled over, ignoring the pain in his back. Krauss pulled his weapon. This was a no-win.

Then Krauss moved. Garrett had one chance. With a grunt, he launched himself at Krauss and shoved him into Strickland. Garrett's weight forced them back toward the edge.

They all teetered on the precipice. Garrett grabbed a protrusion of rock and stopped his fall. Strickland and Krauss disappeared over the side.

Garrett could feel warmth seeping down his back as he climbed up the few feet. He flicked on his flashlight and peered over the side.

The men lay against a rock, motionless. Krauss's neck was bent at an unnatural angle, his eyes wide-open. Dead.

Garrett moved the beam over.

Blood covered Strickland's face. He wasn't moving. Garrett pointed his weapon at Strickland, but the guy didn't move. He wanted to climb down, be sure. He needed to know the truth.

A wave of dizziness stopped him. He fell down to his knees. A beeping noise just to his side grabbed his attention. He picked up a tablet. A red dot blinked. It was *him*. Damn it, how were they tracking him?

He pulled everything out of his pockets. He'd bought the clothes in El Paso. It couldn't be them.

He didn't have time to figure it out.

He took one last look over the edge—Strickland still

hadn't budged. Garrett stumbled to his feet. He had to make sure Laurel and Molly were gone, out of here. Daniel would help.

Garrett didn't know how bad his wound was, but he had to make sure they were safe, and then he had to get as far away from them as he could. Because whoever had sent Strickland and Krauss wasn't giving up.

THE GUNSHOTS HAD STOPPED. Laurel gripped her SIG, planting her hands firmly along the hood of the SUV.

Molly sat in the backseat, hugging Mr. Houdini close. "Where is Sheriff Garrett? He wouldn't leave us."

"He'll be here," Laurel said. He had to be here. She chewed on her fingernail.

Suddenly a figure came stumbling out of the trees. Her finger tightened on the trigger.

He looked up at her. "Garrett!" she shouted.

"Get in," he ordered and bounded into the passenger seat. "Drive," he said, clearing his throat.

Carefully she backed up and turned the SUV around. "Lights?" she asked.

"On," he said. "Get us out of here fast."

The beams hit the dirt road and she hit the gas.

"Why the hell did you wait for me? What if I hadn't come back?"

"I have the number you gave me." Laurel gripped the steering wheel. "I was getting ready to call Daniel Adams."

"I don't know whether to be relieved you were here or turn you over my knee." The SUV bounced and Garrett took a sharp intake of breath. Laurel flipped on the interior lights and looked over at him.

His mouth was pinched and the light leather of his seat was streaked with red.

"You're bleeding."

"Just drive," he ordered. "Get to the main road as fast as you can. Maybe we'll be lucky and those two were the only ones following us. For now."

She urged the vehicle forward.

Molly stuck her head between the seats. "Do you need a Band-Aid?" she asked. "I have princess ones. You can have my favorite if you want. Which princess do you like the best?"

Garrett smiled at her. "You're my favorite princess, sugar. And don't you worry. It's just a scratch. I'll be fine."

Laurel's knuckles tightened on the steering wheel. He was lying to protect Molly. Tears stung Laurel's eyes. She'd fallen hard for this man. He'd saved them yet again, but this time she really didn't know if they'd make it out alive. Blood kept seeping onto the seat. She had to get him help.

The nearest town was Trouble. She'd seen a clinic there. She could go back. Everyone knew him there. Someone would help.

It took forever to reach the county road leading to Trouble. She finally got to the intersection.

"Turn left," Garrett said through clenched teeth.

"I'm glad you agree. I'm getting you to a doctor."

"I can't now." Garrett leaned his head back on the seat. "Keep driving straight."

After about fifteen minutes he turned his head to her. In the light of the interior his face had gone pale. "There's a dirt road not too far from here. Pull over and let me out."

"No way—"

"Do it, Laurel."

Against her better judgment, she pulled to the side and stopped the car.

Garrett gripped the door handle and faced her. "Here's what you're going to do. Take this road. It circles down some back roads until you reach Rural Route 11. Follow that until you hit this highway again. Get to a phone, even if you have to buy a prepaid cell at a convenience store. Call Daniel Adams. Tell him what's happening. He'll take you to Covert Technology Confidential in Carder, Texas. They'll protect you."

Daniel's employer might be the only one that could hide Laurel and Molly from the agency and get away with it.

She shook her head. "I won't leave you. You're hurt."

"Laurel, they're tracking me. I don't know how, but they are. You have to get away."

He opened the SUV door, but as soon as his boots hit the pavement he collapsed.

She shoved open her door and ran around the car. "At least let me stop the bleeding before I leave. You can't do it yourself."

He closed his eyes, then gave her a reluctant nod. Why did the thing that attracted her so much to Garrett have to be the very thing that could kill him?

"There's a T-shirt in my backpack. And a canteen. Wash off the wound and use the cotton as a bandage. Then you have to go."

"Are you fixing Sheriff Garrett, Aunt Laurel?"

"That's right, sugar," Garrett said with a smile. "I'll be good as new."

Liar.

Laurel fished out the material and the water. She lifted his shirt and he passed her the flashlight. She gasped. Dried blood caked part of his back, but fresh still oozed from the wound. She didn't know how he was still standing.

She ripped the T-shirt in two and soaked half in water. She bathed his back, trying to be gentle. He didn't even wince.

Each pass removed more of the blood, revealing the scars. They weren't all that bad. The horror of what he'd experienced far surpassed this permanent reminder.

She worked her way toward the area that still bled. The bullet had hit him near his shoulder blade, near where she'd seen his previous wound and stitches. He looked as if he'd scraped his back raw on the rocks, too.

"Just how many times have you been shot in the back?" she asked.

"Since I met you?" he asked. "Or altogether?"

"Wiseass."

"Aunt Laurel, that's a naughty word." Molly gasped.

"Sorry, Molly." She frowned at his back. "See what you made me do?"

He chuckled. "I'm going to miss you two."

She ripped the clean half of the T-shirt for a second round and dabbed at the wound.

He could use stitches, and the raw skin had rocks and metal flakes embedded in it. She had to scrub a bit harder. He sucked in a breath.

"Too bad I still have some feeling left right there," he said, his voice tight with pain.

"Almost done."

As she cleaned the last bit, a familiar-looking object became visible. Small, metallic. A chip.

"Garrett? Were you ever fitted with a tracking device?"

"Hell, no. If the bad guys caught the frequency…" His head whipped around. "Is one back there?"

"Yes."

"Get it out. Now."

"It's implanted in your back. You need a doctor to cut it out."

"Hand me my backpack."

She dug into her duffel. He tugged out the nylon pack and retrieved a small medical kit, complete with a small scalpel and forceps.

"Yank it out," he said. "We don't have any time to lose. They could be closing in now."

Laurel blinked, staring at the tracking device. She could do this. Her hand shook, and she sucked in a deep breath.

"It's easy. You said there was an incision? Just follow the scar and pull the thing out.

"I don't suppose you have pain medicine in your bag of tricks?"

Molly stuck her head over the seat. She gasped. "Sheriff Garrett, you have lots of boo-boos. You can use all my princess Band-Aids if you need them."

"Laurel, just do it." Garrett smiled up at Molly. "Why don't you find me those Band-Aids, sugar?"

Molly ducked behind the backseat.

"Now," he said tightly.

"Brace yourself."

He gripped the passenger seat. She leaned over him. Taking a deep breath, Laurel pushed the knife into his back and sliced the skin, revealing the entire chip. He didn't say a word, but when she grabbed it with the medical tweezers, his back tightened. Blood flowed from the wound.

She dabbed at it. "Got it."

"Oh, yuck. That's a really bad boo-boo."

"Not so bad, sugar. Maybe you'll be a doctor when you grow up so you can fix people."

Molly's smile brightened. "I want to fix people." She hugged her lion tight.

"Laurel, clean the wound with the Betadine. Put some antibiotic ointment on it and use the butterfly strips to close it," he ordered.

Molly insisted on adding several of her own bandages. When they'd finished, Garrett turned to Laurel. His face had gone pale.

"There's a clinic in Trouble," she repeated.

"We can't go back there. Where is the chip?"

She picked up the small device with the forceps. He took it from her and turned it over in his hand. His jawline throbbed. "Damn him."

"Who?"

He lifted his gaze and met hers.

"Your father requested these chips. As far as I knew, they were never used, but he had one put into me. He would have been the only one to know the frequency."

MIKE STRICKLAND GROANED and pressed his hand to his head. It came away bloody and sticky. He rolled over. His entire body hurt. He tested each limb. Nothing broken, though his head might explode at any moment. Slowly he sat up.

Krauss lay next to him, his neck obviously broken.

He'd been the weak link anyway. A lot like Derek

Bradley. The guy was a fool. If it had been him, he'd have put a bullet in both men's brains…just to be sure.

Strickland struggled to his feet and glared up the steep incline. "I gotta find that guy."

He searched around. No tracking device. "Damn." He hoped Bradley didn't have it.

A phone sounded a few feet from Strickland. His head pounding as if he had an ice pick stabbed in his ear, he followed the sound and bent down, nearly crying out in pain.

The name on the screen caused his stomach to roil. He vomited all over the ground. He should ignore it.

The ringing stopped, then started again.

"Strickland."

"Don't ignore me again, Strickland."

He wiped his mouth.

"Bradley was moving toward Trouble, Texas, and now his signal has vanished. You failed. Again."

"We have a plan," Strickland lied.

"Oh, really? Now that we can no longer track Derek Bradley, he's an even greater threat. Neutralize him."

"I understand."

"Do you, Strickland? Do you really? Because this is your second mistake in as many days. That's one more than anyone else under my command has made—and still lived."

The phone call ended.

He needed a plan. First to get back to his SUV, and then to find Bradley.

Strickland sank to his knees and emptied the rest of the contents of his stomach next to Krauss's body.

He'd never find Bradley this way.

If he couldn't chase after Bradley, he'd just have to find bait that would attract him.

Trouble, Texas, was the way to do it.

Chapter Nine

Laurel wrenched open the door of the SUV. The destroyed chip lay on the ground, along with her shredded heart. "You're wrong about my father," she said, her face hot with anger. "He would never hurt you like that."

"I know what I saw," Garrett said. "First your sister's evidence pointing to James, and now this."

She scooted into the front seat and gripped the steering wheel. It couldn't be. "He might not have been the perfect father or even around much, but he's a patriot through and through. And he's definitely no traitor."

"Well, neither am I," Garrett snapped. "Yet I'm being hunted. He told lies about me, acted like the heartbroken, betrayed mentor, supposedly to save my life. But now I have to wonder. What better way to hide your true leanings than to throw someone close to you to the wolves and mourn the treason?"

She didn't want to admit the plan sounded good—just simple enough and brilliant enough to have her father's name attached to it. But she wouldn't—*couldn't*—believe James McCallister would do that to Garrett.

"Why did he save your life, then?" Laurel shot back,

desperate to convince him—and herself—that her father hadn't betrayed both of them.

"I haven't figured that out yet."

"If my dad really were responsible for all of this, he wouldn't have kept you alive. He wouldn't have given you your new identity." Laurel put her arm on the back of the seat and faced him. "And Dad sure wouldn't have—" she glanced back at Molly "—caused the explosion in Virginia," she said under her breath.

The little girl's wide eyes went back and forth between them, her lip trembling.

"You're making me cry. I don't like fighting."

Garrett's eyes softened. "Sorry, sugar. Your aunt and I didn't mean to scare you."

Molly hunkered back in the seat, hugging Mr. Houdini close. "Mommy and Daddy fighted about her job all the time."

Laurel twisted in the car. "I didn't know that. What did they say?"

"Daddy wanted Mommy to stay at home with me. I wanted her to stay home, too. Now she'll never stay with me." Molly hugged the stuffed animal and picked at its neck. "She said she was doing something 'portant and couldn't stop them."

"I'm sorry, Molly." Laurel shot Garrett a glare. "We won't fight anymore. Will we?"

He shook his head. "I'm not lying to Molly, because we're going to disagree about this." He gave Molly a small smile. "But, sugar, we'll promise to discuss things more quietly next time. Okay?"

Laurel sighed and started the engine. "Fine. Then

where do we go now? Because I need another look at those files."

"To the next town," Garrett said. "I'll pick up a cell phone."

Still disgruntled, she pressed the accelerator and the SUV took off on the lonely Texas highway. "I still can't believe you, of all people, would assume my father is guilty. They made you out to be a traitor, too."

Garrett didn't say anything at first. "I don't want to believe it. But those chips… James had them developed. He wanted to tag each operative. That way he'd know where they were."

"Seems reasonable. If you were captured—"

"It *was* reasonable, except that we already knew there was a leak in the organization. So he ended the program. No one else had access to the technology, yet I was tagged after the explosion. Now someone is trying to kill us. What would you think?"

"What about the person who designed the chips?" Laurel challenged. "Or the organization that funded the program? My father is ops, not administration."

Garrett stroked his chin, where his beard had grown in since they'd left town. It gave him that outlaw look that Laurel, as a CIA analyst on the run for her life, shouldn't find sexy. But she did.

"Interesting," he said. "I always thought of the killer as ops, but you're right. There are too many layers. That requires redirecting funding and resources. Administrative skills and the ability to hide funding transfers." He drummed his fingers on his knee. "But how do we follow that string to this whole conspiracy?"

"What about Fiona?" Laurel said. "She's got to be

going crazy with James missing, and she'd know who has that kind of power."

"I didn't want to involve her, but we're out of options," Garrett said. "It might be time to bring her in. We're running out of leads. And time."

"And we need someone on the inside, Garrett. You know that." They'd eaten up miles of West Texas roads with not a pair of headlights to be seen. Laurel began to relax. Just a little. Still, they needed communication equipment.

"Let's wait and see if the file has something more." Garrett scanned the pitch-dark horizon. "If not, we'll call her."

"I need access to a computer to look at the file."

"We've gone far enough. Find a place to pull over out of sight. With the chip gone, we should be safe. We'll sleep until daybreak, then head for a public library. That's our best shot of opening Ivy's file."

DARKNESS SURROUNDED THE SUV. A gust of wind shook the vehicle. Garrett shifted his shoulder, seeking relief from the pain. The wound hurt, but he'd had worse. Laurel had rounded the car, slipped into the backseat and cuddled Molly next to her.

She might never forgive him, but what was he supposed to think? Who else could possibly have planted a chip in him after the explosion but James?

Laurel and Molly huddled together, looking less than comfortable, but they couldn't risk going to a motel or even going through stoplights in some of the larger towns. People didn't realize how many cameras watched them. Big Brother really did have an eye on them all the time. Especially when whoever was after him had known his location until a few hours ago. The longer they could stay off the radar, the bigger the search pattern the enemies would require.

And the greater chance of a surprise…if Ivy had found something more than Garrett had discovered when he was doing his digging.

He inched open the door and eased out of the front seat. Laurel had been defiant in defending James. Garrett didn't blame her.

If he hadn't seen Ivy's notes and the telltale design of that chip, he wouldn't have suspected James either. But Laurel was smart and made good points.

Fiona had always had James's back. She'd orchestrated difficult ops with knifelike precision, even those deemed impossible. She almost always found a way for the agents to succeed. She would know *all* the players. Maybe she was the person James had pulled in when he'd told Garrett he was getting close.

Laurel was right. They needed an insider. No matter the risk. He let his gaze rest on her, her eyes shadowed while she tried to sleep. Laurel McCallister was one fierce mama bear when riled. He found that quality strangely attractive. She would need it.

But before he called Fiona, he had to put his backup plan into action. Once he called her, his phone would be tracked.

He dialed a number.

"Adams."

"Daniel. It's Garrett. I definitely need your help."

"Thank God you called. What the hell is going on in Trouble?" Daniel barked like a drill sergeant. "I received a call from your deputy a few minutes ago. I guess he kept my number from our last little adventure.

Evidently he's been taken hostage. Along with Hondo and his sister. The men who took them said he'd better find the sheriff. They left an ultimatum."

"What kind?"

"Come to Trouble. Bring the woman and the girl, but no weapons." Daniel paused. "You have an hour left, Garrett, or they start killing people."

A loud curse exploded from Garrett. "It'll take a majority of that time just to get there."

"Then I'd start driving as soon as you can. I'll meet you there."

Garrett looked through the car's window at Laurel and Molly. Innocent, caught up in a deadly game because of James. Now made worse because of Garrett. That scared the hell out of him. He looked at his watch. He needed a few minutes out of their earshot.

"Daniel, do your *friends* from CTC have contacts in the intelligence community?"

"Oh, yeah."

Garrett cleared his throat. "I need help cleaning up a crime scene. There are two guys at the bottom of Guadalupe Gorge."

"You've been busy."

"There's something else." Garrett paused. "You need to know if you're going to help me. My real name is Derek Bradley."

Daniel didn't say a word, but Garrett could tell from the silence Daniel had heard his name before. "I didn't do what's been said about me. I'm no traitor, but I understand if you decide to back out."

"You don't have to convince me. I've seen you in action. A traitor would have turned his back on me and my wife. A traitor would be living on his own island in the Caribbean, not marking time as a sheriff in a place barely passing for a populated town in West Texas."

A baby's cry sounded in the background. Garrett heard the soft voice of Adams's wife, Raven, speaking to the twins, and then a door closed softly.

"Daniel, think long and hard about Raven and those kids before you commit."

"I am. They'd be dead without you. Besides, I believe you. I've seen what men in power can do to protect themselves." He paused. "I can help you, so shut up and tell me what I need to do."

Garrett let out a long, slow breath and made sure Laurel and Molly were still asleep in the SUV. He walked a few more steps away. "First off, I need protection for two witnesses with a target on their backs. I won't lie, Daniel. It's dangerous."

"Why aren't you going back to your organization? There must be someone there you can trust. Someone whose loyalties you're certain of."

"Maybe one person, but the truth is, I can't tell anymore. The man who saved my life could be keeping me alive as a decoy or a weapon." Garrett hadn't said anything to Laurel, but her father had been the best Garrett had ever seen at deception. A month ago, Garrett would have done anything for James. If his mentor had told him that he'd found evidence of who had killed Garrett's family, he would have exacted justice. Swift and uncompromised justice.

"I don't want anyone at the organization involved," Garrett said, scuffing his boot on the dirt. "I need an independent group that has the contacts to keep Laurel and Molly safe if something happens to me."

"You've got it," Daniel said. "When and where do we meet?"

"No other questions?" Garrett asked.

"Like I said, you saved my life, not to mention my wife and daughters. No questions needed. I know what loyalty means, Garrett. You've earned mine. Now, time is passing quickly. What's your plan?"

"I can't leave my witnesses alone. One is a five-year-old girl. I can't watch them all the time and do what needs to be done."

"I understand," Daniel said. "We'll be there, but it'll take more than the hour you have."

"Then I'll make do until then. I don't know who else will be waiting for us, but meet me in Trouble as soon as you can. I can't let anyone else die because of me."

"Wheels up in ten. See you soon."

THE SUV TURNED a corner, waking Laurel. She blinked her eyes against the hazy light of dawn. She glanced at the back of Garrett's head from the backseat. "You shouldn't be driving. You need rest. And a doctor."

Garrett glanced around at her, then at his watch. "No choice. We're going back to Trouble."

He refocused on the road and pressed down the accelerator, lurching the SUV forward. At the urgency in his actions and his tone, Laurel straightened in her seat. She met his gaze in the rearview mirror. "What's happened?"

"Someone tracking us has taken hostages." Garrett's jaw tightened. "My deputy, Lucy and Hondo. They gave us an hour and time is almost up. They're going to kill the hostages one by one."

"Oh, God." Her hand covered her mouth and she kept her voice low. Molly didn't need to hear this.

"I can't let anything happen to them, Laurel. You understand that."

She nodded, wanting to hold Molly even tighter. This couldn't be happening.

Garrett glanced back at her and Molly. "The problem is, the caller who has the hostages wants all three of us."

"Why? I don't understand. What is it that we've done that's so threatening? Especially Molly?"

"The world thinks we're dead, and we potentially know too much. It's safer and easier to eliminate the witnesses."

"I've seen a lot of evil during my time with the CIA, but this— She's just a little girl." Laurel shivered. "We both know if someone wants you dead, eventually they'll succeed. It's too easy. Tampering with brakes, a car bomb, a sniper shot from a thousand feet away."

"Unless they can't find you." Garrett pressed harder on the gas.

Laurel looked over at Molly. "What's the plan for the three of us?"

"I don't know."

"You're lying."

"I'm running options through my head. It will depend on who is waiting for us, how many. Wish I had a sitrep." The SUV sped up and he glanced at his watch. "They'll call in the next five minutes to set up a rendezvous point. I want to try to surprise them. Hopefully it's not too many."

"I can help, Garrett. I may not have field experience, but I'm a good shot. You know I am."

"You need to protect Molly. I have help coming."

"But will they be here soon enough?"

"I don't know."

"Another lie."

"It's not good that you can read me so easily. I'll have to work on that."

"I'm watching your back, Galloway, so get used to it."

A BRIGHT LIGHT blasted into the midnight-dark prison room. James blinked as the beam burned the backs of his eyes.

He tried to squint through the glare, but he could barely see.

"You should have told us about the chip sooner. It might have saved your daughter Ivy and her family's lives. Too bad she had to start digging and learned too much."

James squeezed his eyes shut tight. God, no. Not Ivy. Not the kids. What had he done? He didn't remember revealing anything, just the shot from a hypodermic needle.

A chuckle from across the room lit a fire of hatred. James jerked up his head, not caring how much it hurt. "You won't get away with this."

"I already have. My reputation is impeccable. I'm trusted. People come to me because they know I'll find a way to get them money, resources, equipment. You knew that, too."

"Which *should* make them suspicious of you."

"People see what they want to see, even in the intelligence community."

His captor pulled out a gun and sauntered over to him. The barrel pressed against his temple. "I should kill you now. You're a loose end."

James knew he wouldn't come out of this alive. For

now, he had to try to get a signal to Garrett. There had to be a way.

"Do it."

"You'd like that. Well, it won't be so easy, James." A quick flick of the wrist brought in a beefy man with eyes cold and dead as a snake. "Find out what else he hasn't told us."

James swallowed. The inflamed scar on the man's face was obviously the result of recent burns. He carried an iron rod with him. "Make it easy. I can't stop until you give me something," the man said, touching his cheek.

The man walked over to a heating element and flicked on a switch. A gas flame roared to life and he stuck the tip of iron in the flames, rotating the bar slowly, evenly. After a few minutes the man pulled the red-hot iron from the flame and walked toward James.

"You don't have to do this," James said. "We could leave together."

He let out a harsh laugh. "I just tried. My daughter was killed in a car *accident* yesterday, along with her boyfriend and two others. I have a wife and son, and I've been told what will happen to them if I fail. I won't try to leave again."

He bent over James. "Now tell me something. Anything. Because I *will* protect my family. Even if you have to die for me to do it."

James closed his eyes. He'd already lost one daughter. Just like this man, he would die to protect Laurel. "I can't."

Scorching heat set fire to his skin. James couldn't stop the scream. Blistering pain, unlike anything he'd ever known.

Suddenly it was gone. James sagged in his chair. He caught his breath.

"Tell me," the man said. "I can't stop."

From outside his prison cell, his captor's words filtered through the bars. "You've arrived? Excellent. Strickland failed twice. You know what to do. Kill Bradley and Strickland. I want this hole plugged up today."

THE BUILDINGS OF Trouble, Texas, were one story and far apart. Dawn had come, and the dim light brought with it visibility. For better or worse.

Garrett couldn't afford to drive any closer on the highway. He turned onto the flat desert plain. "I'm not going in through the main drag. I'll drive through the plains and come in on one of the side streets."

"What about your *friends?*"

"They'll be here soon."

"But not before your meeting." Laurel leaned forward. "You need backup, Garrett. You're one of the walking wounded right now."

She was right, but he had to think of Laurel and Molly first. "You have to watch your niece. She can't afford to lose anyone else."

Laurel hugged the little girl closer.

His cell phone rang.

With a quick movement, Laurel tugged at his wrist. He frowned, but eased the phone from his ear so she could hear.

"Galloway."

"You should have answered *Derek Bradley,*" the voice said. "Traitor."

Garrett cursed under his breath. No one knew about Daniel, so that information had to have come from James.

"I don't know what you're talking about."

"Don't play dumb, *Sheriff.* How close are you to your office?"

"Fifteen minutes."

"Five minutes before I'm scheduled to kill your deputy. You're cutting it close. The poor kid just broke into a sweat."

"I said I'll be there."

"You have the woman with you?"

Garrett didn't respond.

"If I don't have your word that I'll see her outside your office in fifteen minutes, the deputy dies now."

He glanced at Laurel. She nodded.

His lips tightened. "She'll be there."

"And the girl?"

"For God's sake, she's only a child."

A shotgun pump sounded through the phone.

"Damn it. All right, Molly will be there, too."

"Excellent. Look, Sheriff, you play this right, and I *might* let the woman and girl live. But you try to double-cross me and I won't hesitate to kill them. I've done it before." The man paused. "I hear you have a lot of scars from the bomb. Too bad it went off before you were in the car with your wife and kid."

"Strickland? You're dead."

"Guess we're both hard to kill."

The phone went dead.

Garrett's mind whirled. He *still* hadn't killed the bastard. What had he done?

Laurel rested her hand on Garrett's shoulder, but he shook her away.

"Strickland killed my family and I let him leave that ravine." Garrett couldn't think, could barely feel. He'd failed. Again. This time Laurel and Molly might pay the price.

"He won't get away with it," Laurel said. She set her SIG on the front seat. "He killed my family, too. He'll pay. Together, we'll make sure of it."

A BLACK ESCALADE pulled two blocks down from the sheriff's office.

"There's Bradley." Shep Warner looked over at his new partner. Léon had an accent Shep couldn't place, but he had some serious skills. The boss wouldn't have brought him on otherwise. "I worked with him. He was good. Too good, I guess."

"The boss wants him dead."

Shep looked through a pair of Zeiss binoculars. "Someone's in the backseat. Two people. A woman and a kid."

Léon stiffened. "No one said anything about killing a kid."

Shep took a quick image with his camera. "Boss will want to know about this."

He hit Send and waited.

Immediately the phone rang.

"Where did you take this?" The computer-filtered voice always gave him a chill, with its inhuman tone. He had no idea who his boss was, just that his bank account was a lot more robust since he'd started the job. It was just business.

His new partner, Léon, unsettled him. Shep couldn't quite pinpoint what felt wrong. He certainly was a surly bastard, like a robot. Well, if he didn't work out, the boss had a means of making more than one person disappear, particularly when the government had already named anyone missing or disavowed.

"Trouble, Texas. She and a kid are in the target's car."

"Strickland's third strike. Our source here isn't talking. Kill them, too, and dispose of the bodies."

"Won't there be questions?"

"Just make them disappear. In the eyes of the world they are already dead."

Léon turned to Shep. "What's the plan?"

"Leave no one alive. Including Strickland."

"The girl?"

"Even the girl."

Chapter Ten

Two blocks from the sheriff's office, Garrett let the SUV idle. Trouble's Christmas lights knocked against the light poles.

The place looked deserted, causing the hairs on his arms to stand on end. He had a bad feeling about this whole thing. Too many unknowns.

He needed a diversion, and with Daniel and CTC still an hour away, he had no choice about who he had to choose. It tore him apart he'd have to put Laurel in danger.

"We're out of time," Laurel said.

"I know." Garrett let out a sigh. "How's Molly?"

"Resting now." Laurel stroked the girl's forehead. "I gave her some acetaminophen. Her temperature popped up last night, so maybe she'll sleep longer. I need to get her checked out by a doctor."

"Hopefully this will be over soon." Garrett studied the sheriff's office. No one was behind the building. Thank goodness. "I have a way to sneak into the back of the building and get to a stash of weapons, but I need a distraction."

"I'll drive," Laurel said, "and park in front of the

sheriff's office. Hopefully they don't have a bazooka in their arsenal."

"Don't even joke about that, Laurel."

"If I don't joke, I'll run screaming from town, Garrett. I'm terrified for Molly."

He turned in his seat. "And I'm scared for both of you.

"When you hear things go bad in that building, you take off to Hondo's place, the Copper Mine Motel. It was on the right as we headed into town. Daniel will be there soon."

"What about you?"

"If it goes well, I'll get to Hondo, Lucy and the deputy. I'll meet you there with the name of the person who ordered these hits. Let's switch places."

Garrett exited the vehicle, leaving the car running to ward off the nippy morning. He rounded the car and Laurel slipped into the front seat. He knocked on the glass and she cracked the window.

"Give me five minutes before you round the corner. Until then, stay down."

She nodded, but tears glistened in her eyes. "You're a good man, Garrett Galloway, so go kick some bad-guy butt and come back to me."

"I promise I want to." He touched Laurel's cheek, then looked over at Molly. "You're going to do great with her," he said.

Her eyes darkened. "That sounded a lot like goodbye. Please don't let it be."

"You know I need to do this."

"For your family," she whispered.

"And for you." He kissed her lips lightly, lingering for just a moment. "For you and Molly and me."

Garrett eased into the alleyway. He took one last

look at Laurel and lifted up a silent prayer. *Please, let them be okay.* He had to focus on the job at hand: take Strickland out, hope he hadn't brought a ton of friends and save Keller, Hondo and Lucy. Not to mention Laurel and Molly.

He scanned the area. He didn't see anything unusual, then paused. One vehicle stood out. The Escalade had to be Strickland's.

Garrett checked his watch. He didn't have time to hesitate. In less than four minutes Laurel would pull the SUV in front of his building.

He rounded the sheriff's office. He had cameras inside and outside, but they required a password to access. He hadn't even given the code to his deputy. Garrett ran his fingers along the bricks at the back of the building. He pulled out a loose one. Inside was a latch to the emergency entrance. Garrett had always thought the whole setup bordered on paranoia, but now he thanked his overly cautious predecessor. Of course, the man had been right, just not careful enough. He was serving twenty for drug trafficking.

Praying Strickland had kept his deputy in the main room, Garrett entered the digital code and the lock clicked. Slowly he eased the door open.

He heard one set of heavy footsteps pacing from the far room to his left, near the jail cells. Had to be Strickland. He wouldn't allow anyone to be moving around.

"Your sheriff is cutting it close, Deputy," Strickland snapped. The footsteps stopped. "You ready to die for a traitor?"

"Sheriff Galloway is on the up-and-up. I'll never believe he did what you said."

"Damn straight, you cow dung," Hondo hollered, rattling the bars of the cage. "He's twice the man you'll ever be."

Hondo should know better. What the hell was he doing? If Strickland lost his temper, he'd start shooting. Garrett had no doubt that if Strickland had his way, no one would be left alive. Not Laurel or Molly. Not Keller, Lucy or Hondo. And certainly not Garrett.

He glanced at the wall safe, opened it and pulled out an extra set of keys to the jail. If nothing else, he needed to get those keys to Keller or Hondo so they had a prayer of escaping.

A loud clatter rang out. Hondo let out a curse. "You trying to break my hand?"

"Shut up," Strickland said. "Or I'll kill you first. I may choose you anyway. You're too damned annoying."

"No, please, no. Now, Lucy, it's going to be okay."

"Make her stop that sniveling, or I take her." Strickland stomped away, toward the front of the building. "Someone's pulling out front."

That had to be Laurel.

Which meant Strickland had his back to the jail.

Garrett hurried outside the emergency exit to the side of the jail. A small window ledge was the only opening. He lifted himself up, then dangled the keys in front of the glass. He grabbed a diamond cutter from his pocket and within seconds had opened a hole. He set the keys in reach.

Garrett tapped lightly.

Keller jerked his head up. His eyes widened. He sidled over to Hondo. The man slid a subtle glance toward Garrett and gave a nod. At the right moment, they'd grab the keys.

Garrett had to trust the ex-marine to get Keller and

Lucy out safely. He returned to the secret entrance and pushed back inside. The easiest thing would be to shoot Strickland in the back of the head. The man deserved it. Garrett had been dreaming of killing the man since he'd woken up from his coma, but that would silence the only lead Garrett had to the identity of the mastermind behind a decade's worth of death and criminal activity.

And Strickland's death wouldn't protect Laurel and Molly in the long run.

That made his job that much more difficult. He needed Strickland alive, which made his every move that much more dangerous.

Hondo hadn't budged. Good man. Playing it smart. Lucy was tucked up on the end of the cot, rocking away. Easy to see how Strickland had gotten the drop on Hondo. Deputy Keller… Well, Garrett would be having a talk with him.

Strickland held an M16 in his hand. He peered through the front window, stepped aside and opened the door.

"The McCallister woman and the girl. But where's Bradley?" Strickland shifted his M16.

"Guess Bradley didn't believe me when I said one of you would die." He pointed the gun at Lucy.

Now or never.

Garrett launched himself at Strickland, knocking the man's weapon from his hand. Garrett landed on his shoulder and nearly cried out in agony even as he grabbed Strickland by the throat. He pressed his forearm against the man's trachea. "I should have killed you."

Strickland grinned up at him. "But you won't, because

someone will keep coming now that the boss knows you're alive. You can't kill me."

The bastard was right.

Garrett pressed harder, blocking the man's air. "Who do you work for? I want a name."

Strickland glared up at him. "Let me go."

"Let me out. Let me out," Lucy shouted.

Out of the corner of his eye, Garrett saw Hondo pluck the keys from the ledge and unlock the door. Lucy raced from the jail cell the moment Hondo opened it.

With that second's distraction, Strickland thrust his arms against Garrett's chest and twisted his body. He broke Garrett's hold and leaned back just in time to avoid Garrett's killing blow to his windpipe.

Strickland leaped to his feet, grabbed Lucy by the hair and dragged her to the front door.

Garrett raised his Beretta. "You won't get out of here alive."

"Stay still, Lucy," Hondo pleaded with his sister.

The poor woman started crying. Strickland's trigger finger flinched.

"What are you going to do now, Sheriff?" Strickland grinned. "Looks like I'm back in charge. Drop your weapon."

Garrett cursed. He had no choice. He slid his weapon over.

Keller circled around Strickland. The man didn't hesitate. He let a bullet fly. Keller went down, his shoulder bloody.

"No more games. Get McCallister and the girl inside, and we'll finish this."

Before the words left his mouth a gunshot echoed through the room.

Lucy screamed.

Strickland fell to the floor, unmoving.

Hondo ran to his sister and cradled her in his arms, turning her away from the dead body. "I was only bringing the deputy cookies," she babbled.

"Everyone down." Garrett raced to the open front door. He stood in the doorway, Beretta drawn. Molly was ducked down in the backseat. Laurel had squeezed under the SUV. "He's dead," Garrett said.

Laurel's eyes widened; she crawled toward him, rose and threw herself into his arms.

"Did he say anything?" she whispered. "Give us any information?"

Slowly Garrett shook his head. "I'm sorry."

"I understand."

But her voice held a resignation that Garrett didn't like. She, too, realized the implications. If Ivy's file didn't give them the name of the person responsible, they were at a dead end. That could cost all three of them their lives.

THE BLACK ESCALADE backed out of sight of the sheriff's office. Shep shoved the gear into Park and glared at Léon. "You should have taken the shot. Strickland was easy, but Bradley was in your sights twice. First when he orchestrated that harebrained scheme with the keys, then through the front door. You could have taken them both out."

His new partner shook his head. "The deputy would have been collateral damage. Plus, I saw movement inside through that front window."

"So what?"

"The boss doesn't want too many bodies that can't be explained. I need to be able to take them out quick, and we have to move in and grab them...or they need to disappear."

"I didn't hear that order."

"Well, I was told when I was brought on board to keep every job out of the papers and low-key. Killing a bunch of people in a sheriff's office will make the news. Trust me, that's how the boss wants it."

"Then how do you expect to get the job done?" Shep asked. This new guy was really starting to bug him. And his accent irritated the hell out of Shep.

"I've got an explosive in the back of the truck that makes C-4 look like Play-Doh. Nothing for forensics to find. We follow them, get them together, blow the car and leave. It'll burn so hot nothing is left. It's cleaner. And we get rid of them all at once."

Shep drummed his fingers on the dash. "Explosives. That's why the boss brought you in. Léon, I may like your style after all."

"Then we're in agreement." Léon peered through his binoculars. "Hmm...looks like we won't have to make Strickland disappear. Our friendly neighborhood deputy's hiding the body."

"Maybe he's taking it to the morgue."

Léon shook his head. "Wrapped the guy in a blanket and dumped him in a pickup. They're getting rid of the body."

"One less task for us to finish."

"One more reason to do this job right, because I refuse to be made into an example of my new boss's desire for perfection."

HONDO'S MOTEL ROOMS were simple, but comfortable. Laurel took a long, slow breath, but her nerves refused to settle. At least the chaos from outside had disappeared.

The group of CTC operatives who had arrived had taken over the motel and the sheriff's office and pretty much secured the entire town. No one went in or out without CTC knowing it.

They'd searched for the man who'd shot Strickland, but the only lead was an unfamiliar black Escalade that had raced out of town. An expensive car carrying a sniper with a good eye.

They'd be back.

Laurel couldn't feel completely safe, even with the armed guards at the door. The two men originally tailing her might be dead, but they'd been replaced. Someone wanted her, Molly and Garrett dead, not to mention they still hadn't heard from her father.

Laurel shifted backward and let her spine rest against the bed's headboard. Molly crawled into her lap, resting against her chest. With a sigh, Laurel hummed the addictive ant song Garrett had sung the night before.

Everything around this room seemed peaceful and safe, but Laurel could feel the tension knotting at the back of her neck. Her gut urged her to run, but she had nowhere to go.

She had to trust Garrett and his friends.

Molly picked at Mr. Houdini, rocking him slightly. She'd gone way too quiet after the latest attack. Would Molly ever be the same? Laurel knew she wouldn't.

Molly snuggled closer and squeezed her lion tightly, playing with its collar.

A knock sounded at the door. Molly jerked in Laurel's arms as the door opened. Laurel palmed her SIG and aimed it at the woman with black hair who stood on the motel's porch. Behind her, Laurel recognized one of the CTC operatives standing guard.

"Who are you?" she asked.

"Raven Adams, Daniel's wife. May I come in?"

The man Garrett trusted so much. One more leap of faith.

Laurel nodded and lowered the SIG, but kept it within reach.

A large reddish-colored dog panted beside Raven. "How about my furry friend, Trouble?" She tilted her head toward her canine companion.

Molly straightened a bit in Laurel's lap and stared closely at the dog, which seemed to smile.

"Come in," Laurel said.

The moment Raven crossed the threshold, Trouble bounded toward Molly, but he didn't jump on the bed. He simply tilted his head and stared at the little girl, then put his big head down on the bed and looked up at Molly with sad brown eyes.

"Your dog's name is Trouble?" Laurel asked.

Raven smiled. "It's a long story. He gets more people out of trouble than into trouble, though."

Molly bit her lip and scooted off of Laurel's lap. "Can I pet him?"

"He'd like that," Raven said. "He especially likes getting his ears rubbed."

Molly reached out a tentative hand and patted Trouble's head. The dog's tail thumped.

"He likes me," Molly said. She moved her fingers to his ears and scratched. The big dog leaned into her and practically groaned with pleasure.

Molly slid off the bed. "He's big." Her lion in one arm,

she wrapped her other around the big dog and hugged him. "I like you."

Raven held up a bag. "Have you had some of Hondo's cookies? He likes you a lot, Molly, so he gave me a few cookies just for you."

Molly's ears perked up even as she rubbed Trouble's nose. "Chocolate chip?"

"Is there another kind of cookie?" Raven opened the bag and passed a cookie to Molly. "Daniel and I wanted to invite Molly to take a ride on a plane and visit my house. I have a swing set in the backyard. It's too big for my little girls, but it might be just Molly's size."

Trouble rolled onto his back and Molly giggled, rubbing the dog's belly. The smile that lit her eyes made Laurel's heart ache.

"She'd be safe with us," Raven said.

Laurel leaned down and patted Trouble. Then she stroked Molly's hair. "When are you leaving?"

"Daniel and Garrett are discussing their plans."

"Really?" Laurel crouched down in front of her niece. "Molly Magoo, I need to go speak with Sheriff Garrett. Do you want to stay here with Trouble?"

Molly nodded.

"Do you mind watching her for a few minutes?" Laurel asked Raven. "She's had a rough time. If she needs me, I'll be right outside."

Laurel started toward the door. Raven took one of Laurel's hands. "You can trust Garrett. He's one of the good ones."

Laurel studied the woman's eyes and recognized the tortured memories of events gone by. Raven had seen things. Laurel looked back at Molly.

"I'll take good care of her. I almost lost my girls. I

don't take their safety for granted." Laurel hesitated. "Look, I know you don't know me from any woman off the street, but Garrett and Daniel saved my life and the lives of my children. There's no one else I'd want in my corner if I were facing the devil himself."

Laurel met Raven's gaze. "We're in a lot of trouble. What if it follows Molly to you?"

"More of Daniel's organization will be stationed at my house. She'll be well guarded. And Trouble will be there, too."

Laurel bit her lip. "I'll think about it."

She walked out of the motel room. Several men with serious faces and equally impressive weapons prowled the area. One tipped his cowboy hat at her. "Ma'am. The sheriff's in the next room over."

Laurel walked in. Garrett sat next to Daniel Adams at a small table near the window, studying the screen of a laptop, deep in conversation.

She strode over to them. "What have you found out from Ivy's information?"

Garrett lifted his head, but the guilt in his eyes gave him away. "We should talk about this later."

"I don't like the secrets," Laurel insisted. "Tell me."

He turned the laptop around and Laurel read through the first page. "This can't be true."

"Ivy's file makes a direct connection between your father and almost every agency leak. It connects gun running, selling of top secret documents and the movement of over a billion dollars into overseas accounts."

Laurel snatched the laptop from him and sat on the bed. She took in page after page. Her shoulders tensed at each new, damning word. "I don't believe Ivy wrote this." Laurel raised her gaze to meet Garrett's. "This is the file I downloaded?"

Garrett nodded.

"She's wrong. She has to be. If anyone saw this—"

"Your father would be convicted of treason."

"He wouldn't do any of this. And I'm not just being naive." She lifted her chin and stared at Garrett.

He knelt beside the bed and held her hand in his. "I don't think so either, but I do believe someone else within the agency is setting him up. Just like me."

"What can we do? Strickland is dead."

Daniel cleared his throat. "After I spoke with Ransom Grainger, the head of CTC, about you, he let me in on some sensitive information. CTC has a contact buried deep in a covert operation within the agency. Ransom had been asked to investigate some irregularities within their overseas operations," he said.

"By who?"

"Let's just say it's someone at the very highest levels of the government. There was a whistle-blower involved."

"Who?" Laurel asked.

"James McCallister."

"Dad?"

"I think this is why he hoped to solve my case," Garrett said.

"Daniel, can you help us identify who wants us dead? Maybe even find out what happened to my father?" Laurel asked. "Can CTC?"

The CTC operative frowned. "Our informant hasn't met face-to-face with the highest level in the organization yet. Evidently, whoever's in charge keeps things very secret, so it's delicate. Any contact with our operative and we risk his life. Too many questions and he'll disappear. Others have."

"So, what do we do until then?" Laurel asked, rubbing the back of her neck to try to get rid of the headache threatening to escalate into agony. "Eventually that sniper will find a way to us. We can't hide forever."

Garrett rose and looked down at her, his expression warning her she wouldn't like whatever he was going to say. "That's why I want you and Molly to disappear for a while with Daniel and Raven."

Laurel took in Garrett's grim face. "You'll come with us, though. You're in danger, too."

"I can't, Laurel. I'm going to—"

"Get yourself killed," Laurel finished.

"I think I'll leave you two to hash this out." Daniel disappeared out the door, closing it behind him.

Garrett plucked the laptop from her and brought her to her feet. He touched her cheek. "I'm going to find James and take this guy down, but I can't focus on the mission if I'm worried about you and Molly. I don't want you hurt, Laurel. Your father would want you out of the cross fire."

"That's playing dirty." She scowled at him, knowing exactly what he was doing and hating him for it.

"I'm telling the truth." He bent down and gently touched her lips with his own. "It has to be this way. For Molly. You know that."

Garrett laced his fingers with hers. She liked the way they intertwined, as if they were one. They'd known each other just a few days, and yet she felt as if they'd been together always. She didn't want to lose him.

"I don't like it."

"But you'll do it." Garrett squeezed her fingers. "For Molly."

"For Molly."

With a soft peck on her lips, he walked to the door and opened it. "Daniel, I need transportation."

Daniel slipped a phone from his pocket. "To D.C.?"

"That's where this thing started. That's where I'll end it."

"Give me a couple of hours to get a plane here. You guys have been up all night. Rest. We'll take care of things for a while."

"Thanks, Daniel. I owe you."

"We're even now," he said. "I'm going to find my wife."

Daniel closed the door on them and Garrett faced Laurel. She could hardly breathe. "I don't like this. It feels wrong. I came to you. I caused you to lose everything."

Without hesitation, Garrett tugged her back into his arms. "You're wrong. You brought me back to life, Laurel."

He stroked her arms, warming the chill that had settled all around her with the knowledge that this might be the last time he held her.

"I'm afraid. For you."

"All I want is for you to be safe. That's all James would want. This is your chance."

She could barely breathe. "Hold me, Garrett. Tight. Please."

"I'll do more than that." Garrett lowered his lips to hers and pressed them open.

With a low groan she wrapped her arms around his waist, pressing her ear to his chest, listening to the strong beat of his heart, memorizing his scent, the feel of him, taking in every moment, terrified that soon it would be over. Soon he would be gone and she would have only this moment to cherish.

When Garrett pulled back slightly, she couldn't stop the moan of protest. But he didn't let her go. He cupped her face this time, the kiss so very sweet, so very loving. So very scary. Like a goodbye.

Without words, he scooped her into his arms and laid her down on the bed, spooning against her back.

He threaded his fingers with hers, breathing in deeply. "If things were different, I would take you away. I would disappear with you. Believe that."

She brought his hand to her chest and squeezed tight. "I'm terrified. For you. For my father. So many people have died." Laurel turned in his arms and touched his cheek, taking in each line of tension, each fleck of gold in his brown eyes. "I don't want to lose you now that I've found you."

"I'll do everything I can to bring your father home, Laurel."

"And you, too. I want you back, Garrett." She clutched the front of his shirt. "You made me feel something these last few days. I've always believed I could only rely on myself. My father taught me that. But you— I feel like I can count on you. I want and need you in my life. Don't die on me."

"I have a whole lot to live for these days," he said softly. "I don't want to leave you." He pulled her closer, and she realized he'd never made a promise that he'd come back. For the first time, the easy lie didn't trip off his lips.

She felt the truth in every word.

GARRETT WATCHED LAUREL sleep for two hours. The rise and fall of her chest, the gentle smile on her face. He wanted nothing more than to take her away and make a new life for all of them, but he knew better. This would never be over, Laurel and Molly would never be safe, his family and Laurel's family would never be avenged until the traitor in the organization was stopped.

Garrett had said goodbye with every kiss, every touch, every caress. Knowing it might be for the last time, he slipped out of the bed with a sigh, pulled on his boots and walked out of the room.

Laurel wouldn't be surprised to awaken and find him gone, but she'd be furious. He knew they were lucky to have survived the past few days. Luck didn't last forever.

He closed the door quietly. Daniel stood on the porch of the Copper Mine Motel in a small pool of sunlight, Raven folded in his arms, a blanket wrapped around her.

Several armed guards nodded at them. Daniel nodded back.

"Any strangers in town?"

"None. And no sign of the Escalade. It looks clear. For now."

"And Molly?"

"Playing on my tablet, using Trouble as a pillow," Raven said with a smile. "She's a tough little thing. Not to mention a girl after my own heart, with her fondness for Hondo's chocolate-chip cookies."

"How are Hondo and Lucy? And Keller?"

Daniel frowned. "Lucy isn't handling it well. Doc gave her a sedative. Keller's going to recover, but he's got a lot of questions."

"Poor Lucy. She's been through hell. You know, I spent the last year in this town playing the waiting game when I wanted to be in the action. Now I've hurt the people who gave me their trust when they shouldn't have. I don't know how to make it up to them."

"You can catch whoever's responsible and make them pay." Hondo's harsh voice came from around the corner. The big man looked devastated.

"Hondo." Garrett stilled. "I'm so sorry about you and Lucy—"

The motel owner raised his hand. "You didn't bring them here. They came after you. Lucy knows better than anyone that evil exists. Her ex-husband's beatings damaged her brain and left her with a childlike innocence. Then a few months ago she was shot and nearly killed. She sees the truth now, though." Hondo handed over another bag of cookies. "Give these to Molly. Lucy wants her to have them. She wouldn't let herself sleep until I brought them out here."

"Again, I'm so sorry."

"Sheriff, you want to make it up to me? Take care of those men, then come back. Obviously Trouble needs a lawman who knows how to handle more than just old man Crowley's drinking binges. We need good men around here, and that's what you are. So get it done."

Hondo disappeared back behind the screen door, then closed and locked it.

Garrett exhaled slowly, shoved his hands into his pockets and looked at Daniel. "I left everything I know about this case on a disk in the top drawer in the hotel room. If I don't come back...use your best judgment."

Daniel nodded.

"Strickland and Krauss are gone, but there are more coming." Garrett pulled Strickland's phone from the

evidence bag. "Once I turn this on, sooner or later someone will track it, or the traitor at the other end will call."

With a solemn nod, Daniel rubbed the back of his
neck. "Then press the button and let's get this damned
thing over with."

GARRETT DROVE THE TRUCK several hours from Trouble
before he pulled off to the side of the road. He didn't
want anyone being led to Laurel.

He dozed, dreaming of lying next to Laurel and cud-
dling her warm body with his. Afternoon sunshine filtered into the pickup. The phone hadn't revealed the
blocked number, so his only choice had been to wait
for the call. He'd signaled Daniel with a text, and CTC
would triangulate the signal.

Just past twelve-thirty the phone rang.

"Derek Bradley, I assume?"

Garrett immediately texted Daniel: The tracking began.

"Strickland and Krauss are dead, I understand. That
must feel good, Mr. Bradley, considering Strickland
blew up your family right in front of you."

"Not particularly. But then again, I don't get off on
killing people."

"Should I even ask what you want, Mr. Bradley? Or
should I call you Garrett?"

"A bargain. For the lives of Laurel McCallister and
Molly Deerfield. They walk away. No one follows them
and they're left alone."

More silence, and a prickle of unease rocked down
Garrett's spine.

"That could be possible. Ivy Deerfield was a better detective than you were, Garrett. She infiltrated my
organization farther than I would have expected. She

collected information I wish returned to me. Returned and destroyed."

"I have her evidence." Garrett waited for several moments. He had to keep the traitor on the phone.

"Your proposition has merit."

Interesting. Whoever was on the other end of the phone felt vulnerable.

"I can come to you," Garrett offered.

"It may very well be time we meet. Then you might begin to understand."

Anticipation coursed through Garrett's blood. He knew he was walking into a trap.

It didn't matter.

"Tell your friends that their attempt to triangulate my location won't work. Besides, you don't have to guess where I'll be, Sheriff. Come to James McCallister's home. Alone. It's a fitting spot for our...reunion. You have until midnight tonight to be here. Or I *will* finish my original plan and eliminate Laurel McCallister and her niece."

Chapter Eleven

Laurel awakened without warmth next to her. She stretched her palm across the motel-room bed, but the sheets were cool to the touch. She didn't have to call out to know Garrett was gone.

Keep him safe.

The silent prayer filtered through her mind. She tucked her legs up. Her skills hadn't brought them the answer. Ivy's investigation had done nothing but incriminate their father, just as he seemed to have done to Garrett. Which was probably why Ivy had thought about leaving the organization.

Garrett would never stop trying to prove his innocence and avenge his wife and daughter, though. And he wouldn't stop now to protect her and Molly.

He was that kind of man. A hero, but the kind of man who could get himself killed in the name of justice.

There had to be something they were missing. That Ivy had missed.

Laurel sat up and rubbed her eyes. How long had she been out?

She slipped on her shoes and opened the door. Daniel stood near her room, his body watchful, his weapon at his side.

"Molly?"

"With Raven and Trouble next door. She's fine."

"I need to see her," Laurel said.

"Sure thing." Daniel took a scan around and met the gaze of a CTC operative at the other end of the motel. "Go on."

Laurel rushed the five feet to the next room and opened the door.

"Aunt Laurel!" Molly grinned, gave Trouble a pat, grabbed her stuffed lion and raced over. "Trouble and me are bestest friends now. Can I have a dog like him? I'll take good care of him and feed him and give him water, and take him for walks, and pick up his poop." She wrinkled her nose. "If I have to. Miss Raven said you were resting. I'm glad you're done. Where's Sheriff Garrett?"

Raven sat cross-legged, hosting a makeshift picnic on the bed.

Laurel fingered Molly's blond hair, able to breathe for a moment, knowing her niece was safe. "He left, Molly Magoo."

Everything within Laurel longed to assure Molly that Garrett would be back soon, but the words simply wouldn't come. Laurel not only couldn't be certain; she feared the worst.

Molly stilled; a frown tugged at the corners of her lips. "He didn't even say goodbye. That's not polite. And I wanted to show him my star. I kept forgetting before. It's just like his when we first met him."

"You have a star?" Laurel asked in confusion.

"Mommy put it on my lion."

Molly held out Mr. Houdini. Laurel stared at the small charm hanging from the lion's collar. She dug into her pocket and retrieved the charm bracelet that her father had sent to Ivy. No charms were missing from it. Every other silver shape had meaning—a seashell representing the last vacation with their mother, a horse for when they'd learned to ride, a ballerina from the terrifying lessons both girls had endured before their mother let them quit.

But a sheriff's star. It had no meaning in their lives.

Except in reference to Garrett.

"When did she put this on, Molly?"

Molly's forehead crinkled in thought. "The day I got sick. She said it was a special star. Grandpa sent it and I had to protect it 'cause I was a brave girl just like the man who wore the star. That's Sheriff Garrett, right?"

"Yes, I think it is." Laurel could barely speak past the thickening of her throat. "Can I borrow it, honey?"

Her niece's face went solemn. "You'll give it back?"

"I promise, Molly Magoo."

Laurel slipped off the lion's collar and returned the animal. She opened the door and motioned Daniel over. "Do you have a magnifying glass or a microscope?"

Daniel's brow rose. "What's up?"

"Maybe nothing. Maybe an answer."

Daniel rounded the back of one of the black vehicles swarmed in the motel's parking lot. He dug into a duffel bag in the back. "Raven is always telling me I carry weird stuff in my bag." He handed her a small magnifying glass. "I've had it since I was a kid. My father taught me to build fires with it."

Laurel sat down at the table in the motel room and laid the charm down. She studied it closely. Molly had carried that lion everywhere. She'd almost left it behind in Virginia when'd they run that very first night.

After studying one side and seeing nothing, she gently turned it over and there it was.

"A microdot." She looked up at Daniel. "We have to find out what's on it, fast. It could save Garrett. And my father."

LAUREL SAT CROSS-LEGGED on the bed, staring at the computer file that the CTC technicians had pulled from the microdot.

Page after page of all the proof she needed that Garrett and her father were innocent. Except for one thing—the true identity of who was behind all the transactions.

But why had her father and Ivy kept it secret?

"Oh, Ivy, where do I go from here? Who were you going to give this to? If only Garrett were here. He might see something unusual."

She opened the motel-room door and called out to Daniel. "Any word yet?"

He shook his head. "They haven't broken radio silence. They will as soon as they can. All I can confirm is that they landed in D.C. a few hours ago."

"D.C.? No. Garrett's walking into a trap." She frowned at Daniel. "You know that."

Worry creased Daniel's forehead. "You have to trust him. I've looked into who Garrett used to be. The man was very good at his job."

Laurel scrubbed her face. This wasn't the same situation. He was a known traitor to the rest of the world. The moment law enforcement recognized he was alive, if someone killed him, not that many questions would be asked.

The answer was in that file. Laurel had to decipher

it. She had to save him somehow. She needed someone who could help her see what she was missing.

She closed the door on Daniel and paced the motel room. She wanted him here, with her. Safe. She longed for him to hold her in his arms, to talk this over with him. She had to call in her last resort.

She toyed with the phone in her hand. Garrett had wanted to keep Fiona out of it, but with the new information from the microdot, Fiona might be the only other person who could help. She could put the word out Garrett was innocent, and that her father was innocent. Save their lives.

Maybe even help Laurel decipher something hidden in the file—something Ivy and James had known about, but that Laurel couldn't identify. Then Garrett wouldn't have to go through with whatever risky plan he and his CTC friends had come up with.

Her finger paused over the numbers. Garrett hadn't wanted to trust anyone else, but even he had recognized Fiona's knowledge. With a deep breath, Laurel dialed Fiona's personal number. No way Laurel could risk her call being recorded.

"Fiona Wylde." The woman's voice was pleasant, welcoming. As it always was. This woman could very well marry her father someday.

"Fiona, it's Laurel."

The woman gasped. "But…I thought… Oh, my God, James and I thought you were dead."

Laurel's knees buckled and she sagged onto the bed. "You've seen my father. Is he okay? Is he safe? I've been so worried about him."

"Oh, honey." A sob came through Fiona's voice. "He's been through hell, but he escaped yesterday and found his way home. We thought…" She could barely choke out the words. "We thought we'd lost everyone."

Laurel's hands trembled. "Can I…can I talk to him?"

"Of course." Laurel heard fierce whispering in the room. "I'll put it on speakerphone. His hands…have been injured. He's weak, but it's all okay now."

"L-Laurel?"

Her father's voice sounded tired, hoarse.

"Dad. Oh, Dad. You're okay?"

"I've been better." He let out a chuckle, then started coughing.

"I have proof you aren't a traitor, Dad. And neither is Garrett."

"But how?" Fiona asked. "We've been trying for so long. I thought we'd have to leave the country. I couldn't find anything but horrible corroboration that your father was dealing with terrorists."

"I-Ivy. You know what happened—?"

Fiona cut Laurel off. "I'm so sorry, Laurel. Look, your father is hurt. Badly. And he has to lie down, but we need to talk—"

A grunt sounded through the phone, then a crash.

"James!" Fiona shouted. "Laurel, your father just fell. I have to go to him." Muffled whispers filtered through the receiver. "James, darling, stay still. You've torn the stitches."

The phone went silent. Laurel gripped the cell tight. "Fiona, is Dad okay?"

"For now. I've had to treat him myself." Worry laced Fiona's breathless voice.

"Garrett Galloway is going to Washington. He needs help. Please."

"I have to get back to your father. I don't know what

I can do. We felt it better to keep James's reappearance and Galloway's identity a secret. I could make it worse. Things don't look good at the agency."

"But if you looked at the file, maybe we can discover who is doing this."

"You have the file? With you?"

"Yes. Please, Fiona."

"Don't send it to me," she said sharply, all business now. "Come to his house, Laurel. I have someone I trust who can bring you. Are you still in the U.S.?"

Laurel took in a deep breath. "I'm in Texas."

"What are you doing—? Oh, Garrett."

"You knew about him?"

"Of course. James and I share everything. But we had to keep it quiet."

"I wish I'd known."

"I understand. Listen to me, Laurel. I *have* to get off this phone. It's been almost three minutes. We can't risk surveillance. I'll send a plane for you. Your father needs to see you." She lowered her voice. "And, Laurel, don't tell anyone where you're going. Anyone. Do you understand? Not until we end this. Once and for all. Trust no one but me."

THE BLACK ESCALADE idled on the side of the road. Shep glared at Léon. "You got us lost. Do you know what the boss does to people who make mistakes?"

"I watched you blow Strickland's head off," Léon snapped. "I get the picture."

"We should have taken out the woman and girl first?"

Léon fiddled with the GPS receiver. "Do I need to explain this in small words, Shep? Galloway's the hard target. We kill him first. He's the biggest risk."

Shep thrust his fingers through his hair. "Well, we're pretty close to finding him right now, aren't we?"

The device in Léon's lap beeped. He smiled. "Maybe I just saved the day."

The tablet blinked on again. Shep let out a curse. "Are you going to be able to fix that thing or not?"

Léon tugged out a small tool set. "I'll fix it. Be patient."

"Tell that to the boss."

The phone sitting between the two men rang.

"Are we bugged?" Shep pressed the speakerphone button. "Yeah, boss?"

"I have a job for you."

"Kill our three targets and dispose of the bodies," Shep repeated.

"No. I want you to pick up your targets just outside of Trouble, Texas, and bring them to me. I'll give you the location."

"We could dispose of them more easily here."

"Are you questioning me, Shep? Strickland started using his brain—that's why you had to blow it away."

"Of course not."

The boss rattled off a rendezvous point. "I want them both alive. I need them unharmed. At least for another few hours." There was a slight pause. "After that, you can use them as target practice."

JAMES MCCALLISTER'S VIRGINIA home appeared deserted.

Garrett glanced at his watch one more time. Five minutes to midnight. He looked over his shoulder. Rafe had parked a second vehicle down the block. They both recognized this was a trap, but they also knew it was important that the mastermind behind this plot believe Garrett had come alone.

He'd taken every precaution he could, because he wanted to survive. He wanted to see if what he'd experienced with Laurel was real. It felt real—almost too good to be true, which made Garrett distrust it all the more—but, oh, how he wanted it to be real.

He'd never thought he could love anyone again, not after his heart had been destroyed when he'd lost Lisa and Ella, but Laurel had put her faith in him, despite the doubts that had to have raced through her mind more than once since they'd met.

They hadn't known each other long, but Garrett had been dead inside long enough to know what he felt. He had two very good reasons to make it out of this op alive.

He glanced at his watch. One minute before the agreed-upon time.

Garrett slammed the door on the vehicle and walked up the concrete sidewalk. When he reached the familiar front porch he hesitated. He might never come out. And he hadn't told Laurel how he felt. He'd tried to show her, but he hadn't been able to say the words. If he died tonight, he didn't want the words haunting her, but right now he wished he'd said something. He prayed she knew how special she was, how much she deserved to be loved with all a man's heart and soul.

He wanted her to know what was between them meant something more than two people seeking comfort. She truly was an amazing woman, and he wanted to see her again. He wanted to tell her he loved her.

Garrett pressed his finger on the doorbell.

The front door slowly opened. His shoulders tightened. Silence greeted him from the house. He stepped inside. Behind the door, tears streaming down her face, Laurel McCallister had let him in.

"What the hell are you doing here?" Garrett reached out to her, but Laurel stepped back.

"I invited her."

Garrett turned around.

"Fiona?"

Fiona Wylde. James's lover. A woman he knew well. Strike that. Based on the gun she had drawn on him, Fiona was a woman he'd *thought* he knew well.

"You're a difficult man to kill." She nodded at a man standing in the shadows. "Disarm him, Léon."

A man gave a quick nod. He walked over to Garrett, patted him down and removed the Beretta from his back, the knife from his ankle holster and the small pistol hidden within his boot.

Léon met Garrett's gaze and patted his other boot, right over where a second knife was hidden. What the hell?

"Cuff him and bring them both downstairs. We'll have a family reunion."

Garrett slid a glance over at Laurel. "Damn it. Why are you here?" She was supposed to be safe, with Daniel, with CTC.

"I found a microdot Ivy left. It contains proof of your innocence and my father's, too," she said, her gaze resigned. "I called Fiona thinking she'd help us."

"Oh, darlings, after tonight, you'll never have to worry again." Fiona led them down to the basement. She hit a code in a panel on the concrete wall. A door to a small room opened up.

James McCallister sat slumped over in a chair, his arms and legs tied in place. He couldn't lift his head.

Garrett saw the flicker of James's eyes, but his clothes

were in tatters, his face bruised. Burns smoldered his pants.

"Dad," Laurel shouted.

"Aunt Laurel?" Molly's cries sounded from behind a door. "Let me out! Please, let me out!"

"Tie them to the chairs," Fiona ordered. "We end this today."

Léon shoved Garrett toward a steel chair and pushed down on his head, indicating for him to sit. The man took nylon rope and secured his hands and feet. A second man did the same to Laurel.

"Why do this, Fiona?" Garrett asked, clenching his muscles against the ropes. He needed room to work if he was going to escape and get Laurel, Molly and James to safety.

"I'm not having a reveal-my-inner-motivations conversation with you, Garrett, because there are none. I'll make it simple. I did it for the money. A *lot* of money."

"He's secure," Léon said. "What about the little girl in the closet?"

"Leave her."

Fiona stalked up the stairs, then whirled around. "I don't want any evidence left behind. Everyone in that room is dead or missing. They aren't to be found." She paused. "And, Léon, this is why I smuggled you into the country. Those explosives should take the house down. Get it down so it's too hot to find even a fragment of bone."

"Where's your loyalty?" Laurel shouted. "To my father, if no one else. He loved you."

"Ah, love and loyalty. How quaint. Almost as heart-warming as Léon's amusing use of handcuffs." Fiona looked down from her perch on the stairs. Her eyes hardened. "Haven't you learned there is no loyalty? The powerful feed off the powerful. And heroes die for nothing. The only thing you have is yourself and your needs. You should have remembered that, Laurel."

Léon and his friend followed Fiona up the stairs. The door closed behind them.

Garrett palmed the key that Léon had placed in his hand. Twisting his wrists, he maneuvered free of the handcuffs, then pulled out of his other boot the knife... the one Léon had left.

Laurel stared at him. "How?"

"Daniel's inside guy. We don't have much time."

Garrett cut through the zip ties around Laurel's wrists. She ran to the door.

"I'm here, Molly."

"Aunt Laurel, help me!"

She tugged on the doorknob. Locked.

"Molly, step back from the door, honey. Hide in the corner."

Garrett gave the lock a hard kick and the door broke free. Laurel scooped up Molly.

"I'll get your father," Garrett said.

Above them an explosion roared. Glass shattered; timbers fell. Laurel raced up the stairs and put her hand on the door. "Fire. Smoke's starting to come through. We're trapped."

"If Léon set the charges, I hope to God he gave us extra time." Garrett knelt in front of James and shook him. "Tell me you followed your own advice, old man. Where's the escape route out of here?"

Laurel hurried down the stairs.

"James, we don't have much time."

The old man blinked. "Behind their mom's picture." His voice croaked.

Garrett spun around, but he didn't see a painting of a woman on the wall. "Where is your mother's picture, Laurel?"

"There's only the mural she painted."

The starry night sky covered one wall.

Murky smoke began to filter into the room. "Get washcloths from the bar area and wet them," Garrett shouted. "Use them to breathe through."

His eyes teared up from the smoke. "Where is it?" He ran his fingers along the brick wall. Finally, at the Big Dipper, he felt a notch at one star. He pressed the button. The brick gave way. He pushed the concealed doorway open.

"It was good of Fiona to have our meeting at midnight. Darkness will help hide us."

Garrett paused at a weapon safe in the corner. He grabbed a hunting knife and a rifle. "Laurel, here you go." He shoved an old Colt .45 at her. "You couldn't have had an Uzi in here, could you, old man?" He pulled a Bowie knife from a drawer and pressed it into James's hands. Even with his injuries, he gripped the weapon.

"Get them out," James choked. "Leave me." He passed out.

"Not on your life." Garrett heaved James over his shoulder in a fireman's carry. "Laurel, let's go."

She clutched Molly to her and followed him out through a short passageway leading up to a tunnel. The gradient rose.

A dim lighting system lit the narrow path. Garrett struggled with James's weight. At the end of the tunnel there was a small door. A key dangled at the edge.

"Thanks, James." Garrett grabbed the key and unlocked the door. It led into what looked like a storage shed. Garrett recognized it from his previous visits.

"I never knew this passageway was here," Laurel whispered.

Garrett didn't turn the light on. He laid James on the ground and propped him up against the rough wooden wall. Garrett peered through a small window in the shed.

Laurel stood at his side, her entire body stiff with resolve.

Flames erupted from James's house, searing through brick and wood. Loud crackling overwhelmed the quiet neighborhood. Smoke billowed into the air and the fire painted the midnight sky red.

Another explosion rocketed through the house.

"That one waited for us to get out," Garrett whispered to her. "Not bad, Léon."

"He's on our side. He can help."

"Rafe Vargas is out there, too." At Laurel's questioning glance, Garrett added, "Another CTC operative. We aren't alone."

"If they haven't been caught," Laurel said. "What's the plan?"

"I'm going out there. Fiona's not getting away with this."

He gripped the old Remington hunting rifle he'd snagged from the safe. "Stay here," he ordered Laurel. "Protect them."

She gripped Garrett's arm. "Be careful. Come back to me."

He gave her a small smile. "Count on it." Then his gaze turned serious. "Have you got your weapon?"

She pulled out the Colt. "I know what to do with it."

He kissed her quickly. "I love you. I should have told you before." Garrett raced out of the building.

A lone figure, carrying an M16, emerged from the smoke. Fiona pointed the weapon at Garrett. "I don't leave witnesses."

Garrett didn't hesitate. He raised his weapon. Before he could get off a shot, a bevy of bullets tore across his body.

He blinked and looked down, then sank to his knees.

Chapter Twelve

A spray of bullets sounded from outside, and then another volley came a moment later. Some pierced the shed. Laurel dragged her father to the ground and covered Molly with her body.

The little girl cried out in fear.

Laurel's heart raced. Garrett hadn't had an automatic weapon.

Please, God, let him live. "Molly," Laurel ordered. "Get over by Grandpa. Hide in the darkest corner."

Molly crawled over toward James, and Laurel quickly stacked a wheelbarrow and other tools in front of them. "Stay here. Take care of each other."

She slipped some metal spikes and a small scythe next to her barely conscious father. It was all she could do for weapons.

"Back up Garrett if he's still—" Her father paused and looked at Molly. "You can't let Fiona escape. Do what needs to be done."

Laurel grabbed the old .45. Handguns were hard to shoot accurately. She'd need to get close.

She opened the shed door slowly, only to see Fiona standing over Garrett's prone body. Behind them, the bodies of her two minions lay on the grass near the burning house.

Fiona pointed her weapon at Garrett again. "You've been damn tough to kill, Bradley, but this head shot ought to do it."

Laurel didn't hesitate. She aimed and fired. Once. Twice. And again, until the gun was empty. Fiona jerked, but she didn't go down. "Stupid woman," Fiona taunted. "Never heard of Kevlar? You're going to pay for that."

Laurel dropped her weapon. She had one chance. If she could get the right angle—

"Aunt Laurel, Aunt Laurel. Come quick. Grandpa's not moving." Molly ran into the yard.

Fiona met Laurel's horror-struck gaze. The woman smiled and swept her gun around, pointing it at the little girl. "Guess the rug rat's next."

Just as Fiona was about to squeeze the trigger, a shot rang out from behind her. The bullet struck her in the head. She hit the ground hard, the wound fatal.

Molly screamed and cowered on the ground.

Laurel's eyes widened. Garrett's arm shook and he dropped the Remington. "She's not the only one who's heard of Kevlar." He coughed. With that, his head dropped to the grass. Laurel grabbed Molly and raced over to Garrett.

Blood pooled at two gunshot wounds.

He glanced down at the red seeping through his shirt. "I needed a bigger size." He looked up at Laurel. "I'm sorry."

Sirens grew louder in the distance.

"Garrett, you're going to be fine. Just hang on. Help is on the way," she said softly, then gasped as his eyes fluttered closed. "Garrett, no!"

"Sheriff Garrett?" Molly whispered. "Please don't go away."

"I'll try, sugar." He coughed.

Laurel leaned down closer. "You told me you loved me, Garrett. You can't leave me now. I love you, too."

There was no response. His chest barely rose.

"Oh, God, no." She didn't know what to do. The vest might be stanching the blood. She needed help.

Suddenly, a crush of police cars, fire engines and ambulances skidded to the curbs. Various personnel carrying hoses, guns and medical equipment came around the house. Laurel yelled to them, "We need help here. A man's been shot!"

She clutched Molly tightly as tears streamed down their faces.

Two paramedics rushed over. "Move back."

Laurel jerked away, hiding Molly's face against her own chest. "My father is in the shed over there." Laurel pointed out the small bullet-ridden structure. "He's badly hurt. Please help him, too."

The paramedics called another of the backup teams to check out the shed.

The yard was complete chaos. The firemen futilely fought the blaze, but whatever had been used to blow up the house did not back off easily.

"Another injured," a cop shouted. "Guy's pinned under a wall."

Men raced around the house. The police hovered over the paramedics, watching them work on Garrett. Others checked the gathering crowds. Still more hurried to where Fiona and the other two bodies lay.

"Hey, this one's alive," someone called out, bending

over one of the men lying near Fiona's body. "I need a medic, quick."

Laurel couldn't tell if it was Léon. She hoped so.

"Please, Garrett. Please make it," she said, clutching Molly to her.

More responders dragged gurneys across the grass to the injured. Laurel stood back, holding Molly, her attention split between Garrett and the activity in the shed. She prayed her father wouldn't come out in a black bag.

What seemed an eternity later, Garrett, her father and Léon were all loaded into different ambulances.

Laurel carried Molly over to the back of the one carrying Garrett and tried to get inside.

"You can't, ma'am."

"Why not? That's my father and Garrett is my…my… fiancé."

A police detective walked up beside her. "Lady, as the only person still standing on a field with multiple dead bodies, you have a lot of explaining to do. I can see the gunshot residue on your hand. We're not letting you near anybody. The kid will have to go with Child Protective Services."

Laurel panicked and held Molly close. "No, she may not be safe without special protection. Please, she's been through so much. Let me call a family she trusts to come take care of her."

"Aunt Laurel," Molly cried. "I want to stay with you. Don't make me leave."

Laurel knelt down in front of Molly so they were face-to-face. "Molly, honey, I have to go with these policemen for a little while to tell them what happened. It's not a place for children."

She shook her head. "You said you wouldn't leave me. Not like Mommy and Daddy."

Laurel couldn't control the tears. "I'm going to call Daniel and Raven. You can stay with them. You could play with the twins, too, and their doggy."

Molly bit her lip. "I like Raven a lot. She gives me cookies. Daniel's nice, too." Then she shook her head. "But I want you and Sheriff Garrett."

Gripping Molly's hands in hers, Laurel met the little girl's gaze. "Please, Molly Magoo. Can you be brave for me one more time?"

"Like Sheriff Garrett?"

Laurel squeezed her niece's hands. "Like Sheriff Garrett. Go to Daniel and Raven."

"You'll come back for me. Promise?"

Somehow she would. "I promise." Laurel looked up at the officer. "Please, let her go to them. You'll understand what's going on soon enough. I cannot have her put through any more trauma."

The detective's brow furrowed. "I got kids of my own," he relented. "Give me the family's info and I'll check them out. Otherwise, the girl goes with CPS."

THE POLICE STATION reeked of the sights and smells of nighttime indigents and criminals. Molly wouldn't let go of Laurel's hand.

She desperately wanted to pace the walkways of the police station, but she had to shield Molly. She glanced over at a tired-looking woman standing in the corner, ever watchful. If Daniel didn't arrive soon, CPS might just take Molly away. Laurel's heart broke at the idea of being separated from her niece.

How could she explain everything that had happened? Would the cops even believe her?

Finally, the door opened and Daniel strode inside, along with another man wearing a patch over one eye, who looked as if he'd been on the wrong end of a fight. She recognized him from somewhere. He walked over and had a few words with the officer assigned to watch Laurel. Her interrogation would start as soon as Molly left.

Laurel finally placed the man's face and scowled. "Exactly *who* is your friend?"

Daniel looked back at the man who was now approaching them. "Laurel, this is Rafe. He's part of CTC, the organization I work for. He was stationed outside the house, but got buried by a wall."

"Is there a problem?" Rafe asked seriously.

"I don't know," she said, her voice full of suspicion. "I saw you driving the ambulance with that man, Léon, inside. You didn't go the same direction as the other ambulances. Why?"

Rafe lowered his voice when he spoke. "Léon is one of ours, too. I took him to some medical facilities that were a little more…discreet. His recovery will take a while and we wanted him safe."

"Great," she snapped. "What about Garrett and my father? What about keeping them safe?" She knew she sounded like an ungrateful witch, but no one would even tell her if Garrett and her father were alive or dead.

"Garrett and your father are alive," Rafe said, "but in critical condition. We have guards both inside and outside their doors, as well as throughout the hospital, keeping watch for intruders. My boss is trying to keep the feds and agency people out of this so they don't have access to Garrett. If they identify him as a fugitive before we prove his innocence, the government will claim him."

Laurel rubbed her face with her hands. "They're alive." Her knees shook.

"I've brought enough evidence that you should be out of here soon, Laurel. Just be patient. I'll take Molly now, and Rafe will wait and handle bail or whatever comes up. He won't let you down, Laurel. I swear it."

Tears filled Laurel's eyes as she hugged Molly and sent her off with Daniel. "Please keep her safe."

"Daniel would give his life for Molly. He'll guard her well."

Just then, a policeman walked over. "Ms. McCallister, it's time."

FROM SOMEWHERE FAR OFF, Garrett heard a sweet female voice calling to him.

"Garrett, please wake up."

He felt a gentle touch on his forehead, but couldn't make much sense out of the soothing, soft words being whispered in his ear.

The dreams had been haunting him again. Strange dreams, where Lisa and Ella were running to him, holding him close, but suddenly they were waving goodbye. *No! Don't go.* Something was wrong. It was very wrong. He fought his way toward consciousness.

The dream changed, colors swirling and spinning in his mind, and this time he was reaching out for Laurel and Molly. He tried to reach them, but they were so far away. They were leaving, too. Sadness in their eyes. The gray returned and pulled him back into the darkness.

The whispering continued, more urgently this time.

The voices were louder. Why wouldn't they leave him alone?

"Garrett. Wake up."

He strained to understand, but each time he tried to open his eyes, they didn't respond at all.

"Come back to me now. You can do this."

Laurel? Was that Laurel trying to get him to do something? He struggled again, forcing the fogginess in his mind away.

A firm hand gripped his, as if to will him to do something. His eyelids were so heavy, but somehow he forced them open for the briefest second. The blaze of sunlight burned his eyes and he groaned, flinching from the light. Even that slight movement sent a spear of fiery pain through his chest.

"He moved!" Laurel yelled. "His eyes opened for a second. Get the doctor in here fast." A firm hand gripped his. "Come on, Garrett. Open your eyes."

"Hurts," he rasped.

"Shut the blinds and turn off the lights. It's too bright," Laurel ordered, then suddenly laughed. "Oh, my God, Garrett. You're waking up. I thought I'd lost you. I love you so very much."

Laurel's voice pulled him from the darkness. He needed to reach her. He had to reach her. He fought with everything inside to open his eyes.

A halo around beautiful brown hair slowly came into focus. He blinked again. She was beautiful. Like an angel.

"Laurel?" His voice sounded strange, hoarse, and when he tried to raise his hand, that blasted pain speared through his chest again.

"Don't move and don't try to talk, Garrett. They just

took the breathing tube out." She put the tiniest ice chip on his tongue to soothe his throat. "You've been in a coma. But you're going to be okay."

Visions came back to him. A little girl holding Laurel's hand, so small and scared. Then outside, in the darkness, an AK-47 pointed at her. "Molly?"

"She's safe. You saved her."

"Fiona?"

Laurel's face went cold. "Dead."

"Good." His eyes closed. "You're all safe." Everything went black and this time he didn't fight it.

LAUREL SAGGED IN the chair when Garrett lost consciousness again.

The doctor strode in.

"The nurse said the patient moved." The man's voice was skeptical. "He looks pretty out of it now. What happened?"

Laurel stood. "He woke up. He spoke to me. He knew me. He remembered some of what happened the night he was shot."

"I didn't expect that much, so it's a good sign. He's been unconscious for two weeks, so don't expect him to go dancing anytime soon." The neurologist leaned over Garrett and checked his vital signs, then his bandages. "The bullet wounds to his chest are healing nicely. His latest MRI showed the swelling has gone down."

"I knew he'd come back to me."

The doctor smiled at her. "Family often knows best. The more you stayed and talked to him, the more you kept his brain stimulated. He may not have known what you were saying, but even in a coma, there is some level of communication happening, especially among loved ones. Your dedication has been important to his recovery. You're going to make him a great wife."

Laurel gulped. She'd never cleared up the misconception that Garrett was her fiancé. The hospital staff never would have let her stay as often or as long as she had.

Legally, she and Garrett weren't family, but in every way that mattered, Garrett had become an integral part of her life. So much had happened. She prayed he'd still want her when he awoke and he could make different choices than the ones she hoped he would.

A short time after the doctor left, Laurel gripped Garrett's hand. If what the doctor said was true, had Garrett heard all the times she'd told him she loved him? There hadn't been time before. But she could no longer imagine life without this man.

"Laurel?" His eyes fluttered open again. With the lights off and window shades drawn, he was able to keep his eyelids somewhat open. "I thought I dreamed—"

His voice gave out and Laurel quickly gave him another ice chip. Several more, spread over the next five minutes, finally allowed him to speak without too bad a rasp to his voice.

"Did James make it?" he asked, watching her warily.

She smiled. "Yes, but he's hurt badly. The burns were..." Laurel stopped, unable to speak further.

"Is he still in the hospital?"

"No. Not this one, anyway. The authorities took him away for a debriefing. I don't know when I'll see him. Your friends at CTC are working on it."

"I'm sorry. You haven't heard anything?"

"Nothing specific, other than that they're angry that he lied about you under oath. It will take time for him to win back anyone's trust. At least my sister's evidence cleared you both of the treason charges. The story has been all over the papers. You're a hero."

"Yeah, right. I almost got you all killed."

"No, Garrett," Laurel insisted, "Fiona almost got us all killed. I've been afraid to take any chances ever since my mother died. My father drilled into Ivy and me that we were only to rely on ourselves. Not anyone else, and sure as hell not him." Laurel hesitated. "Yet a few weeks ago I found myself relying on a man I didn't even know, and every time you proved yourself worthy of trusting."

"You mean when I wasn't lying to you or sneaking out without telling you."

"Yeah, well, we can work on that."

"It was always for your own good," Garrett said.

"Like I said, we'll work on it. Don't push your luck, Sheriff. I was giving you the benefit of the doubt, and you're blowing it big-time."

"Come here." He pulled her gently toward him.

Laurel closed her eyes and leaned forward on the bed. Afraid to jar the wound on his chest, she rested her head gently on Garrett's arm. She longed for those arms to surround her again; she longed for him to hold her close and just talk, just to hear his voice tell her again that he loved her. She wanted to hear him sing that silly ant song once more to Molly in his deep voice. The one that made her feel safe down to her soul.

He stroked her head with his hand. "Why didn't you leave? You didn't have to stay watching over me."

Had he changed his mind about her? She couldn't stop the tears from falling down her cheeks. "I didn't have anywhere else to be," she said. "I figured hanging out in a hospital with you would be a good way to spend Christmas. It's already decorated for the holidays and

Molly's having a wonderful time at Daniel and Raven's. The I-want-a-puppy hints are coming fast and furious. I think a dog is even beating out the princess palace she asked for all year."

Garrett blinked. "Wait a minute. Back up. It's Christmas?"

"Not quite, but close. It's next week."

His eyes went wide. "How long have I been out?"

"Thirteen days, seven hours and twenty-three minutes, but who's counting?" she said, trying for a nonchalance she did not feel.

"You should have left me here," he said. "Molly's so afraid Santa won't be able to find her this year. She needs some normalcy back in her life. She needs you."

His words pierced her heart. Laurel pulled back. "You don't want me here?"

Garrett swallowed and looked at her. "I…I want what's best for you. And Molly."

"You are what's best for me. Can't you see that?"

"I didn't protect you," he said. "You could have died because I didn't plan well enough ahead."

She laughed incredulously. "Garrett, I'm the one who contacted Fiona. If I'd trusted you—"

He gripped her hands. "If we'd trusted each other."

Laurel rose from the bed slowly. "Is this really where we are? Fighting over something this stupid?" She stepped closer. "I am going to give you an ultimatum. Answer it wrong and I will walk away forever."

He struggled to sit up in the bed. "Wait. What are you talking about?"

"I'm talking about us. I love you. Do you hear me? No doubts, no questions on my side. You once told me the same thing, but you thought you were going off to die."

"Laurel—"

"I am not done, mister. Not by a long shot. Derek Bradley's name has been cleared, so if that's the life you want, you can go back to the clandestine, lonely life you led before. But you have a choice. The mayor of Trouble says that you can continue as the sheriff."

Garrett sat staring at her. "The mayor? The mayor hates me because I'm onto his tricks."

"Oh, Daniel had a little talk with that mayor, and he resigned. Hondo took over the job, and he said you can be sheriff as long as he's in office."

Garrett chuckled, then turned serious. "Is that the end of the options available to me? Because it's not a hard choice." Laurel could barely breathe. "Do you think I'd choose anyone or anything but you, Laurel? Where's your faith?"

She couldn't stop the smile from spreading across her face.

"Say the words. When guns aren't blazing and you're not running off to certain death. I need to hear it."

Garrett met her gaze, unwavering, serious. "I love you, Laurel McCallister. I will always love you."

She quivered against him and laid her head on his chest. "I won't ever let you go."

Epilogue

Garrett sat on the floor and placed the last fake flower in the garden of Molly's princess palace.

Laurel walked up to him and handed him a cup of coffee. "You shouldn't be drinking this."

"I won't tell the doctors if you don't." He took a sip of the dark brew and nearly groaned in pleasure. "Some assembly required? That's what the box said. How long have I been at it?"

"Six hours." Laurel chuckled.

"I just hope she likes it. Molly needs some joy."

Laurel knelt down beside him. "She feels safe with you, Garrett. And loved. That's all she needs."

The chime of the clock sounded through the house. "It's six o'clock."

Garrett struggled to get up off of the floor. Laurel held out her hand to steady him. "Take it easy," she said, putting her hands on his waist. "I just got you back."

He kissed her lips, drinking in the taste of her. He stroked his hand down her cheek. "Have I told you lately that you've made my life wonderful?" Her cheeks flushed. "I'm serious. You didn't just love me—you brought Christmas back. You brought joy into this ranch house."

"I could say the same about you, Garrett Galloway."

Laurel wrapped her arms around him, taking his lips. Garrett let himself get lost in her touch. If it weren't for the fact that this was Christmas Day, he'd drag her back to their bedroom and stay there all day long.

A soft knock forced him to raise his head. "Who is that?"

Garrett walked to the door, pulling his Beretta from atop the refrigerator. Slowly he opened the door.

A thin man in a red suit stood on the steps.

"Santa?"

Molly's sleepy voice came from just outside the living room.

The man walked inside.

"Dad?" Laurel whispered.

"Grandpa!" Molly raced to her grandfather.

He swung her up in the air with a grimace. "Molly Magoo!"

She wrapped her arms around him and hugged him tight. "Grandpa, I thought you were gone to heaven like Mommy and Daddy. And Matthew and Michaela."

James hugged Molly and met Laurel's and Garrett's gazes. His eyes were wet. Molly touched one of his tears. "It's okay, Grandpa. They're watching over us all the time. Aunt Laurel and Sheriff Garrett said so."

"I know." The old man cleared his throat. "Hope there's room for an old man on Christmas morning."

"It's Christmas!" Molly wiggled until James put her down. She looked around the room, past the princess palace. Her head dropped. "My letter didn't reach him."

Laurel knelt beside Molly. "Look at the beautiful princess palace. Santa knew exactly what you wanted."

"It's beautiful," she said, tears streaming down her face. "But I wanted to change my Christmas wish list."

Molly's tears broke Garrett's heart. "What do you want, sugar?" he asked gently.

"I want a family," she said, her voice small. "I know my mommy and daddy can't come back, but I don't want to be alone."

Garrett picked Molly up into his arms. He kissed her temple. "I think I can do something about that wish." He walked over to Laurel. "Wait right here."

He walked out the door and within minutes returned with a wrapped gift the size of a bread box. "Sit on the sofa, Molly. You, too, Laurel."

Garrett's nerves were stretched thin. James stood in the corner, a satisfied grin on his face. The old spy knew too much.

With his hand bracing himself, Garrett eased himself down on one knee. "Open the box, Molly."

She lifted the lid and peeked inside. A smile lit her face. A russet-and-white puppy poked its head out.

"For me?"

"You need a friend on this ranch, don't you think?"

Molly hugged the puppy to her. The mixed breed licked her face. "What's his name?"

"Whatever you want it to be, Molly."

She stroked his soft fur. "I love him, Sheriff Garrett."

"What do you think, Laurel?"

Her eyes were wet with tears. "I love him as much as I love you."

"Then maybe you should check out what's around his neck?"

Laurel grabbed the squirming bundle of fur and looked

at his collar. A ring swung back and forth. She stilled. "Garrett?"

"I love you, Laurel. I love Molly. Will you marry me?"

"Yes!" Molly shouted, hugging Garrett around the neck. "We want to marry you. Right, Aunt Laurel?"

"Right." Laurel's voice was thick with emotion. "I do."

"So we're going to live here forever and forever. You, me and Aunt Laurel. And Pumpkin Pie?"

"Who?"

"My doggy. His name is Pumpkin Pie. He told me."

"Yes, sugar, we'll all live together. Sometimes here, but sometimes in town. In Trouble, Texas."

Molly grinned up at them. "I think my daddy and mommy in heaven would like that. They told me almost every day that I was an angel always looking for trouble." She flung herself into Garrett's arms. "And we found it."

Garrett met Laurel's gaze over Molly's head. "Okay with you? If we're a family?"

She slipped the ring on her left hand and kissed his lips gently. "A family for Christmas is the best present ever."

* * * * *

SNOW BLIND

CASSIE MILES

To the brilliant RMFW romance critique group
and, as always, to Rick.

Chapter One

If ninety-two-year-old mogul and client Virgil P. Westfield hadn't died last night under suspicious circumstances, legal assistant Sasha Campbell would never have been entrusted with this important assignment in the up-and-coming resort town of Arcadia, Colorado. She draped her garment bag over a chair and strolled across the thick carpet in the posh, spacious, brand-new corporate condo owned by her employer, the law firm of Samuels, Sorenson and Smith, often referred to as the Three *S*s, or the Three Asses, depending upon one's perspective. Currently, she was in their good graces, especially with her boss, Damien Loughlin, Westfield's lawyer-slash-confidant back in Denver, and she meant to keep it that way. With this assignment, she could prove herself to be professional and worthy of promotion. Someday, she wanted to get more training and become a mediator.

"Where do you want the suitcase?" Her brother Alex was a junior member of the legal team at the Three *S*s and had driven her here from Denver. He hauled her luggage through the condo's entrance.

"Just leave it by the door. I'll figure that out later."

Before the mysterious death of Mr. Westfield, she and Damien had been scheduled to stay at the five-bedroom condo while attending a week-long series of meetings with

the four investors who had financed Arcadia Ski Resort—
Colorado's newest luxury destination for winter sports.

That plan had changed. Damien would stay in Denver,
dealing with problems surrounding the Westfield estate,
and Sasha was on her own at Arcadia. Nobody expected
her to replace a senior partner, of course. She was a legal
assistant, not a lawyer. But she'd been sitting in on the Arcadia meetings for months. They knew and trusted her.
And Damien would be in constant contact via internet
conferencing. Frankly, she was glad she wouldn't have to
put up with Damien's posturing; the meetings went more
smoothly when he wasn't there.

Drawn to the view through the windows, she crossed
the room, unlocked the door and stepped onto the balcony
to watch the glorious sunset over the ski slopes. Though
the resort wouldn't be officially open until the gala event
on Saturday, the chairlifts and gondolas were already in
operation. She saw faraway skiers and snowboarders racing over moguls on their last runs of the day. Streaks of
crimson, pink and gold lit the skies and reflected in the
windows of the nine-story Gateway Hotel opposite the
condo. In spite of the cold and the snow, she felt warmed
from within.

Life was good. Her bills were paid. She liked her job.
And she'd knocked off those pesky five pounds and fit
into her skinny jeans with an inch to spare. Even the
new highlights and lowlights in her long blond hair had
turned out great. She was gradually trying to go a few
shades darker. At the law office, it was bad enough to be
only twenty-three years old. But being blonde on top of
that? She wanted to go for a more serious look so she'd be
considered for more of these serious assignments. Alex
tromped onto the balcony. "I can't believe you get to stay
here for five days for free."

"Jealous?"

"It's not fair. You don't even ski."

He gestured with his hands inside his pockets, causing his black overcoat to flap like a raven's wings. There hadn't been time for him to change from his suit and tie before they'd left Denver. Throughout the two-and-a-half-hour drive, he'd complained about her good luck in being chosen for this assignment. Among her four older brothers and sisters, Alex was the grumpy one, the sorest of sore losers and a vicious tease.

She wouldn't have asked him to drive her, but she'd been expecting to ride up with Damien since her car was in the shop. "This isn't really a vacation. I have to record the meetings and take notes every morning."

"Big whoop," he muttered. "You should send the late Virgil P. a thank-you card for taking a header down the grand staircase in his mansion."

"That's a horrible thing to say." Mr. Westfield was a nice old gentleman who had bequeathed a chunk of his fortune to a cat-rescue organization. His heirs didn't appreciate that generosity.

"Speaking of thank-you notes," he said, "I deserve something for getting you a job with the Three Assses."

The remarkable sunset was beginning to fade, along with her feeling that life was a great big bowl of cheerfulness. "Number one, you didn't get me the job. You told me about the opening, but I got hired on my own merits."

"It didn't hurt to have me in your corner."

Alex was a second-year associate attorney, not one of the top dogs at the firm. His opinion about hiring wouldn't have influenced the final decision. "Number two, if you want to stay here at the condo, I'm sure it can be arranged. You could teach me to ski."

He gave her an evil grin. "Like when we were kids and I taught you how to ride a bike."

"I remember." She groaned. "I zoomed downhill like a rocket and crashed into a tree."

"You were such a klutz."

"I was five. My feet barely reached the pedals."

"You begged me for lessons."

That was true. She'd been dying to learn how to ride. "You were thirteen. You should have known better."

His dark blue eyes—the same color as hers—narrowed. "I got in so much trouble. Mom grounded me for a week."

And Sasha still had a jagged scar on her knee. "Way to hold a grudge, Alex."

"What makes you think you have the authority to invite me to stay here?"

"I don't," she said quickly, "but I'm sure Damien wouldn't mind."

"So now you speak for him? Exactly how close are you two?"

Not as close as everybody seemed to think. Sure, Damien Loughlin was a great-looking high-powered attorney and eligible bachelor. And, yes, he'd chosen her to work with him on Arcadia. But there was nothing between them. "I'd have to call him and ask for an okay, but I don't see why he'd say no."

"You've got him wrapped around your little finger."

Alex made a quick pivot and stalked back into the condo. Reluctantly, she followed, hoping that he wouldn't take her up on her invite. Spending five days with Alex would be like suffocating under an avalanche of negativity.

Muttering to himself, he prowled through the large space. On the opposite side of the sunken conversation pit was an entire wall devoted to electronics—flat-screens, computers and gaming systems.

"Cool toys," her brother said as he checked out the goodies. "Damien is the one who usually stays here, isn't he?"

"Makes sense," she said with a shrug. "He's handled most of the legal work for Arcadia."

"He's kept everybody else away from the project."

"It's his choice," she said defensively. The four Arcadia investors were rich, powerful and—in their own way—as eccentric as Mr. Westfield had been about his cats. They insisted on one lawyer per case. Not a team. The only reason she was in the room was that somebody had to take notes and get the coffee.

"Binoculars." Alex held up a pair of large black binoculars. "I wonder what Damien uses these for."

"He mentioned stargazing."

"Grow up, baby sister. His balcony is directly across from the Gateway Hotel. I'll bet he peeks in the windows."

"Ew. Gross."

Carrying the binoculars, he marched across the room and opened the balcony door. "The guests at that hotel are super rich. I heard there'll be a couple of movie stars and supermodels at the big gala on Saturday."

"Alex, don't." She felt as if she was five years old, poised at the top of the steep hill on a bike that was too big, destined for a crash. By the time she was on the balcony, he was already aiming the binocular lenses. "Please, don't."

"Come on, this is something your darling Damien probably does every night before he goes to bed."

"No way. And he's not my darling Damien."

"I've heard otherwise." He continued to stare through the binoculars. "I'm actually kind of proud. Kudos, Sasha. You're sleeping your way to the top."

She wasn't surprised by gossip from the office staff, but Alex was her brother. He was supposed to be on her side. "I'm not having sex with Damien."

"Don't play innocent with me. I'm your brother. I know better. I remember what happened with Jason Foley."

Jason had been her first love in high school, and she'd broken up with him before they'd gone all the way. But that wasn't the story he'd told. Jason had blabbed to the whole school that she had sex with him. He'd destroyed her reputation and had written a song about it. "How could you—?"

"Trashy Sasha." Her brother recalled the title to the song. "No big deal. You could do a lot worse than Damien Loughlin."

"That's enough. You should go. Now."

He lowered the binoculars and scowled disapprovingly at her. "Even if you weren't having sex with him, what did you think was going to happen this week? You were going to stay here alone with him."

"It's a five-bedroom condo. I have my own bedroom, bathroom and a door that locks." And she didn't have to justify her behavior. "I want you to leave, Alex."

"Fine." He set the binoculars down, stuck his hands into his overcoat pockets and left the balcony.

She followed him across the condo, fighting the urge to kick him in the butt. Why did he always have to be so mean? Alex was the only person in her family who still lived in Denver, and they worked in the same office. Would it kill him to be someone she could turn to?

At the door, Alex pivoted to face her. "I'm sorry. I shouldn't have said anything."

"You got that right."

"You're too damn naive, Sasha. You look around and see rainbows. I see the coming storm. This condo is a first-class bachelor pad, and Damien is a smooth operator. You'd better be careful, sis."

"Goodbye, Alex."

As soon as the door closed behind him, she flipped the

dead bolt, grabbed the handle on her suitcase and wheeled it across the condo into the first bedroom she found in the hallway. Her brother was a weasel for trying to make her feel guilty when she had every reason to be happy about this assignment. The fact that Damien and the other partners trusted her enough to let her take notes at these meetings was a huge vote of confidence. She wasn't going to be a paralegal for the rest of her career, and she'd need the support of the firm to take classes and get the training she needed to become a mediator.

She unpacked quickly. In the closet, she hung the garment bag with the dress she'd be wearing to the gala—a black gown with a deeply plunging neckline. Too plunging? Was she unconsciously flirting? Well, what was she supposed to do? Shuffle around in a burka?

Across the hall from her bedroom, she found a hot tub in a paneled room with tons of windows and leafy green plants. Damien had mentioned the hot tub, and the idea of a long, soothing soak was one of the reasons she'd agreed to this trip. She'd even brought her bathing suit. Following posted instructions, she turned on the heat for the water.

On her way to the kitchen, she paused in the dining area by the back windows. On a bookshelf, under a signed serigraph of a skier by LeRoy Neiman, was a remote control. She punched the top button and smooth, sultry jazz came on. Another remote button dimmed the lights. Another turned on the electric fireplace in the conversation pit. Though she didn't want to think of this condo as a bachelor pad, the lighting and sexy music set a classic mood for seduction.

In the kitchen, she checked out the fridge. The lower shelf held four bottles of pricey champagne. Not a good sign. It was beginning to look as if Alex the grump had been right, and Damien had more than business on his mind.

She should have seen it coming. This was Jason Foley all over again, strumming his twelve-string and singing about Trashy Sasha. If she wanted to squash rumors before they started, she'd get a room at the hotel. As if she could afford to stay there. And why should she run off with her tail between her legs? She hadn't done anything to be ashamed of.

Her fingers wrapped around the neck of a champagne bottle. She was here and might as well enjoy it. She popped the cork and poured the bubbly liquid into a handy crystal flute that Damien had probably used a million times to seduce hapless ladies. And why not? He was single, and they were consenting adults.

"Here's to you." She raised her glass in toast to her absent boss and took a sip. "This is one consenting adult you're not going to bed with."

Taking the champagne with her, she changed into her bathing suit and went to the hot tub, where she soaked and drank. All she had to do was just say no. If people wanted to think the worst, that was their problem.

The windows above the hot tub looked out on a pristine night sky. As she gazed at the moon and stars, her vision blurred. Was she getting drunk? *Oh, good. Real professional.* Clearly, three glasses of champagne were enough.

Leaving the tub, she slipped into a white terry-cloth bathrobe that had been hanging on a peg. Though she wasn't really hungry, she ought to eat. But first she needed to retrieve the binoculars Alex had left on the balcony.

After a detour to the bedroom, where she stuck her feet into her cozy faux-fur boots, she crossed the room and opened the balcony door. The bracing cold smacked her in the face, but she was still warm from the hot tub and the champagne. She picked up the binoculars. Even if Damien was a womanizer, it was ridiculous to think that he might be a Peeping Tom. He probably couldn't see into the hotel at all.

Holding the binoculars to her eyes, she adjusted the knobs and focused on the nine-story building that was a couple of hundred yards away. Only half the windows were lit. The hotel guests might be out for a late dinner. Or maybe the rooms were vacant. The resort wouldn't officially be open until after the Saturday-night gala.

Her sight line into one of the floor-to-ceiling windows was incredibly clear. She saw a couple of beautiful people sitting at a table, eating and drinking. The woman had long black hair and was wearing a white jumpsuit, an elaborate gold necklace draped across her cleavage. She was stunning. The man appeared to be an average guy with dark hair and a black turtleneck. Sasha's view of him was obscured by a ficus tree.

Spying on them ranked high on the creepiness scale, but the peek into someone else's life was kind of fascinating. Sasha noticed they weren't talking much, and she wondered if they'd been together for a long time and were so comfortable with each other that words were unnecessary. Someday she hoped to have a sophisticated relationship like that. Or maybe not. Silence was boring.

Despite telling herself to stop spying, she switched to a different window on another floor, where two men were watching television. In another room, a woman was doing yoga, moving into Downward-Facing Dog pose. Apparently, the floor-to-ceiling windows were in only the front room, which was fine with Sasha. She had no intention of peering into bedrooms.

A shiver went through her. It was cold. She should go back inside. But she wanted one last peek at the dark-haired woman and her male companion. They were standing on opposite sides of the small table. The woman threw her hands in the air. Even at this distance, Sasha could tell she was angry.

Her companion turned his back on her as if to walk away. The woman chased after him and shoved his shoulder. When he turned, Sasha caught a clear glimpse of his face. It lasted only a second but she could see his fury as he grabbed the woman's wrist.

Sasha couldn't see exactly what happened, but when the woman staggered backward, the front of her white jumpsuit was red with blood. Before she fell to the floor, he picked her up in his arms and carried her out of Sasha's sight.

She'd witnessed an assault, possibly a murder. That woman needed her help. She dashed into the condo and called 911.

The phone rang only four times but it seemed like an eternity. When Sasha glanced over her shoulder to the balcony, she noticed the lights had gone out in the would-be murder room. Had she been looking at the fifth floor or the sixth?

When the dispatcher finally picked up, Sasha babbled, "I saw a woman get attacked. She's bleeding."

"What is your location?"

Sasha rattled off the address and added, "The woman, the victim, isn't here. She's at the Gateway Hotel."

"Room number?"

"I don't know." There was no way to explain without mentioning the binoculars. "It's complicated. This woman, she has on a white jumpsuit. You've got to send an ambulance."

"To what location?"

"The hotel."

"What room number?"

"I already told you. I don't know."

"Ma'am, have you been drinking?"

The emergency operator didn't believe her, and Sasha didn't blame her. But she couldn't ignore what she'd witnessed. If she had to knock on every door to every room in that hotel, she'd find that woman.

Chapter Two

Responding to a 911 call, Deputy Brady Ellis drove fast through the Apollo condo complex. His blue-and-red lights flashed against the snow-covered three-story buildings, and his siren blared. From what the dispatcher had told him, the caller had allegedly witnessed an assault at the Gateway Hotel, which seemed unlikely because the hotel was a distance away from the condos. The dispatcher had also mentioned that the caller sounded intoxicated. This 911 call might be somebody's idea of a joke. It didn't matter. Until he knew otherwise, Brady would treat the situation as a bona fide emergency.

He parked his SUV with the Summit County Sheriff logo emblazoned on the door in the parking lot and jogged up the shoveled sidewalk to the entryway. Five years ago, when he first started working for the sheriff's department, this land had been nothing but trees and rocks that belonged to his uncle Dooley. These acres hadn't been much use to Dooley; they were across the road from his primary cattle ranch and too close to the small town of Arcadia for grazing. When Dooley had gotten a chance to sell for a big profit, he'd jumped on it.

Some folks in the area hated the fancy ski resort that had mushroomed across the valley, but Brady wasn't one of them. Without the new development, Arcadia would have turned into a ghost town populated by coyotes and chipmunks. The influx of tourists brought much-needed business and cash flow.

The downside was the 250 percent increase in the crime rate, which was no big surprise. Crime was what happened when people moved in. Coyotes and chipmunks were less inclined to break the law.

Outside the condo entryway was a buzzer. He pressed the button for Samuels, Sorenson and Smith, which was on the third floor. When a woman answered, he identified himself. "Deputy Brady Ellis, sheriff's department."

"You got here fast," she said. "I'll buzz you in."

When the door hummed, he pushed it open. Instead of taking the elevator, Brady climbed the wide staircase. On the third floor, a short blonde woman stood waiting in the open doorway. She wore black furry boots, a white terry-cloth bathrobe cinched tight around her waist and not much else. She grabbed his arm and pulled him into the condo. "We've got to hurry."

He closed the door and scanned the interior, noticing the half-empty bottle of champagne. "Is anyone here with you?"

"I'm alone." Her blue eyes were too bright, and her cheeks were flushed. Brady concurred with the dispatcher's opinion that this woman had been drinking. "What's your name?"

"Sasha Campbell." She hadn't released her hold on his arm and was dragging him toward the windows— attempting to drag him was more accurate. He was six feet four inches tall and solidly built. This little lady wasn't physically capable of shoving him from place to place.

"Ms. Campbell," he said in a deep voice to compel her attention. "I need to ask you a few questions."

"Okay, sure." She dropped his arm and stared up at

him. "We need to move fast. This is literally a matter of life and death."

Though he wasn't sure if she was drunk or crazy, he recognized her determination and her fear. Those feelings were real. "Is this your condo?"

"I wish." Her robe gaped and he caught a glimpse of an orange bikini top inside. "I work for a law firm, and the condo belongs to them. I'm staying here while I attend meetings."

"You're a lawyer?"

"Wrong again. I'm a legal assistant right now, but I'm going to school to learn how to become a mediator and…" She stamped her furry boot. "Sorry, when I get nervous I talk too much. And there isn't time. Oh, God, there isn't time."

He responded to her sense of urgency. "Tell me what happened."

"It's easier if I show you. Come out here." She led him onto the balcony and slapped a pair of binoculars into his hand. "I was looking through those at the hotel, and I witnessed an attack. There was a lot of blood. Now do you understand? This woman might be bleeding to death while we stand here."

He held the binoculars to his eyes and adjusted the focus. The view into the hotel rooms was crystal clear. As unlikely as her story sounded, it was possible.

"Exactly what did you see?"

"Let's go back inside. It's freezing out here." She bustled into the condo, rubbing her hands together for warmth. "Okay, there was a black-haired woman in a white jumpsuit sitting at a table opposite a guy I couldn't see as well, because there was a plant in the way. I think he was wearing a turtleneck. And I think he had brown hair. That's right, brown hair. She had a gold necklace. They were eating. Then I looked away. Then I looked back."

As she spoke, her head whipped to the right and then to the left, mimicking her words. Her long blond hair flipped back and forth. "Go on," he said.

"The woman was standing, gesturing. She seemed angry. The guy came at her. I could only see his back. When the woman stepped away, there was blood on the front of her white jumpsuit. A lot of blood." Sasha paused. Her lower lip quivered. "The man caught her before she fell, and that was when I got a clear look at his face."

"Would you recognize him again?"

"I think so."

The details in her account made him think that she actually had seen something. The explanation might turn out to be more innocent than she suspected, but further investigation was necessary. "Do you know which room it was?"

She shook her head. "They turned out the lights. I'm not even sure it was the fifth floor or the sixth. Not the corner room but one or two down from it."

"I want you to remember everything you told me. Later I'll need for you to write out your statement. But right now I want you to come with me to the hotel."

For the first time since he'd come into the condo, she grinned. Her whole face lit up, and he felt a wave of pure sunshine washing toward him. He stared at her soft pink mouth as she spoke. "You believe me."

"Why wouldn't I?" Immediately, he reined in his attraction toward her. She was a witness, nothing more.

"I don't know. It just seems… I don't know."

"Are you telling me the truth?"

"Yes."

"Get dressed."

She turned on her heel and dashed across the condo to

the hallway. He heard the sound of a door closing. As he moved toward the exit, he checked out the high-end furnishings and electronics. Bubbly little Sasha seemed too lively, energetic and youthful to be comfortable with these polished surroundings. She lacked the sophistication that he associated with high-priced attorneys.

It bothered him that she'd expected he wouldn't believe her statement. Even though she'd related her account of the assault with clear details, she seemed unsure of herself. That hesitant attitude didn't work for him. He was about to go to the hotel and ask questions that would inconvenience the staff and guests. Brady needed for Sasha to be a credible witness.

When she bounded down the hallway in red jeans and a black parka with fake fur around the collar, she looked presentable, especially since she'd ditched the fuzzy boots for a sensible pair of hiking shoes. Then she put on a white knit cap with a goofy pom-pom on top and gave him one of those huge smiles. Damn, she was cute with her rosy cheeks and button nose. As he looked at her, something inside him melted.

If they'd been going on a sleigh ride or a hike, he would have been happy to have her as his companion. But Sasha wasn't his first choice as a witness. At the hotel, he'd try to avoid mentioning that she'd been peeping at the hotel through binoculars.

SASHA CLIMBED INTO the passenger side of the SUV and fastened her seat belt. A combination of excitement and dread churned through her veins. She was scared about what she'd seen and fearful about what might have happened to the woman in white. At the same time, she was glad to be able to help. Because of the circumstance— a strange, unlikely moment when she'd peeked through those binoculars at precisely the right time—she might save that woman's life.

She glanced toward Deputy Brady. "Is this what it feels like to be a cop?"

"I don't know what you mean."

"My pulse is racing. That's the adrenaline, right? And I'm tingling all over."

"Could be the champagne," he said drily.

She'd all but forgotten the three glasses of champagne she'd had in the hot tub. "I've been drunk before, and it doesn't feel anything like this."

When Brady turned on the flashing lights and the wailing siren, her excitement ratcheted up higher. This was serious business, police business. They were about to make a difference in someone's life, pursuing a would-be killer, rescuing a victim.

Her emotions popped like fireworks in contrast to Brady's absolute calm. He was a big man—solid and capable. His jawline and cleft chin seemed to be set in granite in spite of a dimple at the left corner of his mouth. His hazel eyes were steady and cool. In spite of the sheriff's department logo on the sleeve of his dark blue jacket and the gun holster on his belt next to his badge, he didn't look much like a cop. He wore dark brown boots and jeans and a black cowboy hat. The hat made her think he might be a local.

She raised her voice so he could hear her over the siren. "Have you lived in Arcadia long?"

"Born and raised," he said. "My uncle Dooley owned the land where your condo, the hotel and the ski lodge are built."

"You're related to Matthew Dooley?"

"I am."

That wily old rancher was one of the four investors in

Snow Blind

the Arcadia development. Dooley was big and rangy, much like Brady, and he always wore a cowboy hat and bolo tie. During most of the meetings in the conference room at the Three *S*s, he appeared to be sleeping but managed to come alive when there was an issue that concerned him.

"I like your uncle," she said. "He's a character."

"He plays by his own rules."

And he could afford to. Even before the investment in his land Dooley was a multimillionaire from all the mountain property he had owned and sold over the years. Brady's relationship to him explained the cowboy hat and the boots. But why was he working as a deputy? "Your family is rich."

"I'm not keeping score."

"Easy to say when you're on the winning team." Her family hadn't been poor, but with five kids they'd struggled to get by. If it hadn't been for scholarships and student loans, she never would have finished college. Paying for her continuing education was going to be a strain. "What made you decide to be a deputy?"

"You ask a lot of questions."

She sensed his resistance and wondered if he had a deep reason for choosing a career in law enforcement. "You can tell me."

He gave her a sidelong look, assessing her. Then he turned his gaze back toward the road. They were approaching the hotel. "When we go inside, let me do the talking."

"I might be able to help," she said. "I'm a pretty good negotiator."

"This is a police matter. I'm in charge. Do you understand?"

"Okay."

Though she was capable of standing up for herself, she didn't mind letting him do the talking. Not only was he a local who probably knew half the people who worked here, but Brady had the authority of the badge.

After they left the SUV in the valet parking area outside the entrance, she dutifully followed him into the front lobby. In the course of resort negotiations, she'd seen dozens of photographs of the interior of the Gateway Hotel. The reality was spectacular. The front windows climbed three stories high in the lobby-slash-atrium, showcasing several chandeliers decorated with small crystal snowflakes. A water feature near the check-in desk rippled over a tiered black marble waterfall. The decor and artwork were sleek and modern, except for a life-size marble statue of a toga-clad woman aiming a bow and arrow. Sasha guessed she was supposed to be Artemis, goddess of the hunt.

Occasional Grecian touches paid homage to the name Arcadia, which was an area in Greece ruled in ancient times by Pan the forest god. Sasha was glad the investors hadn't gone overboard with the gods-and-goddesses theme in the decorating. She stood behind Brady as he talked to a uniformed man behind the check-in counter. They were quickly shown into a back room to meet with the hotel manager, Mark Chandler.

He came out from behind his desk to shake hands with both of them. His gaze fixed on her face. "Why does your name sound familiar?"

"I'm a legal assistant working with Damien Loughlin. I'll be attending the investors' meetings this week."

"Of course." His professional smile gave the impression of warmth and concern. "I've worked with Damien. His help was invaluable when we were setting up our wine lists."

"Mr. Chandler," Brady said, "I'd like to talk with your hotel security."

"Sorry, the man in charge has gone home for the day. We're still in the process of hiring our full security team."

"His name?"

"Grant Jacobson. He's from one of our sister hotels, and he comes highly recommended."

"Call him," Brady said. "In the meantime, I need access to all video surveillance as well as to several of the guest rooms on the fifth and sixth floors. There's reason to believe a violent assault was committed in one of these rooms."

"First problem," Chandler said, "most of our video surveillance isn't operational."

"We'll make do with what have."

"And I'd be happy to show you the vacant rooms," he said. "But I can't allow our guests to be disturbed."

"This is a police investigation."

"I'm sorry, but I can't—"

"Suit yourself." When Brady drew himself up to his full height, he made an impressive figure of authority. "If you refuse to help, I'll knock on the doors myself and announce that I'm from the sheriff's department."

Chandler's smile crumpled. "That would be disruptive."

Brady pivoted and went toward the office door. "We're wasting time."

She followed him to the elevator. His long-legged stride forced her to jog to keep up. Chandler came behind her.

On the fifth floor, Brady turned to her. "It wasn't the corner room, right?"

She nodded. "Not the corner."

He went to the next door. His hand rested on the butt of his gun.

Hurriedly, Chandler stepped in front of him and used the master card to unlock the door. "This room is vacant. Can you at least tell me what we're looking for?"

Without responding, Brady entered the room and switched on the light. The decor was an attractive mix of rust and sky-blue, but the layout of the furniture wasn't what Sasha had seen through the binoculars. "It wasn't this room," she said. "There was a small table near the window. And a ficus tree."

"You're describing one of our suites," Chandler said. "Those units have more living space and two separate bedrooms."

"I don't see signs of a disturbance," Brady said. "Let's move on."

"The room next door is a suite," Chandler said. "It's occupied, and I would appreciate your discretion."

"Sure thing."

Brady's eyes were cold and hard. It was obvious that he'd do whatever necessary to find what he was looking for, and she liked his determination.

The door to the next room was opened by a teenage girl with pink-and-purple-striped leggings. The rest of the family lounged in front of the TV. Though this didn't appear to be the place, Brady verified with the family that they'd been here for the past two hours.

"No one is booked in the next suite," Chandler said.

"Could someone unauthorized have used it?" Brady asked.

"I suppose so."

"Open up."

Though the layout was similar to the one she'd seen, Sasha noticed that instead of a ficus there was a small Norfolk pine. Brady made a full search anyway, going from room to room. In the kitchenette, he looked for dishes that had been used. And he paid special attention to the bedrooms, checking to see if the beds were mussed and looking under the duvet at the sheets.

"Why are the beds important?" she asked.

"If he carried a body from the room, he might need to wrap it in something, like a sheet."

A shudder went through her. She didn't want to think of that attractive, vivacious woman as a dead body, much less as a dead body that needed to be disposed of. The excitement of acting like a cop took on a sinister edge.

On the sixth floor, they continued their search. As soon as she entered room 621, Sasha knew she was in the right place. There was a table by the window, and she recognized the leafy green ficus that had obscured her view of the man in the turtleneck. The room was empty.

"As you can plainly see," Chandler said, "there are no plates on the table. According to my records, this room is vacant until Friday night."

Brady's in-depth search came up empty. No dishes were missing, the beds appeared untouched, and there wasn't a smear of blood on the sand-colored carpet. But she was certain this had been the view she'd seen. "This is the right room. I know what I saw."

"What were they eating?" Brady asked.

She frowned. "I don't know."

"Think, Sasha."

She closed her eyes and concentrated. In her mind's eye, she saw the dark-haired woman gazing across the table as she set down her glass on the table. She poked at her food and lifted her chopsticks. "Chinese," she said. "They were eating Chinese food."

"I believe you," Brady said. "I can smell it."

She inhaled a deep breath. He was right. The aroma of stir-fried veggies and ginger lingered in the air.

"That's ridiculous," Chandler said. "None of our hotel restaurants serve Chinese food. And I don't smell anything."

"It's faint," Brady agreed.

"Even if someone was in this room," the hotel manager said, "they're gone now. And I see no evidence of wrongdoing. I appreciate your thoroughness, Deputy. But enough is enough."

"I'm just getting started," Brady said. "I need to talk to your staff, starting with the front desk."

Though Chandler sputtered and made excuses, he followed Brady's instructions. In the lobby, he gathered the three front-desk employees, four bellmen and three valets. Several of them gave Brady a friendly nod as though they knew him. He introduced her.

"Ms. Campbell is going to give you a description. I need to know if this woman is staying here."

Sasha cleared her throat and concentrated, choosing her words carefully. "She's attractive, probably in her late twenties or early thirties. Her hair is black and long, past her shoulders. When I saw her, she was wearing a white jumpsuit and a gold bib necklace, very fancy. It looked like flower petals."

One of the bellmen raised his hand. "I carried her suitcases. She's on the concierge level, room 917."

"Wait a minute," said a valet. "I've seen a couple of women with long black hair."

"But you don't know their room numbers," the bellman said.

"Maybe not, but one of them drives a silver Porsche."

"Get me the license plate number for the Porsche." Brady nodded to the rest of the group. "If any of you remember anything about this woman, let me know."

The employees returned to their positions, leaving them with Chandler. His eyebrows furrowed. "I suppose you'll want to visit room 917."

"You guessed it," Brady said.

"I strongly advise against it. That suite is occupied by Lloyd Reinhardt."

The name hit Sasha with an ominous thud. Reinhardt was the most influential of the investors in the Arcadia development. He was the contractor who supervised the building of the hotel and several of the surrounding condos. Knocking on his door and accusing him of murder wasn't going to win her any Brownie points.

Chapter Three

Frustrated by the lack of evidence, Brady wished he had other officers he could deploy to search, but he knew that calling for backup would be an exercise in futility. For one thing, the sheriff's department was understaffed, with barely enough deputies to cover the basics. For another, the sheriff himself was a practical man who wouldn't be inclined to launch a widespread manhunt based on nothing more than Sasha's allegations. Brady hadn't even called in to report the possible crime. Until he had something solid, he was better off on his own.

But there was no way he could search this whole complex. The hotel was huge—practically a city unto itself. There were restaurants and coffee shops, a ballroom, boutiques, a swimming pool and meeting areas for conferences, not to mention the stairwells, the laundry and the kitchens—a lot of places to hide a body.

Sasha tugged on his arm. "I need to talk to you. Alone."

He guided her away from Chandler. "Give us a minute."

In a low voice, she said, "There's really no point in going to the ninth floor. The man I saw wasn't Mr. Reinhardt. He was taller and his hair was darker."

"How do you know Reinhardt?"

"From the same meetings where I met your uncle." She shook her head, and her blond hair bounced across her forehead. "There are four investors in Arcadia—Uncle Dooley, Mr. Reinhardt, Katie Cook the ice skater and Sam Moreno, the self-help expert."

He nodded. "Okay."

"Mr. Reinhardt isn't what you'd call a patient man. He's going to hate having us knocking on his door."

Brady didn't much care what Reinhardt thought. "What are you saying?"

"It might be smart for me to step aside. I don't want to get fired."

He tamped down a surge of disappointment at the thought of her backing out. During the very brief time he'd known Sasha, he'd come to admire her gutsiness. Many people who witnessed a crime turned away; they didn't want to get involved. "Have you changed your mind about what you saw?"

"No," she said quickly.

"Then I want you to come to room 917, meet this woman and make sure she isn't the person you saw being attacked."

"And if I don't?"

"I think you know the answer."

"Without my eyewitness account, the investigation is over."

"That's right." He had no blood, no murder weapon and no body. His only evidence that a crime had been committed was the lingering aroma of Chinese food in an otherwise spotless room.

"A few hours ago," she said, "everything in my life seemed perfect and happy. That's all I really want. To be happy. Is that asking too much?"

He didn't answer. He didn't need to. She understood what was at stake. As she considered the options, her eyes took on a depth that seemed incongruous with a face that was designed for smiling and laughter.

"It's your decision," he said.

"I've always believed that life isn't random. I don't know why, but there was some reason why I was looking into that room at that particular moment." She lifted her chin and met his gaze. "I have to see this through. I'll come with you."

She was tougher than she looked. Behind the fluffy hair and the big blue eyes that could melt a man's heart was a core of strength. He liked what he saw inside her. After this was over, he wanted to get to know her better and find out what made her tick. Not the most professional behavior but he hadn't been so drawn to a woman in a long time.

Chandler rushed toward them. Accompanying him was a solidly built man with a military haircut. He wore heavy boots, a sweater and a brown leather bomber jacket. Though he had a pronounced limp, his approach lacked the nervousness that fluttered around the hotel manager like a rabble of hyperactive butterflies.

"I'm Grant Jacobson." The head of Gateway security held out his hand. "Chandler says there was some kind of assault here."

When Brady shook Jacobson's hand, he felt strength and steadiness. No tremors from this guy. He was cool. His steel-gray eyes reflected the confidence of a trained professional with a take-charge attitude. Brady did *not* want to butt heads with Grant Jacobson.

"Glad to meet you," Brady said. "I have some questions."

"Shoot."

"What can you tell me about your surveillance system?"

"It's going to be state-of-the-art. Unfortunately, the only area that's currently operational is the front entrance." A muscle in his jaw twitched. "By Friday everything will be up and running with cameras in the hallways, the meeting rooms and every exit."

If the hotel security had been in place, they'd have had a visual record of anyone who might have entered or exited room 621. "Was there a security guard on duty tonight?"

"There should be two." Jacobson swiveled his head to glare at the hotel manager. "When law enforcement arrived on the scene, those men should have been notified."

Chandler exhaled a ragged sigh. "I contacted you instead."

"Apparently, we have some glitches in our communications." Jacobson looked toward Sasha. "And you are?"

"A witness," she said. "Sasha Campbell."

"It's a pleasure to meet you, Sasha." When he returned her friendly grin, it was clear that he liked what he saw. "And what did you witness?"

Wanting to stay in control of the conversation, Brady stepped in. "We have reason to believe that a woman was attacked in her room. Right now we're on our way to see someone fitting her description."

"Where?"

"Room 917."

"Reinhardt's suite," Jacobson said. "I'll come with you."

With a terse nod, Brady agreed. He could feel the reins slipping from his grasp as Grant Jacobson asserted his authority. The head of security was accustomed to giving orders, probably got his security training in the military, where he had climbed the ranks. But this was the real world, and Brady was the one wearing the badge.

Jacobson dismissed the hotel manager, who was all too happy to step aside as they boarded the elevator. The doors closed, and Jacobson asked, "Where did the assault take place?"

"One of the suites on the sixth floor," Brady said.

"I assume you've already been to that suite."

"We have, and we didn't find anything."

"What about the Chinese?" Sasha piped up.

He shot her a look that he hoped would say *Please don't try to help me.*

"Chinese?" Jacobson raised an eyebrow.

Brady jumped in with another question. "What can you tell me about the key-card system?"

"Why do you ask?"

"No one was registered to stay in that room."

"And you're wondering how they could get access," Jacobson said. "The hotel has only been open a week on a limited basis, which means the new employees are being trained on all the systems. In the confusion, someone could have run an extra key card for a room."

"You're suggesting that one of the employees was in that suite."

"It's possible." Jacobson shifted his weight, subtly moving closer to Sasha. He looked down at her. "Are you staying at the hotel?"

"I'm in a corporate condo," she said. "I work for the Denver law firm that's handling the Arcadia ski-resort business."

"Interesting." His thin lips pursed. "How did you happen to witness something on the sixth floor?"

Before Brady could stop her, Sasha blurted, "Binoculars."

"Even more interesting." He hit a button on the elevator control panel, and they stopped their upward ascent. The three of them were suspended in a square box of chrome and polished mirrors. They were trapped.

Jacobson growled, "Do you want to tell me what the hell is going on?"

"Police business," Brady asserted. "I don't owe you an explanation."

For a long five seconds, they stood and stared at each other. Their showdown could have gone on for much longer, but Brady wasn't all that interested in proving he was top dog. He had a job to do. And his number-one concern was finding a victim who might be bleeding to death. Though his instinct was to play his cards close to the vest, he needed help. He'd be a fool not to take advantage of Jacobson's experience in hotel security.

"Here's what happened," Brady said. "Ms. Campbell happened to be looking into the suite. She saw a man and woman having dinner—"

"With chopsticks," Sasha said.

Brady continued, "There was an argument. Ms. Campbell didn't see the actual attack, but there was blood on the woman's chest. She collapsed. The man caught her before she hit the floor."

"A possible murder," Jacobson said. When he straightened his posture, he favored his left leg. "How can I help, Deputy?"

Ever since they got to the hotel, Brady had been moving fast and not paying a lot of attention to standard procedures. At the very least, he should have taped off the room as a crime scene. There was enough to think about without Sasha distracting him. "You mentioned that you had two men on site. I'd appreciate if you could post one of them outside room 621 until we have a chance to process the scene for fingerprints and other forensic evidence."

"Consider it done." Jacobson pulled a cell phone from the pocket of his leather jacket and punched in a number. While it was ringing, he asked, "What else?"

"I want to check the surveillance tapes from the front entrance," Brady said.

"No problem." Jacobson held up his hand as he spoke into the phone and issued an order to one of his security men. As soon as he disconnected the call, he turned to Brady again. "Anything else?"

"Where's the closest place to get Chinese food?"

"Don't know, but that's a good question for the concierge on the ninth floor." He pushed a button on the elevator panel, and they started moving again. "Now I have a request for you. I'd like to do most of the talking with Reinhardt."

"Why's that?"

Jacobson's brow furrowed. "Because this is his fault."

WHEN THE ELEVATOR doors opened, an attractive woman with her white-blond hair slicked back in a tight bun stood waiting. Sasha's friendly smile was met with a flaring of the nostrils that suggested the woman had just poked her nose into a carton of sour milk.

"This is Anita," Jacobson said as he guided them off the elevator. "A top-notch concierge. She's been in Arcadia for less than a week, and I'll bet she knows more about the area than you do, Deputy."

His compliment caused Anita to thaw, but only slightly. Her voice dripped with disdain. "Mr. Chandler said you want to see Mr. Reinhardt, but I'm afraid that will not be possible. Mr. Reinhardt asked not to be disturbed."

"You're the best," Jacobson said, "always protecting the guest, always operating with discretion. But this is a police matter."

"Can't it wait until tomorrow?"

"I'm afraid not," Jacobson said.

Brady showed his badge. "We'll see him now."

Anita stared at one man and then the other as though she was actually considering further resistance. Changing her mind, she pivoted, led the way to the door of room 917 and tapped. "Mr. Reinhardt, there's someone to see you."

She tapped again, and the door flung open.

Sasha found herself staring directly at a red-faced Lloyd Reinhardt. She assumed his cherry complexion was the result of sunburn from skiing without enough sunscreen. The circles around his eyes where his goggles had been were white, like his buzz-cut hair. The effect would have been comical if his dark eyes hadn't been so angry. His face resembled a devil mask, and he was glaring directly at her.

Through his clenched jaw, Reinhardt rasped, "What?"

Sasha gasped. She had no ready response.

Jacobson stepped in front of her. "We had a conversation last week, and I warned you that the hotel shouldn't open for business until I had all security measures in place."

"I remember. You wanted a ridiculous amount of money to keep the computer and electronics guys working around the clock on the surveillance cameras."

"And you turned me down," Jacobson said. "Now we have a serious situation."

"I hope you aren't interrupting my evening to talk business," he said. "How serious?"

"Murder," Jacobson said.

Reinhardt narrowed his eyes to slits. With his right hand resting on the edge of the door and his left holding the opposite door frame, his body formed a barrier across the entrance to his room. The white snowflake pattern on his black sweater stood out like a barbed-wire fence. "I want an explanation."

"May we come in?" Jacobson asked.

Reinhardt glanced over his shoulder. It seemed to Sasha that he was hiding something—or someone—inside the room. He wasn't having an affair, because—as far as she knew—he wasn't married. But what if the dark-haired lady was somebody else's wife? Or what if she was the victim, lying on the carpet bleeding to death? Sasha cringed inside. Nothing good could come of this.

Reinhardt stepped aside, and they entered. The luxury suite on the concierge level had more square footage than her apartment in Denver. The sofas and chairs were upholstered in blue silk and beige suede. There was a marble-top dining table with seating for eight. In the kitchen area, a tall woman with long black hair stepped out from behind the counter. She wore white slacks and a white cashmere sweater that contrasted with her healthy tan.

Though she wasn't the woman Sasha had seen through the binoculars, this lady could have been a more athletic sister to the other. After she introduced herself as Andrea Tate, Sasha glanced at Brady and whispered, "It's not her."

The conversation between Reinhardt and Jacobson grew more heated by the moment. Jacobson had advised against opening until all the security measures were in place and his staff was adequately trained. He blamed Reinhardt for everything. For his part, Reinhardt was furious that someone dared to be murdered in his hotel.

Reinhardt turned away from Jacobson and focused on her. "I need to speak with Damien as soon as possible. There are liability problems to consider."

"Yes, sir." She hadn't even considered the legal issues.

"Who was killed?"

Sasha froze. Her lips parted but nothing came out. She couldn't exactly say that a murder had been committed. Nor did she have a name. And she was reluctant to point to the sleek black-haired woman and say the victim looked a lot like her.

Brady spoke for her. "I can't give you a name."

Reinhardt whipped around to face him. "My public-

ity people need to get on top of this situation right away.
The grand opening is Saturday. Who the hell got killed?"

"We don't know," Brady said, "because we haven't
found the body."

Though it didn't seem possible, Reinhardt's face turned
a deeper shade of red. He punched the air with a fist. "A
murder without a body? That's no murder at all. What kind
of sick game are you people playing?"

Panic coiled around Sasha's throat like a hangman's
noose. She wanted to speak up and defend herself, but
how? What could she say?

Jacobson sat in one of the tastefully upholstered chairs
and took an orange from the welcome basket. He gestured toward the sofa. "Have a seat, Reinhardt. I'll explain everything."

While Reinhardt circled the glass coffee table and lowered himself onto the sofa, Brady took her arm. "We'll
be going."

"Wait for me outside," Jacobson said.

They made a hasty retreat. As soon as the door to
Reinhardt's suite closed behind her, Sasha inhaled a huge
gulp of air. It felt as if she'd been holding her breath the
whole time she'd been in the suite. She shook her head
and groaned.

"You look pale," Brady said. "Are you okay?"

"I'm in so much trouble."

"You did the right thing," he reassured her.

That wasn't much consolation if she ended up getting fired. Reinhardt had said that she needed to contact
Damien, and she knew that was true. But she wanted to
be able to tell him something positive. "Is there anything
else we can do?"

"I've got an idea."

He crossed the lounge to the concierge desk where

Anita sat with her arms folded below her breasts and a smug expression on her face. "I warned you," she said. "Mr. Reinhardt doesn't like to be interrupted."

"Jacobson said you know this area better than anyone."

"It's my job," she said coolly.

"If I wanted Chinese food, where would I go?"

"There's a sushi bar scheduled to open next month. Right now none of the hotel restaurants serve Asian cuisine. And I'm sure you know that the local diners specialize in burgers, pizza and all things fried."

Sasha walked up beside him. Her legs were wobbly, but she'd recovered enough to understand what was going on. Anita was acting like a brat as payback for them not listening to her earlier. The concierge would be in no mood to help. The best way to get through to her was to be even snottier than she was.

"She doesn't know," Sasha said, not looking at Anita. "She's not as good at her job as she thinks she is."

"I beg your pardon."

"Well, it's true." Sasha flipped her hair like a mean girl. "If one of the people up here on the concierge level requested *moo shu* pork, you'd just have to tell them to suck an egg."

"For your information, missy, I've been providing gluten-free Asian food fried in coconut oil for a guest and his entourage since last Saturday. One of the chefs in the Golden Lyre Restaurant on the first floor of the hotel cooks up a special batch. I had it tonight myself."

"Who's the guest?" Brady asked.

"Sam Moreno, the famous self-help guru. He has a special diet."

Sasha should have guessed. One of the main investors of the Arcadia resort, Mr. Moreno was always requesting special foods and drinks. "He's picky, all right."

Anita leaned across the desk and whispered, "And he's staying right down the hall."

Of course he was. Sasha groaned. She just couldn't catch a break.

Chapter Four

Three hours later Brady drove Sasha back to the corporate condo. His shift was over, and there didn't seem to be anything more he could do at the hotel. He'd tracked the evidence to a dead end, leaving the matter of the assault-slash-murder unsolved and the hotel staff irritated.

The logical thing would have been for him to drive home to his cabin behind the horse barn on Dooley's ranch, yank off his boots and go to bed. But he was reluctant to leave Sasha. Halfway through his investigation, it had occurred to him that she might be in danger. If she had, in fact, witnessed a murder, the killer might come after her next.

When he parked his SUV in front of her building, she turned to him with the grin that came so naturally to her. "Thanks for the ride."

"Hold on, I'll walk you in."

"That's not necessary."

He hoped she was right and he was overreacting to the possibility of a threat. "Not a problem."

A porch light shone outside the door to the condo entrance, and a glass panel beside the door gave a view inside. Nothing appeared to be out of the ordinary. When she unlocked the outer door, he followed her inside. She hit the button on the elevator and the doors swooshed open.

The interior of the elevator was extra large to accommodate skis and other winter sports equipment.

As she boarded, Sasha said, "I should apologize. I think I got you in trouble."

The sheriff had been none too pleased when Brady had asked for a couple of men to fingerprint and process the suite on the sixth floor. It hadn't helped that the room was clean. They'd found nothing to corroborate Sasha's story.

"Not everybody was ticked off," he said. "Grant Jacobson was real pleased with the way things turned out."

Jacobson had used the incident as a learning tool to train his newly hired staff. Investigating a possible homicide also gave him an edge in talking to Reinhardt about the importance of security at a top-rated hotel. His budget had been tripled.

"Jacobson is intense," she said as she got off the elevator at the third floor. "What's his story?"

"He's former military, Marine Corps." He was a man to be respected. "Did you notice his limp? He lost his left leg above the knee in Afghanistan."

Her blue eyes opened wider. "I didn't know."

"According to his staff, he snowboards and skis. One of the reasons he took this job at Gateway was the availability of winter sports."

"I'm just glad he's on our team."

When she reached toward the lock on the condo door, he took the key from her. "I'll open it. I should go first."

"Why?"

"In case there's someone inside."

She took a step back, allowing his words to sink in. "You think someone might have broken into the condo and might be waiting for me."

"I don't want to alarm you." He kept his voice low and calm. "But you're a witness to a possible murder."

"And he might want me out of the way."

She was a loose end. An efficient killer would come back for her. Brady drew his weapon before opening the door. "Wait here until I check the place out."

As soon as he entered, he hit the light switch. At first glance, the condo appeared to be empty, but he wasn't taking any chances. This possible killer had already outsmarted him once tonight.

Quickly, he went from room to room, taking a look in the corners and the bathrooms and the closets. The only bedroom that was occupied was the first one on the right, where Sasha had unpacked her suitcase. It smelled like ripe peaches, a sweet fresh fragrance that reminded him of her and got under his skin. The only other room that had been used was the hot tub, where a damp towel hung from a rack by the door.

"All clear," he said as returned to where she was standing.

"Good. I've had more than enough excitement for one night." She peeled off her parka and hung it on a peg by the door. In her white sweater and red jeans, she reminded him of a pretty Christmas package waiting to be unwrapped. "Are you hungry?" she asked.

"I had some Chinese."

"Me, too. I felt guilty eating it and thinking that this might have been the last meal for the black-haired woman."

In the restaurant kitchen at the hotel, it hadn't taken long for them to locate the off-the-menu Chinese food. A cooking station had been set up near the rear exit with fried rice, gluten-free noodles and organic stir-fry veggies available to anyone who came by and scooped a serving into a carryout box.

"That was our best clue," he said.

"How do you figure? None of the kitchen staff remembered who had stopped by and loaded up on free food."

"And that's the clue. The killer was nobody remarkable. He was somebody the staff had seen before."

"And what does that prove?"

"It's likely this is an inside job."

"Somebody who works at the hotel?" she asked.

"Or somebody who has been around this week. A workman. A consultant."

"It's a long list of possible suspects."

He'd gathered a lot of information tonight but hadn't had a chance to put things together or draw conclusions. Tomorrow when he wrote his report, there'd be time enough to figure things out. He followed her to the kitchen, where she opened the door to the fridge and peeked inside.

She looked up at him. "There's nothing in there but condiments and champagne."

"Try the freezer," he said. "Some of these condos stock up on gourmet frozen deliveries when they're expecting guests."

"I'm not hungry enough for a full meal." She moved to the cabinets above the countertops. "Maybe just a cup of tea. Would you like some?"

His boots were pointed toward the exit. He should go home. He'd delivered her safely and done all that could be expected. "I ought to call it a day."

She held up a little box of herbal tea bags. "I can make you a cup in just a minute."

"Good night, Sasha."

"Wait." With the tea box clutched in both hands like a precious artifact, she took a step toward him. "Please don't go."

The pleading tone in her voice stopped him in his tracks. He saw tension reflected in her baby-blue eyes, and the upturned corners of her mouth pulled tight. Until now she'd managed to hold her emotions in check. Not that she lacked passion. Her moods flitted across her face with all the subtlety of a neon billboard. This was different, darker. "What is it?"

Her brave attempt at a smile failed. "I don't want to be alone. Tea?"

"Sure." How could he refuse? He shucked off his dark blue uniform jacket and sat on a stool at the kitchen counter. "I hope I didn't scare you when I did a room-to-room search in here."

"I'm glad you did." Looking away from him, she continued as though talking to herself. "I'd told myself that I didn't have anything to worry about, but I couldn't help thinking about what it meant to be a witness. That guy could come after me. But I know I'm safe here. All the doors and windows are locked. This is a secure building."

"It's okay to be scared."

Still holding the tea, she rested her elbows on the opposite side of the counter and leaned toward him. "When I'm worried, it helps to talk about it. Do you mind?"

"Starting from the beginning?"

"We don't have to go that far back," she said. "I've already decided that I'll never drink champagne again."

He remembered her flushed cheeks and bright eyes when he first came to the condo. "Were you drunk earlier?"

"No, but I was silly and unprofessional. If I hadn't had a glass or two—" she winced "—or maybe three, I might not have picked up the binoculars and looked into the hotel. I wouldn't have seen anything."

"Is that what you'd want?"

"Not knowing would be easier. If I hadn't seen the attack, I could have watched TV and gone to bed and had pleasant dreams." When she looked down at the tea box in her hand, her blond hair fell forward, hiding her expression. "I have no regrets. I'm glad I saw. That man can't get away with murder."

He reached across the counter to comfort her. He clasped her hand in his, rubbing the delicate skin of her palm with his thumb. In a casual way, they'd been in physical contact all night as he guided her through the hotel and bumped against her in the elevator. But this touch felt significant.

Her gaze lifted to meet his eyes, and he felt an instant, deep connection to her. At that moment, she became more than a witness. His instinct was to pull her into his arms and cradle her against his chest until her fears went away.

No way could that happen.

She'd blamed the champagne for making her behave in a less-than-professional manner. What was his excuse? He knew better than to get personal with a witness, especially someone who was only passing through Arcadia. Reining in his instincts, he released her hand and sat back on his stool. "What did you want to talk about?"

"I'm not sure when it started," she said, "but I've been having that weird feeling you get when someone is watching. You know how it is? The hairs on the back of your neck stand up and you see things in your peripheral vision."

"When did the feeling start?"

"Not when we first arrived at the hotel. Not when we were going through the rooms. It was after we saw Reinhardt and I swallowed my tongue." Her voice broke. "Talk about being in trouble. I'm up to my armpits. I don't know how I'm going to find the nerve to show up for that meeting tomorrow."

"You didn't do anything wrong."

"Oh, but I did. It's my job to facilitate the discussion and make things easier for the investors. Instead, I created a big fat problem." A tear slipped over her lower lashes and slid down her cheek. "I'm going to get fired for sure."

He wanted to wipe away her tears and tell her that everything was going to be all right, but he wasn't a liar. He was a cop, and the proper procedure for answering a 911 call didn't include cozying up to the witness.

Circling the counter, he rifled loudly through the cabinets until he located a stainless-steel teakettle, which he filled with water and placed on the burner. When he faced her again, she had regained her composure.

"Okay," he said, "skip ahead to the time when you felt like you were being watched."

She thought for a moment. "When we were at the front desk, finding out how the key cards for the hotel rooms worked, I started to take my parka off. I shivered. Then I felt the prickling up and down my arms. It was like a warning. I looked around, but I didn't notice anybody watching me."

The front desk was located in the wide-open atrium area where dozens of people came and went. Plus there was a balcony overlooking the marble pond and the statue of the huntress. They could have easily been spotted. "Why didn't you tell me?"

"I didn't want to interrupt. It seemed like we were making some progress. The key cards were a pretty good clue."

Using the computerized system, they'd learned that key cards had been made for the suite on the sixth floor. The key had been activated prior to the time when she saw the couple having dinner, indicating that someone could have been in the room. "If the security cameras in the hallway had been operational, we'd have this all wrapped up."

"Do you think he was planning to kill her from the start?" She bit her lower lip. "That the murder was premeditated?"

"I don't know."

"I think it was," she said. "It took some planning for him to get her alone in that room without anybody knowing."

Premeditation made sense to Brady. The slick way the body had been whisked away without leaving a trace seemed to indicate foresight. For the sake of argument, he took a different view. "He might have just wanted a free night at a classy hotel, eating free food and enjoying the view."

"When I was first watching them, I thought they were a couple. They weren't talking much, and I thought it was one of those comfortable silences between people who have been together for a long time."

"Like a husband and wife?"

"Not really." She shook her head. "The woman was all dolled up, and that made me think they were on a date. Her fancy gold necklace isn't the kind of thing a wife would wear."

"Why not?"

"It's too formal. I think she wanted to impress him with her outfit, and he was doing the same by taking her to the expensive suite." As she chatted, she began to relax. "If he was trying to impress her, he wasn't planning to hurt her."

"And his attack wasn't premeditated." He found a couple of striped mugs in the cabinet above the sink, and she popped a tea bag in each. "Is that your theory?"

"That's one theory," she said. "But it leaves a lot of details unexplained. I saw him pick her up in his arms. He must have gotten blood on his clothes. How could he risk walking through the hall like that?"

The teakettle whistled, and Brady poured the boiling

water over the tea bags. He had a couple of theories of his own. "When the forensic guys went over the room, they didn't find a single drop of blood. Not even when they used luminol and blue light. He was tidy. He could have covered the blood with a jacket and slipped on a pair of gloves."

She nodded. "And he could get rid of those clothes when he left the hotel."

Brady didn't often handle complicated investigations, and he appreciated the chance to discuss the possible scenarios. He probably shouldn't be having this talk with her, but there wasn't anybody else. Due to the lack of evidence, the sheriff was going to tell him to forget about this investigation. Jacobson might be inclined to throw around a few ideas, but his plate was full with getting the hotel security up and running.

Brady sweetened his tea with sugar and took a sip. The orange-scented brew tickled his nostrils. "His real problem was disposing of the body. If he carried her any distance, there would have been a trail of blood drops."

When she lifted the mug to her lips, her hand was trembling so much that she set it down again.

"Sasha, are you all right?"

"It's okay." She lifted her chin. "Keep talking."

Her struggle to control her fear was obvious. He didn't want to make this any harder for her. "Maybe we should go and sit by the fireplace."

"I said I was fine." Her voice was stronger. "You were talking about a blood trail."

"If he'd planned the murder," he said, "he could have arranged to have one of those carts that housekeeping uses to haul the dirty sheets."

"That doesn't seem likely. How could he explain having a maid's cart standing by?"

"It's hard to imagine that he wrapped her up in a sheet

or a comforter and didn't leave a single drop of blood. What if he ran into someone in the hallway?"

"But he didn't have to go far," she said, "only down the hall to the elevator. That goes all the way down to the underground parking."

Brady preferred the idea of the maid's cart. "He could have been working with someone else."

A shudder went through her, and she turned away from him, trying to hide the fear that she'd denied feeling a moment ago. "Would there be a lot of blood?"

He didn't want to feed her imagination. "There's no way of knowing. This is all speculation."

"The red blood stood out against her white clothing. It happened so fast. One minute she was fine. And the next…"

Witnessing the attack had been hard on Sasha, more traumatic than he'd realized. And he was probably making it worse by talking about it. He set down his tea and lightly touched her back above the shoulder blade. "I shouldn't have said anything."

She spun around and buried her face against his chest. Her arms wrapped around him, and she held on tight, anchoring herself. Tremors shook her slender body. Though she wasn't sobbing, her breath came in tortured gasps.

"I'm sorry, Brady, really sorry. I don't want to fall apart."

"It's okay."

"I can't forget, can't get that image out of my head."

Her soft, warm body molded against him as he continued to hold her gently. He wished he could reach into her mind and pluck out the painful images she'd witnessed, but there was no chance of wiping out those memories. All he could do was protect her.

Chapter Five

The next morning, Sasha put on a black pinstriped pantsuit, ankle-length chunky-heel boots and a brave face. After her breakdown last night, she felt ready to face the day. Being with Brady had helped.

Not that he had treated her like a helpless little thing, which she would have hated. Nor had he been inappropriate in any way, which was kind of disappointing. He was sexy without meaning to be. She wouldn't have objected to a kiss or two. Usually, she wasn't the kind of woman who threw herself into the arms of the nearest willing male, in spite of what her obnoxious brother thought. But Brady brought out the Trashy Sasha in her.

In the condo bathroom, she applied mascara to her pale lashes and told herself that she was glad that he hadn't taken advantage. He was different. Brady believed her, and that made all the difference.

She checked the time on her cell phone. In fifteen minutes, Brady would stop by to pick her up. He still had concerns about her safety and wanted to drive her to her meeting with the four investors, and she was excited to see him. As for the meeting? Not so much.

It'd be great if the partners treated her the way they usually did, barely noticing her existence. But she feared they'd be critical about her behavior last night, accusing her of not acting in the best interests of the resort. Applying a smooth coat of lipstick, she stared at her reflection in the bathroom mirror and said, "I can handle this."

Her cell phone on the bathroom counter buzzed. She read a text message from Damien that instructed her to conference with him. In the kitchen, she opened her laptop and prepared for the worst.

Damien Loughlin's handsome face filled the screen. His raven-black hair was combed back from his forehead. He was clean-shaven and ready for work in a white shirt with a crisp collar and a silk necktie.

"What the hell were you thinking?" he growled. It was so not what she wanted to hear.

"I'm not sure what you're referring to."

"Spying on the hotel through binoculars." Unfortunately, he had it right. "Why would you do that?"

She didn't even try to explain. "I witnessed an assault, a possible murder."

"And then you traipsed over to the hotel and got everybody worked up."

"By *everybody,* I'm guessing you mean Mr. Reinhardt."

"Damn right, I mean Reinhardt. He's one of my most important clients, and you brought a cop to his doorstep."

Damien hadn't asked if she was all right or if she needed anything at the corporate condo, but then again, that really wasn't his problem. She was his assistant, and her job was to fulfill his needs in the investors' meeting.

"Last night," she said, "I was working with the police, following a lead."

"You're not a cop, Sasha." His dark eyes glared at her with such intensity that she thought his anger might melt the computer screen. "I expect more from you."

"You won't be disappointed," she said. "I'm prepared for the meeting today."

"If anyone asks about last night, I want you to tell them that it's being handled by local law enforcement. You're not to be involved in any way. Is that clear?"

"I understand." But she couldn't promise not to be part of the investigation. Witnessing a crime meant she had an obligation to help in identifying the killer or, in this case, the victim.

Hoping to avoid more instructions, she changed the topic. "How is Mr. Westfield's family?"

Damien leaned away from the computer screen and adjusted the Windsor knot on his necktie, a move that she'd come to recognize as a stalling technique. When he played with his tie, it meant he wasn't telling the whole story. "The family is, of course, devastated by his unfortunate death. Virgil P. Westfield was in his nineties but relatively healthy. He had several good years left."

Sasha tried to guess what Damien wasn't saying. "Are the police investigating his fall down the staircase?"

"They are," he admitted, "and you're not to share that information with anyone, especially not the Arcadia investors."

She hadn't been aware of a connection between Westfield and the people who founded the ski resort, but there were frequent crossovers among the wealthy clients of Samuels, Sorenson and Smith. Damien also represented Virgil's primary heir, a nephew. "Are there any suspects?"

"Let's just say that we're looking at the potential for many, many billable hours."

That was a juicy tidbit. Was the heir a suspect? For a minute, she wished she was back in Denver working on this case with Damien. If the nephew was charged with murder, the trial would turn into a three-ring circus, given that Westfield was a well-known eccentric and philanthropist who had left a substantial bequest to a feral-cat shelter.

Criminal cases were much more interesting than property disputes and corporate law.

"I'll stay in touch today," she said.

"No more drama," he said before he closed his window and disappeared from the screen.

No more drama. The last thing she wanted was more trouble.

TUCKED INTO THE passenger seat of Brady's SUV, she fastened her seat belt and watched as he took off his cowboy hat and placed it on the center console. He combed his fingers through his unruly dark brown hair. He looked good in the morning. Not all sleek and polished like Damien but healthy, with an outdoorsy tan and interesting crinkles at the corners of his greenish-brown eyes. She wondered how old he was. Maybe thirty? Maybe the perfect age for her.

He gave her a warm grin. "You look very—"

"Professional?" She turned up the furry collar on her parka. "That's what I was going for."

"I was going to say pretty. I like the way you've got your hair pulled back in a bun."

"A chignon," she corrected, "which is just like a bun, only French."

"And I especially like this." When he reached over and tucked an escaped tendril behind her ear, his fingers grazed her cheek. "Your hair is a little out of control."

"Like me." His unexpected touch sent a spark of electricity through her. She pushed that sensation out of her mind. They weren't on a date. She continued, "I'm a little out of control but very professional."

"If you say so."

He drove through the condo parking lot and turned onto the main road. Today his features were more relaxed, and his smile appeared more frequently. The optimism she'd felt when she first came to Arcadia returned full force. Who could be glum on a blue-sky day with sunlight glistening on the snow?

"Anything new on the investigation?" she asked, even though Damien had specifically told her not to get involved.

"The sheriff doesn't want anything to do with it. He says looking into a murder without a body is a fool's errand. Then he said it was my assignment. I guess that makes me the fool."

"Ouch."

"It's not so painful," he said. "I'd rather be hanging out at the hotel than writing up speeding tickets. If I plan it right, I might even find a reason to investigate on the ski slope."

"Are you a skier or snowboarder?"

"Both," he said. "You?"

"Neither."

"Are you a Colorado transplant?"

"I'm a native, born in Denver, the youngest of five kids. Our family moved around a bit when my dad changed jobs, but I came back here for college. I just never got into skiing. Lift tickets are too expensive."

"So you're a city girl."

"But I'm in pretty good shape." Thanks to a corporate membership in a downtown Denver gym, she took regular yoga classes and weight training. Neither of those indoors exercises would impress Brady. "I do a little figure skating."

"You can show me. That's where we're headed, right? The brand-new Arcadia ice rink?"

"As if I'd get on ice skates in front of Katie Cook." Sasha scoffed at the thought. "Ms. Cook has won tons of championships. She was with the Ice Capades."

Katie Cook was one of the four investors. Her agenda for the Arcadia development had been crystal clear from the start. She wanted a world-class ice-skating rink capable of hosting international events and rivaling the facilities in Colorado Springs, where many athletes trained.

The first meeting was scheduled to be held in the owners' box overlooking the ice. Construction costs on the rink with stadium seating had gone over budget, and Sasha suspected that Ms. Cook intended to placate the other three business investors by showing how well her ideas had turned out.

The drive took them past the ski lodge and hotel into the town. At eight thirty-five several vehicles were parked at a slant on the wide main street that split the town of Arcadia. Unlike the gleaming new facilities for the lodge and hotel, the town was plain and somewhat shabby, with storefronts on either side of the street and snow piled up to the curbs. Brady pointed out the Kettle Diner. "They have really good banana pancakes."

"I'm not really a fruit person, but I love bananas."

"Why's that?"

"I like something I can peel."

"Me, too."

She'd like to peel him, starting with his hat and working her way all the way to his boots. Before she got completely sidetracked with that fantasy, she looked over at the small grocery store on the corner.

"I should stop there," she said. "I need some basic food supplies for the condo."

"We'll do that after your meeting. I'll be back at the rink at noon to pick you up."

Having him chauffeur her around seemed like a huge inconvenience to him, especially on a gorgeous day when she couldn't imagine anything bad happening. "Maybe I should arrange for a rental car."

He pulled up at a four-way stop and turned toward her. "Until we know what's going on, I'm your bodyguard. You don't leave your condo without me."

"Do you really think that's necessary?"

"I'm not taking any chances with your safety."

She didn't bother arguing. His stern tone convinced her that he wasn't joking. She remembered how she'd felt last night in his arms—safe, secure and protected. "I've never had a bodyguard before."

"Then we're even. I've never needed to protect anyone 24/7."

"Really?"

"Arcadia isn't like the big city. The last time we had an unsolved murder up here was over ten years ago. That was before I became a deputy."

"You were a cowboy." She picked up his hat and would have put it on but didn't want to mess up her chignon.

"I never stopped being a cowboy."

"What does that mean?"

He combed through his wavy hair again. "Once a cowboy, always a cowboy. It's who I am. Growing up on a ranch is different than the city. The pace is slow but there's always plenty to do. You learn to watch the sky and read the clouds to know when it's going to rain or snow. As soon as I could walk, I was on a horse."

"What about friends?"

"I mentioned the horse."

"It sounds lonesome," she said.

"I spent plenty of time alone. I like the quiet."

On the outskirts of town, she spotted the Arcadia Ice Arena—a domed white building with a waffle pattern and arched supports across the front. A marquee in front welcomed new guests to the grand opening this weekend, featuring a special show by Katie Cook.

The large parking lot in front had been snowplowed. Only a few other vehicles—including an extralong Hummer—were parked at the sidewalk leading to the entrance. As Brady drove closer, she felt a nervous prickling at the nape of her neck under her chignon. A shiver trickled down her spine.

She glanced to the left and to the right. She saw a maintenance man with a shovel and the driver for the Hummer, who leaned against the bumper. Keeping her nerves to herself might have been prudent, but she didn't want to take any chances.

"I've got that feeling again," she said. "It's like somebody is watching me."

Brady leaned forward and looked across the front. "I'll find an entrance that's closer."

He drove parallel to the sidewalk until they were beside the young man wearing a parka with an arm patch indicating he was maintenance. "Is there a back entrance to the arena?" Brady asked through the open window of his SUV.

"Yeah, but it's locked. I'll open it with my key."

"Hop in."

With the maintenance man in the backseat, Brady circled the parking lot to the less impressive rear of the arena. The vehicles parked in this area were trucks and unwashed cars.

Brady turned to her. "I'll escort you inside. Stay in the car until I open your door."

Though her feeling of apprehension lingered, she needed to be on time for the meeting. She clutched the briefcase holding her laptop and note-taking equipment against her chest. "We have to hurry. I need to find the owners' box."

The maintenance man said, "I can show you where it is."

"You go first," Brady told him. "We'll follow."

After the maintenance man unlocked the rear door, Brady rushed her into a huge kitchen with gleaming appliances and stainless-steel prep tables. She recognized the chef from the hotel who made the Chinese food for Sam Moreno. He was arguing with a tall woman dressed in a black chef's jacket.

Sasha checked her wristwatch. Six minutes until the meeting was supposed to start. She nudged the maintenance man and said, "Which way do we go?"

"Out that door." He pointed.

They dashed through the swinging door from the kitchen into another room and then into a concrete corridor that curved, following the outer edge of the arena. At the far end of the curve, she glimpsed a figure dressed all in black. He had something in his hand. A gun?

Brady stepped in front of her. His weapon was in his hand.

"Don't move," he shouted. "Sheriff's department."

The figure disappeared.

Chapter Six

Brady took off in pursuit. The curved corridor had narrow windows on the outer wall, admitting slashes of sunlight across the concrete floor. The opposite side was lined with spaces for vendors and entrances into the arena. He glanced over his shoulder and saw Sasha and the maintenance guy running behind him. As a bodyguard, he should have dropped back and made sure she was protected. But he was also a cop, and he sure as hell didn't want this guy to escape.

The only way the man in black could have vanished so quickly was by diving through an entrance to the arena. Brady made a sharp left and charged through the open double doors nearest where he'd seen the man standing. Inside, the tiers of stadium seating were in darkness, but the massive ice arena was spotlighted. A Zamboni swept around the edges of the ice. In the center, a delicate woman in a sparkling green costume spun on her skates.

Sasha, followed by the maintenance man, ran up behind him. "Did you find him?"

"Not yet." He scanned the dark rows of seats. The man in black had to be hiding in here; there was nowhere else he could have gone.

"I beg your pardon," said a tenor voice with a light British accent. "I believe there's been a misunderstanding."

Brady pivoted on his boot heel and looked up to see a man in black standing on the tier of seats above the entryway. When Brady started to raise his weapon, Sasha held out the arm holding her briefcase to block his move.

With her free hand, she waved at the suspicious figure. "Good morning, Mr. Moreno. I'd like to introduce Deputy Brady Ellis."

So this was Sam Moreno, the self-help guru who preached a philosophy about turning one's goals into reality with positive thinking and regular attendance of his seminars. Brady wasn't familiar with Moreno's program, but he suspected a scam. In his experience, the best way to reach a goal was hard work. And he really didn't like the way Moreno demanded special treatment, ranging from the food he ate to the hours of sleep he required. Last night Brady had wanted to question the guru about his menu of organic Chinese food but had been convinced by Sasha not to disturb the supposed genius.

Brady holstered his gun and climbed the stairs to shake hands. Up close he noticed Moreno's fine, smooth olive complexion. His features were as symmetrical as an artist's drawing of a face and he sported neat black bangs across his forehead. He stood nearly as tall as Brady, and his body was trim, almost too thin.

"Pleased to meet you," Brady said. "Why did you run?"

"I make it a point to be punctual. Our meeting was scheduled to start."

"For future reference, when a law enforcement officer tells you to stop, you should obey. I thought that cell phone in your hand was a weapon."

"Rather a large mistake on your part." Moreno's smile stopped just short of a smirk. "Deputy, I'm sensing some anxiety on your part."

"No, sir." Brady wasn't anxious; he was irritated by this

self-important jerk and his phony accent. Given the slightest provocation, Brady would be happy to arrest the self-help celebrity. "I have some questions for you."

"Regarding what?"

"Murder," Brady said.

Citing a violent crime usually got someone's attention, but Moreno didn't react. "I have nothing to hide."

"Where were you last night?"

"In my suite at the Gateway Hotel. I had dinner at six, meditated until seven-thirty and worked on my next book with my secretary until nine when I went to bed."

"Did you leave the suite?"

"I don't believe I did." He gave a thin smile. "You can check with the concierge."

"Okay," Sasha said. "Which way to the owner's box?"

Moreno gestured over his shoulder toward a long glass-enclosed room at the top of the lower seating area. Lights shone from the inside. Standing in the center was Lloyd Reinhardt and his black-haired female companion, who was, according to introductions last night, an assistant.

The public address system crackled to life, and a woman's voice boomed through the speakers. "Good morning, everyone. It's me, Katie Cook, and I'd like for you all to come down to the edge of the rink."

After her announcement, she stood in the middle of the ice, preening like the champion she was, waiting for the others to do her bidding. Brady didn't know how Sasha could work with all these egomaniacs. Each one seemed worse than the last.

Uncle Dooley was the next voice he heard. The old cowboy came out of the box, cleared his throat and called out, "Hey there, Katie. I ain't going nowhere until somebody turns on the lights. I can't see a damn thing in here."

As the Zamboni drove off the ice, Katie gestured to

a high booth at the end of the ice. The arena lights came to life, and Brady had a chance to see the interior seating that rose all the way up to the rafters. This vast area could represent a threat to Sasha. There were a lot of places for an attacker to hide. "How big is this place?"

"Six thousand seats," Sasha said.

"Do you still feel like you're being watched?"

"I'm nervous." Her slender shoulders twitched. "I know it's cool in here but I'm sweating like I'm in the Bahamas."

"Maybe we should get you away from this place."

"No," she said with a shake of her head. "My nerves aren't because I feel like I'm being watched. I'm scared because this meeting isn't going the way I expected. How am I supposed to keep track of what people say if we're hanging out by the skating rink? I wonder if I should check in with my boss."

"He probably doesn't expect you to record every word."

"You're right. That's logical." Unexpectedly, she grasped his hand and gave a quick squeeze. "Thanks, Brady."

He doubted she was in danger. The killer wouldn't risk an attack with all these witnesses. "Go get 'em, tiger."

"I can do this," she said as she drifted toward the rink.

His uncle tromped down the concrete stairs and stood beside him. "Hey, Brady, I understand you raised a ruckus at the hotel last night."

"Just doing my job."

"Did you come here to cause more trouble?"

"Maybe," Brady said.

"I suggest you start by harassing Simple Sam Moreno. He's as slippery as a river otter but not as cute."

Brady watched as the three other investors gathered beside the ice. Katie Cook was joined by two male skaters in black trousers and tight-fitting long-sleeved shirts with matching sequin patterns. Reinhardt brought his attractive assistant with him. And Moreno had an entourage of five, all of whom were dressed in simple but expensive black-and-gray clothing.

It occurred to Brady that he might get the inside scoop on these people by observing them in action. Not that he had much reason to suspect they were involved in the random assault of the woman with black hair. He asked Dooley, "Mind if I tag along with you?"

"I'd be glad for your company. This bunch drives me crazy." He descended the stairs and spoke to the group. "Brady is going to join us."

"Why?" Reinhardt demanded. "We don't need a cop."

"He's not just a deputy. He's my nephew," Dooley said, "and I want him here."

"It's all right with me," Katie said. "I have skates here for all of you, and I want you to put them on and join me on the ice so you can get the full experience of the Arcadia Ice Rink."

"Not necessary," Reinhardt grumbled. "I can get the experience just fine from where I'm standing."

"Be a good sport," she cajoled. "This is my one day to talk about my special contribution, and it's important for you to understand my perspective."

Moreno and his crew were already putting on their skates. He glanced at Reinhardt. "I suggest you cooperate. I'd like to deal with our business here as quickly as possible, and Katie seems to have a plan."

Still muttering to himself, Reinhardt sat on a rink-side bench to put on the skates.

Uncle Dooley wasn't going to play. He stepped up to the edge of the rink and leaned across the railing. "Sorry, Katie, but I can't skate, and I'm not going to risk a broken hip."

She patted his cheek. "I understand, Dooley."

The old man took a seat, and Brady sat beside him. He nudged Dooley with his elbow. "You don't seem to mind being around Katie Cook."

"She ain't bad to look at. As a pro athlete in her forties, she's past her prime, but she's got a nice shape."

Brady seconded that opinion. With her trademark short haircut and long legs, Katie had a pixie thing going on. She'd piled on too much makeup for his taste, but she was cute.

He watched as the others stepped onto the ice. In a display of showmanship, Katie and her two companions glided and twirled across the glistening white surface, seemingly immune to gravity as they leaped through the air. Others were more hesitant. A couple of people fell and shrieked as their butts smacked the ice. His focus went naturally to Sasha.

Her neat pinstriped business suit wasn't meant to be an ice-skating costume, but she looked good as she set off skating down to the far end of the rink and back. Moving more like a hockey player than an ice dancer, she picked up speed as she went. Her forward momentum started a breeze that tousled her tidy chignon. Her cheeks flushed pink with exertion, and she was beaming. Her smile touched something deep inside him.

"That one's real pretty," Dooley said. "How'd you get hooked up with our little Sasha?"

"She's a witness to a possible murder. And I'm not hooked up with her."

"Don't lie to me, boy. The only other time I've seen that goofy look on your face was when you were twelve years old and your daddy bought you that roan filly named Harriet."

The fond memory made him grin. "Harriet was a beauty."

"It's about time you started looking at women that way. How old are you? Thirty?"

"Thirty-one," Brady said, "old enough that I don't need advice on women."

"Yeah? Then how come you're still living alone in that cabin of yours?"

"Maybe I like it that way."

"Your aunt says you're the next one in line to get married and start popping out babies for her to play with. She'd be over the moon if I told her you had a serious girlfriend."

Brady couldn't imagine Sasha living with him in his isolated cabin. She was a city girl. Her work at the Denver law firm was important to her, and she wanted to be a professional. Living on a ranch would bore her to tears.

That was what had happened with his mom. Though she'd tried her best to adjust to country life, she needed the stimulation of the city, and she'd divorced his dad when Brady was ten years old. Mom had stayed in touch, even after she started a new family in Denver, where she had a little flower shop. He'd wanted to stay angry at her, even to hate her. But he couldn't. She was different from Brady and his dad, but she wasn't a bad person.

"You know, Dooley, not everybody is meant to get married."

"Not according to your aunt. She wants everybody matched up two by two."

It hadn't worked that way for his parents. Divorce was probably the best thing that happened for them.

Eight years ago, when his dad passed away, his mom had come to Arcadia and stayed with him. Though he was a grown man who didn't need his mommy, he'd appreciated her support through that rough time. She'd encouraged him to follow his heart and find work that was meaningful. That was when he became a deputy.

Though born and raised a cowboy, Brady had always wanted a job that allowed him to help other people. Joining the sheriff's department was one of the best moves he'd ever made.

He looked down at the ice where Sasha was swirling along. She was bright, energetic and pretty. Not meant for ranch life. He turned to Dooley and shook his head. "She's not my girlfriend."

FOR A COUPLE of minutes, Sasha allowed herself to enjoy the pure, athletic sensation of liquid speed as she flew across the ice in the cool air of the arena. Looking up into the stands, she spotted Brady sitting by his uncle. Both men seemed to be watching her, and she liked their attention. Maybe she wasn't as graceful as Katie Cook but she was coordinated. Earlier she'd mentioned to Brady that she knew how to skate, and she was tempted to try a fancy leap. Or not. Showing off usually got her into trouble.

Reinhardt's companion, Andrea Tate, zoomed up beside her and asked, "Do you have any idea what's going on here?"

"Not a clue." And Sasha was a little bit worried about her responsibilities for the meeting. Her boss wasn't going to be pleased with this impromptu skating event. "It seems like we should be sitting around a conference table talking."

"Boring," Andrea said with a toss of her head that set her long black ponytail swinging.

Though Sasha agreed, she couldn't say as much. "But necessary. How did you meet Mr. Reinhardt?"

"I sell real estate. He's a developer." She lowered her voice. "For an old guy, he's got a lot of energy."

Sasha looked across the ice to where Reinhardt was

standing, bracing himself against the waist-high wall at the edge. His stance seemed uncertain. "Bad ankles?"

"Guess so," Andrea said. "Race you to the other end."

"You're on."

Together they took off. Sasha's thigh muscles flexed, and she used her arms to ratchet up her speed as she charged down the ice, nearly mowing down one of Moreno's minions. She and Andrea hit the far end of the rink in a tie. Laughing, she shook hands with the other woman. Her excitement dimmed as she realized how much Andrea resembled the victim. It didn't seem right to forget about her.

She spotted Katie Cook nearby and swooped toward her, hoping she could get the actual meeting started. After a fairly smooth stop, she clung to the edge of the rink. "Ms. Cook, this is a beautiful arena."

"Please call me Katie, dear. You're not a bad skater."

"It means a lot to hear you say that. I saw you once in an Ice Capades show, and you were magical."

Katie's pale green eyes sparkled inside a ring of extralong black lashes. "Was that the ballroom-dancing show?"

"Forest creatures," Sasha said. She'd been only ten at the time and didn't remember it well but had looked up the show online to make sure she could talk to Katie about it. "You were a butterfly and were lowered from the ceiling."

"Such fun." Katie combed her fingers through her pixie-cut hair and rested her hand on her hip. Her pose seemed studied, as though she were arranging her body to show off her curves.

"Could you tell me what you're planning for the meeting?" Sasha asked. "I want to make sure I can record everything for Mr. Loughlin."

"What a shame that Damien couldn't be here," she said. "I was looking forward to seeing him on skates."

"He sends his deepest regrets."

"Poor old Virgil P. Westfield." Her head swiveled, and her pale green eyes focused sharply. "I've heard rumors that the police are investigating his death."

This topic was exactly what Damien had told her *not* to talk about. Sasha clenched her jaw. "I really can't say."

"But Damien is the Westfields' attorney, isn't he?"

"Yes."

Sasha felt herself being drawn into a trap and was grateful when Sam Moreno joined them. He skated as well as he did everything else; she'd seen him pull off a single axel leap without a wobble.

He asked, "What are you ladies talking about?"

"Westfield," Katie said.

"So tragic." He shook his head and frowned. "The police think he was murdered."

Sasha silently repeated her mantra: *say nothing, say nothing, say nothing.*

"I knew it," Katie said. "My husband consulted with his cardiologist last year. I know for a fact that Virgil P. had the heart of a man half his age."

Apparently, the ice-skater didn't have a problem with sharing confidential medical information. Sasha pinched her lips together, refusing to be drawn into the conversation.

"Westfield's mind wasn't sharp," Moreno said. "I heard he wanted to leave his fortune to his cat. Is that right, Sasha?"

It wasn't. She wanted to speak up and defend Mr. Westfield, who hadn't been senile in any way. *Say nothing, say nothing.* She tried to change the subject. "I wasn't aware that you all knew each other."

"My relationship with Westfield was long-standing and true," Moreno explained. "Like many people who have spent their lives accumulating property, he neglected the inner growth that would make his life truly meaningful."

"And profitable," Katie said cynically. "I'm sure you told him how to invest."

"I advised," Moreno said. "He listened."

Sasha had been involved with the investors long enough to understand the subtext. All of them made their money with real estate. Dooley got his land the old-fashioned way: he had inherited thousands of acres in the mountains. Reinhardt was a developer. Katie Cook and her surgeon husband owned commercial buildings in downtown Denver. And Sam Moreno reaped commissions for turning land into cash on a house-by-house basis.

The Arcadia project was supposed to be a nest egg for all of them. Their plan was for the resort to continue to turn a profit without much in the way of further investment. Sasha wasn't sure how Westfield fit into this picture.

She heard Brady calling her name and turned toward the far end of the ice, where he was waving to her. Happily, she grabbed the excuse and skated away from Katie and Mr. Moreno.

When she reached the edge, she leaned toward Brady. "Thanks for giving me an excuse to get away from them."

"You're welcome, but that wasn't my intention."

"What is it?" she asked.

"Your briefcase is ringing." He held it up.

She scrambled off the ice and sat on a bench before opening it. The last thing she needed was to spill the documents inside or to break her laptop.

This call had to be from Damien. She didn't expect good news.

Chapter Seven

"The reason I wanted you all to skate," Katie Cook said, "was so you could experience the very impressive potential of the Arcadia Ice Rink for yourselves. Not only is this an outstanding facility for skating and training, but the six thousand–seat venue can be used as a stadium for special events."

Sasha adjusted the screen on her laptop, where the face of her boss stared out at the investors and their entourages. Damien hadn't wanted to conduct the first part of the meeting here, but Katie hadn't offered him an alternative.

Still wearing her skates, Katie pushed away from the edge of the rink toward the center. This must have been a signal because the man who had been operating the PA system started playing the opening to Ravel's *Boléro*. After an impressive two-minute version of her famous routine, Katie skated back toward them. Her message was clear: *I've still got the moves.*

"My connections in the skating world are excellent," she said. "I intend to host a national championship at the Arcadia Ice Rink this year, with television coverage, but I will need other revenue streams to make this a profitable endeavor."

"I'm in," Sam Moreno said. "I'll host a minimum of two

seminars at this location. If the partners agree to finance my ashram, I will do more."

"Your what?" Reinhardt demanded. "Ashram?"

"It's a retreat devoted to meditation and study with live-in residents."

"Here we go," Reinhardt growled. "I've been waiting to hear some half-baked scheme from you that was going to cost me money."

"Your investment will be minimal," Moreno assured him, "and far outweighed by the benefits."

"Gentlemen," Damien said from the computer. "May I have your attention?"

His computerized voice was less than commanding, and Reinhardt ignored him. "I'm not putting one penny into financing some hippie-dippie ashram."

On Damien's behalf, Sasha spoke up, "Excuse me."

"What?" Reinhardt said.

She held up the computer. "Mr. Loughlin has something to say."

On the screen, her boss straightened his necktie in his classic stalling move. Then he said, "Today the stage belongs to Katie Cook. We need to stay on topic. I suggest that we adjourn to the owners' box. Immediately."

As they lumbered off the ice and changed into street shoes, Sasha turned the computer screen toward herself. "Any suggestions, boss?"

"I need to go. Try to keep the talks on track. Only contact me if it's absolutely necessary."

The screen went blank. She was glad that he trusted her enough to leave her on her own. At the same time, she was completely freaked out. These people were all strong personalities who could trample her like a herd of wild rhinos. Somehow she had to maintain control.

On the way to the owners' box, she stopped where Brady was standing and looked up at him. If he came with her to the meeting, she'd feel as if she had at least one person on her side. "Are you going to stay?"

He fired a quick glance around the ice rink. "I think you'll be safe here with all these witnesses."

"I'm not worried about being physically attacked." His presence gave her confidence. He was strong and solid and trustworthy—the opposite of most of the partners. "I don't know how I'll keep this meeting on track."

"You'll manage." He gave her a wink. "You're a professional."

Though she straightened her spine, she didn't feel in control. She'd already made the mistake of allowing Katie Cook to lure them onto the ice. Damien wouldn't be pleased if she didn't cover all the items on the agenda. "Tell me again."

He held her upper arms and looked directly into her eyes. "You're a pro. You'll handle these people and be done by noon. Then I'll take you out for a cheeseburger and fries."

"Nice incentive," she said with a nod. "I love cheeseburgers."

"I had a call from Jacobson and need to head back over to the hotel."

"A clue?"

"Maybe." He stepped away from her. "I'll be back to pick you up. Don't go anywhere alone. Don't leave without me."

She was sad to see him go. Her feet were itching to run after him and pursue the investigation. In some ways, tracking down a mysterious killer felt far less dangerous than being locked in a boardroom with the business leaders.

AT THE HOTEL, Brady didn't have to look hard to find Grant Jacobson. The head of Gateway Hotel security was striding toward him before Brady reached the front desk. Jacobson greeted him with a nod and jumped directly to what he wanted to say; he wasn't the kind of guy who wasted time with "hello" or "goodbye."

"I've apprised the staff on the day shift about the black-haired victim. A couple of them identified Andrea, the woman who was with Reinhardt."

"How do you know it was Andrea?" Brady asked.

"They saw her with Reinhardt. He's the big boss, so people notice what's going on with him."

In his casual but expensive leather jacket, Jacobson fit in well with the hotel guests who were on their way to a late breakfast or early lunch in one of the hotel's cafés. He continued, "Since last night, we've searched this place from top to bottom looking for evidence, like a blood trail or a piece of jewelry or a purse."

Brady caught a hint of self-satisfaction in Jacobson's attitude. "You found something."

"Come with me."

They exited onto the street, where the valets turned toward them and backed off when Jacobson indicated with a quick gesture that he didn't need their assistance. The former military man had already trained the staff to understand his needs and to know how to respond. A born leader, Jacobson could have been running a battalion rather than security for a hotel. This job might be a kind of retirement for him with the beautiful surroundings and lack of problems.

"Speaking of Reinhardt," Brady said, "has he given the go-ahead on getting your electronic surveillance operational?"

"You bet he has." Jacobson's expression was grim. "There's nothing like a tragedy to focus attention. Reinhardt agreed to several upgrades, and I have a full contingent of electricians and computer techs on the case. By tonight I'll have the hallways, elevators and underground parking area wired."

Leaving the entryway, Jacobson led the way around to the sidewalk on the right side of the building. It was sunny and warm today. The artificial snow–making machines would be working overtime on the slopes tonight. Halfway down the block, on the other side of the ramps leading to underground parking, Jacobson stopped at the curb beside a dark green SUV.

"This vehicle was here overnight," he said.

As far as Brady could tell, the parking spot was legal. The SUV didn't have a ticket tucked under the windshield wiper. "How do you know it was here?"

He nodded toward the entrance to underground parking. "My parking space is down here, and I saw that SUV when I came in last night. When I left, it was the only vehicle parked on the block. It was still there this morning."

A car parked on the street hardly counted as evidence, but Brady was grasping at straws. Until now he'd had nothing but Sasha's testimony to go on. "I'll run the plates."

"I already did." Jacobson shrugged. "I don't want you to think I'm stealing your thunder, but I have a couple of connections, and I thought I could check it out and save you the time if it wasn't relevant."

Brady squared off to face him. Jacobson had seriously overstepped his authority. "This isn't your job. You're not a cop."

"I understand."

"And I don't have to tell you proper procedure."

"Yeah, yeah, I should have notified you first."

"Damn right you should have."

When Jacobson locked gazes with him, Brady knew

better than to back down. Maybe he wasn't getting much
help from the sheriff. And maybe he was a newbie when it
came to homicide investigations. But he was still in charge.
If this killer got away, Brady would take the blame.

Jacobson gave a nod. "I like you, kid. If you ever decide to leave the sheriff's department, you've got a job
with me."

"I'm glad you're on my side," Brady said, echoing the
statement Sasha had made earlier. "Show me what you
found."

Jacobson pulled a computer notepad from his inner
jacket pocket and punched a few buttons. "The plates belong to Lauren Robbins of Denver. This is her driver's license."

The photo showed an unsmiling thirty-seven-year-old
woman with brown eyes and long black hair. She fit the
description Sasha had given.

IN THE LUXURIOUS owners' box at the Arcadia Ice Rink,
Sasha helped the catering staff clean up the coffee mugs,
plates and leftovers as the meeting wrapped up. No surprise decisions had been made. The discussion among the
business partners had been relatively calm and rational. It
seemed that the three men were more than happy to leave
control of this operation to Katie Cook as long as she didn't
exceed her stated budget.

Sasha's main contribution had been to make sure everything was recorded for future reference. She also kept
the coffee fresh and the juice flowing, made sure the fruit
was organic and sorted the gluten-free pastries for Moreno
and his minions.

Her boss had joined them for the last couple of minutes
via computer. "To summarize," Damien had said from his
computer screen, "existing contracts are still in order. And

I will prepare a new agreement that will allow Moreno to use the arena facilities for two recruitment sessions."

"At a sixty-five percent discount," Moreno said.

Katie Cook rolled her heavily made-up eyes. "Fine."

"Tomorrow," Damien said, "we meet at Dooley's ranch. For those of you who don't want to drive, a van will be waiting outside the hotel at eight-thirty."

"Are you joining us?" Katie Cook asked.

"I'm sure as heck going to try," Damien said.

"Is there anything we can do for Virgil P. Westfield's family?" she asked. "When is the funeral?"

"Your condolences are appreciated. The funeral won't be until next week."

Katie smirked as though she'd discovered a clever secret. "No funeral is scheduled because there's going to be an autopsy. Am I right?"

"Yes," Damien said hesitantly.

"I knew it," she crowed. "The police suspect murder."

"Cause of death was a blow to the head caused by falling down the grand staircase in his home. The coroner will perform an autopsy to determine if he fell because of medications he was taking."

"Or if he was pushed," Katie said.

"At present," Damien said, "the police consider Westfield's death to be an accident. That's all I can say for now. If you have concerns or questions, don't hesitate to ask Sasha and she'll be in touch with me."

As Damien had requested, Sasha turned off the computer screen and officially closed the meeting. She gave the group a reassuring smile and said, "I'll see you all tomorrow. Have a great day."

She noticed that Brady had entered the room and was talking with his uncle as the others exited. Reinhardt and Andrea approached the two cowboys. In his usual gruff manner, Reinhardt demanded information about the supposed hotel murder. Brady told him he was following up on several leads.

"But you still don't have a body," Reinhardt said.

"Not yet."

"Waste of time," Reinhardt muttered.

In short order, the room was empty except for her and Brady. The tension in the air dissipated, and it was quiet. Sasha exhaled a sigh of relief, rotated her shoulders and stretched her arms over her head. Since most of her hair had already escaped the chignon, she pulled out the last few clips and tossed her head.

Being done with the meeting reminded her of the feeling she'd had as a kid when the final bell rang and school was over for the day. She wanted to skip or run or twirl in a circle. *I'm free!* Even better, she was in the company of somebody she liked. Better still, they were going to get cheeseburgers.

Her natural impulse was to give Brady a big hug, but she stopped herself before grabbing him. "Thanks for coming."

"I wasn't going to leave you here unprotected." The dimple at the left corner of his mouth deepened when he grinned. She'd like to kiss that dimple. "Good meeting?"

"No yelling. No huge arguments. Katie had a chance to name-drop every superstar in the ice-skating world. Reinhardt was satisfied with the numbers, especially since Katie's rich hubby has agreed to take up any slack. Moreno hinted about this ashram he wants to build. And then there's your uncle Dooley."

"Who slept through it," Brady said.

"Good guess."

"He's never really sleeping. He hears everything."

"I know," she said.

"That's kind of like you," he said. "You pretend to be

busy filling coffee mugs but you're really keeping track. I came in early enough to hear you give the summary for your boss. Very complete and concise."

"Thank you."

His compliment made her feel good. In her position as a paralegal, few people even acknowledged her presence. Brady listened to everyone, including her. That was a useful attribute for a cop.

He sat at the table and patted the seat of the chair next to him. "Are you ready for some bad news?"

"Not really." But she sat beside him anyway.

As he scrolled through several entries on his cell phone screen, he said, "Jacobson noticed a car on the street that hadn't moved since last night. He checked out the license plate and found the owner."

He held the screen so she could see the driver's license. The photograph showed an attractive black-haired woman. Though Sasha was somewhat relieved to know that she hadn't imagined the attack, she hated to think of what had happened to her.

He asked, "Is this the woman you saw?"

"I think so. It's hard to say for sure from this little picture. Who is she?"

"Her name is Lauren Robbins. One of the other deputies has been doing research on her but hasn't found much. She lives alone in the Cherry Creek area in Denver."

"Those are pricey houses," Sasha said.

"She's a self-employed real-estate agent who works out of her home office, so we can't talk to her employer to get more information. We also know she doesn't have a police record."

"I could check with my office," she offered. "We do a lot of real-estate work, and she looks like somebody who handles high-end properties."

"That's not your job."

That was exactly what Damien would have told her. "I want to help."

"I promise to keep you updated. For now, let's get lunch."

She really wished there was a valid reason to spend more time with him. She liked watching him in action and especially liked the way she felt when she was with him. For now, she'd just have to settle for a juicy cheeseburger.

Chapter Eight

At the Kettle Diner on Arcadia's main street, Sasha dunked a golden crispy onion ring into a glob of ketchup and took a bite. There was probably enough gluten and trans fat in this one morsel to put Sam Moreno into a coma, but she wasn't hypervigilant about her diet. Moreno and his minions considered their bodies to be their temples. Hers was more like a carnival fun house.

Across the booth from her, Brady watched as she mounted a two-handed assault on her cheeseburger. "Hungry?" he asked.

"Starved." She glanced down at the onion rings. "Want one?"

"I've got fries of my own," he said. "When was the last time you ate?"

"I grabbed some munchies during the meeting." But she hadn't had a decent meal all day. "As you know, there's not much food in the condo."

"We'll stop at the grocery before I take you home. Is your boss going to be joining you this afternoon?"

"He hasn't told me." She hesitated and set her amazing cheeseburger down on her plate. Though there was no need for further explanation, she wanted Brady to understand the arrangement at the condo. "When Damien gets here, he'll stay in his bedroom and I'll stay in mine. There's nothing going on between us."

"I didn't think there was."

She was a little bit surprised. Everybody else seemed quick to assume that she was sleeping with the boss. "Well, you're right. How did you come to that conclusion?"

"You're easy to read." He washed down a bite of burger with a sip of cola. "When you look at your boss on the computer screen, your expression is guarded and tense. There's no passion. It's not like the way you look at those onion rings."

Or the way she looked at him. "So, bodyguard, will you be staying with me for the rest of the day?"

"I'd like that."

"Me, too."

"But I'd better take you back to the condo. It's got a security system. You'll be safe there."

He was right. The smart thing would be to go back to the condo and review the files for tomorrow's meeting. Hanging out with Brady wouldn't be professional, and Damien had specifically told her not to get involved with the police. But she wanted to get involved—in a more personal way—with Brady.

"After lunch," she said, "what are we going to do?"

"We'll get you some groceries, then I want to take you by the hotel. Jacobson put together some surveillance footage of the front-desk area during the time when you felt like someone was watching you."

"And you think I might see the killer on the tapes."

"Does that scare you?"

"I don't think so." When she was with him, she felt safe. "If there's anything else I can do, I'm up for it. It's such a gorgeous day. I want to be outside. Even though I'm working, this trip to Arcadia is kind of a vacation for me."

"Is that so?" He swallowed a bite of burger. "I've never thought of my job as a vacation."

"If I come with you, I promise not to get in the way."

"We'll see."

His gaze met hers and, for a moment, he dropped his identity as a cop. He looked at her the way a man looked at a woman, with unguarded warmth and interest. She could tell that he wanted to spend time with her, too.

By bringing her to the local diner in Arcadia rather than going back to the hotel or the condo, he was sharing what his life was like in this small community. Half the people who came through the door of the Kettle Diner greeted him with a smile or a friendly nod. These were the locals—the ranchers and the skiers and the mountain folk. The laid-back atmosphere fit her like an old moccasin and was a hundred times more comfortable than the thigh-high designer boots worn by the guests at the Gateway Hotel.

"I'm looking forward to seeing Dooley's ranch tomorrow," she said.

"I don't know what he's got up his sleeve, but it'll be nothing like Katie Cook's presentation at the ice rink."

"No *Boléro?* No cowboys in matching sequin shirts?"

"All he wants is for his fellow investors to understand the needs of the community."

Dooley's viewpoint had been consistent throughout the planning and negotiations. Of course, he'd jumped into the development for the money, but he also wanted to protect the environment and to make sure the locals weren't misused. "I don't think he likes Moreno's idea of building an ashram where his followers could live."

"Dooley won't mind. We've got a long tradition of weird groups seeking shelter in the mountains."

"Like what?" she asked.

"Back-to-nature communes, artist groups, witch co-

vens." He shrugged. "You never know what you're going
to find when you go off the beaten path. There's room in
these mountains for a lot of different opinions, as long as
everybody respects each other."

Brady's cell phone rang, and he picked up. After a few
seconds of conversation, his easygoing attitude changed.
Tension invaded his body. His hazel eyes darkened. She
could tell that something had happened, something important.

Sasha finished off the last onion ring and watched him
expectantly as he ended the call.

"We have to go," he said.

"What is it?"

"They've found a body."

BRADY SHOULD HAVE taken her back to her condo, but it
was the opposite direction from the canyon where they
were headed. Also, he couldn't drop Sasha off without entering the condo and making sure the space was secure.
This would take time they didn't have, and he wanted to
be among the first at the crime scene.

Beside him in the passenger seat, Sasha cleared her
throat and asked, "Are you sure this is our victim?"

"The 911 dispatcher seemed to think so." The report
had mentioned a woman with black hair. "We don't get a
lot of murders up here."

"What happens next? Are you still in charge?"

"I'm not sure."

The sheriff had been happy to send him on a fool's errand, but finding a body meant that this was a legitimate
murder investigation. No doubt the state police would be
involved. The body had to be sent to Denver or Grand
Junction for autopsy since the local coroner was an elected
official who didn't have the training or facilities for that

type of work. Brady had the feeling that everything was about to go straight to hell.

"I wonder," Sasha said, "if there's anything I can do to minimize the negative publicity for the resort."

As he guided the SUV onto a two-lane mountain road, he glanced over at her. "You're doing some corporate thinking."

"I know." Her grin contradicted the image of a cool professional. She held up her pink cell phone. "Is it okay if I call my boss and tell him that a body has been found?"

"You'd better wait until we have confirmation on her identity."

She dropped the phone. "Just tell me when."

He drove his SUV onto a wide shoulder on the dirt road and parked behind a state patrolman's vehicle. On the passenger side, a steep drop-off led into a forest where nearly half the trees had been destroyed by pine beetles and stood as dry, gray ghosts watching over the new growth. There wasn't much room on the narrow road. When more law enforcement showed up, it was going to get crowded.

He turned to Sasha. "You have to stay in the car."

"Let me come with you. I won't get in the way."

He'd seen how deeply traumatized she'd been by witnessing the attack, and he didn't want to give her cause for future nightmares. "This isn't something you should have to see."

"I'll look away."

"A curious person like you?" He didn't believe that for a minute. "This is my first murder investigation, but I've seen the bodies of people who died a violent death. It's not like on TV or in the movies, where the corpse has a neat round hole in their forehead and otherwise looks fine. Death isn't pretty."

"Are you trying to protect me?"

"I guess I am." He added, "And I don't want to be distracted by worrying about what's happening to you."

"Aha! That's the real reason. You think I'll get into trouble."

She did have a talent for being in the wrong place at the wrong time. "This is a crime scene. Just stay in the car."

Reluctantly, she nodded. "Okay."

"With the doors locked," he said.

"Can I crack a window?" she muttered. "If I was a golden retriever, you'd let me crack a window."

"I'll be back soon."

He exited his vehicle and strode through the accumulated snow at the edge of the road to where two uniformed patrolmen were talking to an older couple dressed in parkas, waterproof snow pants and matching knit wool caps with earflaps. Their faces were as darkly tanned as walnuts.

After a quick introduction, the woman explained, "We only live a couple of miles from here and we cross-country ski along that path almost every day."

She pointed down the slope to a path that ran roughly parallel to the road. Though this single-file route through the forest wasn't part of an organized system of trails, the path showed signs of being used by other skiers.

Just down the hill from the path, he saw a gray steamer trunk with silver trim leaning against a pine tree. The subdued colors blended neatly with the surroundings. If these cross-country skiers hadn't been close, they might not have noticed the trunk.

"That's a nice piece of luggage," the woman said. "It looks brand-new."

"So you went to take a closer look," Brady prompted.

"That's right," her partner said. He was almost the same height as she was. Though they had introduced themselves as husband and wife, they could have been siblings. "We figured the steamer trunk had fallen off the back of a truck. You can see the marks in the snow where it skidded down the hill."

His observation was accurate, but Brady added his own interpretation. He imagined that the killer had pulled off the road, removed the luggage from the trunk of his vehicle and shoved it over the edge. This wasn't a heavily populated area, and there was very little traffic. If it hadn't been for the cross-country trail, the trunk could have gone undiscovered for a very long time.

"Did you open it?" he asked.

"We did," the man said. "The only way we could hope to find the owners was to see what was inside. I used my Swiss Army knife to pop the locks."

His wife clasped his hand. "I wish I hadn't seen what was in there. That poor woman."

"Can we go?" the man asked. "We did our civic duty and called 911. Now I want to get back to our cabin, chop some firewood and try to forget this ever happened."

One of the patrolmen stepped forward. "Come with me, folks. I'd like for you to sit in the back of my vehicle and write out a statement for us. Then I can drive you home."

Brady appreciated the willingness of the state patrol to help out. He knew both of these guys, had worked with them before and didn't expect any kind of jurisdictional problems. Truth be told, he doubted that any of the local law enforcement people would be anxious to take on a murder investigation.

His cell phone rang, and he checked the caller ID. Sasha was calling, probably bored from sitting alone. Ignoring the call, he turned to the patrolman who was still standing at the side of the road beside him. "How'd you get here so fast?"

"Me and Perkins happened to be in the area when the alert went out. You're the deputy who searched the Gateway Hotel for a missing dead body. Brady Ellis, right?"

Brady nodded and scraped through his memory for the patrolman's name. "And you're Tad Whitestone. Weren't you about to get married?"

"We did the deed two months ago, and she's already pregnant."

"Congrats," Brady said.

"Yeah, lucky me."

"Have you climbed down to take a look inside the trunk?"

"Not yet."

"What's stopping you?"

Officer Whitestone pursed his lips. "We were kind of waiting for you, Brady. I've done a training session on homicide investigation, but I don't know all the procedures and didn't want to get in trouble for doing it wrong."

Brady didn't make the mistake of thinking that the state patrol guys respected his expertise. When it came to homicide procedure, he was as clueless as they were. But he wasn't afraid to take action. A cold-blooded murder had been committed, and he intended to find the killer.

"Let's get moving. Do you have any kind of special camera for taking crime-scene photos?"

Whitestone shook his head. "All I've got is my cell phone."

"We'll use that." Brady grabbed the phone from his fellow officer.

As they descended the slope, he took a photo of the skid marks from the road and another of the track made by the cross-country people. Halfway down the hill, they were even with the steamer trunk. It was large, probably three feet long and two feet deep. The lid was closed but both of the silver latches on the front showed signs of being pried open.

Brady snapped another photo. Using his gloved hand, he lifted the lid. A woman dressed in white was curled inside with her legs pulled up to her chin. Her wrist turned at an unnatural angle. Her fingers were like talons. Dried blood smeared the front of her pantsuit, streaked across her arm and splattered on the gold necklace encircling her throat. Her black hair was matted and dull. Her blood-smeared face was a grotesque mask. Her lips were ashy gray. Her eyes were vacant and milky above her sunken cheeks.

There were broken plates thrown in with her, and also a fork and globs of Chinese food and wineglasses with broken stems. The killer had cleaned up the hotel room and dumped everything in here. He was disposing of the trash, treating a human life like garbage.

"Damn," Whitestone said, "that's a lot of blood."

"She must have bled out while she was in the trunk." For some reason, he recalled that the average woman had six to seven pints of blood in her body. He couldn't help but shudder.

"Do you think she was still alive when he locked her in there?"

"I hope not."

If the murder had happened the way Brady imagined, the killer had stabbed her and stuffed her in this trunk immediately afterward so he wouldn't leave any bloodstains behind. The steamer trunk must have been standing by, ready to use, which meant the crime was premeditated.

He looked away from the dead woman and up at the road. Two more police vehicles had arrived. This situation was about to get even more complicated. After Brady snapped several photos from several different angles, he closed the lid.

"I'm going back to the road," he said. "I'll wait until the sheriff gets here before I do anything else."

"No need to call an ambulance," the state patrolman said.

But there was a need, a serious need, to get this investigation moving forward. This killer was brutal, callous. The sooner they caught him, the sooner Sasha would be out of danger.

When he reached the road, he went directly to his SUV to check on her. He yanked open the driver's-side door.

Sasha was gone.

Chapter Nine

Cradling her cell phone against her breast, Sasha crept along the twisting two-lane road. If she took two giant steps to the right and looked over her shoulder, she could see Brady's SUV and the police vehicles. Standing where she was, beside a stand of pine trees, they couldn't see her and vice versa.

In spite of the noise from that group, she felt as if she was alone, separated, following her own path. Maybe she should turn around and go back. Maybe she'd already gone too far.

A gust of wind rattled the bare branches of a choke-cherry bush at the edge of the forest to her left. The pale afternoon sun melted the snow on the graded gravel road, and the rocks crunched under her boots when she took another step forward.

Was she making a huge mistake?

When Brady had left her in the SUV, she had fully intended to stay inside with the doors locked, but she'd been staring through the windshield and noticed movement in the forest. She'd wriggled around in her seat and craned her neck to see beyond the state patrol vehicle parked in front of them. From that angle, she'd seen what looked like a man dressed in black. He had moved in quick, darting steps as though he was dodging from shadow to shadow in the trees.

And then he had disappeared.

She'd wondered if she was looking at the murderer. Had he come back to the scene of the crime? Who was he? A witness? Had she actually seen anything at all?

After the embarrassing disbelieving response she'd gotten when she witnessed the attack through the hotel window, Sasha hadn't wanted to make a mistake. She didn't want to be the girl who cried wolf when there was nothing there.

That was her reason for opening the door to the SUV and stepping into the snow at the edge of the road. In the back of her mind, she'd heard Brady's voice telling her to keep the doors locked and to stay out of trouble. But it wasn't as though she'd been planning to run off and get lost. As long as she stayed fairly close to the SUV, she ought to be okay.

She'd gone around the front of the state patrol car in the opposite direction from where Brady and the two officers had been talking to two elderly people who resembled garden gnomes. Squinting against the sunlight reflected off the snow, she'd tried to see the shadowy figure again. If she didn't see him, she'd run back to the SUV and hop inside and Brady would never know that she'd disobeyed his instructions.

When she'd spotted him again, the state patrolman had been escorting the gnomes into the back of his vehicle. Instead of addressing the patrolman and possibly spooking the shadow man, she'd darted across the road and hidden behind a granite boulder. At that point, it had occurred to her that if she was looking at the killer, she might be in danger.

Using her cell phone, she'd called Brady. He hadn't

answered, and the shadow man had been moving farther away from where she stood. Sasha had made the decision to follow him and find out where he was going. If she kept a distance between herself and him, she ought to be safe. And if he suddenly turned and came toward her, she could always yell for help.

She'd gone around one twist in the road and then another. Still close enough to see Brady's SUV, she moved cautiously forward, trying to see the man in black. The wind had died, and the forest had gone still. There was no movement, not even the shifting of branches. The shadow man was gone.

There had been a whir as an engine started up. Not a motorcycle in this much snow—it was probably one of those all-terrain vehicles. Should she try to follow him? Would he come back in this direction?

"Sasha!"

She heard Brady call her name and turned toward the sound. Chasing after a shadow made no sense, especially if he'd taken off on an ATV. She jogged back down the road to where Brady stood beside his SUV. He looked worn-out and tired. His mouth pulled into an angry scowl with no sign of dimples.

Immediately, she regretted causing him to worry. "I'm sorry."

"Where were you?"

"I thought I saw someone sneaking around in the forest, and I got out of the SUV to get a better look."

"Why?"

"I was trying to be helpful. I thought maybe this guy was a witness."

"Or the killer," Brady said coldly. "You put yourself in danger."

"No, I didn't." She'd been cautious. "I kept my distance.

If he'd come toward me, I would have had plenty of time to run back to the car."

"What if he'd had a gun? Tell me how you were planning to outrun a bullet."

It hadn't occurred to her that he might be armed. If this was the killer, he'd used a knife to attack the black-haired woman, but that didn't mean he couldn't have a gun. "I thought about the danger," she said. "That's when I called you, and you didn't answer."

"Because I trusted you to stay in the car," he said. "I don't understand. One minute you're scared. The next you're tracking down the killer."

"Yesterday I witnessed an attack and nobody believed me. I didn't want to go through that again. That's why I went after him. I wanted to be sure. Can you understand that?"

"Barely."

She reached toward him. When he didn't respond, she dropped her hand to her side. "For what it's worth, he was headed in that direction and I heard an engine starting up."

"A car engine?"

"More like a motorcycle," she said. "Like an ATV."

A siren blared, and red-and-blue lights flashed as another SUV from the sheriff's department joined them. She counted five vehicles. The road was blocked in both directions.

Sasha had the distinct feeling that she didn't belong here. These law enforcement guys had their jobs to do, and she was in the way. Without another word, she walked past Brady on her way to his SUV, where she would sit inside with the windows rolled up like a good little golden retriever. When she came even with him, he caught her arm and leaned close to talk to her.

"I believe you. Again, I believe you saw a man and heard an engine."

When she turned her head, her face was only inches away from his. She wished with all her heart that she could be someone he trusted. "You're the only one."

"When I saw that you weren't in the car, I was scared." His voice dropped to a whisper. "If anything bad had happened to you, I'd never forgive myself."

She wanted to lean a little closer and brush her lips across his. A kiss—even a quick kiss—wasn't acceptable behavior, but she couldn't help the yearning that was building inside her. "Do you want me to go back to the car?"

"I want you where I can see you. Stay with me."

She positioned herself beside him and put on her best attitude. At the firm, she was accustomed to meeting all kinds of big shots, shaking hands and then quietly fading into the wallpaper.

Brady introduced her to Sheriff Ted McKinley, an average-sized guy with a bit of a paunch, slouchy shoulders and a thin face. He shook her hand and gave her a grin. At least, she thought he was smiling. His bushy mustache made it hard to tell. "You're the little lady who caused all this trouble."

"All I did was call 911," she said.

"Well, you sure got Deputy Ellis all fired up."

He clapped Brady on the shoulder. Though the two men weren't openly hostile, she could tell they didn't like each other. Brady had a cool, easy confidence. In spite of his less-than-official uniform, he was every inch a deputy—the man you'd want to have around in a crisis. By contrast, the sheriff, who wore regulation clothes from head to toe, seemed unsure of himself. He had a nervous habit of smoothing his mustache.

Brady got right down to business. "The body resembles

the woman in the driver's license photo, Lauren Robbins. Is there any more information on her?"

"Not yet."

"Did you assign anybody to do that background research?"

The sheriff pulled on his mustache. "Are you telling me how to do my job?"

"No, sir."

"I wanted more to go on before I started a full-scale investigation. My resources are limited. You know that."

Brady's jaw tensed. She could tell that he was holding back his anger. If she'd been in his position, she would have lashed out. The sheriff's reluctance to act was causing them to waste time.

"How long," Brady asked, "before we have an ID on the dead body?"

"Not long." The sheriff glanced toward the edge of the road where other deputies were climbing down the slope. "We're using that mobile fingerprint scanner so we can confirm her identity real quick."

"Is that equipment working?"

"It's pretty handy." He scowled. "Did you talk to the couple who found the body?"

Brady nodded. "The state patrol took their statement."

Another vehicle pulled up, and the sheriff grumbled, "Look at this mess! And it's only going to get worse. You know what they say about too many cooks."

"They spoil the broth," Sasha said. She understood how the sheriff might be frustrated and would have felt sorry for him, but this wasn't a cooking class; it was a murder. He needed to take charge.

"I knew something like this would happen when the new ski lodge was built," he said. "I told your uncle Dooley."

"I know," Brady said.

"We used to have a nice quiet little county. Crime rate was next to nothing. Now we've got ourselves a damn murder."

She could tell from the annoyed look on Brady's face that he'd heard this story before. He asked, "Sheriff, what do you want me to do?"

"Hold tight for a couple of minutes. We're waiting for the coroner. The state police are going to loan us some expert forensic investigators. And I've already contacted mountain rescue so they can bring the steamer trunk up in a rescue basket. It's a hell of a thing, isn't it? Stuffing a body inside a piece of luggage?"

He looked to Sasha for a response, and she nodded. "It's awful."

"You work for Damien Loughlin, don't you?"

Another nod.

"Well, you can tell him not to worry. We've got everything under control."

Or not. In her view, the situation at the crime scene was teetering on the brink of chaos.

Brady stepped forward. "If you don't mind, Sheriff, I'd like to follow up on another lead. I thought I heard an ATV starting up. Maybe I can follow the tracks and find a witness."

"You go right ahead." The sheriff sounded relieved. "There's nothing for you to do here but stand around and watch."

Brady wasted no time before directing her to his SUV. It took some maneuvering to separate his vehicle from the others, but they were on their way in a few minutes, and she was glad to leave the crime scene in their rearview mirror.

The state patrolmen, the deputies, the sirens and the flashing lights created a wall of confusion between her and the truth. A woman had died in a horrible way. Like it or not, Sasha was part of that death. She needed to make sense of the terrible thing that had happened, to fit that piece into the puzzle of her life.

Alone with Brady, her mind cleared. She relaxed, safe in the belief that he would protect her.

"Sheriff McKinley seems…overwhelmed," she said.

"But he's still coming up with cutesy sayings about too many cooks spoiling the broth."

"How did a man like that get to be sheriff?"

"It's an elected position, and he's a nice guy, so people vote for him. Being sheriff used to be easy. McKinley spent most of his day sitting behind his desk with his feet up. The Arcadia development changed all that."

"Is he capable of investigating a murder?" she asked.

"He's got as much experience as any of us. Which is to say—none."

She found it hard to believe that Brady had never done anything like this before. Last night he had approached people with an unshakable attitude of authority. He'd asked the right questions and looked for evidence.

"What about you?" she asked. "Would you want to be sheriff?"

"I want to keep things safe." He pulled over to the edge of the road. "Is this the area where you heard the engine?"

She pointed to the left side of the road, the opposite side from where the body was found. The snow-covered land rose in a gentle slope with ridges of boulders and scraggly stands of pine trees. In her business suit and boots with chunky heels, she wasn't dressed to go tromping around the mountains. "Do we have to hike up there and look around?"

"If I was a real homicide detective, I'd send six forensic

experts to comb the hill for clues and track down that ATV. I'd have a suspect in custody before the day was over."

"But all you've got is me."

"And it doesn't seem worth the effort to search the whole mountain for a track that may or may not have been left by the guy you saw." He slipped the SUV into gear. "There's a dude ranch not far from here, and they've got several ATVs. Let's start there."

"Good plan," she said gratefully. She didn't want to do too much unnecessary hiking in these boots.

"The old man who owns the dude ranch is buddies with my uncle."

"Is he in favor of the ski resort development or opposed?"

"He's prodevelopment." He glanced toward her. "Seems like you've caught the gist of our local politics."

"It's hard to miss."

"Most people in Arcadia are glad to have the new opportunities and the employment, but there are many—like the sheriff—who think the ski resort is nothing but trouble."

"Change is hard," she said.

"But necessary. Slow waters turn stagnant."

He drove out of the forest into a wide snow-covered valley surrounded by forested hills and rocky cliffs. In the distance, a spiral of smoke rose from the chimneys of a two-story log house with a barn and other outbuildings. Several horses paced along the fence line in a field.

Though she spotted two ATVs racing across the meadow, she forgot about the investigation for a moment. These mountains took her breath away. She was, after all, a city girl. Being here was like visiting another world. "It's beautiful."

"I used to come to the dude ranch all the time when

I was a kid to help out with the horses." He cranked the steering wheel and made a quick right turn onto a single-lane dirt road. "I want to show you something."

When the SUV turned again, she didn't see anything resembling a road. The tires bumped across a stretch of field, and she bounced in the passenger seat. "Where are we going?"

"This area is dotted with hot springs and artesian pools." He parked at the foot of a cliff, flipped open the glove compartment and took out a flashlight. "I'm taking you to a place I used to go as a kid. A cave."

She jumped from the vehicle and chased after him as he hiked up a narrow path. Afternoon sunlight glared against the face of this rocky hillside, and the snow was almost entirely melted. Even in her chunky-heeled boots, she was able to keep up with him.

This little detour was totally unexpected. _A cave?_ Until now Brady had been straightforward and purposeful. Though she loved a surprise, she asked, "Why are we going to a cave?"

He turned to face her. "I need to catch my breath."

"I'm not sure what that means."

"There's a lot going on. I need to slow down so I can think." He pointed to a dark shadow against the rock face. "This is the entrance."

When she looked closer, she saw a narrow slit that was only as high as her shoulders. If she hadn't been standing right beside it, she wouldn't have noticed the entrance. She looked up at his broad chest. "How are you going to fit in there?"

"Carefully." He ducked down, took off his hat and turned on the flashlight.

After she wedged herself through the entry, she felt his hand on her arm as he pulled her forward and halted. With the flashlight beam, he swept the walls of a small chamber with a rock floor. The ceiling was just high enough for him to stand upright. The air was thick and moist…and warmer than outside. "Is this a hot spring?"

"Not hardly. The temperature in here is a steady fifty-three degrees, summer and winter." He guided her forward. "Be careful where you step. The footing is uneven."

He led her through the first chamber into a second room that was longer. The flashlight beam played across the wall and landed on a jagged row of stalagmites rising from the floor in weird milky formations. Other stones dripped down from the ceiling.

"It looks like teeth," she said, "like the teeth of a giant prehistoric monster."

"Listen," he said.

She cocked her ears and heard nothing but the beating of her own heart. "Perfect silence."

"Hold on to me." He wrapped his arm around her. "I'm going to turn off the flashlight."

She slipped her hand inside his jacket and pressed against him. Absolute darkness wrapped around them.

Chapter Ten

With the impenetrable darkness came a sense of disorientation. Brady held Sasha close to him. Though the interior of the cave was utterly black, he closed his eyes. He'd never practiced meditation, but he suspected it was something like this. An emptiness. A feeling of being suspended in space, not knowing which way was up and which was down.

Breathing slowly, he tried to rid his mind of chaos and confusion. Specifically, he wanted to erase the image of the dead woman stuffed inside the trunk.

"Brady?" Sasha's sweet voice called to him. "Are you all right?"

"I'm fine," he said, not wanting to alarm her.

There had been so much blood. Her pristine white jumpsuit had been soaked with it. Her lips were gray. Her cheeks sunken. Her eyes dull and vacant. The fingernails on one hand were broken. Had she been alive when he forced her into the trunk? Had she struggled?

He held Sasha tighter, absorbing the gentle warmth that radiated from her. Her arms were inside his jacket, embracing him. He leaned down and inhaled the ripe peach fragrance of her shampoo.

"You're so quiet," she said.

"Thinking." He couldn't release the image of death.

Maybe he wasn't meant to forget. Maybe he needed to be reminded, to keep that memory fresh throughout the investigation.

"Would you mind turning on the flashlight while you think?" she asked. "The dark is kind of creeping me out."

He turned on the light. In the glow, he looked down at her delicate features, her wide blue eyes and her rose-petal lips. Before the intention had fully formed in his mind, he was kissing those lips.

Her slender body nestled against him just the way he had imagined it would. Even through layers of clothing, they fit together perfectly. He glided his free hand around her throat to the nape of her neck, where his fingers tangled in her silky hair. He tasted her mouth again. So sweet.

He shouldn't be kissing her but had no regrets. When they separated, his gaze held hers for a long moment. In the damp, mysterious atmosphere of the cave, they shared a silent communication. The attraction that was building between them didn't need words.

His hand clasped hers, and he aimed the flashlight beam toward the end of the long room. "This goes back thirty feet, and then it links with another through a narrow split in the rock."

"Are we going there?" she asked.

"Not today. These caves twist and turn for a long distance. I've never been to the end."

"I'd like to come back and explore," she said.

"Maybe we will."

But now they needed to return to the real world. When he wriggled through the small opening leading from the cave, the late-afternoon sun seemed strangely cold and harsh. Out here they had very little protection from the brutal killer who had taken a woman's life. So far this investigation was reaping more questions than answers.

Brady straightened his shoulders. He had to make the best of a bad situation with a sheriff who couldn't tell his ass from a hole in the ground and a killer who always stayed several steps ahead. No matter how much he wished he'd been better trained for a homicide investigation, Brady had to work with the tools he'd been given.

"After we're done at the dude ranch," he said, "I want to go back to the hotel and look at those surveillance tapes. Our best chance of finding the killer is if you can identify him."

"I hope I can," she said.

"And I wouldn't mind talking through the investigation with Jacobson. He's got good insights."

"I've got insights," she said. "You can talk to me."

"I know. And you're smart."

"Smart and professional."

"But I don't want to drag you any deeper into this." His number-one priority was to protect her. "I don't suppose there's any way I could talk you into going back to Denver."

"And lose my job?" She shook her head. "I'm staying right here until the meetings are over."

In the SUV, he backed up, turned and drove back toward the road leading to Jim Birch's dude ranch. He couldn't help but notice that Sasha was staring at him. She was a chatty person who liked to talk things through, and he really hoped that she didn't feel compelled to discuss the meaning of that kiss in the cave. It had happened. As far as he was concerned, they should leave it right there.

When she cleared her throat, he braced himself. All he could tell her was the truth. He liked her a lot, and that kiss seemed like the right thing to do in the moment.

She said, "What do people do at a dude ranch?"

Relief surged through him. He liked her even more.

"They want the Old West experience. Riding horses and eating beans and burgers from a chuck wagon around a fire. The owner of this place, Jim Birch, plays a guitar and sings."

"Sounds like the Old West in a movie. Do real cowboys do any of those things?"

"I ride," he said. "I've eaten beans. And I even play the guitar a little."

He parked his SUV in a line of other vehicles at the side of a long bunkhouse. There seemed to be a lot of guests at the dude ranch. Together he and Sasha walked toward the main house, where Jim Birch and two other old cowboys were sitting on the front porch drinking from mugs. It was a little too chilly to be outside, and Brady guessed that Jim's wife had shooed the men out of the kitchen while she prepared dinner.

Jim rose to greet him. "I haven't seen you in a while. Is deputy work agreeing with you?"

"Can't complain."

"Sure you can." Jim Birch was big and tall and everything about him was boisterous, from his thick red muttonchop sideburns to his silver rodeo belt buckle the size of a serving platter. "I'd complain if I had to see Sheriff Ted McKinley every day. That man has the vision of a cross-eyed garden slug."

His buddies on the porch chuckled and raised their mugs. Brady figured they were drinking something stronger than coffee.

Jim gave Brady a hug and welcomed Sasha, telling her that she was as pretty as a sunflower in spring. Jim was known for having a way with the ladies. All the women loved him, but Brady knew for a fact that Jim had never betrayed his marriage vows. His wife—an energetic little woman who was as plain as a peahen—was the love of his life.

Brady said, "I saw a couple of your ATVs out in the field. Do you have many guests staying here?"

"Only one family. The rest are visitors." He lowered his voice. "You can tell your uncle Dooley that he's not the only one getting rich off the new development. I'm thinking of selling this place."

"Who's the buyer?"

"I've got a couple of buyers on the hook. One of them is kind of flaky and wants to turn the ranch into a sanctuary for unwanted house pets. The other is serious. I'm not supposed to say who he is until the deal is final, but he's one of the partners in the Arcadia project."

"Sam Moreno," Sasha said. "He wants to develop an ashram where his followers can live."

"How'd you guess that?"

"I work for the law firm handling the resort business."

"You're a lawyer?"

"Legal assistant," she said.

Jim patted her shoulder. "Smart and pretty. Brady should hang on to you."

"How'd you get to know Moreno?" Brady asked.

"I can tell you one thing," Jim said. "It wasn't from taking any of his seminars. That stuff is a truckload of hooey."

Brady agreed. He'd taken an immediate dislike to the smooth, handsome Moreno when he first met the guy, and that hostility deepened when he thought of the dude ranch being turned into a New Age enclave. "Has Moreno been visiting you this afternoon?"

"Him and a bunch of his people. They seem okay for city folks. They wear too much black for my taste, but they took to riding the ATVs like kids on a playground."

THEY FOLLOWED JIM into the house, where his wife provided steaming cups of strong coffee and a plate of sliced zucchini bread. She barely had time to say hello before she rushed back into the kitchen to deal with one of Moreno's people, who was making sure the food met all the organic standards the guru required.

Sitting at the dining room table with Jim Birch, Brady asked, "If you sell this place, what will you do?"

"For one thing, I'll quit worrying about paying my bills. It's been a rough couple of years with the economy slowing down and people cutting back on their vacations." He rested his elbows on the table and shrugged. "What's your uncle going to do?"

"I'm not sure." Brady looked toward Sasha. "I'll bet she can tell you more than I can."

"He won't quit ranching," she said. "He's made that clear from the very start."

"There you go," Jim said. "Maybe I'll go to work for Dooley. Wouldn't that be something? Us two codgers out riding herd."

Sasha excused herself from the table. "I just checked my phone, and I have a couple of messages I should answer."

As soon as she left the room, Jim gave him a grin and wiggled his eyebrows. "You're sweet on her."

"She's a witness."

"And a pretty young woman," he said. "Is there anybody else you're seeing right now?"

Brady glared at the grizzled old man with red sideburns. "Who do you think you are? Dr. Phil of the Wild West?"

"It's about time for you to settle down and start raising a family."

No way was he discussing his personal life with Jim

Birch. "I didn't see a for-sale sign on your property. How did Moreno know to get in touch with you?"

"I've been quietly shopping around. There's a couple of people from Denver who are interested. I talked to my real-estate lady this afternoon, and she thought she might be able to get the buyers into a bidding war."

"What's her name?"

"Andrea Tate."

She was Reinhardt's black-haired companion. An interesting link. "How long have you been working with her?"

"I met her a couple of years ago. She showed up when the Arcadia development was under way, looking for more property that could be used for condos."

The dude ranch and the acres attached to it wouldn't be suitable for skiers, who would want to be closer to the slopes. The drive from here on the road that followed Red Stone Creek was twenty minutes in good weather. And it would be a shame to tear down the big house and the barn, which were kept in good repair.

When Sasha came back into the room, her mouth was tight, and twin worry lines appeared between her eyebrows.

"That was the property manager at the condo," she said. "There's been a break-in."

SASHA WAS GLAD that Brady put her problem first. Though he had intended to wait at the dude ranch until he had a chance to question Moreno, they left immediately to survey the damage at the condo.

The route he took avoided the high road where the body had been found. Instead, the SUV zipped along a snow-plowed asphalt road that followed the winding path of a creek. The late-afternoon sunlight shimmered on the rushing water as it sliced through a landscape of bare cottonwoods and aspens. After two days of good weather, the snow had partially melted away, leaving the rocks bare.

Brady used the police radio on his console to contact the sheriff and tell him about the change in their plans. After a quick discussion, Sheriff McKinley decided to let the security company employed by the property manager investigate the break-in, dusting for fingerprints and picking up forensic clues.

Though Brady didn't look happy about the decision, he had no choice but to accept it. All the deputies working for the sheriff's department were busy at the crime scene or dealing with a three-vehicle accident on the highway. This small county wasn't equipped to handle complicated investigations.

"One more thing," the sheriff said over the radio. "We have an ID on the body. You were right. She's Lauren Robbins, age thirty-seven, from Denver."

"I'll stay in touch," Brady said.

When he ended the call, his jaw was tight. The moment of calm they'd experienced in the cave had been replaced by a new layer of tension. She wished she could do or say something to help him relax, but the situation seemed to become more and more frustrating.

The only bright moment had come when he'd kissed her. Holding her in the darkness, he'd been so amazingly gentle. At the same time, she'd felt the power of their attraction as though they were drawn together, as though they belonged together. She knew better than to expect another kiss. Not while there was so much going on. He glanced over at her. "How are you doing? Are you okay?"

"I've been better." She looked down at the laptop she held on her lap, thinking that she should contact Damien and tell him what had happened. "What if you had dropped me off at the condo instead of taking me with you to the crime scene?"

His brow tightened. "I don't want to think about it."

"Was the intruder after me?"

"The break-in wasn't a coincidence," he said. "I don't care what the sheriff says or how stretched our manpower is. Until this is over, you are my assignment. I'm your bodyguard 24/7. Remember? That's our deal."

Did that mean he was going to stay at the condo tonight? In spite of a logical ration of fear, her heart took a happy little leap. Spending the night with Brady wouldn't be the worst thing that had ever happened to her.

"Tell me about the phone call from the property manager," he said.

"She said that the security company notified her as soon as the alarm went off."

"When was that?"

"She gave me a precise time, but I don't remember what it was. A few minutes before she called me." Sasha liked to have things right. She should have written down the time. "She went directly to the condo. There isn't any damage that she noticed, but she's waiting for me to get there before she files a report."

"How did the intruder get in?"

"They picked the lock on the balcony door." She clutched her laptop to her chest. "I'm glad I had my computer and the Arcadia files with me."

Brady glanced over at her. "To enter through the balcony, the intruder would have had to climb up the side of the building to reach the third floor."

"That's crazy," she said. "Who would do that? A ninja?"

In spite of the tension, he chuckled. "Yeah, that's it. You're being stalked by ninjas."

And she hoped they'd left some kind of clue.

Chapter Eleven

At the condo, Sasha spoke to the property manager and took a look at the balcony door. Since the lock had been picked, the door didn't show any damage. If the security firm hadn't received an electronic alert, she might never have known that the place had been broken into.

Brady was talking to the security men, who were shining some kind of blue light on the wall, dusting for fingerprints and inspecting the side of the building where the intruder had climbed from one floor to the next. Now was her chance to take her laptop into the bedroom for a private conversation with Damien. She placed the computer on a small table by the window and sat in a chair facing it. The bed would have been more comfortable, but she needed to look professional.

Every time she talked to Damien, it seemed as if she was telling him about another problem. Her job was to avoid negative situations, not to create disasters. The least she could do was present a neat appearance. She even took a moment to brush her hair and apply a fresh coat of lipstick.

It took a few minutes to pull her boss out of a meeting with the Westfield family. When his face popped up on the screen, he looked angry.

"I'm busy, Sasha. What is it?"

She didn't apologize for interrupting him. He needed to know about damage to corporate property; her call was appropriate. "The condo was broken into."

"What? Why?"

She was painfully aware that the break-in could be blamed on her involvement in the murder investigation, but she didn't want to spin it that way. "Nothing appears to be stolen, but I'm not familiar with everything that's in here. Could they have been looking for something valuable?"

"You mean like a safe? Or documents?" He frowned as he thought. "Not as far as I know. I'll check with the other partners at the firm."

"When I fill out the insurance claim, I'll reserve the right to add more items until after you've had a chance to make an inventory." She'd handled forms like this before. It shouldn't be a problem. "The intruder came through the balcony door, and the lock isn't damaged. Should I have it changed anyway?"

"I want a dead bolt installed," he said. "And I want it done this afternoon."

"I'll inform the property manager." So far, so good. She might be able to end this conversation without mentioning the murder. "I'll take care of it."

"Wait a minute," he said. "Were you there when the break-in occurred?"

"No, sir, I wasn't."

"Where were you?"

The accusing tone in his voice irritated her. Shouldn't he be concerned about her physical safety? She tried not to glare at his image on the computer screen. "I was at a crime scene. The police discovered the body."

"Oh, yes." His upper lip curled in a sneer. "Is this about the apparent murder you witnessed?"

"It's a real murder." She could accept his dismissive

attitude toward her, but she wouldn't allow him to belittle the horrible crime that had been committed. "She was killed in a callous and cold-blooded manner. They found her remains stuffed inside a piece of luggage. Her name was Lauren Robbins."

His eyes widened and he drew back from the screen. "What was that name again?"

"Robbins, Lauren Robbins. She's thirty-seven and lived in Denver."

"She's Lloyd Reinhardt's ex-wife."

Stunned, she felt her jaw drop. "No way."

"Damn it."

"Did you know her?"

"An attractive woman with long black hair, very classy. She looks a lot like her cousin, who is also in real estate. In fact, I think they worked together for a while."

"Andrea Tate." She choked on the name. "Her cousin is Andrea Tate."

"Yes," he said.

"She's here in Arcadia, staying at the hotel. She's dating Mr. Reinhardt."

Damien's face got bigger as he leaned close to the screen. "Listen to me, Sasha. Our firm can't be involved with this investigation. You need to back away from this as quickly as possible."

She wished that she could. "That won't be possible."

"Why the hell not?"

"I have to cooperate with the police."

"That doesn't mean you have to be in their pocket. Stay as far away from the investigation as you can."

What about Brady? What about her need for a bodyguard? She wanted to keep her job, but she wouldn't risk her life to stay employed. Her brain clicked through possibilities. "Do you think Mr. Reinhardt will be a suspect?"

"Cops always go after the ex-husband."

"Then it's important for me to stay on their good side," she said. "I witnessed the murder, and I know Reinhardt didn't do it. I'm his alibi."

WHEN SASHA STUMBLED out of the bedroom, she'd changed out of her business suit, which was much the worse for wear after hiking along the dirt road and climbing into a cave. She'd slipped into comfortable hiking shoes, jeans and a maroon ski sweater with a snowflake pattern on the yoke.

Damien hadn't fired her, but she could feel it coming. Her neck was on the chopping block and the axe was about to fall. Not only would she be losing a job, but she couldn't count on a good recommendation. Somehow she had to get back in her boss's good graces. Finding the murderer would be a good start. Damien couldn't fire her if she proved that Reinhardt was innocent…if he was innocent and hadn't hired someone to kill his ex-wife.

She approached the dining table in front of the balcony window where Brady was talking to a guy wearing a black baseball cap with Arcadia Mountain Security stenciled across the front. If she'd been alone with Brady, she would have jumped into his arms and clung to him while she poured out her fears about losing her job.

But there were other people around, and she needed to behave in an appropriate manner. First she spoke to the property manager and arranged to have a dead bolt installed on the balcony door. Sasha also explained that she'd like to wait before filing an insurance claim, per Damien's request.

The property manager made a note in her pad and asked, "Will you continue to stay at the condo?"

It was a good question, one that she couldn't answer for

sure. The place had already been broken into; it might be targeted again. "Let's assume that I am. Is there any way you could stock the refrigerator? Nothing fancy, just cold cuts and bread and fruit."

"Of course," she said. "Damien has a standard list of food supplies when he comes up here, but he didn't mention anything for this trip."

Thanks, Damien. "His standard list will be fine."

While the property manager hurried off to do her duties, Sasha sat at the table beside Brady. Her desire to be close to him was so strong that she actually leaned toward him and bumped her shoulder against his arm. He glanced toward her and flashed a dimpled grin. "I think we finally got lucky."

"How so?"

He introduced the security guy. "This is Max. We went to high school together."

Reaching over, she shook Max's hand. "Nice to meet you."

"Max has already done the fingerprinting and found nothing. Not a big surprise. When we checked out the balcony, we found signs that the intruder climbed from one level to the next, and he used some kind of grappling hook."

"I've never seen anything like it before," Max said. "It's good to know about. We'll make sure all our properties have better locks on the balcony doors."

"If the sheriff had been handling this, it would have taken hours, waiting for one of the two guys who handle our forensics." Brady leaned his elbows on the table. "I don't mean to bad-mouth Sheriff McKinley, but every deputy in the department should be equipped with simple forensic tools and trained on how to use them."

"Things are changing around here," Max said. "A lot

of us think it's time to elect a new sheriff. Maybe some-body like you, Brady."

"Yeah, yeah," he said as he brushed the suggestion aside. "Even better news is that Max's security firm has surveillance video of the balconies. We're waiting for it to be transferred to his digital screen."

"So we can actually see the guy breaking in?"

"That's right."

He laced his fingers together, put his hands behind his head and leaned back in his chair, looking pleased with himself. She hated to burst this bubble of contentment, but she'd already decided to tell him what Damien had said. The victim's relationship to Reinhardt and Andrea wasn't privileged information, and Brady would find out soon enough even if she didn't speak up.

"I mentioned the name of the victim to Damien Lough-lin."

"That's okay. It's about to become common knowledge."

A lazy grin lifted the corners of his mouth. The way his gaze lingered on her face made her wonder if he'd been having the same thoughts about touching and being close. She hoped so. She wanted another kiss, just to make sure the first one hadn't been a fluke.

She blurted, "Lauren Robbins was Reinhardt's ex-wife. Her cousin is Andrea Tate."

Brady snapped to attention. In the blink of an eye, he lost the lazy cowboy image as he pushed away from the table and took out his cell phone. "I'd better inform the sheriff."

The thought of paunchy old McKinley wiggling his mustache at the ferocious Lloyd Reinhardt worried her. Reinhardt would eat the sheriff alive. "It might be best if you're the one who breaks the news to Reinhardt."

"I'll bet that news has already been broken. You told Damien, Reinhardt's lawyer."

Obviously, Damien would call his top client to inform him of the investigative storm cloud headed in his direction. She hadn't seen the problem from that perspective. "I shouldn't have said anything."

As Brady walked away to make his phone call, he shrugged. "It's okay. You didn't know."

Once again she'd stumbled into a mess. Balancing between the police and the lawyers was a tricky business. Investigating leads would be even more complicated. She'd seen the killer and could say for certain that it wasn't Lloyd Reinhardt. He hadn't wielded the knife that had killed his ex-wife, but he surely could have hired the man who had.

AFTER BRADY FINISHED his call to the sheriff, he took his seat at the table to watch the surveillance video from Max's security company. The fact that Reinhardt and his companion had been part of the victim's life didn't bother him as much as their connection to Sasha. Less than an hour ago, he'd found Sam Moreno in an area where Sasha thought she'd seen a stalker. Now Reinhardt was a suspect. It felt as if danger was inching closer, reaching out to touch her. The killer knew who she was and what she had seen.

When he glanced at her, he saw the worry in her eyes. Quietly, he said, "Don't let this get to you. I'll keep you safe."

"I feel bad for telling Damien."

"That's not your problem," he said.

"I wasn't planning to say anything to him. The words just kind of spilled out."

Max placed the computer screen in front of them. "Ready?"

"Okay," she said as she sat up straight in her chair and

focused those pretty blue eyes on the screen. "How does this work?"

"On most of the properties we're hired to protect, we set up stationary digital surveillance cameras on several angles. They record continuously, have night vision and store twelve terabytes of data. The feed for this camera was accessed at our office and transferred here to me."

"That's what I'm talking about," Brady said. He loved gadgets. "The sheriff's office could use a bunch of these."

"To do what?" she asked.

"We could put them at banks or high-crime areas." Referring to a "high-crime area" in this quiet little county might be exaggerating a bit. Most of their arrests took place outside the two taverns at the edge of town. "Or on the traffic lights."

"And how many traffic lights are there in Arcadia?"

"Five," he said. "Every one of them could have a camera."

The screen came to life, showing a wide high-resolution picture of the back side of the condo building. The trees bobbed in the wind. There was no one around.

"I'll zoom in," Max said.

The picture tightened on the three balconies in a vertical row. The floor of the lowest was over an attached garage, about ten feet off the snow-covered ground. A tall pine tree partially hid the view.

Brady saw a figure dressed in black wearing a ski mask. "There he is."

With quick, agile movements, the intruder tossed a hook attached to a rope over the banister on the first balcony and climbed up. He used similar moves to get to the third floor. His entire climb took only about ten minutes.

"He's good," Sasha said. "I thought I was kidding about ninjas."

"Could be a rock climber," Max said. "Looks like he's wearing that kind of shoe."

Brady was impressed with both the skill of the intruder's ascent and the speed he showed in picking the lock. "This isn't the first time he's done this. When it comes to break-ins, this guy is a pro."

Almost as quickly as he'd entered, he appeared on the balcony again.

"It doesn't look like he's carrying anything," Max said. "He didn't come here to commit a robbery."

Brady knew why the intruder had made this daring entry into the condo. He was after Sasha. His intention had been to find her and silence her.

On his climb down, the figure in black slipped at the lowest balcony and took a fall. When he rose and moved away from the building, he was limping.

"I hope his leg is broken," Sasha said.

Brady looked toward Max. "Did your cameras pick up his escape? Did you see a vehicle?"

"Sorry, there wasn't anything else."

This footage was enough to convince Brady of one thing. Sasha was in very real danger. There was no way she could stay at this condo by herself.

Chapter Twelve

Brady had insisted that Sasha pack her suitcase and leave the condo. It hadn't taken much to convince her that she'd be safer somewhere else. That video of the guy in black creeping up the wall like a spider was all the motivation she needed.

The best plan, in his eyes, would be for her to come home with him. Not the most appropriate situation, but the most secure. As they drove to the hotel to look at the security tapes, he mentioned that possibility.

"Maybe you should spend the night with me…at my cabin." A warm flush crawled up his throat, and he was glad that the afternoon sunlight had faded to dusk. He didn't want her to see him turning red. "I have an extra bedroom."

"Wouldn't that be a problem for you? Since I'm involved in the investigation."

"It's not like you're a suspect. I wouldn't be harboring a fugitive." People would talk, but he didn't mind the wagging tongues and finger-pointing. Maybe she did. "Your boss might not approve."

"He's not happy with me." She exhaled a long sigh. "I'll be lucky to get out of this investigation without being fired."

"You haven't done anything wrong."

"Actually, it was a big mistake for me to pick up a pair of binoculars and look through somebody's window."

"If you hadn't witnessed the murder, we wouldn't have learned about it for a long time. The killer cleaned up after himself too well."

"You would have found out today," she said. "The cross-country skiers would still have discovered the body."

"Maybe or maybe not," he said. "Because we were poking around last night, the killer might have been in a hurry to dispose of the body. He might have chosen the most expedient dumping site rather than the best place to hide that steamer trunk."

For a moment, Brady put himself in the killer's shoes. At first the murder had gone according to his plan. He'd stabbed the victim and dumped her into the trunk without spilling a single drop of blood on the floor. After he'd cleaned up the room, throwing everything into the trunk, he'd wheeled the steamer trunk into the hall and down to the parking garage. If anyone had seen him, it wasn't a problem. Nobody would question a man with a suitcase in a hotel.

The killer must have been pleased with himself, thinking he'd gotten away with a nearly perfect crime. And then, less than an hour after the attack, an eyewitness appeared and a deputy started asking questions. The killer's careful planning had failed. He must have been reeling from shock.

"If we ever catch this guy," Brady said, "it will be because you happened to be looking in the right place at the wrong time."

She reached across the console and touched his arm. "That makes me feel better."

Her touch reminded him of the other reason he wanted her to stay at his cabin tonight. He needed another kiss. To be honest, he craved more than kissing. He wanted Sasha in his bed. Every moment he spent with her heightened that longing. He had memorized the shape of her face and the way her eyes crinkled when she smiled. His ears were tuned to the warm cadence of her voice and her light, rippling laughter. He wanted to hold her close and inhale the peachy scent of her shampoo. No matter how inappropriate, he wanted her. It was taking a full-on exertion of willpower to hold himself in check.

He swallowed hard. "What do you say? My cabin?"

"I won't stay at the condo."

He held his breath. "And?"

"I should get a room at the hotel." At least she didn't sound happy about it. "If Jacobson has all the surveillance in place, it ought to be safe."

Rejected. He decided not to take it personally. "I'll arrange it."

"I'd rather be with you."

He knew that. A couple of times today, he'd caught her looking at him with a sultry heat in her eyes. "My offer stands."

"I've got to be professional, to concentrate on my job."

"I understand. Don't worry about the cost of the hotel. The sheriff's department can spring for a room to protect a witness."

When he drove toward valet parking outside the Gateway Hotel, he spotted the sheriff's SUV. "McKinley is already here, probably questioning Reinhardt."

She groaned. "That's not going to go well."

"I think we should join them."

"We?" Her voice shot up a couple of octaves. "You mean both of us?"

"Andrea just lost her cousin. She might appreciate having another woman to talk to."

"But there's a confidentiality thing," Sasha said. "I'm not a lawyer, but the firm I work for represents Reinhardt and the other investors. If they say anything to me in private, I should tell Damien first."

"Not a problem. We'll make sure you're not alone when you talk to them." He parked the SUV and turned to her. "That's a good rule. Until we know who hired the ninja, you can't be alone with any of the partners or their people."

"You suspect all of them? Even Katie Cook?"

"She could have hired a killer."

"But why? What's her motive?"

"Something to do with real estate," he said. "Didn't she have two male skaters with her? Two guys wearing black?"

"And sequins," Sasha said. "Not many ninjas wear sequins."

He wouldn't have been surprised by anything. This investigation had taken more twists and turns than the road over Vail Pass.

WHEN SHE AND Brady entered Reinhardt's suite on the concierge level of the Gateway Hotel, she could feel tension shimmering in the air. Sheriff McKinley and another deputy stood in the middle of the room, holding their hats by the brims and looking confused, as though they couldn't decide if they should apologize to Reinhardt or arrest him.

Pacing back and forth, Reinhardt was easier to read. He was outraged with a capital *O*. As soon as he saw Sasha, he came to a stop and jabbed his index finger at her.

"She can straighten this out," he said. "She works for my lawyer, and my lawyer told me not to say a damn thing to the cops until he gets here. Tell them, Sasha."

Heads swiveled, and all eyes turned toward her. Though trained as a paralegal and familiar with these simple legal parameters, Sasha wasn't accustomed to having anyone seek her opinion. It was time for her to rise to the occasion.

She inhaled a breath and spoke clearly. "Mr. Reinhardt is correct. He's not required to talk to the police without having his lawyer present."

"When's the lawyer getting here?" the sheriff asked.

"Tomorrow." She *hoped* Damien would be here tomorrow.

"What about you?" McKinley was almost whining. His mustache drooped dejectedly. "You're present. Doesn't that mean he can talk to me now?"

"I'm not an attorney, just an assistant."

"You're wasting your time," Reinhardt said. "I haven't done anything wrong. Lauren was my ex-wife, but that doesn't mean I didn't care about her. When you came in here and told me that she was murdered, it hurt."

"Shut up, Lloyd." Andrea rose from the chair where she'd been curled up with a wide-bottomed whiskey glass cradled in both hands. "You were over Lauren."

"I didn't hate her."

"Probably not." Andrea wobbled on her feet. "You gave her a good settlement and always sent the alimony checks on time. Lauren was the bad guy in your divorce. I loved my cousin, but she spent money like a wild woman. Wouldn't listen to anybody."

Sasha could see that Andrea was on the verge of a crash. When she got closer to her, she caught a whiff of strong alcohol. "I'm sorry for your loss. Is there anyone I can contact for you?"

"My mom." A tear skidded down her tanned cheek. "Lauren's parents are dead. My mom is the one who handles all the family business. She lives in Texas, but she'll hop a plane and be here quick."

"Come with me into the bedroom," Sasha said, "and we'll make that phone call."

"Oh, God, there's going to be a funeral. Lauren would want an open casket. How did she look? No, don't tell me. I don't want to know." Andrea plunked back into the chair and held up her glass. "I need more of this."

Sasha didn't argue. She took the glass and went across the suite to the wet bar, where a bottle of amber whiskey stood on the counter. All the men were watching her, and she sensed their uneasiness when it came to comforting a nearly hysterical woman. For Sasha this kind of situation wasn't a big emotional stretch. She came from a big family where somebody was always in crisis.

Though she hadn't planned it, she was in charge. "I have an idea about how we can handle the legal situation. I can contact Mr. Loughlin on my computer, and he can take part in the talks with Mr. Reinhardt."

"Do it," Reinhardt said.

After delivering the drink to Andrea, she whipped open her briefcase and set up the communication with Damien. The sheriff, the other deputy and Reinhardt sat around the table with the computerized version of Damien overseeing the conversation.

Sasha returned to Andrea. "Let's make your phone call."

"She didn't deserve to die." The strong, attractive lines of her face seemed to be melting. "Lauren did some real stupid things, but she wasn't a bad person."

Sasha signaled for Brady to join her. "I could use some help here."

Together they guided the black-haired woman across the suite and into the bedroom, where she threw herself facedown on the bed and sobbed. Sitting beside her, Sasha patted her back and murmured gentle reassurances. When

Brady started to leave, she waved at him and mouthed the words *You have to stay.*

He shook his head and silently said, *No.*

She couldn't let him go, not with the confidentiality problem. She mouthed, *Please, please, please.*

Scowling, he leaned his back against the wall and folded his arms across his chest.

When the storm of weeping had subsided, Sasha said, "Brady is going to stay in here with us, okay?"

"Whatever." Andrea levered herself up to a sitting position but was still slouched over so her hair fell forward and covered her face. "Brady's okay. I've heard about him."

"From Jim Birch," Sasha guessed.

"He's a sweet old guy." She inhaled a ragged breath and pushed her hair back. In spite of her tears, she was still attractive. "He always tells me I look like an Apache maiden, wild and beautiful."

The colorful compliment sounded exactly like something Jim Birch would say. "Have you known him long?"

"I've been working with him for a couple of years. I met him when I came up here with Lloyd to check on the development at Arcadia. I had time to explore while Lloyd was fussing around with the construction crews."

"Was he still married to Lauren then?"

"No, they've been divorced for five years. Lauren was actually working with me when I first started talking to Jim Birch about selling his property. She tried to steal his listing away from me, the bitch." Her hand flew up to cover her mouth. "I shouldn't say that now that she's dead."

"I won't tell."

Sasha wrapped her arm around the other woman, encouraging her to lean against her shoulder. She hoped the physical contact would bring some comfort.

Sasha couldn't get over the similarities between Andrea

and the victim. The hair. The sense of style. It wasn't surprising that Reinhardt had gone from one cousin to the other. "Are you and Mr. Reinhardt in a serious relationship?"

"We're just dating. He's a little old for me, but I like powerful men. And I've been attracted to Lloyd for a long time, even when he was still married to Lauren." She swiped at her swollen eyes. "Brady, can you get me an aspirin from the bathroom?"

Though he did as he was asked, he stayed within earshot, and she was glad that he did. She figured that they were going to get more information from Andrea than the sheriff would uncover in his interrogation of Reinhardt.

"Don't get me wrong," Andrea said. "I never made a move on Lloyd when he was married. That's not how I roll."

"Dating married men is never a good idea."

"Not like you and Damien," Andrea said. "Wasn't he voted one of Denver's most eligible bachelors?"

"Not my type." Sasha didn't want to go through this song and dance again. "We aren't dating."

"But you were going to be together at the corporate condo."

"I'm moving to the hotel tonight."

Andrea accepted three aspirin tablets and a glass of water from Brady. She looked from him to Sasha and back again. "Poor Damien. I think you found something more interesting in the local scenery."

Sasha glanced over at Brady. She was anxious to shift the topic back toward the investigation. "Tell me about you and Lloyd."

"We started spending more time together about three months ago. It was just after Lauren tried to pull a fast one and steal Jim Birch. She had a buyer who was perfect for

the dude-ranch property, and she took him up for a showing without telling me. When I found out, I started a bidding war using my contact with Sam Moreno."

"That was three months ago?"

"Give or take." Andrea swallowed the aspirin.

The timing was interesting. At the investors' meetings,
Moreno had never spoken of his intention to buy the dude-
ranch property. The first mention of his ashram was today.
For some reason, he'd kept this plan a secret.

Reinhardt had the most to lose from Sam Moreno breaking away from the group to set up his own development, as
he was the one the business partners had agreed would su-
pervise all new construction. Was it pure coincidence that
he'd started dating Andrea at that time? Was he using her?

She gave Andrea a smile. "Are you ready to make that
call to your mom?"

"Might as well get it over with."

"If you want, I'll stay with you."

She tossed her head, and her long black hair fell back
over her shoulders. "I'll do it alone."

"Don't hesitate to give me a call if you want to talk."
Sasha rose from the bed. "Again, you have my deepest
condolences."

She was at the bedroom door when Andrea called to
her. "Here's a little something that you and Brady might
be interested in knowing."

"What's that?"

"The person in the bidding war with Moreno was none
other than Virgil P. Westfield."

That little tidbit was more than unexpected. It was a
bombshell. Sasha knew that several of the investors had
ties to Westfield but hadn't suspected that they were actually doing business with him. At ninety-two, how much
business did he undertake? "Was he Lauren's client?"

"You bet he was. She had that old man tied up in knots."

And now that old man was dead.

Sasha caught a glint of awareness in Andrea's eye. The supposedly grief-stricken cousin knew exactly how important this information was to the investigation. Apparently, Andrea wasn't above doing a bit of scheming on her own.

Chapter Thirteen

Returning to the meeting at hand, Sasha felt the need to inform the computerized version of Damien that she needed to view some surveillance tapes in the hotel security office. As usual, he brushed her off, telling her that he still had important matters to discuss with Reinhardt and the sheriff.

How typical! His conversation with the others was important. And her role as an eyewitness—the only witness—wasn't.

She held her tongue as she and Brady went past the concierge desk on their way to the elevator. There was no sign of ice-cold Anita, the concierge, and Sasha was glad. The last thing she needed was another condescending comment. When she hit the button to summon the elevator, she couldn't contain her frustration for one more moment. She exploded. "I can't believe this."

"What?"

"Damien didn't tell me that Mr. Westfield was working with Lauren Robbins. Those should have been the first words out of his mouth."

"Are you sure he knew?"

She'd never been more sure of anything in her life. "Westfield was one of his big clients. If he was planning to buy a huge parcel of mountain property, Damien would know everything about it."

"Maybe he didn't think it was important."

"Don't you dare defend him!" She hit the elevator button again. "I've been doing the best I can in a messy situation, and my boss is holding back information, treating me like a lackey. Which, I suppose, is how he sees me. I'm *not* another attorney, not a colleague. I'm just the girl who gets coffee."

"Hey." He held up a hand to stop her rant. "I just watched you take charge with a sheriff, two deputies and a billionaire developer. You're doing a hell of a good job."

Those were exactly the words she needed to hear. Together they entered the elevator. The instant the doors whooshed closed, she went up on her tiptoes, threw her arms around his neck and kissed him hard. With his hands at her waist, he anchored her against his hard, muscled body.

Though she had initiated the kiss, he took charge. His mouth was firm and supple, not at all sloppy. When his tongue penetrated her lips, he set off an electric chain reaction. Her entire body trembled. Her heart raced.

Too soon the elevator doors opened on the first floor. She gave a frantic little gasp as she pulled herself together and stepped away from him.

Standing directly outside the elevator was Grant Jacobson. His stern features were lit with a huge grin.

"Let me guess," Brady said. "The surveillance in the elevators is operational."

"And I can transfer the picture to this portable screen." He held up a flat device slightly larger than a cell phone. "Too bad I'm not in the blackmail business."

"It's nice to see you again," Sasha said. She was trying

her best not to be embarrassed…and failing. The thrills hadn't stopped. Her mouth tingled. If her lipstick hadn't already been worn off, it would have been smeared across her face.

Jacobson chuckled. "Oh, but the pleasure was all mine."

"Did you have some surveillance for me to look at?"

"Right this way."

There were desks, computers, filing cabinets and a large wall safe in the front area of the hotel security area. Through another door was an array of screens and graphics that displayed every inch of Gateway property.

"We're wired," he said. "Every public space, all the hallways and the parking lots are covered. Nothing happens here that I don't notice."

"I'm impressed," she said. "You got this done in a day?"

"It's amazing how fast problems go away when you throw handfuls of money at them."

Brady meandered through the desks with separate consoles, occasionally leaning down to check out various switches and dials. He stood in front of the big screen in the front of the room where several camera feeds were playing simultaneously. "Nice stuff."

"Top-of-the-line."

"Later I want a detailed tour. But right now we're in kind of a hurry."

"Give me the time and the place you want to look at," Jacobson said. "I'll pull up the relevant camera feed on the big screen."

"Front lobby," he said. As he guessed at the time, she realized that all this had happened in a twenty-four-hour time span. She had witnessed a murder, had had her life threatened, was probably going to lose her job and had kissed an incredible man…twice. It hardly seemed possible that her life had changed so radically in one day.

A split-screen picture appeared. Last night there had been two cameras in the lobby, both showing wide views. Right away she spotted herself and Brady standing together behind the check-in counter. If she recalled correctly, the hotel manager had been giving them a lecture on the key-card system and how it worked.

She looked at herself on the screen. The highlights in her hair looked great, but there wasn't a lick of styling, just messy curls, and her clothes looked as if she'd gotten dressed in the dark. Standing beside Brady, she seemed petite and maybe a little timid. On the other hand, he was confident, strong and altogether terrific—a movie star with his big shoulders and his cowboy hat. It was hard to take her eyes off him, but she glanced around at the other people milling in the lobby. None of them seemed particularly suspicious, but she recalled the creepy feeling of apprehension, as though someone was watching her.

"I don't see him," she said.

"Keep watching," Jacobson said. He froze the picture. A laser pointer appeared in his hand and he aimed the red dot at a man who was talking on his cell phone. "How about this guy? He seems to be standing around for no reason."

She shook her head. "He's too tall."

For another ten minutes, she watched people coming and going, stopping beside the statue of Artemis the huntress, meeting and saying goodbye. Nothing stood out. It had been a long shot to think that she'd see the killer strolling through the lobby, but she had hoped for an easy solution.

Behind her back, Brady was telling Jacobson about the break-in at the condo. "Climbed up the wall like a ninja and picked the lock in two minutes flat."

"Sounds like a pro," Jacobson said.

"Exactly what I said."

"You're not going to let her go back there alone, are you?"

"She thought it would be best if she stayed at the hotel."

Sasha wanted to interrupt and tell them that she'd changed her mind. Spending the night with Brady sounded like a wonderful idea. From a logical standpoint, it made sense because the meeting tomorrow morning was at Dooley's place. From an emotional perspective, she wanted to take those kisses to the next level.

Usually, she wasn't so quick to fall into a man's arms and allow herself to be swept away. The days of Trashy Sasha had made her wary, and she hated the way other people were so quick to judge. Even Andrea thought she was sleeping with her boss.

But Brady was different. He was a decent man and would never purposely do anything to hurt her. Frankly, she wouldn't mind if rumors started. He was someone she'd be proud to be with.

Before she could speak up, Jacobson and Brady had arranged for her room at the Gateway. Jacobson guaranteed her safety and promised to have one of his men regularly patrol her floor.

As they made their way back to the concierge level to pick up her computer, she thought she might remind Brady of his duties as a bodyguard and hint that he might want to stay in her hotel room tonight…just to be sure she was safe. But she didn't want to push too hard.

Computer in tow, they entered her appointed room. It wasn't fancy, just a very nice suite with windows facing the ski slope, where the snow machines were now working full blast. She pulled the curtain and turned toward him.

Brady wasn't sidling around the bed. He was much too masculine to be shy, but he seemed to be avoiding the largest piece of furniture in the room as he leaned his hip against the dresser. "I'll be back tomorrow morning to pick you up for the meeting," he said.

"You don't have to. I can ride in the van with the others."

"I want you to stay away from the investors," he said. "I didn't much like these people before, but now they're all suspects."

"It's crazy, isn't it? I mean, what are the odds? I witness a murder and it turns out that the people I'm working with are suspects."

"I would have said the same thing, but I checked with Jacobson. This week, before the grand opening, over half the people staying at the hotel are connected with the resort partners. They're employees or consultants or independent contractors."

"Or minions," she said, thinking of Moreno.

"He's got a mob of followers."

She peeled off her jacket and tossed it over a chair. Sitting on the edge of the bed, she took off her boots. Though they were comfortable shoes, taking them off felt like heaven. She stretched her feet out and wiggled her toes. "Uncle Dooley isn't a suspect."

"Don't be so sure. Virgil P. Westfield has been around for a long time. Dooley might know him." Brady grinned. "But my uncle isn't a subtle man. If he had a beef with Westfield or our victim, he'd come after them with six-guns blazing."

"What about Katie Cook?"

"She knew Westfield, and she was real interested in the status of the police investigation into his death."

A thought occurred to her. "Could these two deaths be related?"

"It's possible." He shrugged. "But we don't know for sure that Westfield was murdered. Did Damien mention anything to you?"

"Not much." Her boss didn't talk things over with her—not even the legal issues related to the partners and their meetings. "As far as he's concerned, I'm a tape recorder with legs. My job is to listen and keep track of what's being said. Not to think for myself."

"I'd like to hear your opinion."

Talking about the murders was draining all the sexiness out of the room, which was probably for the best. Though she hadn't given up on more kissing, she liked the part of their relationship where they talked to each other.

Hopping off the bed, she went to the chair where she'd dropped her jacket and sat. "If both of these people were murdered within a day of each other, it seems like there has to be a connection."

"The only thing we know is that they were working together in a bidding war for the dude-ranch property."

"Lauren might have been involved in other real estate purchases with him," she said. "Mr. Westfield made his fortune buying and selling commercial properties in Denver. He owned much of the land where the Tech Center is now located."

"His work was similar to what Reinhardt does."

"You're right." She hadn't made that connection before because Westfield and Reinhardt had the kind of profession that didn't really fit a category. "Lauren Robbins must have learned all about that buying and selling when she was married to Reinhardt. Being part of Westfield's operation was a natural step for her."

When Brady took off his cowboy hat and raked his fingers through his unruly brown hair, it was all she could do not to reach out and touch him. Talking was interesting and even productive, but she was itching to get closer. The light reflecting from his hazel eyes enticed her. If she gave in to her desires, she'd fly across the hotel room and into his arms.

"Do you remember," Brady asked, "what Andrea said about her cousin having the old man wrapped around her finger?"

She nodded. "That makes me think their relationship wasn't strictly business."

"Was Westfield married?"

"His third wife died four years ago."

If Lauren Robbins was aiming to be the next Mrs. Virgil P. Westfield, that would be a whole other motive for murder. No matter how vigorous Mr. Westfield was, the man was ninety-two years old. His heirs wouldn't be happy if he married again.

"How about kids?" Brady asked. "Did he have children?"

"Never had any of his own. His greatest love was for his cats. He always had five or six running around the mansion, and he built an incredible cat condo that went up two stories. They were all strays." She remembered a pleasant afternoon with the old man while he discussed a property sale with Damien. They drank tea and the cats had cream in matching saucers. "He used to say that the cats were his real family."

"What's going to happen to his inheritance?"

"He has a nephew who works for the family foundation and is his primary heir. But there's a big chunk of change set aside for a cat shelter."

Brady grinned. "That's a man who goes his own way. I like that."

"I liked him, too."

A stillness crept into the room. Her sweater seemed too warm. Her clothing too confining. She couldn't keep her gaze from drifting toward the king-size bed, which seemed even bigger and more dominating. She wished they could lie beside each other, not necessarily to do anything else. Yeah, sure, who was she trying to kid? She wanted the whole experience with Brady.

He moved away from the dresser. "I should be going."

Silently, she begged him to stay. Could she ask that of him? What if he said no? Not knowing what to say, she stammered, "I g-g-guess I'll see you in the morning."

He was at the door. His hand rested on the knob. "As soon as I leave, flip the latch on the door. Don't let anybody else in the room. Promise me."

"I'll be careful."

He opened the door. "Pleasant dreams."

As she watched the door close behind him, the air went out of her body, and she deflated like a leftover balloon at a party. Was it too late for her to run down the hall and tackle him before he got into the elevator? She bounced to her feet but didn't take a step. She wasn't going to chase him down. She'd missed her chance for tonight.

Following his instruction, she flipped the latch on her door, protecting herself from accidental intrusions by maids and purposeful assaults from ninjas. Nobody would come after her in the hotel, would they? Jacobson had surveillance *everywhere*. She was safe.

On the way to the bathroom, she peeled off her sweater. Underneath, she wore a thermal T-shirt, and she got rid of that, too. What she needed was a nice long soak in the tub, and then she'd fall into that giant bed. Stripped down to her underwear, she heard a knock on the door to her room. Her heart leaped. Was it Brady coming back? She could only hope that he'd gotten down to his SUV, realized that he needed to spend the night with her and returned.

She grabbed an oversize terry-cloth robe from a hook in the bathroom and dashed to the door. On her tiptoes, she peeked through the fish-eye.

It was Sam Moreno.

Chapter Fourteen

Panic bubbled up inside her. Sasha's fingertips rested on the door. Only this thin barrier separated her from a man who might have plotted two murders. And now he was coming for her. When he knocked again, she jumped backward and clutched the front of her bathrobe.

"Sasha, it's me, Sam Moreno. I wanted to talk to you."

"This isn't…" She heard the tremor in her voice and started over. She didn't want him to know she was scared. "This isn't a good time."

"It's important."

The logical side of her brain—the left side—told her that she was overreacting. She didn't *know* that he was the killer. She had no compelling reason to believe that he was guilty. But she'd be a fool to invite him into her room. If they stood in the hallway, Jacobson's surveillance camera would be watching and Moreno wouldn't dare try anything.

She grabbed her cell phone and held it so Moreno would see that she was in constant contact with others. As she opened the door, her heart beat extra fast. She couldn't help thinking of how quickly the man in black had killed Lauren Robbins. One slash of his knife, and she was dead.

Sasha stepped into the hallway. "What's wrong, Mr. Moreno?"

His clothing wasn't all black for a change. He wore a dark rust-colored turtleneck under a black thermal vest. His olive complexion was ruddier than usual, making his dark eyes bright. Though he was a very good-looking man, he wasn't very masculine. His smile was almost too pretty. She reminded herself not to be charmed by that smile. She'd seen Moreno in action at one of his seminars and had been amazed at his charisma. People wanted to believe him, especially when he told them that they were empowered and could have anything they dreamed of.

"May I come into your room?" he asked.

"I'd be more comfortable here," she said. Her left hand had a death grip on the front of her robe, and she held up the cell phone in her right. "You said this was important."

"I came to you as soon as I heard the name of the murder victim," he said. "I knew Lauren Robbins."

His timing surprised her. Since she and Brady had received confirmation on the victim's identity a couple of hours ago, it seemed as if everybody else should know. "How did you hear about this?"

"When we got back to the hotel, one of my assistants told me that the sheriff was questioning Reinhardt. That's when I heard Lauren's name. I came looking for you immediately."

"Why me?" She glanced down the hallway. Though she saw no sign of the surveillance camera, she knew it was there.

"I'll be truthful with you." His lightly accented voice held a practiced ring of sincerity. In the self-help business, everything was based on trust. "Damien Loughlin is the lawyer, but you're the person who really gets things done. Isn't that right?"

His question had a double edge. Of course, she wanted to be respected as a proactive person, but she knew better than to criticize her boss. "Is there something you wanted to tell me about Lauren Robbins?"

"I want you on my side." There was the disarming piece of honesty, accompanied by his smile. "Lauren was handling a real-estate transaction for me at Jim Birch's dude ranch. Earlier today you and Brady were there."

His smile and the persuasive tone of his voice were working their magic. She felt her fear begin to ebb. "If you know anything about the murder, you should talk to the police. And I'm certain that Damien would want to be present when you do."

"Am I a suspect?"

Echoing the words she'd read in every detective novel, she said, "Everybody is a suspect."

"Rest assured that I didn't do anything wrong. I'm here to help the investigation. That's all." He held out both hands with the palms up to indicate he had nothing to hide. "I knew Lauren well. She was a strong woman, tough and perhaps too ambitious. Her dream of wealth clouded her other perceptions and made it difficult for her to find peace."

In his description, she recognized several of his catch-phrases. "I'll pass that along."

"You remind me of her," he said, "in a good way."

She knew that he was dangling a carrot in front of her nose. Thousands of people were his followers and hung on his every word. Why shouldn't she get a free reading? "How so?"

"You have ambitions, Sasha. And you must honor those ambitions. If you conceive it, you can achieve it. And you're also a caretaker. I'd guess you came from a big family with four or five siblings. Are you the youngest?"

"Yes." For half a second, she wondered how he had

known about her family. Then she realized that personal information wasn't hard to come by on the internet.

"You like the balance offered by a legal career," he said, "but you don't like the restrictions of law. You're more suited to a profession like mediation."

He was accurate. She felt herself being drawn in.

Moreno continued, "Don't worry if you lose the job with Damien. You're the type of person who finds opportunities. With your optimism and enthusiasm, you'll be hired again." He paused. "I could help you. I could be your mentor."

He reached toward her and made contact with the bare flesh of her hand holding the phone. His touch was warm and meant to be soothing. He wanted her to trust him. That was what this conversation was about. He wanted her to be on his side.

But she pulled her hand away. She'd seen him in action and knew his routine too well. Sasha wasn't suited for the role of minion. She didn't look good in all black. "I appreciate that you came forth with this information, and I'll pass it on to Damien."

Down the hall, the elevator opened. She saw Grant Jacobson striding toward them and almost cheered.

Jacobson greeted Moreno and turned to her. "Step inside with me, Sasha. We have something to discuss."

Relief swept through her. She bid Moreno good-night, went into her room with Jacobson, closed the door and leaned her back against it. "Thank you."

He glared. "Didn't Brady tell you not to open the door for anyone?"

She nodded. "But I knew you'd be watching. That's why I didn't let him into the room."

"You can't take chances like that. It's not safe."

"I won't do it again."

There was nothing soft or comforting about his presence. Jacobson didn't lead by gently convincing his followers; he demanded respect. And she had no intention of disobeying him. She thanked him again, and he left.

After she showered and changed into a soft cotton nightshirt, she snuggled between the sheets and turned out the light. Lying in the dark, her mind ping-ponged from one thought to another. She remembered the moments of tension and considered the web of complications that stretched from the murder of Lauren Robbins to the suspicious death of Virgil P. Westfield. Were they connected? Or not? Connected? Or not?

And she thought of Brady. Her memory conjured a precise picture of his wide shoulders, narrow hips and long legs. He was totally masculine, from the crown of his cowboy hat to the soles of his boots. The hazel color of his eyes darkened when he was thinking and shimmered when he laughed. And when he kissed her… She sank into the remembrance of his kiss, and she held that moment in her mind. When she slept, she would dream of him.

BRADY WOKE AT the break of dawn. The light was different today; there was more shadow and less sun. A storm was coming.

Farmers and ranchers had the habit of checking the weather before they did anything else. He was no exception to that rule. Looking out his bedroom window, he watched the clouds fill up the sky. Though he was no longer a cowboy responsible for winter chores, the snowy days were vastly different from the brilliant, sunny ones they'd been having. For a deputy, the snow meant more traffic accidents and a greater likelihood of hikers being lost in the backcountry.

He glanced back at his bed, extralong so his feet didn't

hang off the end, and wished she was there. He understood why she'd turned him down when he asked her to come home with him. Spending the night with him wouldn't be appropriate for either one of them. His *only* assignment today would be protecting Sasha. Though he was glad, he had hoped to be more involved in the investigation. Last night Sheriff McKinley had told him that the Colorado Bureau of Investigation was taking over. It made sense. The CBI had the facilities and the trained personnel for autopsy and forensics. With the proper warrants, they could search the financial records of the suspects to find out if they had made payments to hired killers.

Still, Brady hated to give up jurisdiction. Stepping back and letting the big boys take over felt like failure. This was his county, his case. As a lawman, he wanted to see the investigation through to the end.

Usually, he made his own coffee in the morning. But he knew Dooley would be having the investors over for a meeting in a couple of hours. There might be some special tasty baked goods in the kitchen of the big house that was down the hill, about a hundred yards away from his two-bedroom log cabin.

He got dressed and sauntered along the shoveled path leading to the big house. As soon as he opened the back door, he was hit by the aroma of cinnamon and melted butter mingled with the smell of freshly ground coffee.

Clare and Louise, the women who did most of the cooking on the ranch, gave him a quick greeting and shoved him toward the dining room, where the table was filled with plates of cinnamon rolls and muffins, as well as regular breakfast foods—platters of bright yellow scrambled eggs, bacon and hash-brown potatoes. Five or six cowboys sat around the table, eating and drinking from steaming mugs of coffee. Chitchat was at a minimum. This was a working ranch, and they were already on the job.

Brady followed the same protocol. When he sat, the guy on his left nudged his shoulder. "I heard you found a dead body."

"That's right."

"Somebody got murdered at that fancy hotel."

"Yeah."

The cowboy across the table leaned back in his chair. "I bet McKinley is pulling his mustache out."

"Pretty much," Brady said.

"How about you? Are you playing detective?"

Brady sipped his coffee. "The CBI is stepping in to take over."

"That's a damn shame." Dooley appeared in the doorway from the kitchen. "We don't need a bunch of CBI agents in suits to come prancing around and solving our problems."

Brady loved his great-uncle, the patriarch of their family, and he agreed with him. They weren't the sort of people who gave up. "We've got no choice. The state investigators have trained experts and fancy electronic investigation equipment. With our budget, we can barely afford gas for the vehicles. The sheriff's department needs help."

"I think we need a new sheriff," one of the cowboys said. "Somebody like you, Brady."

Why did everyone keep saying that? Running for sheriff was a heavy responsibility and a long-term commitment for someone his age. "You just want a free pass on parking tickets."

"Amen to that."

"It doesn't take a budget to solve a crime." Dooley hitched his thumb in his belt. "You need what we used to call poker sense. If you want to find a liar, look him straight in the eye. If he blinks, he's got something to hide."

"And how does that work in a court of law?"

"You got to trust your gut," Dooley said. "You've met all these suspects, Brady. Now you go with your gut. Ask yourself who did it, and you're going to get a reply. And you'll probably be right."

The name that popped in his head was Lloyd Reinhardt. He didn't know why, didn't have a shred of proof, but somehow his subconscious had picked Reinhardt, the ex-husband, the man with a lot of money invested. "In the meantime, my assignment is to make sure our key witness is safe."

"Sasha Campbell," Dooley said. "Watching her all day shouldn't be too hard."

The cowboy next to him perked up. "Is she that cute little blonde?"

Because Brady knew how hard Sasha worked to be thought of as professional, he said, "She's more than cute. She works for the law firm with the partners at Arcadia, setting up the meetings and recording what goes on."

"Brady's right," Dooley said. "She's ten times smarter than her boss. But she's also nice to look at."

He couldn't argue.

On the drive over to the hotel to pick her up, he tried to reconcile his different images of Sasha. Her warmth and her smiles were natural, and she liked to think the best of people. But she wasn't a pushover. Though she didn't dress in low-cut blouses or wear sultry makeup, she had that girl-next-door kind of sexiness that made a man sit up and take notice. When she was being professional, she was smart and efficient, whipping out her laptop computer and keeping everyone on track.

Thinking about her ever-present briefcase reminded him

of how much she relied on electronics to do her job. Everybody did. It was only the dinosaurs like Dooley who figured you could count on your gut feelings. The rest of the world was plugged in, including Lauren Robbins. She was a businesswoman. Where were her electronics? Her cell phone had been recovered with her body, but where were her computer and her electronic notepad? She wouldn't have left those items at home. Not if she'd been planning to do business in Arcadia.

At the hotel, he circled around to the side where her car was still parked at the curb. He'd told McKinley about the vehicle, but the sheriff apparently hadn't had time to get it towed. And the CBI hadn't taken notice.

Brady parked his SUV in front of her car. Had Lauren left anything inside? He should tell someone else to check it out.

Or maybe he should do a tiny bit of investigating on his own.

In the back of his SUV, stored inside his locked rifle case, were the low-tech tools used to break into a car when somebody had accidentally lost their keys.

He unlocked the gun case and took out a wooden wedge and a metal pole with a hooked end. Over the years, he'd helped lots of folks who had gotten stuck in bad places without their keys, and he was good at breaking in. Many of the newer vehicles were impossible to unlock but this dark green American-made SUV wouldn't be a problem for him.

He used the wedge to pry open a narrow space at the driver's-side window, stuck the pole inside and wiggled it around until he could manipulate the lock. There was a click. He opened the door.

The SUV was a little beat-up on the inside, showing its age, and he wondered if Lauren wasn't as successful as she tried to appear in her gold necklace and classy outfit. She might have parked out here on the street so the valets wouldn't notice her less-than-glamorous car.

Wearing his gloves, he made a quick search of the car, front and back and under the seats. When he opened the glove compartment, he found a black patent leather notebook about the size of a paperback novel. He snapped a couple of photos on his phone of the notebook inside the glove box. Then he removed it. Bulging with Post-its and scribbled notes, the sides were held together with a fat rubber band.

The notebook was the nonelectronic, messy way people used to keep track of their appointments and phone numbers. Lauren Robbins had hung on to these scraps of paper and notes to herself for some reason.

His fingers itched to search through the pages. He should turn this evidence over to the CBI, but it wouldn't hurt to take a look inside first. At least, that was what he told himself.

Chapter Fifteen

Brady knocked only once on the door to Sasha's hotel room before she flung it open. She grabbed the front of his jacket and pulled him inside—a surprising show of strength for such a tiny little thing.

"I'm staying with you tonight," she announced. "I'm all packed and ready to go. We can drop my suitcase off at your cabin after the meeting at Dooley's."

"Fine with me." Better than fine—this was exactly what he wanted. "What changed your mind?"

"I don't want to be accessible to these people. Last night Moreno showed up at my door. Then I got a call from Andrea, begging me to come up to her room. She really laid on the guilt, talking about how it's so hard to be a woman working in a man's world, and how ambition killed her cousin. Maybe I should have gone to her, but I was too scared."

"You were smart."

"I don't feel safe here." Her shoulders tensed. "I saw a woman get killed in this place. This hotel doesn't exactly whisper 'home, sweet home' to me. I was even too nervous to call room service this morning."

"So you haven't had breakfast?"

"I attacked the minibar and had a couple of granola bars and some orange juice."

"There's plenty to eat at the ranch."

He grabbed the handle on her suitcase. Before they left the hotel room, he inhaled a deep breath. "Peaches, smells like peaches."

"It's my shampoo."

Light glinted off the golden highlights in her hair. For a moment, he pretended that they weren't caught up in a murder, that they were just a couple planning to spend the night together. Too bad that life wasn't that easy.

They left the room and went down the hall to the elevator. In the lobby, Moreno separated from a small group of his followers and came toward them. Trying to read his expression, Brady concentrated on his intense dark brown eyes. Moreno hardly seemed to blink. He circled Sasha like a great white shark.

His mesmerizing gaze fastened on her. "Did you sleep well?"

"Well enough," she said politely. "And you?"

"I required two meditation sessions to relax my mind enough to achieve REM sleep. It's difficult to process a murder. The energy in the hotel needs a psychic adjustment."

"Better not let Reinhardt hear you say that," she said. "Not while he's getting ready for the grand opening."

"I was concerned about you."

Brady's protective senses went on high alert. If Moreno so much as touched Sasha, he'd knock the guru flat on his buttocks.

Moreno continued, "You shouldn't stay here, Sasha. This place is not conducive to your goals and aims. You've made great progress for someone your age, and I'd hate to see you hurt. My people and I will be moving to Jim Birch's dude ranch. I propose that you come with us."

"I've made other arrangements," she said.

"Please reconsider. I have your best interests at heart."

Brady inserted himself between them. "She's made other plans. Back off."

Moreno's eyes flared with anger. The corner of his mouth twisted into a scowl. He wasn't accustomed to being told he couldn't have what he wanted. Turning his shoulder to exclude Brady, he spoke to Sasha. "When you need me, I'll be here for you."

He pivoted and rejoined his people, who waited in a dark cluster like a flock of crows.

In a low voice, Brady said, "I don't trust that guy."

"Same here."

"What was he saying about your ambitions?"

"The usual line. If you conceive it, you can achieve it."

He took her elbow and walked her through the lobby. "Do you believe that?"

"Sure I do. That's the thing about Moreno. Most of his philosophy makes sense, and I like taking a positive approach. But you can't control everything. Sometimes you win, sometimes you lose. And sometimes you look through a window and see a murder being committed."

Across the lobby, he spotted Sheriff McKinley accompanied by two strangers carrying suitcases. Brady guessed they were the agents from CBI. The appointment notebook he'd picked up in Lauren's SUV burned against the inner pocket in his jacket. Police procedure dictated that he turn the evidence over to them, but he wanted a chance to look at it first. He hustled Sasha toward the exit, hoping to avoid the agents.

"Wait a minute," she said. "I'd like to get a cup of coffee before we go."

A reasonable request. He had no logical reason to say no. Still, he tried to divert her. "We could stop at the diner."

"No need to go to extra trouble." She veered in the

direction of an espresso kiosk that was set up near the black marble waterfall. "The aroma is calling to me."

Keeping his back to the check-in desk, he went to the kiosk. With any luck, they could grab a coffee and get the hell out of the lobby before the sheriff saw him. If Brady was introduced to the CBI agents, he'd have no excuse for not handing over Lauren's notebook. He would be purposely obstructing their investigation.

At the kiosk, Sasha stared up at the dozens of possible combinations. "Let's see. What do I want?"

"Coffee, black," he suggested.

She licked her lips. "I'll have an extralarge double-shot caramel macchiato with soy milk."

He groaned. "I almost forgot you were a city girl."

"My neighborhood barista knows me by name." She stared through the glass case at the pastries. "And throw in one of those low-fat blueberry muffins."

Brady felt a tap on his shoulder. Slowly, he turned to face Sheriff McKinley. Standing to his left were two men in conservative jackets and sunglasses.

"I thought that was you," McKinley said. "Deputy Brady Ellis, I'd like to introduce Agent Colton and Agent Zeto from the CBI."

Brady shook their hands and tried to tell himself that he wasn't really lying. Yes, he was withholding evidence. But it was only temporary. Sooner or later he'd hand over the notebook. "Pleased to meet you."

When Sasha was introduced, her beaming smile lightened the mood.

Agent Zeto held her hand a few seconds too long. "We'll need to take a statement from you."

"No prob," she said. "Right now I have to run. But after the meeting with the resort investors, I'm totally available."

"We'll be in touch."

On that less-than-promising note, Brady whisked her through the lobby. They'd be seeing the agents again. He'd have to come up with an excuse for why he'd mishandled evidence. Maybe there wouldn't be anything useful in those pages, and he could ignore the notebook altogether. But that wasn't the way police procedure worked. He had to take responsibility.

Outside, the temperature had dropped and snowflakes dotted the air. He bundled Sasha into the SUV and set out on the familiar route to Dooley's ranch. Though there was less traffic than usual on the streets, more skiers were out. Some were riding a shuttle to the lodge by the gondola and chairlift. Others were walking with their gear in tow.

Sasha sipped her fancy coffee drink. "Anything new with the investigation?" she asked.

"Nothing I'd know about."

"What does that mean?"

His natural inclination was to keep his mouth shut. She didn't need to be bothered by his problems, but she'd find out soon enough when Agent Zeto interviewed her. "I'm off the case."

"Why?"

"The sheriff handed jurisdiction to the CBI. They have better resources."

"What about me? Are you still my bodyguard?"

"You bet I am."

He'd demanded that position. McKinley wanted to assign Brady to traffic duty, but he'd flat out refused. Sasha needed his full-time protection.

Even if he hadn't been attracted to her, he'd have felt the same way about protecting a witness. The main reason he'd gone into law enforcement was to keep people safe. It might be corny, but he still believed that it was his duty to serve and protect.

"It doesn't seem fair," she said. "You've already made a lot of headway."

He wanted to believe that was true. Though he lacked the formal training to conduct a homicide investigation, he had a lawman's instincts and an innate ability to see through alibis and find the truth. Like his uncle had said, poker sense. Brady needed to learn to trust his gut.

"There's only one thing that's important," he said, "finding the killer and making sure no one else gets hurt."

"You're not giving up, are you?"

He glanced over at her. She was as pretty and as sweet as a cupcake with sprinkles, but her big blue eyes were serious. "You ask the hard questions."

"Well, it's important to me. As you keep pointing out, I'm in danger. I could get killed. And you could…" Her voice faded, and her delicate hand fluttered.

"What? What could I do?"

"I haven't known you for a long time, but I believe in you. I believe you're a good detective." She shrugged. "At the risk of sounding like Moreno, you need to believe how good you really are."

"You're saying I shouldn't quit."

"That's what I'm saying."

"I'll try to work with the CBI." Even if giving up juris-diction made him feel like a second-string player, he had a unique perspective on the crime. Because of his uncle and Sasha, he was intertwined with the suspects. Answering the 911 call meant he'd literally been in at the start.

Even if he wanted to, he couldn't quit his investigation.

WITH EVERYONE GATHERED in the huge front room at the big house on the ranch, Dooley took a position in front of the big moss-rock fireplace where a gas fire radiated heat. Brady stood at the back of the room, watching. Moreno sat on a heavy leather chair that looked like a throne while three of his minions perched in a row on the sofa, drinking herbal tea. Katie Cook and her distinguished white-haired husband shared a love seat. Reinhardt, looking as tense as a clenched fist, sprawled on another sofa, with Andrea Tate sitting as far away from him as she could at the opposite end.

Sasha had set up the computer with Damien Loughlin's face on a table near the fireplace.

Dooley hitched his thumbs in the pockets of his jeans and started talking. "I was planning to saddle up a bunch of horses and get all of you outside where you could appreciate this mountain land and understand the need to preserve our resources. But I'm not going to drag you out in the snow."

"Thank you," Katie said. "I would have been concerned about being injured."

"Wasn't worried about you," Dooley said. "I didn't want any of the horses to take a tumble."

Brady stifled an urge to chuckle. His plan had been to watch the start of the meeting and then go into Dooley's office, where he could study the contents of Lauren's notebook. But he'd changed his mind. His uncle was up to something, and he wanted to know what it was.

"I figure you all know what I want out of this partnership," Dooley said. "I've been consistent. Every time we talk about our needs, I tell you that I want a percent of profits to go into land management."

"And we're on your side," Reinhardt said. "We all agree that we need to hire a qualified person to coordinate with the BLM, the EPA and the Forest Service. It's in everybody's interest to care for the land and the wildlife."

There were murmurs of support that ended with the

computerized version of Damien saying, "Now that we have that wrapped up, I'd like to discuss our current problem."

"Whoa there, counselor." Dooley bent down to talk to the computer screen. "I've got something more to say. We had a murder in Arcadia. And our sheriff's department ain't equipped to handle the investigation. Law enforcement needs to expand, and we need to pay for it."

"I disagree." Reinhardt raised his hand. "That's a problem for the county."

"You're a fine one to talk. If you'd had your hotel security up and running, we'd have arrested the killer."

"I paid for it," Reinhardt grumbled. "My security man, Grant Jacobson, has complete surveillance on the hotel. Hey, that's an idea. Instead of funding the local law enforcement, why not hire Jacobson to handle security for all the ski resort properties."

"Including the condos?" Damien asked.

"Most of them already employ a security company."

"What about the ice rink?" Katie asked.

"And outlying areas," Moreno said.

"Relax." Reinhardt spread his hands in an expansive gesture. "Jacobson is a pro. He could set up a police force that would make this the most secure area in Colorado."

Brady didn't like where this conversation was headed. The very idea of a private police force should be nipped in the bud. If Dooley didn't say something to put them on the right track, he'd have no choice but to step forward.

"How much would this cost?" Moreno asked.

One of his followers piped up, "It'd be worth the price. We have high-profile people who attend our seminars—movie stars and politicians. Their safety is of paramount concern."

"Same here," Katie said. When it came to name-dropping, she would not be outdone. "I'm bringing in famous athletes and champion skaters, many of whom need bodyguards."

From across the room, Dooley met his gaze and gave him a grin. "Let's hear what Deputy Brady Ellis has to say."

Brady stepped away from the wall. "First of all, let me make it clear that I appreciate Grant Jacobson's skills, his leadership ability and his experience. He's a hero."

"Damn right," Reinhardt said.

"But the Arcadia partners can't set up their own private vigilante force. You can't station armed guards on every street corner, and you wouldn't want to."

"He's right," Katie said. "Arcadia should be about recreation and fun. I'm acquainted with many athletes from Russia and China, and their bodyguards are very subtle. We should consult with them."

Ignoring her, Brady continued, "Our sheriff's department usually works just fine. The 911 system is efficient. Our efforts are well coordinated with mountain rescue, helicopter evacuations and ambulance services. Still, Dooley has a point. We could use more personnel, more equipment and more funding."

"If I'm going to pay for it," Reinhardt said, "I want to be in charge."

"That's exactly why a private police force doesn't work," Dooley said in his deceptively soft drawl. "If you run the police, it puts you above the law."

"What are you saying?"

"You're a suspect in this murder."

Reinhardt surged to his feet. "Wrongly accused. I've been wrongly accused."

"I understand why the police are looking at you," Katie

chirped. She almost sounded cheerful. "Lauren Robbins was your ex-wife."

"I didn't kill her. Tell them, Andrea."

Without looking up, she murmured, "He was with me."

"You people have it all wrong. I didn't hate Lauren." He glared like a trapped animal. "I respected her. She was more than a wife. We worked together. She wasn't much of a salesperson, but she was the best bookkeeper I've ever had."

Sasha stood. "Excuse me. Damien has something to add."

"Wait," Moreno said. "I want to hear more from Reinhardt. If he's charged with murder, it tarnishes all our reputations."

"What murder charges?" Reinhardt snapped.

"I heard the police were about to arrest you."

"You heard wrong."

"Excuse me," Sasha said more loudly. "Please take your seats."

Grumbling, they did so. She turned up the volume for Damien's computer image. "Thank you," he said.

They muttered a hostile response.

He continued, "Over the next few days, you're all going to be questioned by the police and the CBI. Do not—I repeat—do not speak to anyone without having me present. Even if you choose to bring in your own attorney, I wish to be included at all of these interviews."

"How are we supposed to do that?" Dooley gave a snort. "You're a hundred and seven miles away."

"I'm leaving Denver within the hour," Damien said. "I'll be in Arcadia this afternoon. In the meantime, may I remind you that there's a law enforcement officer in the room with you? Do not speak of the crime in his presence. Is that clear?"

Their heads swiveled as they turned toward Brady. He put on his hat and gave a nod. "I was just leaving."

He stepped onto the front porch, closed the door behind himself and inhaled a deep breath. The killer was one of them. He knew it and so did they.

Chapter Sixteen

Sasha took her laptop into Dooley's office—a large space filled with oak file cabinets, a giant desk and half a dozen mounted heads on the walls. Avoiding the marble-eyed gazes of the taxidermy collection, she sat behind the desk and placed the screen on the desktop so she could talk to Damien.

As soon as his computerized face appeared, he asked, "Are we alone?"

She looked up at a snarling bobcat. "Kind of."

"What does that mean?"

She turned the computer so he could see the collection. "Dooley is big on protecting the environment, but I guess he's also a hunter."

"What the hell is that thing?"

She followed his computerized gaze. "Moose. He's got a beard. Did you know mooses had beards? That doesn't sound right, does it? *Mooses?* Should it be *meese?*"

"Sasha, pay attention. Are there any other people in the room?"

"No, sir."

Reinhardt and Andrea were already on their way back to the hotel. Moreno and his entourage were in the dining room sharing tea and special gluten-free coffee cake with

Katie and her husband. Brady had made himself scarce after Damien pointed out that he was the enemy.

Though she understood that attorneys and police sometimes had different agendas when it came to crime, she'd always thought they were after the same thing: justice. Damien would tell her that she was being naive. So would her brother Alex. They'd remind her that the duty of a lawyer was to represent their client, whether they were guilty or not.

But it didn't feel right. If Reinhardt was responsible for the murder of his wife, Sasha wanted to see him in prison. Maybe she was in the wrong profession.

Outside the window, the wind whooshed around the corner of the big house. The snow had begun to fall in a steady white curtain.

She confronted computerized Damien. "If you're coming up here this afternoon, you should get on the road. The weather is starting to get nasty."

"Duly noted."

"I spoke to the property manager at the condo this morning. She stocked the refrigerator with your standard food order."

"And there's champagne for us in the fridge, right?"

For us? "Three bottles."

"There were supposed to be four."

"I opened one the first night," she said.

"You naughty girl," he said with a smirk. "Did you try the hot tub?"

"Yes." Hoping to squelch any flirting, she added, "I remembered to bring my bathing suit."

"Clothes aren't really necessary. Not in the privacy of the condo."

She was beginning to feel as if the proper attire for a spin in the hot tub with Damien would be a suit of armor.

"Anyway, the condo is ready for you. The property manager assured me that the dead bolt on the balcony door has been installed."

"Why are you telling me this? Aren't you staying there?"

"After the ninja break-in, I didn't feel safe. I booked a room at the hotel last night."

She was certain that Damien wasn't going to appreciate her plan to spend tonight with Brady, but her mind was made up. When it came to her job, she'd do what was required, but her sleeping arrangements were her own private business.

"I'll be at the condo tonight," he said. "You can move back."

"I have other plans." Hoping to avoid a discussion of where she'd be sleeping, she changed the topic. "What time do you think you'll be arriving? I can set up appointments with the CBI agents."

"What are these plans of yours?"

"Staying with a friend."

"Don't be ridiculous, Sasha. I was looking forward to spending time with you. We could discuss your future with the firm."

Talking about her career goals with a senior partner was a hugely tempting opportunity. She'd been employed at the Three *S*s for only a year. Most legal assistants went forever without being noticed. Damien hadn't actually said anything that would cause her to mistrust him. "I'd like to have that talk. I hope to get started taking classes to learn mediation in the spring."

"I'm sure you do." When he straightened his necktie, playing for time, she knew there was something he wasn't telling her. "Right now we'll focus on the needs of the Arcadia investors. Reinhardt and his sexy little real estate agent, Andrea, are the top suspects. They both have motive. If you hadn't witnessed the murder, he'd be in custody right now."

"What's their motive?"

"The oldest in the book," he said smugly. "Money and revenge. Pay attention, Sasha, you might learn something."

She put up with his condescending attitude to get information. "Tell me all about it."

"Reinhardt's ex-wife was receiving alimony, and she kept digging into his finances, finding bits and pieces he might owe her. She did the same with Andrea."

"They were partners," Sasha recalled.

"It bothers me that Lauren was also working for Westfield," he said. "The autopsy showed that he was murdered. He took a blow to the skull before he fell down the stairs."

She gasped. It was hard to imagine someone killing that sweet, elderly man who loved his cats so dearly. "That's horrible."

"The Denver homicide cops are looking into any connection between that murder and the death of Lauren Robbins. They figure one murder leads to another."

"What could possibly be the motive for killing Mr. Westfield?"

"I don't know. There's some question about a dude-ranch property that Westfield wanted to acquire. Do you know anything about it?"

"I've been there," she said quickly. "Moreno is also interested in buying the dude ranch to set up an ashram for his followers."

"The same property?"

She nodded. "Andrea is the real-estate agent, and I think she was setting up a bidding war between Moreno and her cousin."

"And Reinhardt?"

"I haven't heard anything about him and the dude-ranch property," she said. "It's too far from the ski lodge to be a good development for condos."

"That's good. He doesn't need any more strikes against him." Damien's hand reached toward the screen, preparing to close down their communication. "I should be in Arcadia by three o'clock. When I arrive, we'll make appointments with the CBI. We'll have a nice dinner and a soak in the hot tub."

His face disappeared. Though she hadn't actually told him that she wouldn't be waiting for him at the condo, Sasha was even more convinced that she didn't want to put herself in that position. She might be naive, but she wasn't fool enough to think Damien was interested in discussing her career.

During the conversations she'd had with him over the past few days, he hadn't once asked about her safety. The only time he'd perked up was just now when he talked about champagne and hot tubs. Her brother had it right when he'd said that the condo was a bachelor pad; Damien wanted her alone with him so he could seduce her. The never-forgotten chords of "Trashy Sasha" played in her head.

She closed the computer and looked up at the bobcat on the wall and snarled back at it, baring her teeth. *No way, Damien.* She'd sleep outside in the snow before she spent the night under the same roof with him.

In the hallway outside the office, Brady was waiting for her. Seeing him immediately brightened her mood. Leaning against the wall opposite the office, he squinted down at a small notebook, concentrating hard. For some reason, he was wearing purple latex gloves. Looking up, he gave her a crooked grin. "Either I need glasses or I finally found somebody with worse penmanship than mine."

"Let me see." She held out a hand. "I've gotten pretty good at translating chicken scratches for lawyers."

He hesitated. "This is evidence. I shouldn't let you look at it. Matter of fact, I shouldn't be looking, either."

"Evidence, huh? That's why you're wearing the gloves. You don't want to leave fingerprints."

He held up a purple hand. "I've been carrying a boxful of these around in my SUV for a couple of years. This is the first time I've worn them."

"They're cute."

"That's what I was going for." He held the notebook toward her. "Can you tell what this says? It looks like something about a Dr. Cayman at an office in a southern bank."

She glanced at the scribbled abbreviations. The letters *D* and *R* were in capitals. In small letters, it read "off-s-bnk." She took her cue from the one clear word.

"Cayman," she said, "might refer to the Cayman Islands, a place with many offshore banks."

"I got it." He nodded. "Off-s-bnk. What about the doctor?"

"I'm not sure, but I think that's an abbreviation used by auditors for a discrepancy report, referring to an accounting problem."

"What kind of problem?"

"A discrepancy," she said, "is a difference between reported transactions and actual money. If we could access Lauren's business records for that date, we might have more information."

He snapped the book closed. "Grab your jacket. I need to get back over to the hotel and talk to the CBI agents."

Since the investors' meeting was officially ended, Sasha had no particular reason to hang around at Dooley's ranch, especially since she and Brady would be returning here later. They made a speedy exit through the kitchen door and hiked through the snow toward the barn.

His SUV was parked outside a rustic little two-story log cabin nestled under a spruce tree. "Your house?"

"I never gave you the grand tour," he said. "Well, that's the barn. Over there is a bunkhouse. This is my place. Me and my dad built it when I was a teenager. Tour over."

She climbed into the passenger side of the SUV. "Did your dad live at the cabin, too? I don't understand the whole family dynamic here at the ranch."

"Nobody does," he said. "This property has been in our family for over a hundred years, so it gets kind of twisted around. The bottom line is that Dooley owns most of the acreage and runs the ranch. He's been a widower for seven years but has a lady friend who lives in Arcadia. Dooley has four kids, but only one of them is interested in ranching."

"That would be Daniel," she said, recalling the name from some documents. "And he's married with three kids."

Brady drove along the narrow road toward the front of the big house. "Daniel and his wife have a spread of their own where she trains horses. Their kids are off in college. When he's in town, Daniel works with Dooley. Someday he'll inherit the ranch."

"What about you? What do you inherit?"

"I don't really think about it." He peered through the windshield at the steadily falling snow. "I'll always help out at the ranch, but it's not my whole life. When I was a kid, all I wanted to do was be a rancher like Uncle Dooley. I loved riding and being outdoors. I still do."

His words ended on a pensive sigh. Brady didn't often talk about himself, and she wanted to hear more. "What changed your mind?"

"I want to make a difference." He gave a little shrug.

"Being in law enforcement makes that happen. When people get in trouble, I'm the first one they call."

She thought of the first time she'd seen him, when he responded to her 911 call. His presence had been a huge relief. When she saw his wide shoulders and determined eyes, she'd known that he had come to help her. "You like your work."

"That's why I hate giving up on this murder. I want to make it right."

At the moment, she was less interested in the murder and more focused on the lawman who wanted to solve it. He was so deeply involved in his work that it was an extension of him. Sasha had never felt that way about her job. Sure, she liked the prestige of being employed by a high-power law firm, and the paycheck was decent. But she lacked a passion for the law.

"There must have been something in your childhood," she said, "that made you want to be a deputy."

"I always used to root for the underdog, always took care of the runt in the litter." He tossed her a grin. "If I hadn't become a deputy, I would've been a vet."

"Tell me about your dad."

"He died eight years ago in a car accident. His death was mercifully fast, unexpected. One day he was here. The next he was gone forever. It left me with unanswered questions. I don't think I ever really knew my dad. He was a good man. Quiet. Kindhearted. He loved being a cowboy."

Though his expression barely changed, she felt the depth of his emotion. "And you loved him."

"Yeah, I love both my parents. You remind me of my mom. She's a city gal, real pretty and real smart."

A gentle warmth made her smile. "You think I'm pretty."

"And smart."

At the intersection with the highway, he turned right. On a clear day, the chairlift and the ski lodge would have been visible in the distance. Through the snowfall, she could hardly see beyond the trees at the edge of the road. "Do people ski in this weather?"

"It's a winter sport."

"You never told me why it was so important to see the CBI agents."

"The evidence in the notebook," he said. "I didn't obtain it in the usual manner. I kind of swiped the notebook out of the glove compartment in Lauren Robbins's car, and it's been weighing on my conscience like a twelve-ton boulder."

Obviously, he had already gone through the notebook. "Did you find any clues?"

"The best one is that offshore bank note," he said. "Other than that, it's just random jotting. She only had a few big clients like Westfield and she took them out to dinner and to sports events. Andrea owed her money but not a lot. And she really hated Reinhardt."

"How could you tell that from an appointment book?"

"On his birthday, she sent him dead roses and cheap wine."

Sasha chuckled. "That's pretty funny."

"Maybe for the first year after the divorce or the second, but they've been split up for five years. It was time for her to move on."

"Unless she saw him with her cousin and that triggered her anger." Sasha tried to put herself in Lauren's shoes. Being betrayed by a girlfriend could be painful. She remembered Damien's words. "The oldest motives in the book are money and revenge."

"But Lauren didn't kill anybody. She was the victim."

"I don't know if this helps or not, but Damien told me

that the Denver police have classified Westfield's death as a homicide. And they think it might be connected to Lauren's murder."

"It adds a new wrinkle." He hooked into his hands-free phone. "The sheriff won't be answering his radio. I'm going to try to get him on the cell phone to find out where the CBI agents are."

As they drove the last few miles toward the hotel, she realized that she'd blabbed confidential information. It wasn't a big deal, really. Brady was a cop. He'd know what other cops had discovered.

As Brady drove into the valet parking area at the hotel, he finished his phone call to Sheriff McKinley. He turned to her. "We've got a problem."

"What's that?"

"The CBI is on their way to arrest Reinhardt."

Chapter Seventeen

Brady rushed into the lavish hotel lobby with Sasha right beside him. Unless the CBI had come up with conclusive proof, he thought the arrest of Reinhardt was premature. His gut told him that Reinhardt was a tough contractor who had earned his millions the hard way and knew that murder was bad business. Reinhardt had already figured out the way to handle his ex-wife. When Lauren gave him trouble, he paid the woman off.

Waiting for the elevator, his cell phone jangled. It was McKinley.

Brady answered. "What is it, Sheriff?"

"We're up here on the concierge floor, and Reinhardt is gone. We've got to assume he's making a run for it. If you see him, arrest him on sight."

Even before he disconnected the call, Brady had a pretty good idea where he would find Reinhardt. When he'd searched for the body of Lauren Robbins, he'd been all over the hotel, but he knew better than to start combing the back hallways and the laundry room. The interior and part of the exterior of the hotel were visible on surveillance cameras, and there was only one man who could make a fugitive disappear from these premises: Grant Jacobson.

He glanced down at Sasha. "Stick close to me."

"What are we doing?"

"We'll know when we get there."

He went to the security offices behind the front desk. In the room with all the camera feeds, he found Jacobson sitting alone, watching the monitors. Brady ushered Sasha inside and closed the door.

"Grant Jacobson, your name came up at a meeting this morning."

"Did it?"

As Jacobson pushed back from the desk and stood, his gaze darted toward his private office at the back of the room. That glance was what Dooley would call a "tell." Jacobson was concerned about something in that rear office.

"Somebody suggested that we should have a private police force to secure and protect the resort, and that you should run it. I had to tell them it was a bad idea. A sheriff's department is different from private security." Brady nodded toward the closed door to Jacobson's private office. "Is he in there?"

Jacobson rubbed his hand across his granite jaw. "You're pretty smart for a cowboy."

"He's not a cowboy," Sasha said. "He's a cop."

"Tell me, Brady. How did you know?"

"It didn't take a lot of brainpower," he said. "I've seen your surveillance setup. The way I figure, you've probably engineered a successful escape from this hotel."

"And why would I do that?"

"Because you know it might be necessary." Brady didn't make a move toward the office. Getting in a fight with Jacobson would be a supremely dumb move, and he wasn't sure he could win. "But the CBI agents made their move too quickly, and you haven't had time to get Reinhardt away from here."

"In another ten minutes, he would have been in the

wind," Jacobson said. "What's the evidence they've got against him?"

Brady took out his phone. "I'll find out."

Sheriff McKinley answered right away. His voice was high and nervous. "Did you see him?"

"Not yet." On the surveillance video screen for the concierge level, Brady watched the sheriff and the two CBI agents searching the rooms on that floor. "Can you tell me about the new evidence?"

"Fingerprints. The victim's purse was with her inside the steamer trunk, and the forensic people found Reinhardt's prints on a couple of quarters in her wallet."

"Sounds kind of circumstantial," Brady said.

"He said he hadn't seen her in months. What are the odds that she's been carrying those quarters around for months?"

That was a valid point. "I'll call you if I find him."

Brady ended the call and turned toward Jacobson. "Reinhardt has some explaining to do."

"Let's talk."

When Jacobson strode across the room, Brady had to remind himself that the man had a prosthetic leg. His gait was steady and determined. If Brady had been in the market for an assassin, he would have put Jacobson at the top of the list.

Using an optical scanner, Jacobson unlocked his private office. They entered the small room that was neatly furnished with a desk, two computers and several file cabinets.

Reinhardt sat behind the desk with his brawny arms folded on the surface in front of him. "I can't believe this. Lauren is reaching out from the grave to make my life miserable."

"Don't blame yourself." To Brady's surprise, Sasha

circled the desk and gently patted Reinhardt's heavy shoulders. "You and Lauren had an intense, passionate relationship."

He shot her an angry glare. "How the hell would you know?"

"As the only woman in the room, I'm kind of the resident expert on this stuff."

Brady was both amused and intrigued by the way Sasha had waltzed in here and taken charge. "What's your evidence, Sasha?"

"It's been five years since the divorce, and they still can't stop poking at each other. He's still paying her off." She looked directly into Reinhardt's eyes. "Not to mention that Andrea looks an awful lot like your ex-wife."

"You could be right," he said grudgingly. "I never got that woman out of my system. She drove me crazy, but there's no way I wanted her dead."

Brady stepped in. Before they all started talking about their feelings, he wanted to get a take on the *real* evidence, namely Reinhardt's fingerprints on the quarters in Lauren's purse. "When was the last time you saw her face-to-face?"

Reinhardt looked at Sasha. "Shouldn't I have Damien here?"

She nodded. "Sorry, Brady. He's right."

"Understood." Brady stepped back. "A bit of advice. Never run away from the cops. It makes you look guilty."

Reinhardt stood behind the desk. "I'll tell you this, off the record. I had breakfast with Lauren in Denver last week. She wanted an advance on her alimony, claimed to be dead broke."

"Did you believe her?" Brady asked.

"Hard to say. She always exaggerated." He looked toward Sasha. "What do you call that?"

"She was a drama queen?"

"That's right. When the bill for breakfast came, she insisted on paying for the tip and calculated the amount down to eighteen percent. She put a couple of coins on the table to show how broke she was."

"And what happened to those coins?"

"I scooped them up and dumped them back in her wallet. Then I wrote her a check for the alimony advance."

That was a simple explanation for the fingerprints. If Reinhardt was lying about his intense relationship with his ex-wife, he was a pretty good actor. It seemed more likely that Andrea would have wanted her annoying cousin out of the way.

Brady arranged for the sheriff and the CBI to meet with Reinhardt right here in the security office while Sasha got Damien on the computer for their session of questioning. He was already on his way in the car, but this situation required his immediate attention.

In the outer room with Jacobson, Brady waited and watched normal hotel activities flitting across the many security screens. From the arriving guests to the maids cleaning up the rooms to the busy kitchens behind the restaurants, this complex was a beehive, a world unto itself. Jacobson was responsible for protecting these people and keeping them from harm.

"Do you like your work?" Brady asked.

"It satisfies me."

His priorities were clear. Take care of the guests, the employees and…the owner. "If I hadn't guessed where Reinhardt was hiding, would you have helped him go on the run?"

"I would have tried to talk him out of it. Like you said, running makes you look guilty."

"What if he insisted?"

"If I believed he was a killer, I'd turn him in. But I think the guy is innocent. And I go with my gut."

So did Brady.

BY FOUR O'CLOCK in the afternoon, the snow was coming down hard. Seven inches had already fallen, and there was no sign of a break. Riding in the passenger seat of Brady's SUV, Sasha had just gotten off the phone with Damien, who was running late and didn't expect to arrive at the condo until nightfall.

She'd managed not to tell him where she was staying, putting him off with a promise to meet with him tomorrow morning at the condo at eight o'clock so they could plan their day. Moreno would be in charge of the investors' meeting program.

Tucking her phone into a special pocket in her briefcase, she leaned back and exhaled a sigh. "That should take care of business for the rest of the day."

"I won't believe that unless you turn off your phone and your computer and unhook yourself from the rest of the world."

"Sorry, I can't. What if Damien needed to reach me? What if something came up at the Denver office?"

"There was a time, city girl, when people weren't on-call twenty-four hours a day."

"I'm not like that," she protested. "I'm not one of those people who are always checking their phones and answering emails."

"Professionals," he said. "That's what you want to be."

A few days ago, she might have agreed with him. She'd always been a little bit envious of the plugged-in people who were so much in demand that they couldn't take two steps without talking on their phone. But she wasn't so sure anymore.

He drove the SUV down the snowplowed road to the big house at Dooley's ranch. Though it wasn't late in the day, clouds had darkened the sky, and the pure white snowfall dissolved all the other colors into shadows. Lights shone on the porch of the big house and at the front of the barn. In spite of the whir of the heater inside the vehicle, a profound silence blanketed the land.

"It's not like this in the city," she said. "Snow means traffic jams and sloppy puddles in parking lots."

"The best place to enjoy new snow is indoors," he said as he drove past the big house to his cabin by the spruce tree, "with a fire on the grate and extra blankets on the bed."

It was the first time he'd mentioned bed, and a shiver of anticipation went through her. They hadn't talked about sleeping arrangements for tonight, and she wasn't sure what was going to happen. Their kisses whetted her memory. She usually didn't fall into bed with a guy until after they knew each other very well. But there was something different about Brady. He wasn't just *any* guy. He'd saved her life. He'd believed in her when no one else did. And she'd be kidding herself if she tried to believe that she wasn't attracted to his six-foot-four-inch frame and his long legs and that teasing dimple at the corner of his mouth.

He parked the SUV inside an open garage at the side of the cabin and turned to her. "I put your suitcase inside this morning."

Looking into his greenish-brown eyes, her heart thumped. "All I have is my briefcase. I can carry it myself."

She hopped out of the SUV into the cold and dashed to the porch, which was covered by the overhanging roof but still blanketed by an unbroken sheet of snow.

He unlocked the door, and they rushed inside. The corporate condo in Arcadia had the sleek atmosphere of a high-class bachelor pad. Brady's cabin was the opposite. It felt comfortable and cozy, and she was glad to see that he didn't share his uncle's fondness for animal heads. The walls were creamy stucco, decorated with framed photographs of landscapes. And there were shelves filled with well-read books and a couple of rodeo trophies. The floors were rugged wood covered by area rugs in Navajo designs. The furniture looked heavy and handcrafted but comfortable with thick wool-covered cushions.

Her suitcase stood by the door as though it hadn't decided whether it needed to be in the guest room or sharing the main bedroom with Brady.

"A warning," he said. "If you want to take a shower, you've got to move fast. My hot-water tank is kind of small."

"I'd rather shower in the morning," she said.

"Me, too."

"Then we'll really have to move fast…unless we shower together."

He met her gaze and then quickly looked away. "That's always an option."

She wandered into the adjoining kitchen and turned on the overhead light. "Should I make some coffee?"

"That'd be great. I'm going to get a fire started."

On the ceramic tile counter, she found a coffeemaker. The necessary beans, grinder and filter were stored in the cabinet directly above. As she went through the movements, she wondered if he was as hesitant and confused as she was about what would happen between them tonight.

It might be up to her to make the first move. Brady was so incredibly polite. He was an "aw, shucks" cowboy with a slow, sheepish grin. If she really wanted anything to happen, she might have to pounce.

The question was: Did she want anything to happen?

Keeping her distance might be for the best. There wasn't a possibility for them to have any kind of long-term relationship with her living in Denver and him being a deputy in Arcadia. Their life trajectories were worlds apart.

After she finished setting the coffee to brew, she went into the front room, where he'd started a fire and placed a screen in front of the blaze. He'd taken off his jacket and hat, tossing them onto the sofa. The sleeves of his uniform shirt were rolled up on his muscular forearms. Still hunkered down in front of the grate, he hadn't turned on any of the other lights in the cabin, and the glow from the fire danced in his unruly brown hair and highlighted his profile.

He beckoned to her. "Come over here and get warmed up."

"That's okay. I'm not cold."

He turned his head and reached toward her. "Come."

His direct gaze sent a tingle of excitement through her. He wasn't asking her to join him. He was telling her. There was no way she could refuse.

Sasha placed her hand in his and allowed him to pull her down onto the handwoven wool rug in front of the fireplace. The warmth from the flames mingled with a churning heat that came from inside as he took her into his arms and kissed her with a fierce passion that she hadn't felt from him before.

His kiss consumed her. A thousand sensations rushed through her body. Never had she been kissed like this, never. She hadn't expected fire from him, but somehow she'd known from the first that he was everything she'd ever wanted.

Sasha surrendered herself to him.

Chapter Eighteen

After a few intense moments, Sasha found herself lying on her back in front of the fire with Brady beside her. His leg was thrown across her body, holding her in place, while he took his time kissing her and unbuttoning her blouse. His knuckles brushed against the bare flesh of her torso, setting off an electric reaction. There was magic in his touch. When he ran his fingers across the lace of her bra, she felt as if she was going to jump out of her skin.

She reached for his chest and grabbed a handful of material. "Take off your shirt."

"I've got a better idea," he murmured. "Why don't you do it for me?"

He leaned back, giving her access to his dark blue uniform. She definitely wanted the shirt off, but stripping him wasn't so easy. Her fingers were trembling so hard that she couldn't get the buttons through the holes. Even worse, there was a thermal undershirt under the uniform. It might take her hours to get rid of all these clothes. Biting her lower lip, she concentrated.

"Hah," she said, "got one."

"Need some help?"

"I can do this." She shoved him onto his back and straddled him while she worked on the shirt. This wasn't the best position for her to maintain concentration. The hard bulge inside his jeans pressed against her inner thigh, and she couldn't help rocking against him. What had ever made her think this man was shy?

As he rose to a sitting position, he grasped both of her wrists in his large hands. "Let me take care of your clothes."

"Do I have a choice?"

"Only if you want me to stop," he said.

"Absolutely not."

While desire had turned her into a total klutz, Brady was smooth; he seemed to know exactly what he was doing as he held her gently against his warm chest. He reached toward the sofa, grabbed a soft woolly blanket and spread it on the rug in front of the fire. Then he stretched her out on the blanket, stroked the hair off her forehead and gazed into her eyes. "Lie still."

"Why? What are you doing?"

"First I'm taking off your boots."

She stared up at the reflection of firelight across the ceiling. Her pulse was rapid, excited. Her senses were on high alert. The crackling of the fire sounded as loud as cannon fire. The scent of burning pine tickled her nostrils.

He pulled off her boots and socks, and the soles of her feet prickled. When he lay beside her, she was grateful to see that both his uniform and his thermal shirt were gone.

Her hands glided over his chest, tracing the pattern of springy black hair that spread across his muscular torso. Touching him gave her much-needed confidence. Dipping her head down, she kissed his hard nipples, and she knew she was having an effect on him because she could feel his body grow tense. Her fingers slid lower on his body. When she touched his belt buckle, he made a growling noise deep in his throat—a dangerous sound that both excited and pleased her.

Before she could reach farther, he had slipped off her shirt and her bra. Suddenly aggressive, he tightened his grasp and held her close. Her breasts were crushed against his chest.

Her mouth joined with his for another mind-blowing kiss. Gasping, she rubbed her cheek against his, feeling the rough beginnings of stubble.

Her clumsiness was gone. She was self-assured and focused. She wanted to explore his body, to learn every inch of him intimately. His male scent aroused her. All man, Brady was all man. And he was hers.

In the back of her mind, she wondered if they should talk about what was happening, to discuss their feelings, and she pushed words through her lips. "What are we doing?"

"I don't know about you, but I'm making love."

"But is this…?" Was it smart? Was it right? Should they reconsider? Should they try to understand?

"It's natural," he said.

And that was enough for her. Her questions and reservations could wait. She forgot everything else. For now, she would live in this moment when they were together, bathed in the flickering light from the fireplace.

His big hands were gentle as he cupped her breasts and teased her nipples into hard nubs. When he lowered his mouth to suckle, a shock wave tore through her. She arched her back, yearning to be one with him.

"You're beautiful, Sasha." His voice was a whisper. "A beautiful woman."

With quick, sure movements, he unfastened her waistband and slid her slacks down her legs. Her white lacy underpants followed. She felt his heated gaze on her body, caressing her from head to toe. And she felt beautiful.

When he lay beside her again, he was naked. She saw

him in firelit glimpses. His long muscular thighs. The expanse of his chest. The sharp definition of muscle in his arms. His rock-hard erection pressed into her hip, and she reached down to grasp him. Her touch sent a shudder through his body.

His arms tightened. She felt his strength and his urgency. As she stroked him, her leg wrapped around his thigh and she opened herself to him. A throbbing heat spread from her core to her entire body.

"I need a condom," he whispered.

"Yes."

"I have one in my wallet."

"Behind your badge?"

He sat up beside her on the floor and pawed through his jeans until he found what he was looking for. When he took her in his arms again, he was sheathed and ready.

He mounted her, taking control, and she arched into his embrace. Before, they had been doing a slow dance of lovemaking. Now the rhythm changed. As he pushed against her most intimate place, she heard the blood surging through her veins. She needed to feel him inside her. When he made that first thrust, she cried out in pure pleasure.

This was better than she'd imagined, better than she had dreamed of. She writhed under him, driven by passion. His hard, deep thrusts went on and on, taking her beyond mere satisfaction.

Sasha wasn't very experienced when it came to making love, and she tended to hold back. Not now. Not with Brady. An uncontrollable urge consumed her, and she desperately clung to self-control. She didn't want these sensations to end but didn't know how long she could hold on. Hot and cold at the same time, every muscle in her body tensed. And then…release. Fireworks exploded behind her eyelids. It felt as though she was flying, that she'd left her body to soar.

Afterward she lay beside him, breathing hard. She felt as if there was something she ought to say but all she could manage was a soft humming noise.

"Are you purring?" he asked.

"Maybe."

"I like it."

BRADY LIKED HER a lot. Making love in front of the fireplace hadn't been a plan or a strategy. He didn't think that way. He had just seen her coming toward him from the kitchen and had wanted to take her into his arms. Why? He couldn't say. Maybe it was because in his cabin, he felt safe and could relax his vigilance in protecting her. Or maybe it was because he wasn't sure how long their passion would last. Every minute with her had to count.

"Are you okay?" he asked.

"The floor is a little hard."

He dropped a light kiss on her cheek, lifted her off the floor, wrapped the edges of the soft woolly blanket around her and snuggled her into the big chair closest to the fire.

"I'll bring you coffee," he said. "Let me see if I remember. A double-shot macchiato with soy milk, right?"

"Or plain black coffee, no cream or sugar."

"I can do that."

On his way to the kitchen, he grabbed his jeans and pulled them on. He was still warm enough from their love-making that he didn't need a shirt. In the kitchen, he filled two mugs and returned to the front room, placing hers on the wooden arm of her chair. Looking down at her gave him a burst of pleasure. She meant a lot to him, more than he would have thought possible after knowing her for only a few days. He hated to think of her leaving, going back to the city.

He carried his steaming mug to the window where he looked out at the snow. Forecasters had predicted the storm would continue through the night and maybe into tomorrow morning, which ought to make the people at the ski lodge happy. The ski slopes had a good base, but more snow was welcome this early in the season.

Taking a taste of coffee, he reflected. So many things were changing. Arcadia was transforming from a quiet backwater town into a destination point. They needed to step up and prepare for new challenges. All the folks that kept urging him to run for sheriff were going to increase the pressure, and he ought to be seriously thinking about taking on that responsibility.

But there was only one thing on his mind: the pretty woman who was curled up in the chair by his fireplace. She was special. Different. When he made love to her, he actually believed that he wouldn't spend the rest of his life alone.

Crossing the room, he turned on a couple of table lamps before he sat on the sofa next to her chair. She smiled at him across the rim of her coffee mug, and the sparkle in her blue eyes brightened the whole room.

"I want you to stay in Arcadia," he said. "Give me a week, and I'll teach you how to ski and how to ride horses."

"I can't."

"Sure, you can. Call it a vacation."

"Maybe later this winter," she said. "It's not like I'm going to the moon. I'll only be a couple of hours away in Denver."

"But you'll be busy with your professional life. You were going to start taking classes."

"I'm not so sure about that." She leaned forward and

placed her mug on the coffee table. Under the blanket, she was naked, and he caught a glimpse of her smooth white breast before she pulled the blanket more snugly around her.

He swallowed hard. "No classes?"

"I don't know if law is the right career path for me. I mean, what if Reinhardt is guilty?"

"What if he is?"

Brady had managed to turn over Lauren's notebook to the CBI agents with a minimum of explanation. They were glad to have a direction of inquiry and would be studying Reinhardt's finances for offshore accounts. More than likely, the murder would be solved when the CBI figured out who had withdrawn enough money to pay the killer.

"If he's guilty," she said, "our law firm would have to defend him anyway."

"That's how the system works."

"How could I represent somebody like that, a person who could commit murder?"

She snuggled under the blanket as though hiding behind the soft folds, protecting herself. Was she scared? Sasha was one of the least fearful people he'd ever met. Her bravado could last for days, which, he suspected, came from being the youngest of five kids. She'd learned not to show her fear.

Gently, he asked, "What are you thinking about?"

"The killer's face." She avoided looking at him. "Shouldn't my memory start to fade after a couple of days? Why do I see him so clearly? The lines across his forehead, the sneer on his mouth, every wrinkle, every shadow seems to get sharper. Is that even possible?"

"Yes."

He believed her. He had suggested to the CBI agents that they arrange for Sasha to look through mug shots.

With their databases and their technology, they could put together a digital array of suspects for her to identify.

They hadn't been interested in his idea. Eyewitnesses were notoriously unreliable, and Sasha had caught only a glimpse of the killer through binoculars. Other people doubted her ability to recall.

But he believed her. Today he would insist on that digital array. "I'll set it up so you can look at photos. He's not going to get away with this."

She turned in her chair to face him. The hint of fear was gone. "Here's what I hate. Why should a lawyer have to defend him?"

Brady said nothing. She wasn't really expecting a response. He sat back and drank his coffee.

She continued, "I know that justice needs to be balanced and every criminal deserves a defense. But I don't think I could be the one who speaks for a guilty person. I'd blurt out to the judge and jury that they should lock him up and throw away the key."

"Are you thinking of changing jobs?"

"Oh, I couldn't. I was really lucky to get this job, and I need the salary. But I'm not convinced that I want to move on in the legal profession."

"Then my work is done," he teased. "I've gotten one more lawyer off the market."

"Are cops and attorneys always adversaries?"

"In theory, we're working on the same side." But he'd had his share of situations when a high-powered lawyer swooped in and got charges dismissed, turning a drunk driver back out on the road or letting a rich kid think it was okay for him to commit vandalism.

"I'd rather track down the bad guys," she said, "than figure out what happens to them afterward."

Before they sank into a complicated discussion of the law, he asked, "How do you feel about dinner?"

"That depends," she said. "I don't want to go anyplace else. Do we have to leave the cabin to get food?"

"I've got plenty of supplies right here."

"Then, yes, I'm hungry." With the blanket wrapped around her like a toga, she rose from the chair. "I should probably get dressed."

"Don't bother on my account."

He grinned when he suggested that she stay nude, but he was only halfway kidding. Her nearness and the way that blanket kept slipping was beginning to turn him on.

She lifted her chin. "Show me where I'll be sleeping."

"You have a choice."

"Show me your bedroom."

He grabbed her suitcase and wheeled it down the hall to his bedroom—a big, comfortable space with a chair by the window for reading and a flat-screen television mounted on the wall over the dresser for late nights when he couldn't fall asleep.

"Your bed," she said, "is gigantic."

"Extralong so my feet don't hang off the end."

She climbed up onto the dark blue comforter and primly tucked her feet up under her. Peering through her lashes, she gave him a flirtatious glance. "We never discussed sleeping arrangements."

"I want you here. In my bed."

She dropped the blanket from one slender shoulder. "Let's try it and make sure we fit."

He didn't need another invitation.

Chapter Nineteen

As she drifted from dreams to wakefulness, Sasha felt warm, cozy and utterly content. She loved being under the comforter in Brady's giant bed. As she snuggled against him, his chest hairs tickled her nose and made her giggle.

She should have been tired; they'd made wild, passionate, incredible love four times last night, which had to be the equivalent of running a marathon. But her body felt energized and ready to go.

"Are you awake?" he asked.

She peeked through her eyelids. "It's still dark."

"There are a couple rays of sunlight. It's almost seven."

And she was supposed to meet Damien at eight o'clock at the condo to plan their day. A jolt of wake-up adrenaline blasted through her. The agenda for her day wasn't one happy event after the next. It was the opposite. Damien was sure to be angry about not having her at his beck and call at the condo. The investors' meeting today with Moreno promised to be full of problems since the guru couldn't allow his sterling reputation to be smeared by an inconvenient murder. Oh, yes, and she was still in danger from the killer-slash-ninja.

She tilted her head back and kissed Brady under the chin. "I wish we could stay here all day."

"We could try," he said.

"But it wouldn't work. I can't bail out on my job. And you need to be involved in the investigation." She threw off the comforter and sat up in the bed. Since she hadn't gotten around to unpacking her suitcase last night, she was wearing one of his T-shirts as a nightie. "How long will it take to get to the condo?"

"Half an hour in the snow."

"So I've got only half an hour to get ready."

He sat up beside her, completely naked and not a bit self-conscious. "We'll have to share the shower. To save time and hot water."

She liked that plan but didn't want to rush through a shower with him. Soaping him up and rinsing the suds away should be done slowly and meticulously, giving her the chance to savor every steely muscle in his body. "You go ahead. I'm just going to throw on clothes. I can't be late."

There was only one bathroom in his cabin—a large expanse of tile with a double sink and an old-fashioned claw-footed tub with a see-through circular shower curtain. With Brady in the shower, steam from the hot water clouded the mirrors above the sinks as she splashed water on her face and brushed her teeth.

The awareness that he was naked behind that filmy curtain was driving her crazy. But she was determined to be on time. "Hurry up."

"There's room in here for you."

She groaned with barely suppressed longing. Oh, she wanted to be in that shower. Damien had better appreciate her sacrifice.

"I SHOULD FIRE YOU."

Sasha gaped. She'd knocked herself out to get here on time. She and Brady had entered the condo at five minutes until eight o'clock. Damien had asked Brady to wait outside the front door, which was insulting but necessary to keep the deputy from overhearing any privileged information.

He'd sat her down at the counter in the kitchen, refreshed his own coffee without asking her if she wanted any and made his announcement.

"Why fire me?" she asked.

"This shouldn't come as a surprise." In the absence of a necktie to adjust, he straightened the collar on his gray sweater. "You could have stayed here last night, but you chose otherwise."

She had expected a reprimand, but threatening to fire her was way over-the-top. No way would she let him get away with it. "Are you saying that you'd fire me because I wouldn't spend the night with you?"

"Certainly not," he said in the cool baritone he used to mesmerize juries. "That would be sexual harassment, and I have no intentions toward you other than expecting—no, demanding—a professional performance of your duties."

"But I've been professional," she protested. She'd run the meetings in his absence, recorded them and made sure he was hooked in via computer when his presence as an attorney was required.

"I'm disappointed in you, Sasha. I've gone out of my way to nurture your career at the firm. Some people might think I was expecting a quid pro quo where I scratch your back and you scratch mine, but—"

"Did you lead anyone else to believe in this quid pro quo?" She translated into the non-Latin version: sleeping with him to get favors on the job.

He lifted his coffee mug to his unsmiling lips. "Smallminded people draw their own conclusions when they see an attractive twenty-three-year-old woman rising so quickly through the ranks."

Her jaw tightened. She hadn't been goofing off. As his legal assistant, she'd put in hours and hours of overtime doing research and filing court documents. All her good work was going up in smoke. "You still haven't told me why you'd terminate my employment."

"Let's start with whatever idiotic urge compelled you to spy on the Gateway Hotel through my binoculars."

"That wasn't smart," she conceded, "but the consequences turned out well. Because I witnessed the murder, I could state, unequivocally, that our client was innocent."

Damien shrugged. "I'd be willing to forgive if that was your only indiscretion, but you failed on a more important level. You betrayed the sacred bond between client and attorney."

"Confidentiality," she said.

"Do you deny that you shared information you obtained from me or from one of our clients with Deputy Brady Ellis?"

She couldn't categorically say that she hadn't told Brady about a few details he'd shared with her about the investigation. She knew that she'd mentioned that the Denver police considered Westfield's death to be murder. "I've said nothing that would affect or harm our clients."

"That's not for you to decide," he said. "Confidential means you keep your mouth shut. I partially blame myself for your failure. I should have counseled you about how difficult it can be for attorneys to work closely with law enforcement, especially when the cop in question is a tall, good-looking cowboy."

Her lips pressed together, holding back a scream of frustration. *What a sleazeball.* He was insinuating that Brady had seduced her to get information, which was patently ridiculous. "He was acting as my bodyguard."

"I'm sure he kept his eye on your body."

She couldn't pretend that she and Brady hadn't slept together last night. Nor could she claim a lack of culpability. Damn it, she'd broken confidentiality. She should have known better. And so should Brady.

Her job wasn't the most important thing in her life, but she didn't want to lose it. Not like this, anyway. She didn't want that stain on her record.

Straightening her shoulders, she faced the sleaze and asked, "How can I make this right?"

"I'm afraid it's too late."

"You're going to need my help at the meeting." He had no idea what she actually did to record those sessions and make sense of them.

"You bring up an interesting but irrelevant point," he said. "There won't be any more meetings with the Arcadia investors. Moreno has pulled out because he doesn't want the association with Reinhardt and the murder. Thanks to you, my negotiations are falling apart."

As soon as he spoke, she got the full picture. Damien was setting her up to take the blame for the collapse of the Arcadia partnership and the possible loss of revenue to the firm. He could twist every contentious issue and every argument to look as if it was her fault. Given this scenario, she wasn't just losing the job with the Three Ss. Nobody would ever hire her again.

"I have a proposition," she said.

He chuckled. "You're joking."

"What if I could convince Moreno to come back into the fold? I know he's staying at the dude ranch and he wants to buy that property. I might be able to show him how it would be to his benefit to maintain ties with the resort."

"And why would he listen to you?"

That was a fair question, and she didn't have an answer. For the past couple of days, Moreno had been going out of his way to talk to her. If she stopped and listened, she might be able to change his mind. "I'd like to try."

Damien's cool but slimy gaze rested on her face. Never again would she think of him as handsome or eligible. He was a self-serving creep who, unfortunately, had a vast influence over her future employment. Even if she wasn't working for him, she'd need his recommendation.

"Talk to Moreno," he said. "If you can get him back on board, you can keep your job."

She jumped to her feet. "You won't be disappointed."

Halfway to the exit from the condo, he called after her. "Sasha."

Now what? She turned. "Yes, sir."

"Leave the notes and your briefcase."

His words stung. She'd gotten so accustomed to carrying her briefcase that it was like an extension of her arm. Returning to the kitchen counter, she opened the briefcase, took out her personal cell phone and her wallet and placed them in the pockets of her parka.

"These are mine." She also had a small makeup case, but she didn't want to dig through the briefcase to find it. "You can keep the rest. Is there anything else?"

"Be careful what you say to your deputy."

She ran for the door.

In the hallway outside, Brady stood waiting. Too fired up to wait for the elevator, she grabbed his arm and dragged him down the staircase. She charged through the lobby and burst through the exit door. Outside, the snow had given up for the day. Hazy blue skies streaked behind the snow clouds above the condo complex.

It must have been cold, but she didn't feel the chill as she stormed down the shoveled sidewalk. Distance— she wanted to put enough distance between herself and Damien that he wouldn't hear if she exploded. With Brady trailing in her wake, she marched to the end of the side-walk and climbed over the accumulated snow piled up at the curb. Her boots slipped on the packed ice in the parking lot, but she kept going. If the way had been clear, she would have run for a hundred miles until the anger inside her was spent.

At the next corner, she dug her toe into the snow and climbed onto another sidewalk. Icy water was already seeping through the seams into her boots, which really weren't made for outdoor activities. They were going to be ruined, and she didn't care, didn't care about anything.

Brady caught her arm, bringing her to a sudden halt. "Where are you going?"

"Let go." She wrenched her arm, but he held tight. "Let go of me, right now."

"Talk to me, Sasha."

"I'm in trouble," she shouted. In the still morning light, those words sounded like an obscenity. "Damien almost fired me."

Unsmiling, he asked, "How can I help?"

"You can't. And why would you want to?" She turned on him, unleashing her rage. "You hate my job."

"There must be something we can do."

"You've done quite enough, thank you very much. You're the reason I'm nearly unemployed."

His jaw tensed, and his head pulled back as though she'd slapped him. She knew that she was being unfair. No matter how furious she was, she couldn't blame Brady. Less than an hour ago, she'd been in his bed, in his arms, coming awake from a dream that reflected their night of lovemaking. How could she stand here and accuse him? What was wrong with her?

"Brady, I'm sorry."

"It's okay. Let's get out of here."

He placed his hand at the small of her back to guide her down the sidewalk, but his touch didn't soothe her. She felt empty and alone with no one on her side, no one to help her. She'd been playing with the big kids, and she'd lost.

"I don't deserve to be fired," she said, "but Damien has a valid reason. He accused me of breaching confidentiality when I talked to you, and he was one hundred percent right. I passed on information."

"You never revealed anything that would cause me to suspect Damien's clients."

"Technically, it doesn't matter. I should have kept my big mouth shut."

Her only hope for redemption was to convince Sam Moreno to change his mind and rejoin the Arcadia partnership.

Chapter Twenty

Before Brady agreed to chauffeur Sasha to the dude ranch to see Moreno, he insisted that they stop for coffee and breakfast. His concern wasn't to feed her; Jim Birch's wife always had something fresh from the oven at the dude ranch. Brady wanted Sasha to take her time and calm down.

Sitting in a booth at the Kettle Diner in Arcadia, he wasn't happy to see her drain her coffee cup in a few gulps. The last thing she needed in her agitated state was caffeine.

He understood why she'd exploded on the sidewalk outside the corporate condo. She was angry. And he knew she hadn't meant to blame him. She'd been lashing out, and he'd been little more than a bystander. Not innocent, though—he couldn't claim that his presence had no effect on Damien's threat to fire her. If Brady hadn't been there to listen to her privileged information, Sasha never would have been in trouble.

The waitress delivered each of them a plate of banana pancakes topped with bits of walnut, powdered sugar and maple syrup.

Sasha tasted and gave a nod. "These might be the best pancakes I've ever had."

"Are you sure they're gourmet enough for you?"

"Is that some kind of dig?"

"I'm just saying that you don't have to sound surprised when the food tastes good. We're pretty civilized up here."

"And a little bit touchy." She gestured with her fork.

"Maybe." He filled his mouth with pancake, not wanting to set off another eruption. One volcano a day was plenty for him.

Her voice dropped to that low, husky alto he'd come to associate with passion. "I'm sorry, Brady. I've already said it once, but I'll say it again. Sorry."

"I'm not mad."

But he was hurt, and he hated that feeling, that weakness. Last night when they'd made love, he'd made the mistake of opening himself up to her. She was more to him than a date or a one-night stand. She was someone he could spend a long time with.

It was pretty damn obvious that she didn't feel the same way. The possibility of losing her job had broken her heart. Picking up a paycheck at a fancy Denver law firm was more important to this city girl than being with him. Fine, he could live with that as long as he didn't gaze too deeply into her liquid blue eyes. He could forget what it felt like to hold her in his arms. He shoveled more pancakes into his mouth, trying to erase the memory of her soft, sweet lips.

"I need a plan," she said. "When I see Moreno, I need to figure out what to say to him. Any ideas?"

"Not really."

"He's been following me around, encouraging me to join his group. I've got to wonder why."

"Could be he's attracted to you."

"Nope, I don't get that feeling from him." She tossed her head, sending a ripple through her blond hair. "A woman knows."

"Is that right?"

"I knew with you," she said. "Maybe it was wishful

thinking, but as soon as I met you, I knew there was chemistry between us."

He didn't want to think about the fireworks when they touched. He focused on the problem at hand. "You've spent a lot of time around Moreno, and you've seen how he operates. How does he recruit his followers? What does he get from them?"

"Mostly money," she said. "People pay a lot for his advice. They think they're going to get rich or become powerful."

"And what happens when they don't?"

She leaned back in the booth and sipped her coffee. "I had a long talk with one of his minions. This guy had given up his job and lost his savings to follow Moreno. I thought he'd be angry. But no. He was even more devoted, more willing to hang on for the next big success. He recruited friends and family members to join the guru."

"Contacts," Brady said. "Maybe he wants to get close to you because of your contacts."

"But I don't know anybody."

"You work at a big law firm," he reminded her. "Moreno might want a connection inside your firm."

She rewarded him with a huge smile. "That's got to be right. In his eyes, having me at the Three *S*s is important. That's where I'm going to start with him."

Her sketchy logic made sense, but Brady wasn't comfortable with it. His gut told him that Moreno was dangerous and not to be trusted.

BACK AT JIM BIRCH's dude ranch, Sasha was pumped and ready to go. Raw energy coursed through her veins. She felt as if she could convince Moreno of anything. Sure, he was a world-renowned motivational speaker who boasted hundreds of thousands of followers. But she was motivated to get through to him.

Unfortunately, Moreno was nowhere in sight. He and a couple of his guys were out riding snowmobiles and ATVs across the new-fallen snow, taking advantage of a break in the weather. Sasha had no choice but to sit and wait at the kitchen table with Jim Birch and Brady.

Birch leaned forward and rested an elbow on the table-top. With his other hand, he pensively stroked his red mut-tonchops. "I'm going to take the deal," he said.

"Big decision," Brady said. "Are you sure you want to give up the ranch?"

"Moreno is offering a fair price. Not as much as when Westfield was bidding against him. Andrea thinks I could get more, but it seems fair to me."

"And how does the missus feel about it?"

"She's already got her bags packed and has made plane reservations to Florida. It's time we retire."

Though Sasha tried to stay engaged in the conversation, she couldn't stay focused. Under the table, her toe was tapping on the floor.

"We'll miss you around here," Brady said.

"In the summer, we'll be back for visits. But to tell you the truth, I'm not looking forward to another winter in the mountains. Life's too short. Poor old Virgil P. Westfield said he always wanted to retire in the mountains, and now he's dead." He shot Brady a glance. "Folks are saying he was murdered."

"That's what the sheriff told me this morning," Brady said. "The Denver P.D. told McKinley about the autopsy results. The killer clunked Westfield on the head and shoved him down the stairs."

"Did those Denver cops arrest anybody?"

Blake shook his head. "They haven't even got a suspect.

Mr. Westfield was alone in his house when it happened. His body wasn't found until the next morning."

Sasha felt a pang of guilt. She hadn't given a thought to the murders all day. "Was it a robbery? A break-in?"

"The alarm system wasn't on, and the back door was unlocked." Brady focused a steady gaze on her. "They think it was a professional killer."

Another possible link to Lauren's murder. A professional assassin had murdered Virgil P. and stabbed Lauren and climbed into the corporate condo like a ninja. And he—if it was only one killer—was still at large. "When did you talk to the sheriff?"

"While I was waiting for you outside the condo."

She gave a curt nod, not wanting to think about those moments when Damien had been running her life through the shredder. She ought to be more worried about her personal safety, but all she could think about was her next job interview when she had to explain why she might be fired. If she told her future employer that she was being chased by a ninja, would it hurt her prospects?

She pushed away from the table, went to the sink, dumped the remains of her coffee and rinsed the cup. Through the window she saw distant peaks etched against a fragile blue sky. Sunlight glistened on rolling fields of white snow, unbroken except for the tracks of snowmobiles. There was no other sign of Moreno and his minions.

She couldn't wait one more minute. Returning to the table, she gave Jim Birch a smile. "Do you have any snowmobiles that aren't being used right now?"

"I was wondering when you'd ask," he said. "You've been as jumpy as a long-tailed cat in a roomful of rocking chairs. It might do you good to get outside and blow off steam."

"That's not a bad idea," Brady said as he stood. "Jim, have you got some heavy-duty gloves we can borrow?"

"You know I do. I keep a stock of everything for the dudes that visit the ranch with nothing more than cute little mittens. Help yourself. You know where everything is."

Finally, it felt as if she was doing something. She followed Brady's instructions as he outfitted her in the mudroom off the kitchen. With waterproof snow pants over her jeans, gloves with cuffs that went halfway up to her elbows and heavy boots that were a size too big, she felt as though she was preparing for a trip to the moon. "Is all this really necessary?"

"Baby, it's cold outside." He studied her with a critical eye. "You should swap your parka for something heavier."

"I'll be fine." She had her wallet and cell phone in her parka. Not that she was planning to use them. "Is it hard to learn how to snowmobile?"

"It's kind of like riding a dirt bike."

With a shudder, she remembered her brother pushing her down the hill outside their house. "The first time I rode a bike, I nearly killed myself."

"I won't let that happen."

Was he beginning to forgive her? Someday things might be all right between them again. But probably not today.

In the dark recesses of her mind, she realized that she might have lost out on the chance to be with Brady. Their relationship had just begun, and it might already be over. She might never make love to him again. She didn't dare to think about that loss. *One disaster at a time.* She trundled out the back door behind him, tromping in his footsteps through new snow that rose higher than her ankles.

In one of the outbuildings near the big barn, Brady showed her a collection of ATVs and snowmobiles. "Jim says he keeps these for the tourists, but I know better.

When he goes out on a snowmobile, he's like a big kid with hairy red sideburns."

"He does have a Yosemite Sam thing going on," she said. "It's ironic that his idea of retirement is to leave this place. So many others, like Mr. Westfield, want to live here."

"Working at a dude ranch is different from visiting."

She sat on a racy blue machine that reminded her of a scooter with skis instead of tires. "Can I use this one?"

"If it has keys, you can take it." He picked a blue helmet off the wall and handed it to her. "You'll need this."

"Why? Am I going to be falling a lot?"

"Count on it."

He ran through the basic instructions, showing her how to use the throttle to give more gas and telling her to lean into the turns.

"It'll take a while for you to get the feel of how fast you should be moving. You need enough speed to go uphill. But you've still got to stay in control. Keep in mind that there are rocks and tree stumps buried under the snow."

She fastened the chin strap on her helmet, started the snowmobile and chugged out the door. As he'd promised, it was fairly easy. By the time they got away from the barn, she was beginning to understand how to ride. As she and Brady went past the corral, a couple of horses looked up disinterestedly and nickered.

Beyond the fences, they hit the wide-open fields. She watched as Brady took off, standing on the floor boards of his snowmobile and flying over the bumps and hills in the field. He let out whoops of pure exhilaration as he swept in a wide circle back to her and stopped, kicking up a spray of snow.

He flipped back the visor on his helmet. "Your turn, city girl."

"I can do this. I'm not a sissy."

"Show me."

As she drove into the snow, the earth seemed to shift under the skis of her snowmobile. She felt out of control and off-balance as she toiled to reach the top of a small rise. And then she went faster. And faster. And faster. The pure sensation of speed hyped her adrenaline as she accelerated over a hill and caught air on the other side. Swerving, she almost turned on her side but managed to right herself.

When she stopped, Brady was right beside her. She flipped her visor up. "This is the best."

"I thought you might like going fast."

"I love it."

"I want to show you a view. Follow me."

"Right behind you, cowboy."

Surrounded by unbelievable, spectacular mountain scenery and revved by excitement, she almost forgot why she was here. She wanted a snowmobile. She wanted to feel like this every day for the rest of her life.

While she and Brady swept across the hills, she lost track of time but still had a sense of direction. The landscape was vaguely familiar. The cliff with the cave he'd shown her two days ago was to her right.

Brady was near the edge of the forest when she saw two other riders coming toward her. It had to be Moreno and his henchman. It was time to put on her game face.

He stopped beside her and flipped his visor up. "I'm surprised you're here, Sasha."

"I've been looking for you." She lifted her own visor. "In the past couple of days, it seems like you've been trying to tell me something. I'm ready to listen."

"You're perceptive," he said smoothly. "I've been trying to get you alone."

She couldn't tell if this was going well or not. With a

determined grin, she asked, "Why do you want to see me? Is it because of my contacts at the law firm?"

"Guess again."

He wanted to play games? Well, fine. She'd humor him. "You can't be looking to me as an investor, because we both know I'm a paralegal with a fixed salary."

"Why would I want to get you alone?"

She glanced over her shoulder toward the forest where she'd last seen Brady. "You want to ask me out on a date?"

Moreno laughed out loud. "I'm a careful businessman, Sasha. I don't like to leave loose ends…or eyewitnesses."

His companion flipped up his visor.

She was staring at a face that was branded into her memory and haunted her nightmares. It was him, the man who had killed Lauren Robbins.

Chapter *Twenty-One*

From the top of a ridge at the edge of the forest, Brady saw her metallic blue snowmobile trapped between two others. It had to be Moreno. Brady had been looking for him and the minions but hadn't caught sight of them until this moment. The timing bothered him. It was as though they'd been waiting until he was far from Sasha and unable to come to her aid.

He tore off his glove, opened his parka and drew his handgun. He might be making a mistake, but this time he'd go with his gut. Raising his weapon, he fired into the air.

The result was immediate and unexpected. Sasha's snowmobile took off. She raced across the field, headed toward the cliff. *The cave.* She was running for cover.

Gunfire ripped across the valley and echoed. One of the men was shooting at him.

"That's right," Brady muttered under his breath as he fired back. "Focus on me. Forget her."

They didn't come after him. They followed Sasha.

He needed to get to her first.

The powder snow at the edge of the forest wasn't as deep as in the field. His snowmobile shot across the land at top speed. He took a hard jolt and struggled to right himself. If he fell, he wouldn't be able to get up in time to stop them. He couldn't fall, couldn't pause. His bare hand clutching the gun was freezing cold.

But he was making headway. He was within a hundred yards of Sasha when she stopped at the foot of the cliff and leaped from her snowmobile. She scrambled up the path leading to the cave. He didn't know what had inspired her. Hiding in the cave was smart because they couldn't get to her. But she'd be trapped. There was only one way in or out.

He saw her disappear behind the boulder that hid the entrance to the cave. For the moment, she was safe.

And he was closing in. He slid to a stop beside her snowmobile, dismounted and dropped to one knee to aim his handgun. With his fingers half-frozen, he couldn't accurately hit the broad side of a barn, but the other two on the snowmobiles didn't know that. When he snapped off three shots, they slowed and stopped, preparing to return fire.

He dashed up the cliff, following Sasha's path. When he got to the safety of the cave, he'd call for backup. Not to Sheriff McKinley. Unless one of the deputies happened to be close, it'd take too long for law enforcement to get here. He'd call Jim Birch.

Likely, Birch had already heard the gunfire and was wondering about it.

In his bulky snow clothes, Brady squeezed himself through the small opening to the cave. "Sasha, are you all right?"

"I saw him," she said. "The man with Moreno is the killer."

She was using the LED function on her cell phone as a flashlight. In the bluish glow, he saw the fear she'd managed to keep mostly under wraps. He nodded to the phone. "Did you call for help?"

"I've got no reception in here."

He should have figured as much. "Move around. There might be a place you can get through."

She'd already peeled off her extra layer of snow clothes, and he did the same. If they couldn't call out, they'd have to make a stand in here, and they needed to be mobile.

From outside the cave, he heard Moreno's voice. "Are you in there, Deputy?"

"Step inside and find out."

If Moreno poked his head into the cave, Brady had the advantage. While they were squeezing through, he could shoot.

After a moment, Moreno said the obvious. "Looks like we have a standoff."

"Not for long. I called for backup." Brady had his phone in hand. *No reception.* But Moreno didn't know that. "You might as well give up right now."

"You underestimate me. I've gotten out of worse situations than this."

Brady's best hope was that Jim Birch would come looking for them. When he saw the abandoned snowmobiles, he'd know something was wrong. Until then, he'd try to keep Moreno distracted.

"I've got a question for you, Moreno. Why'd you kill Virgil Westfield?"

"The man was in his nineties. His death should have been chalked up to old age. I don't know why everybody got so worked up about it."

Because he was murdered. "What did he do to you?"

"He knew too much. When he and Lauren started digging into my financial background to undermine my bid on the dude ranch, they uncovered a few nasty details about my offshore businesses. I was actually impressed.

Lauren was one hell of a good bookkeeper. Too bad she got greedy."

"She tried to blackmail you," Brady said.

"It's about more than just the money. If my finances don't look clean and pure, I lose credibility with my followers. I need for them to believe in me."

"If you conceive it," Brady said, "you can achieve it."

"Ninety-nine percent of the time, it's true. Getting rid of Lauren and the documentation she tried to use against me would have been easy. Her death would have gone unnoticed for weeks if Sasha hadn't been looking through that window. This brings us to the current situation. Something must be done."

The craziest thing about Moreno was that he sounded sane. He talked about multiple murders the way other people made dinner plans.

"I'm leaving you now," Moreno said. "I'll have to take care of damage control and arrange for you to both disappear without a trace. In the meantime, my friend will keep watch outside the cave. Sooner or later, you'll have to come out."

And then, Brady supposed, Moreno's friend would kill them. There didn't seem to be an escape.

STILL HOLDING HER cell phone for light against the intense darkness of the cave, Sasha stepped into Brady's arms and melted against him. Fear had robbed her of strength. Her legs trembled with the effort of merely standing. "I guess losing my job isn't the worst thing that could happen."

He lifted her chin, tilted her face toward his. "I guess not."

Gazing up at him, she saw the dimple at the corner of his mouth. For some reason, that gave her hope. If Brady could still smile, all was not lost. His lips brushed hers, and fear receded another step. He kissed her more powerfully, pulling her close against him, and she felt life returning to her body. She wasn't ready to give up. Not yet. Not when she had something to live for.

She heard a rustling near the entrance to the cave. Brady must have heard it, too. He turned his head in that direction, lifted his handgun and casually fired a shot, reminding Moreno's friend that they weren't helpless.

Her hand glided down his cheek. "There's nothing like facing death to get your priorities straight."

"I was thinking the same thing."

"My job isn't such a big deal," she said. "And it doesn't matter if I live in a city or in the mountains. Other things are more important. People are important."

When she'd been snowmobiling across the field, the threat of danger had become real. And she wasn't thinking about her employment possibilities or her salary. She thought of him. She thought of long nights in front of the fireplace and waking up with him in the morning. "Brady, you are important to me."

"Same here. You're more important than I ever would have thought possible after only knowing you a couple of days." His breath was warm against her cheek. "I love you, Sasha."

"If I have to die…" Her voice trailed off. "I'm glad we're together."

"Nobody's going to die. Not on my watch."

He gave her another quick kiss and then went into action, gathering up rocks from the floor of the cave. "Help me out. We're going to pile these up by the entrance. Anybody who tries to sneak in will make a lot of racket."

Still holding her phone, she did as he said. Within a few minutes, they had a stack of loose rock that was two feet high.

"Now what?" she asked.

"We've got to find another way out."

"Didn't you say that you'd explored these caves when you were a kid? You didn't find another exit then."

"I wasn't as motivated then as I am now. You go first. We'll use your cell phone until it goes dark. Then we'll switch to mine."

Losing the light from the cell phone would be terrible. The dark inside the cave felt palpable and thick, almost like being underwater. He pointed the way through the darkness, but she took the first steps, passing the stalagmites that looked like dragon's teeth.

Too soon it seemed as if they had come to the end of the caverns that were large enough to stand upright in. Brady felt along the walls, looking for a break or a fissure. "Bring the light over here."

She knelt and aimed her phone at the bottom side of an overhang. Peering into the narrow horizontal space, she said, "I can't tell if this leads anywhere or not."

"Only one way to find out."

He flattened himself on the floor and stretched his arm into the opening. "I don't feel another rock."

"You can't fit in there. It's barely big enough for your shoulder."

She wasn't claustrophobic but didn't relish the idea of squeezing herself into a narrow space without knowing where it went. "Is there any way to tell how far it goes?"

"No, and that's why I'll go first. I don't want you to get hurt. Sometimes these gaps in the rock lead to other rooms. Sometimes the floor disappears and you fall into a pit."

Reluctantly, she pointed out the flaw in his logic. "I should go first. For one thing, I'm smaller. For another, if I start slipping into a pit, you're strong enough to haul me back up."

Placing the cell phone on the floor, she maneuvered around so she could wriggle feetfirst into the space below the overhang. He laced his fingers through hers, holding tightly as the lower half of her body disappeared into the fissure.

"That's enough," he said.

"There's more space. I can keep going."

"I don't want to lose you. I've barely just found you. If you disappeared from my life, I couldn't stand it."

"I feel the same. And I can't believe that I do. This is happening so fast." She blew the moist cave dirt away from her mouth. "I can count on one hand the number of men I've cared about. And that was after weeks and weeks of dating."

"Fast is good," he said.

"I love you, Brady."

They heard the crash of rocks coming from the front entrance. Moreno's friend had grown tired of waiting. He was coming after them.

Brady yanked her away from the overhang and turned off the light on her cell. Total darkness surrounded them, and she was immediately disoriented.

"Stay on the floor," he whispered.

When she heard him moving away from her, she wanted to grab his ankle and hold on. She curled into a ball. Her hand rested on the side of the cave.

A flash of light drew her attention. Someone was using a cell phone to find their way. It had to be the killer. She didn't see Brady.

The sound of gunfire crashed against the rocks. Two guns shooting. Then one. Then silence.

She pinched her lips together to keep from making any noise. Her heart drummed against her rib cage. The darkness was stifling.

The light from a cell phone flared.

She was looking into the murderer's face. He lifted his gun.

From behind his back, Brady fired first. His first bullet tore through the other man's shoulder, causing him to drop his weapon. The second shot was centered in the murderer's chest. He fell to the floor of the cave.

It was over.

Epilogue

At the Gateway Hotel, the gala grand opening for the ski lodge was keeping the valets hopping. As Sasha exited the limo Dooley had rented for the occasion, she knew she looked pretty spectacular in her black gown with the plunging neckline, especially since she was draped in a fake fur coat that Jim Birch's wife had given to her. Jim's missus said she wouldn't need fur in Florida, which was where they were going even though the deal with Sam Moreno had fallen through.

Moreno was in police custody, as was his "friend," who hadn't died in the cave.

Everything that had happened after he was shot was kind of a blur. She and Brady had climbed out of the cave into the chilly afternoon light, and he'd put in the call for backup. As it turned out, Sheriff McKinley had already been on his way. Jim Birch had called him when he heard gunfire. The CBI agents had taken responsibility for Moreno's arrest.

She strolled across the red carpet at the entrance with her hand lightly resting on Brady's arm. In his black suit and white linen shirt, he was her best accessory. She was proud to be Brady and Dooley's guest for this event.

When they entered the lobby, Katie Cook rushed toward her and took her hand. "Sasha, darling, how are you?"

She'd never gotten that kind of enthusiastic greeting when she was only a legal assistant. Moreno's dramatic arrest had turned her into a local celebrity. "I'm very well, thanks. Do you remember Brady?"

"The deputy?" Katie squinted as though she couldn't believe this sophisticated-looking man was the rugged lawman who had given them all so much trouble.

He gave her a dimpled smile and a nod. "It's a pleasure to see you, ma'am."

"Dooley's nephew," she said. "Of course, I remember you."

Politely, Sasha asked about the Arcadia partnership and how their negotiations were going, but she really didn't care. She wasn't part of the law firm anymore. Though she'd left two phone messages for Damien, he'd never bothered to call her back.

Katie scanned the crowd, looking for someone more impressive to talk to. Offhandedly, she asked, "What are your plans?"

"I'm going back to school."

"Law school?"

No way. Sasha wasn't cut out to be a lawyer. She wanted to help people and to pursue justice in another way. "I'm going to study forensic science."

"Whatever for?" Katie asked.

Brady answered for her. "I'm planning to run for sheriff in the next election. And my first order of business will be to upgrade local law enforcement."

He'd stepped into the role of taking on authority as though he was born to it. Every day she spent with Brady, she found something else to love about him.

As he took her coat, she spotted Damien in his tuxedo. He was standing near the statue of Artemis. "Will you excuse me, Katie?"

"Of course, dear." She was already waving to someone else. "Don't be a stranger."

Sasha looked up at Brady. "There's something I need to say to Damien."

"Do you want backup? I'd be happy to shoot him in the foot or kick his sorry behind."

"I can handle this myself. Like a professional."

She stalked through the lobby until she was standing directly in front of the man she would forever think of as a giant sleaze. When he opened his mouth to speak, she held up her hand to stop him.

"Two words," she said. "I quit."

She spun on her heel and walked back to Brady. By the time she reached his side, Damien was forgotten. She'd never been so happy or so much in love.

* * * * *

CHRISTMAS AT THUNDER HORSE RANCH

ELLE JAMES

This book is dedicated to my fans who kept writing, asking when Dante would have his book. Without my fans I wouldn't be pursuing the career I love. Thank you for reading and falling in love with my characters. May all your lives be blessed!

Chapter One

Big sky…check. Flat plains…check. Storm clouds rolling in…check.

Like ticking off his preflight checklist, Dante Thunder Horse reviewed what was in front of him, a typical early winter day in North Dakota before the first real snowstorm of the season. It had been a strange December. Usually it snowed by Thanksgiving and the snow remained until well into April.

This year, the snow had come by Halloween and melted and still the ground hadn't yet grown solid with permafrost.

Based on the low temperature and the clouds rolling in, that first real snow was about to hit their area. The kids of Grand Forks would be excited. With the holidays just around the corner, they'd have their white Christmas after all.

A hundred miles away from base, flying the U.S.-Canadian border as an air interdiction agent, or pilot, for the Customs and Border Protection, Dante was on a mission to check out a possible illegal border crossing called in by a concerned citizen. A farmer had seen a man on a snowmobile coming across the Canadian border.

He figured it was someone out joyriding who didn't realize he'd done anything wrong. Still, Dante had to check.

He didn't expect anything wild or dangerously crazy to happen. The Canadian border didn't have near the illegal crossings as the southern borders of the United States. Most of his sorties were spent enjoying the scenery and observing the occasional elk, moose or bear sighting.

Chris Biacowski, scheduled to fly copilot this sortie, had come down with the flu and called in sick.

Dante was okay with flying solo. He usually liked having the quiet time. Unless he started thinking about his past and what his future might have been had things worked out differently.

Three years prior, he'd been fighting Taliban in Afghanistan. He'd been engaged to Captain Samantha Olson, a personnel officer who'd been deployed at Bagram Airfield. Every chance he got he flew over to see her. They'd been planning their wedding and talking about what they'd put on their dream sheet for their next assignments.

After flying a particularly dangerous mission where his door gunner had taken a hit, Dante came back to base shaken and worried about his crew member. He stayed with the gunner until he was out of surgery. The gunner had survived.

But Dante's life would be forever changed. When he had left on his mission, his fiancée had decided to go with a few others to visit a local orphanage.

On the way back, her vehicle hit an improvised explosive device. Three of the four people on board the military vehicle had died instantly. Samantha had survived long enough to get a call through to the base. By the time medics arrived, she'd lost too much blood.

Dante had constructed images in his mind of Samantha lying on the ground, the uniform she'd been so proud to wear torn, a pool of her own blood soaking into the desert sand.

He'd thought through the chain of events over and over, wondering if he'd gone straight from his mission to Bagram, would Samantha have stayed inside the wire instead of venturing out? Had their talk about the babies they wanted spurred her to visit the children no one wanted? Those whose parents had been collateral damage or killed by the Taliban as warning or retribution?

Today was the third anniversary of her death. When Chris had called in sick, Dante couldn't cancel the flight, and he sure as hell couldn't stay at home with his memories haunting him.

For three years, he'd pored over the events of that day, wishing he could go back and change things so that Samantha was still there. How was he expected to get on with his life when her memory haunted him?

The only place he felt any peace whatsoever was soaring above the earth. Sometimes he felt closer to Samantha, as if he was skimming the underbelly of heaven.

As he neared the general area of the farm in the report, movement brought his mind back to earth. A dark shape exploded out of a copse of trees, moving swiftly into the open. It appeared to be a man on a snowmobile. The vehicle came to a halt in the middle of a wide-open field and the man dismounted.

Dante dropped lower and circled, trying to figure out what he was up to. About the time he keyed his mic to radio back to headquarters, he saw the man unstrap what appeared to be a long pipe from the back of his snowmobile and fit something into one end of it.

Recognition hit, and Dante's blood ran cold. He jerked the aircraft up as quickly as he could. But he was too late.

The man on the ground fired a rocket-propelled grenade.

Dante dodged left, but the grenade hit the tail and exploded. The helicopter lurched and shuddered. He tried to keep it steady, but the craft went into a rapid spin. Realizing his tail rudder had probably been destroyed, Dante had to land and if he didn't land level, the blades could hit first, break off and maybe even end his life.

The chopper spun, the centrifugal force making it difficult for Dante to think and move. He reached up and switched the engines off, but not soon enough. The aircraft plummeted to the ground, a blade hit first, broke off and slammed into the next blade. The skids slammed against the ground and Dante was thrown against the straps of his harness. He flung an arm over his face as fragments of the blades acted like flying shrapnel, piercing the chopper's body and windows. The helicopter rolled onto its side and stopped.

Suspended by his harness, Dante tried to key the mic on his radio to report his aircraft down. The usual static was absent, the aircraft lying as silent as death.

Dante dragged his headset off his head. Frigid wind blew through the shattered windows and the scent of fuel stung his nostrils.

The sound of an engine revving caught Dante's attention. The engine noise grew closer, moving toward his downed aircraft. Had the predator come to finish off his prey?

He scrambled for the harness releases, finally finding and pulling on the quick-release buckles. He dropped on his left side, pain knifing through his arm. Gritting his teeth, he scrambled to his knees on the door beneath him and attempted to reach up to push against the passenger door. Burning pain stabbed his left arm again and he dropped the arm and worked with his good arm to fling the passenger-side door open. It bounced on its hinges and smashed closed again, nearly crushing his fingers with the force.

He hunched his shoulder and nudged the door with it, pushing it open with a little less force. This time, the door remained open and he stood, his head rising above the body of the craft. As he took stock of the situation, a bullet pinged against the craft's fuselage.

Dante ducked. A snowmobile had come to a stop a hundred yards away, the rider bent over the handlebars, pointing a high-powered rifle in his direction. With nothing but the body of the helicopter between him and the bullets, Dante was a sitting duck.

He sniffed the acrid scent of aviation fuel growing more potent as the time passed and more bullets riddled the exterior of the craft. If he stayed inside the helicopter, he stood a chance of the craft bursting into flames and being burned alive. If the bullets sparked a fire, the fuel would burn. If the flames reached the tanks, it would create a tremendous explosion.

Out of the corner of his eye, he could see the bright orange flicker of a flame. In seconds, the ground surrounding his helicopter was a wall of fire.

Amid the roar of flames, the snowmobile revved and swooped closer.

Debating how long he should wait before throwing himself out on the ground, Dante could feel the heat of the flames against his cheeks. If he didn't leave soon, there wouldn't be anything left for the attacker to shoot.

The engine noise faded, drowned out by the roar of the fire.

With fire burning all around him, Dante pulled himself out of the fuselage one-armed and dropped to the ground. His shoulder hit a puddle of the flaming fuel and his jumpsuit ignited.

Rolling through the wall of flames, Dante couldn't get the flame to die out. His skin heated, the fuel was thoroughly soaked into the fabric. He rolled away from the flame, onto his back, unzipped the flight suit and shimmied out of it before the burning fabric melted and stuck to his skin.

Another bullet thunked into the earth beside Dante. Wearing nothing but thermal underwear, Dante rolled over in the snow, hugging the ground, giving his attacker very little target to aim at.

Covered in snow, with nothing to defend himself, Dante awaited his fate.

EMMA JENNINGS HAD spent the morning bundled in her thermal underwear, snow pants, winter jacket, earmuffs and gloves, one of them fingerless. Yes, it was getting colder by the minute. Yes, she should have given up two days ago, but she felt like she was so close, and the longer she waited, the harder the ground got as permafrost transformed it from soft dirt to hard concrete.

The dig had been abandoned by everyone else months ago when school had started up again at the University of North Dakota. Emma came out on weekends hoping to get a little farther along. Fall had been unseasonably warm with only one snowfall in late October that had melted immediately. Six inches of snow had fallen three days ago and seemed in no hurry to melt, though the ground hadn't hardened yet. The next snowfall expected for that evening would be the clincher, with the predicted two feet of snow.

If she hadn't set up a tent around the dig site months ago, she never would have come. As it was, school was out and she'd come with her tiny trailer in tow, with the excuse that she needed to pull down the tent and stow it for the winter. If not for the steep roof, the tent would easily collapse under the twenty-four inches of white powder. Not to mention the relentless winds across the prairie would destroy the tent if it was left standing throughout the wicked North Dakota winter.

Each weekend since fall semester began had proved to be fair and Emma had gone out to dig until this weekend. Some had doubted there'd be snow for Christmas. Not Emma. She'd lived in North Dakota all her life, and never once in her twenty-six years had the snow missed North Dakota at Christmas.

So far, the dig had produced the lower jawbone of a *Tyrannosaurus rex*. Emma was certain if she kept digging, she'd find the skull of the animal nearby. The team of paleontologists and students who'd been on the dig all summer had unearthed neck bones, and near the end of the summer, the jawbone. The skull had to be close. She just needed a little more time.

There to tear down the tent before it was buried in knee-deep drifts, she'd ducked inside to find the ground smooth and dry and the dirt just as she'd left it the weekend before. She squatted to scratch away at the surface with a tool she'd left behind. Before she knew it, she'd succumbed to the lure of the dig. That had been two days ago.

Knowing she had to leave before the storm hit, she'd given herself half of the last day to dig. Immersed in her work, the sound of a helicopter cut through her intense concentration and she glanced at her watch. With a gasp, she realized just how long she'd been there and that it was nearing sunset of her last day on the site.

She still needed to get the tent down and stowed before

dark. With a regretful glance at the ground, she pushed the flap back and ducked through. High clouds blocked out any chance for warmth or glare from the sun.

The thumping sound of blades churning the air drew her attention and she glanced at the sky. About a mile away, a green-and-white helicopter hovered low over the prairie.

From where she stood, she couldn't see what it was hovering over. The ground had a gentle rise and dip, making the chopper appear to be almost on the ground. Emma recognized the craft as one belonging to the Customs and Border Protection.

There was a unit based out of Grand Forks and she knew one of the pilots, Dante Thunder Horse, from when he'd taken classes at the university. A handsome Native American, he had caught her attention crossing campus, his long strides eating up the distance.

He'd taken one of her anthropology classes and they'd met in the student commons on a couple of occasions and discussed the university hockey team games. When he'd finally asked her out, she'd screwed up enough courage to take him up on it, suggesting a coffee shop where they'd talked and seemed to hit it off.

Then nothing. He hadn't called or asked her out for another date. He must have finished his coursework at the university because she hadn't run into him again. Nor did she see him crossing campus. She'd been disappointed when he hadn't called, but that was at the end of last spring. The summer had kept her so busy on the dig, she wouldn't have had time for a relationship—not that she was any good at it anyway. Her longest one had lasted two months before her shyness had scared off the poor young man.

Emma wondered if Dante was the pilot flying today.

She marveled at how close the helicopter was. In all the vastness of the state, how likely was it that the aircraft would be hovering so near to the dig? Then again, the site was fairly close to the border and the CBP was tasked with protecting the northern border of the United States.

As Emma started to turn back to her tent to begin the job of tearing it down, a loud bang shook the air. Startled, she saw a flash in her peripheral vision from the direction of the helicopter. When she spun to see what had happened, the chopper was turning and turning. As if it was a top being spun faster and faster, it dropped lower and lower until it disappeared below the rise and a loud crunching sound ripped the air.

Her heart stopped for a second and then galloped against her ribs. The helicopter had crashed. As far away from civilization as they were, there wasn't a backup chopper that could get to the pilot faster than she could.

Abandoning her tent, she ran for the back of the trailer, flung open the utility door in the rear, dropped the ramp and climbed inside. She'd loaded the snowmobile on the off chance she couldn't get the truck all the way down the road to the dig. Fortunately, she'd been able to drive almost all the way to the site and had parked the truck and trailer on a hardstand of gravel the wind had blown free of snow near the edge of the eight-foot-deep dig site.

Praying the engine would start, she turned the key and pressed the start button. The rumble of the engine echoed off the inside of the trailer but then it died. The second time she hit the start button, the vehicle roared to life. Shifting to Reverse, she backed down the ramp and turned to face the direction the helicopter had crashed.

A tower of flames shot toward the sky, smoke rising in a plume.

Her pulse pounding, Emma raced across the snow, headed for the fire.

As she topped the rise, her heart fell to her knees. The helicopter was a battered heap, lying on its side, flames rising all around.

Gunning the throttle, Emma sped across the prairie, praying she wasn't too late. Maybe the pilot had been thrown clear of the aircraft. She hoped she was right.

As she neared the wreck, movement caught her attention. Another snowmobile was headed toward the helicopter from the north. *Good,* she thought. Maybe whoever it was had also seen the chopper crash and could help her free the pilot from the wreckage and get him to safety. She waved her hand, hoping the driver would see her and know she was there to help. He didn't give any indication he'd spotted her. But the snowmobile slowed. The rider pulled off his helmet, his dark head in sharp contrast to his white jacket. He leveled what appeared to be a rifle across the handlebars, aiming at something near the wall of flames.

Emma squinted, trying to make out what he was doing. The pop of rifle fire made her jump. That's when she noticed a dark lump on the ground in the snow, outside the ring of fire around the helicopter. The lump moved, rolling over in the snow.

The driver of the other snowmobile climbed onto the vehicle and started toward the man on the ground, moving slowly, his rifle poised to shoot.

Emma gasped.

The man was trying to shoot the guy on the ground.

With a quick twist of the throttle she sent her snowmobile skimming across the snow, headed straight for the attacker. At the angle she was traveling, the attacker wouldn't see her if he was concentrating on the man on the ground.

Unarmed, she only had her snowmobile and her wits. The man on the ground only had one chance at survival. If she didn't get to him or the other snowmobile first, he didn't stand a chance.

Coming in from the west, Emma aimed for the man with the gun. She didn't have a plan other than to ram him and hope for the best.

He didn't see her or hear her engine over the roar of his own until she was within twenty feet of him. The man turned the weapon toward her.

Emma gave the engine all it could take and raced straight for the man. He fired a shot. Something plinked against the hood of the snowmobile engine. At the last moment, she turned the handlebars. Her machine slid into the side of his and the handlebars knocked the gun from his hand.

She twisted the throttle and skidded sideways across the snow, spinning around to face him again.

Disarmed, the attacker had turned as well and raced north, away from the burning helicopter and the man on the ground.

Emma watched as the snowmobile continued into the distance. Keeping an eye on the north, she turned her snowmobile south toward the figure lying still on the ground.

She pulled up beside him and leaped off the snowmobile into the packed snow where he'd rolled.

A man in thermal underwear lay facedown in the snow, blood oozing from his left arm, dripping bright red against the pristine white snow.

Emma bent toward him, her hand reaching out to push him over.

The man moved so quickly, she didn't know what hit her. He rolled over, snatched her wrist and jerked her flat onto her belly, then straddled her, his knees planted on both sides of her hips, twisting her arm up between her shoulder blades.

Until that point, she hadn't realized just how vulnerable she was. On the snowmobile, she had a way to escape. Once she'd left the vehicle, she'd put herself at risk. What if the man shooting had been the good guy? In the middle of nowhere, with a big man towering over her, she was trapped and out of ideas.

"Let me up!" she yelled, aiming for righteous contempt. Her voice wobbled, muffled by a mouthful of snow it sounded more like a frog's croak.

She tried to twist around to face him, but he planted his fist into the middle of her back, holding her down, the cold snow biting her cheek.

"Why did you shoot down my helicopter?" he demanded, his voice rough but oddly familiar.

"I didn't, you big baboon," she insisted. "The other guy did."

His hands roved over her body, patting her sides, hips, buttocks, legs and finally slipping beneath her jacket and up to her breasts. His hands froze there and she swore.

Emma spit snow and shouted, "Hey! Hands off!"

As quickly as she'd been face-planted in the snow, the man on top of her flipped her onto her back and stared down at her with his dark green eyes.

"Dante?"

"Emma?" He shook his head. "What the hell are you doing here?"

Chapter Two

"Well, I'm sure not on a picnic," Emma said, her voice dripping with sarcasm.

Dante stared down at the pretty young college professor he'd met when he'd taken classes at the University of North Dakota, working toward a master's degree in operations management.

She stared up at him with warm, dark chocolate-colored eyes, her gaze scanning his face. "What happened to you?" She reached up to touch his temple, her fingers coming away with blood. "Why was that man shooting at you?"

"I don't know." Dante's brow furrowed. "Did you get a good look at him?"

"No, it was all a blur. I thought he was coming to help, but then he started shooting at you. I rammed into him, knocking his gun out of his hands. Then he took off."

"You shouldn't have put yourself in that kind of danger."

"What was I supposed to do, stand by and watch him kill you?"

"Thankfully, he didn't shoot *you*. And thanks for saving my butt." Dante staggered to his feet and reached down with his right hand and helped her up. "He shot down my helicopter with an RPG and would have finished me off if you hadn't come along." A bitterly cold,

Arctic breeze rippled across the prairie, blowing straight through his thermal underwear. A shiver racked his body and he gritted his teeth to keep them from chattering.

Emma stood and brushed the snow off her pants and jacket. "What happened to your clothes?"

"I fell into a puddle of flaming aviation fuel when I climbed out of the helicopter." He glanced back at the inferno. "We need to get out of here in case the fire ignites the fuel in the tank."

He climbed onto her snowmobile.

"You should take my coat. I bet you're freezing." Emma started to unzip her jacket.

He held up his hand. "Don't. I can handle it for a little while and no use in both of us being cold." He moved back on the seat and tipped his head. "Get on. I don't know where you came from, but I hope it's warmer there than it is here."

Her lips twisted, but she didn't waste time. She slipped her leg over the seat and pressed the start button. She prayed the bent skid, damaged in the collision, wouldn't slow them down.

Once she was aboard, Dante wrapped his arms around her and pressed his body against her back, letting her body block some of the bitter wind.

It wasn't enough. The cold went right through his underwear, biting at his skin. He started shaking before they'd gone twenty yards. By the time they topped a rise, he could no longer feel his fingers.

Emma drove the snowmobile along a ridge below which a tent poked up out of the snow. A truck and trailer stood on the ridge, looking to Dante like heaven.

When she pulled up beside the trailer, Emma climbed off, looped one of Dante's arms over her shoulder and helped him into the trailer. It wasn't much warmer inside, but the wind was blocked and for that Dante could be very grateful. The trailer consisted of a bed, a sink, a small refrigerator and a tiny bathroom.

"Sit." Emma pushed him onto the bed, pulled off his boots and shoved his legs under the goose down blanket and a number of well-worn quilts. She handed him a dry washcloth. "Hold this on your shoulder so you don't bleed all over everything."

"Yes, ma'am," he said with a smile.

Her brows dipped. "Stay here while I get the generator running." She opened the door, letting in a cold blast of air.

"Keep your eyes open," he said through chattering teeth.

"I will." She closed the door behind her and the room was silent.

Dante hunkered down into the blankets, feeling as though he should be the one out there stirring the generator to life. When Emma hadn't returned in five minutes, he pushed the blankets aside, wrapped one around himself and went looking for her.

He was reaching for the doorknob when the door jerked open.

Emma frowned up at him, her dark hair dusted in snowflakes. "The generator's not working."

"Let me look at it," he insisted.

She pushed past him, closing the door behind her. "It won't do any good."

"Why?"

"The fuel line is busted." She held up the offending tube and waved him toward the bed. "Get back under the covers. At least we have a gas stove we can use to warm it up a little in here. I don't recommend running it all night, but it'll do for now."

"Why don't we get out of here?"

"It's almost dark and it started snowing pretty hard, I can barely see my hand in front of my face. It's hard enough to find my way out here in daylight. I'm not trying in the dark and especially not in North Dakota blizzard conditions."

"I need to let the base know what happened." He glanced around. "Do you have any kind of radio or cell phone?"

"I have a cell phone, but it won't work out here." She shrugged. "No towers nearby."

His body shook, his head ached and his vision was hazy. "I need to get back."

"Tomorrow. Now go back to bed before you fall down. I'm strong, but not strong enough to pick up a big guy like you."

Dante let Emma guide him back to the bed and tuck him in. When she smoothed the blankets over his chest, he grabbed her hand.

Her gaze met his as he carried her hand to his lips and kissed the back of her knuckles. "Thanks for saving my life."

Her cheeks reddened and she looked away. "You'd have done the same."

"I doubt seriously you'd be shot down from the sky. Your feet are pretty firmly on the ground." He smiled. "Paleontologist, right?"

She nodded.

"Isn't it a little late in the season to be at a dig? I thought they shut them down when the fall session started."

She shrugged. "With our unseasonably warm weather, I've been working this dig every weekend since the semester started."

"Until recently."

"Since it snowed a few days ago, I figured I'd better get out here. I'd heard more snow was coming, and I needed to dismantle my tent and bring it in." She stared toward the window as if she could see through the blinding snow.

"I take it you didn't get the tent down in time."

She gave him a little crooked smile. "A downed helicopter distracted me."

"Well, thank you for sacrificing your tent to be a Good Samaritan."

Her cheeks reddened and she turned away. "Let's get that shoulder cleaned up and bandaged."

She wet a cloth and returned to the bedside. Pushing the fabric of his thermal shirt aside, she washed the blood away.

Her fingers were gentle around the gash.

"It's just a scratch."

Her lips quirked. When she'd washed away the drying blood, she applied an antiseptic ointment and a bandage. "As it is, it was just a flesh wound, but it wouldn't do to get infected." Patting the bandage, she stepped back, the color higher in her cheeks. "I'll make you a cup of hot tea, if you'd like."

Studying her face, Dante found he liked the way she blushed so easily. "Have any coffee?"

"Sorry. I didn't expect to have guests."

"In that case, tea would be nice." Dante glanced around the tiny confines of the trailer. "Aren't you afraid to come out to places like this alone?"

Emma reached for two mugs from a cabinet. "Why should I be? It's not like anyone else comes out here."

"What if you were to get hurt?"

She shrugged. "It's a chance I'm willing to take."

"As close as it is to the border, you might be subject to more than just an elk hunter or farmer."

"I have a gun." Emma opened a drawer and pulled out a long, vintage revolver.

Dante grinned. "You call that a gun?"

She stiffened. "I certainly do."

"It's an antique."

"A Colt .45 caliber, Single Action Army revolver, to be exact."

Nodding, impressed, Dante stated, "You know the name of your antiques."

Her chin tipped upward. "And I'm an expert shot."

"My apologies for doubting you."

The wind picked up outside, rocking the tiny trailer on its wheels.

Emma struck a long kitchen match on the side of a box and lit one of the two burners on the stove. A bright flame cast a rosy glow in the quickly darkening space. She filled a teakettle with water from a large water bottle and settled it over the flame. "I have canned chili, canned tuna and crackers. Again, I hadn't planned on staying more than a couple of nights. I was supposed to head out before the weather laid in."

Despite his injuries, Dante's stomach grumbled. "I don't want to take your food."

She leveled her gaze at him. "I wouldn't offer if I didn't have enough."

"Then, thank you."

She opened two cans of chili and poured them into a pot, lit the other burner and settled the food over the flame.

Before long the teakettle steamed and the rich aroma of tomato sauce and chili powder filled the air. Emma moved with grace and efficiency, the gentle swell of her hips swaying from side to side as she moved between the sink and the stove. Dante's groin tightened. Not that she was his typical type.

Emma appeared to be straitlaced and uptight with little time in her agenda for playing the field, as proved by their one date that had gone nowhere. Still, it didn't give him the right to go after her again.

He shoved aside the blanket and tried to stand. "I should be helping you." A chill hit him, penetrating his long underwear as if he wore nothing at all.

"Stay put." She waved in his direction. "There's little enough room in the trailer without two people bumping into each other. And I've got this covered." She shed her jacket and hung it on a hook on the wall.

"I can at least get the plates and utensils down and set the table." He glanced around. "Uh, where is the table?"

Emma grinned. "It's under the bed. You were lying on it."

He gave her a half bow. "Where do you propose we eat?"

"On the bed." She grinned. "Picnic-style."

"Do you always eat in the bed?" Images of the slightly stiff Emma wearing a baby-doll nightgown, sitting on the coverlet, eating chocolate-covered strawberries popped into Dante's head. He tried but failed to banish the thought, his groin tightening even more. The slim professor with the chocolate-brown hair and eyes, and luscious lips tempted the saint right out of him. And the kicker was that she didn't even know she was so very hot.

"I don't usually have company in my trailer. I can eat wherever I want. In the summertime, I sit on a camp stool outside and watch the sun set over the dig."

He could picture the brilliant red, orange and mauve skies tinting her hair. "I'll consider it an adventure." He reached around her and opened one of the overhead cabinet doors. "Where are the dishes and utensils?" As he leaned over her, the scent of roses tantalized his nostrils. Her hair shone in the light from the flame on the stove as much as he thought it might in the dying embers of a North Dakota sunset. Despite having shed her coat, the thick sweater, turtleneck and snow pants hid most of her shape. But he could remember it from the class he'd audited while attending the university in Grand Forks.

He tucked a hair behind her ear. "Why was it we only went out once?"

Her head dipped. "One has to ask for a second date."

Dante gripped her shoulders gently and turned her slowly toward him. "I didn't call, did I?" He stared down at her until she glanced up.

Her lips twisted. "It's no big deal. We only went out for coffee."

Dante swallowed hard. He remembered. It had been shortly before a particularly harsh bout of depression. One of his buddies from the army had been shot down in Afghanistan. He'd wondered if he'd stayed in the army if he could have changed the course of events, perhaps saved his friend or if he would have died in his place. Losing his fiancée and his friend so soon afterward made him question everything he'd thought he'd understood— his role in the war on terrorism, his patriotism and his faith in mankind. It had been all he could do to get out of bed each morning, go to work and fly the border missions.

"I'm sorry." He brushed a thumb across her full lower lip and then bent to follow his thumb with his mouth. He'd only meant to kiss her softly, but once his lips touched hers, he couldn't stop himself. A rush of hunger like he'd never known washed over him and before he realized it, he was crushing her mouth, his tongue darting out to take hers.

When he raised his head, he stared down at her through a haze of lust, wanting to drag her across the bed and strip her of every layer of clothing.

Her big brown eyes were wide, her lips swollen from his kiss and pink flags of color stained her cheeks.

Dante closed his eyes, forcing himself to be reasonable and controlled. "I'm sorry. I shouldn't have done that."

"I don't—" she started.

The teakettle whistled.

Emma jerked around to the stove, one hand going to the handle of the kettle, the other to her lips.

Dante retrieved bowls from the cabinet and spoons from a drawer and stepped back, giving her as much space as the interior of the trailer would allow.

The wind churned outside, wailing against the flimsy outer walls, the cold seeping through.

As she poured the water into the mugs, Emma's hand shook.

Kicking himself for his impulsive act, Dante vowed to keep his hands—and lips—to himself for the duration of their confinement in the tight space.

Since resigning his commission, Dante hadn't considered himself fit for any relationship. He'd come back to North Dakota, hoping to reclaim the life he'd known growing up. But the transition from soldier to civilian had been anything but easy. Every loud noise made him duck, expecting incoming rounds from hidden enemies. Until today, it had only been noise. Today he'd been under attack and he hadn't been prepared.

Emma dipped a tea bag in each mug until the water turned the desired shade. Then she pulled the bags out and set them in the tiny sink. "I'm sorry, I don't have milk or lemon." She held out a mug to him. "Sugar?"

The way her lips moved to say that one word had him ready to break his recent vow. "No, I'll take it straight."

When she handed him the mug, their hands touched and an electric surge zipped through him. He backed away and his knees bumped into the mattress, forcing him to sit and slosh hot tea on his hand. The scalding liquid brought him back to his senses.

Emma spooned chili into bowls and handed one to him. "Who would shoot you out of the sky?" She cradled her bowl in both hands, blowing the steam off the top.

"I have no idea."

"As a border patrol agent, have you pissed off anyone lately?"

He shook his head. "Not anyone who would have the firepower that man had. He used a Soviet-made RPG from what I could tell. How the hell he got ahold of one of those, I don't know."

"How'd he know you'd be here?"

"I was responding to a call from my base that a man had crossed the U.S.-Canadian border on a snowmobile in this area. I can only assume it was him."

"Could be someone with a gripe against the border patrol."

"Yeah. I wish I could get word to my supervisor. They'll be freaking out right about now. A missing helicopter and pilot is a big deal."

"Would they send out a rescue team?"

"In this weather, I don't see how."

"Hopefully, it'll be gone in the morning." She stirred her chili. "If they don't come looking for you, we'll do our best to drive out and find a farmer with a landline so that you can call back."

He nodded. "A lot of people will be worried. That's an expensive piece of equipment to lose."

"Seems to me that a skilled pilot is harder to replace." Emma took a bite of her chili and chewed slowly.

Dante shrugged. Everything would have to wait until tomorrow. In the meantime… "It's getting colder outside."

"I have plenty of blankets for one bed." She stared at her empty bowl and a shiver shook her body. "Without the generator, we'll have to share the warmth." Her gaze clashed with his, hers appearing reserved, wary.

His lips thinning, Dante raised his hands. "I'm sorry about the kiss. I promise to keep my hands to myself."

Before he finished talking, Emma was shaking her head. "It's going to get really cold. The only way to stay warm is to stay close and share body warmth."

Dante swallowed hard, his body warming at the thought.

He set his empty chili bowl in the sink and took hers from her, laying it on top. "We're adults. This doesn't have to be awkward or a big deal," he said while his body was telling him, *Oh, yes it does!*

Chapter Three

Emma stared at the bed, her heart thumping against her ribs, her mouth going bone-dry. If it wasn't so darned cold in the trailer, she'd sit up all night on the camp stool.

No, she wasn't afraid of Dante. Frankly, she was afraid of her body's reaction to being so close to the tall, dark Native American.

Too awkward around the opposite sex in high school, she'd focused instead on excelling in her studies. While girls her age were kissing beneath the bleachers, she was playing the French horn in band and counting the minutes until she could go back home to her books.

College had been little better. At least her freshman roommate in the dorm had seen some potential in her and shown her how to dress and do her hair and makeup. She'd even set her up on a blind date, which had ended woefully short when she had yanked her hand out of his when he'd tried to hold it.

For all her schooling, she was remarkably unschooled in the ways of love.

The wind moaned outside, sending a frigid chill raking across her body. Her hands shaking, she pushed the snow pants down over her hips and sat on the side of the bed to pull off her boots, slipping the pants off with them. Then she slid beneath the covers in her thermal underwear, sweater and turtleneck shirt and scooted all the way to the other side of the small mattress.

What man could lust after a woman covered from neck to feet? Not that she wanted him to lust after her. What would she do? Heaven help her if he should find out she was a virgin at the ripe old age of twenty-six.

Emma lay on her back, the blankets pulled up to her chin and her eyes wide in the dim glow of the stove's fire. "You'll need to turn off the flame before we go to sleep." Perhaps in the dark she'd felt less conspicuous and self-conscious.

Dante reached for the knob on the little stove and switched it off. The flame disappeared, throwing them into complete darkness.

The blanket tugged against her death grip, and the mattress sank beneath the big man's weight. "Don't worry. I promise not to touch you."

Damn, Emma thought. With a man as gorgeous as Dante Thunder Horse lying next to her, what if she wanted him to touch her? Then again, one close encounter with her bumbling, shy inexperienced self and he'd disappear, just like he had the last time she'd gotten up the courage to go out for coffee with him.

He stretched out alongside her, his shoulder and thigh bumping against her.

A ripple of anticipation fluttered through her belly, followed by a bone-rattling shiver as the cold seeped through the three blankets, her sweater and thermal underwear.

"This is foolish. We won't last the night in the frigid cold without heat." He turned on his side and reached around her.

"W-what are you doing?" she squeaked as his hand brushed across her breast.

"We're both fully clothed, which, by the way, isn't helping matters. We're both adults and we're freezing. The best way to warm up is to share heat."

"That's what we were doing."

"Not like this." He rolled her onto her side, pulled her against him and spooned her backside with his front, his arm draped around her middle. "Better?"

Her pulse pounded so loud she could barely hear him, but she nodded and whispered, "Better." Far too much better.

As she lay in the dark, cocooned in blankets and a handsome man's arms, part of her was freaking out, the other part was shouting inside, *Hallelujah!*

"Let's go to sleep and hopefully the storm will have passed by morning."

Sleep? Was he kidding? Every cell in her body was firing up, while her core was in meltdown stages. Little shivers of excitement ignited beneath her skin with his every movement. His warm breath stirred the tendrils of hair lying against the side of her throat and all she could think of was how close his lips were to her neck. How likely was he to repeat the kiss that happened just a few moments ago?

If she turned over and faced him, would he feel compelled to repeat the performance? Did she dare?

"You smell nice. Like roses." His chest rumbled against her back, his arm tightening around her middle.

"Must be my shampoo. It was a gift from a friend." As soon as she said it, she could have kicked herself. Why couldn't she just say *thank you* like any other woman paid a compliment?

"Am I making you nervous?" he asked.

"I'm not used to having a man…spoon me."

"Seriously?" His thighs pressed against the backs of

her legs and one slid across hers. "They were missing out. You're very spoonable."

She bit her bottom lip, afraid to admit she was a failure at relationships and scared off the men who'd ever made an attempt to get to know her. "I'm not good at this."

"It's as natural as breathing," he said, his big hand spanning her belly. "Speaking of which, just breathe," he whispered against her ear.

His words had the opposite effect, causing her breath to lodge in her throat, her heart to stop for a full second and then race to catch up.

Her arm lay over his and she wasn't sure what to do with her hand. When she let it relax, it fell across his big, warm one.

"Your fingers are so cold," he said.

She jerked her hand back. "I'm sorry."

"Don't be. Let me have them." He felt along her arm until he located her hand and enveloped it in his. "Tuck it beneath your shirt, like this." He slipped his hand with hers under the hems of her sweater and thermal shirt, placing them against the heat of her skin. "You're as stiff as a board. Are you still cold?" He moved his body closer.

"Yes," she lied. Inside she was on fire, her nerve synapses firing off each time he bumped against her.

His fingers curled around hers, his knuckles brushing against her belly. "You really haven't ever snuggled with a man?"

Not trusting her voice, she shook her head.

"Then you haven't found the right one." Dante's lips brushed the curl of her ear.

She lay for a while basking in the closeness, letting her senses get used to the idea of him being so near, so intimate.

Without the heat from the stove top, the trailer's

interior became steadily colder and Dante's hand holding hers inched upward beneath her shirt. "Just tell me if you want me to stop."

Oh, heck no. If anything, she wanted him to move faster and cup her breasts with that big, warm hand. A shiver of excitement shook her.

"Still cold?"

"Yes." So it was a half truth. The parts of her body against his were warm, the others were cold and getting colder.

"Sharing body heat works better when you're skin to skin." His knuckles nudged the swells of her breasts.

Her breath caught in her throat when she said, "I know." Emma bit her bottom lip, wondering if Dante would take her words as an invitation to initiate the next move.

"I don't know about you, but it's getting pretty damn cold in here. If we want to keep warm all night, we'd better do what it takes." He removed his hand from her belly and rolled onto his back.

The cold enveloped her immediately and she scooted over to lie on her back as well, tugging the blanket up to her nose.

Dante sat up next to her, tugging the blanket aside, letting even colder air beneath.

"What are you doing?" she said through chattering teeth.

"Getting naked." His movements indicated he was removing his thermal shirt and stuffing it beneath the covers down near his feet. He slid his long underwear over his hips, his hands bumping into her thigh as he pushed them all the way down to his feet.

"Now your turn." He reached for the hem of her sweater and dragged it over her head.

"Are you crazy? It's f-freezing in here." She tried to keep her turtleneck shirt on, but he was as determined to remove that as he'd been with the sweater.

"Again, we're adults. If it helps, just think of me as a big electric blanket to wrap around you." He stuffed her shirt and sweater into the space around her feet and went to work on the long thermal underwear, dragging them down over her legs.

By the time he had her stripped to her bra and panties, she was shaking uncontrollably. "I was w-warmer b-before you s-started," she said through chattering teeth.

"You'll be warm again. Come here." He dragged the blanket over them and pulled her close, crushing her breasts against his chest, his big arms wrapping around her back, tucking the blanket in as close as he could get it.

Their breath mingled, the heat of their skin, touching everywhere but her bra and panties, helped to chase away the chills. But Emma still couldn't stop shaking. She'd never lain nearly naked with a man. She had trouble breathing and couldn't figure out where her hands were supposed to be. Planting them against his chest was putting too much space between them and allowing cold air to keep her front chilled. She tried moving them down to her side, but her fingers were cold and she wanted them warm. When she slipped them around to her belly, they bumped against a hot, stiff shaft.

As soon as she touched it, she realized it was his member and before she could think, her hands wrapped around it.

"Baby, only go there if you mean it," he warned her. "As close and naked as we are, it wouldn't take much to set me off."

"I thought you were just an electric blanket," she whispered, reveling in a surge of power rolling through her.

She had caused him to be this way. Her body against his was making him desire her in a way she'd only dreamed about.

For a moment, all her awkward insecurities disappeared. Her fingers tightened around him and slid downward to the base of his shaft.

His arms squeezed around her and his hips rocked, pressing himself into her grip.

Blood hummed through her veins. For that moment, she forgot the chill in the air and the fact they could freeze to death. Her focus centered on what she had in her hands and, in connection, what it could lead to.

Dante moaned. "Do you know what you're doing to me?"

"I think so," she responded. Her hand glided up his shaft to the velvety tip, her core heating, liquid fire swirling at her center, readying her to take him.

"I didn't get us naked in order to take advantage of you."

Her hands froze. "Am I taking advantage of *you?*"

"Oh, hell no."

Her finger swirled across the tip, memorizing him by touch. "Just say so and I'll stop," she repeated his words.

"Are you sure you want to do this?" He ran his hands over her back and down to smooth over her bottom.

She laughed, emboldened by the complete darkness. "I've never been more sure of anything in my life." Something about the anonymity of the dark gave her the confidence to continue. Then she hesitated. "Unless you don't want to. You're the injured party."

"I've wanted this since I stole that kiss." He hooked the elastic of her panties and slid them down her legs.

She kicked them off, loving the way his member

pressed into her curly mound. Just a little lower and he'd be there.

"I don't have protection," he said.

"I'm clean of STDs if that's what you're saying." How could she not be when she'd never made love to a man?

"So am I." He nuzzled her neck, his lips pressing against her pounding pulse. "But we shouldn't do this without protection."

"Can't you withdraw at the last minute?"

"Withdrawal isn't one-hundred percent safe."

"You can't stop now." Surely she couldn't get pregnant on her first time. Her first time. Wow. With a man as gorgeous and gentle as Dante, maybe she'd finally overcome her awkward shyness. She trembled, her body shaking like an engine when it first starts.

"Are we going to do it?" she asked, her hand tugging on him, guiding him to her center.

He chuckled softly. "Say the word."

She inhaled and let out the single word on a breath of air, "Please."

Dante hesitated for less than a second, and then he rolled on top of her, nudged her legs apart with his knees and settled between her thighs, his member pressing to her opening.

But he didn't enter, not immediately. He started with a kiss. One similar to the one he'd stolen at the stove. This time, Emma kissed him back, finding his tongue and sliding hers along the length of his. She curled her fingers around the back of his neck and dragged him closer, loving the feel of his smooth chest against her fingers. She reached behind her and unclasped her bra, wanting her naked breasts to feel what her fingers had the pleasure of.

Dante tore it away and slid it beneath her pillow, then he pulled the blanket over their heads and moved down her body. Inch by inch, he tasted her with his tongue, nipping her with his teeth, settling first on one breast, sucking the tip into his mouth and rolling the tight bud around. He moved to the other and gave it equal attention before he inched lower, skimming across her ribs and down past her belly button to the tuft of hair at the apex of her thighs.

Emma held her breath, wondering what he would do next. His mouth so close to home, she couldn't move, frozen to the sheets, waiting.

With his big, rough fingers, he parted her folds and stroked that sensitive strip of skin.

"Oh, my!" she exclaimed, her heels digging into the mattress, raising her hips for more.

He swirled, tapped and flicked, setting her world on fire. When she thought she couldn't take any more, he moved up her body, and pressed into her.

At the barrier of her virginity, he paused.

Emma wrapped her legs around his waist and dug her heels into his buttocks, urging him deeper. "Don't stop," she pleaded.

"But…"

"Just do it. Please." She tightened her legs.

He thrust deeper, tearing through.

She must have gasped, because he pulled back a little. "Are you all right?" Dante asked.

She laughed shakily. "I'd be better if you didn't stop."

After hesitating a moment longer, he slid slowly into her and began a steady, easy glide in and out.

The initial pain lasted but a moment, and soon Emma forgot it in the joy of the connection between them. So this was what all the fuss was about. Now she understood and dropped her feet to the mattress to better meet him thrust for thrust.

When Dante stiffened, he stopped, his hard member buried deep inside her. A moment later, he dragged himself free and lay down beside her, pulling her into the warmth of his arms.

The heat of his body and the haze of pleasurable exhaustion washed over her and she melted against him. "Mmm. I never knew it would be that good."

He lay with his arms around her, his body stiff. "You cried out. Why?"

Heat rose into her cheeks. "Did I?"

For a long moment, Dante held her without talking. "You were a virgin, weren't you?" When she refused to answer, he continued, "Why didn't you tell me?"

Emma rested her hand on his chest, feeling the swift beat of his heart against her palm. "I was embarrassed. Besides, what difference does it make?"

"We wouldn't have done it." He smoothed a hand along her lower back.

"Are you sorry you did?" she asked, her lips so close to his nipple, she tongued the hard little point, liking the way it beaded even tighter.

"No."

She smiled in the darkness and relaxed against him. "Me, either. Virginity is way overrated."

He tipped her chin up with his finger. "Then why are—*were*—you still one?" His breath warmed her.

"Like I told you. I'm not good at relationships. I could never get past a first date."

She could feel his head shaking side to side. "Inconceivable," he said, then captured her mouth with his.

When he broke the kiss, Emma lay in his arms, basking in the afterglow, their bodies generating enough combined heat that, along with the cocoon of blankets, they held off the cold.

"Just so you know, I'm not good at relationships, either," Dante said into the darkness. "I can offer you no guarantees."

"I understand." The warmth she'd been feeling chilled slightly. What did she expect? Sex was sex. No matter how good it felt, it didn't necessarily come with emotional commitment.

She couldn't expect Dante to fall in love with her just because she'd given him her virginity. "Don't worry. I won't stalk you or make any demands of you. The 'no guarantees' thing goes both ways."

His hand paused the circular motion he'd begun on her naked back.

She added to boost her own self-confidence, "Thank you for getting me over my awkwardness. I won't be so hesitant with my future dates." As soon as she said the words, she could have kicked herself. Would he consider them flippant and insensitive, or worse? Would he think she was loose and easy with her body?

Despite his announcement that he'd give no guarantees, she'd harbored a wish, a dream and a raging desire to repeat what had just happened. When the storm cleared and they made it back to civilization, she hoped he'd ask her out again. Though sex with Dante had been magical to her, he certainly wouldn't be impressed enough for a repeat performance with an awkward ex-virgin?

Chapter Four

Dante pressed himself as close as he could get to the jagged hulk of his crashed helicopter; his copilot lay at an awkward angle, still strapped to his seat, dead from a broken neck sustained upon impact. He didn't recognize the copilot, his face was hidden in shadows.

A movement at the edge of the village where he'd crashed caught Dante's eye. The flap of a dark robe fluttered in the desert breeze. There. The man he'd seen at the last minute, pointing an RPG at him, stood at the corner of a mud hut.

Staying low behind the metal wreckage, Dante leveled his 9 mm pistol, aiming at the man, waiting for him to step out of the shadows and come within range.

The sound of an engine made his blood run cold. An old, rusty truck rumbled down the middle of the street between the buildings, loaded with Taliban soldiers wielding Soviet-made rifles.

Alone, without any backup, it was him with a full clip against the Taliban. If he wanted to live, he had to make every shot count.

The truck barreled toward him and stopped short. The soldiers leaped over the side. He fired, hitting one, then another, but they kept coming as if the truck had an endless supply. One by one, he fired until the trigger clicked and the clip was empty.

Taliban men grabbed his arms and pulled him from the wreckage, shouting and shooting their weapons in the air. The hum of the truck engine growled louder as they dragged him closer.

"Dante."

How did they know his name? He struggled against their hold, kicking and shoving at their hands.

"Dante, wake up!"

He opened his eyes. The sand and desert disappeared and dim light seeped in around the blinds over a window.

"Dante?" a soft feminine voice called out and it all came back to him.

"Emma?" he said, his voice hoarse.

She leaned over him, her naked body pressed against his, her breasts smashed to his chest, her thigh draped over his. She smelled of roses mixed with the musky scent of sex.

It took him a moment to shake the terror of being captured and dragged away by the Taliban, and even longer to return to the camp trailer on the North Dakota tundra.

Then he noticed a red mark on Emma's cheek. "What happened to you?" He reached up to gently brush his thumb around the mark.

She smiled crookedly. "You were having a bad dream."

"I did that?" His chest tightened and he pushed to a sitting position. "Oh, Emma, I'm so sorry."

"It doesn't hurt." She pressed her fingers to the red welt. "I'm more worried about the engine noise I hear outside."

Dante sat still and silent, focusing on the noise from outside. Just as she'd said, an engine revved nearby.

Dante threw back the covers. "Get up. Get dressed."

"Why?" She asked, scrambling off the bed, gooseflesh rising on her naked skin.

"We don't know if the man who shot me down yesterday is back."

"Damn." Emma grabbed her sweater, tugged it over her naked breasts and slipped into her snow pants and boots.

Dante only had his thermals to pull on and his boots.

When he reached for the door handle and twisted, it didn't open. "Is there some kind of lock on this?"

"It should open when you twist the handle."

He tried again.

About that time, the trailer lurched, sending him flying across the floor, slamming into the sink.

Emma fell across the bed. "What the hell?"

"The door lock is jammed, and someone's driving your truck with the trailer still attached. Hold on!"

The vehicle lurched and bumped over the rough terrain.

"He's backing us up!" Emma shouted. "If he goes much farther, we'll end up in the ditch my team has been digging." She staggered to her feet and flung herself across the room to the door. Another bump and her forehead slammed into the wall.

She slipped, her hands grabbing for the door latch. "We have to stop him."

Dante staggered across to her. "Move!" He picked her up and shoved her to the side. Bracing himself on whatever he could hold on to, he slammed his heel into the door. The force with which he hit reverberated up his leg. The door remained secure. He kicked again. Nothing.

Emma grasped the sink and ripped the blinds from the window. "Oh, my god. We're going to fall—"

The trailer tipped wildly. Everything that wasn't nailed to the floor, including Dante and Emma, was flung to the back of the trailer as it tumbled down the near-vertical slope of the dig site. The rear end of the trailer slammed into the ground, crumpling on impact. Cold air blasted through the cracks and glass broke from the windows.

Dante landed on the mattress as it slid toward the back of the trailer. "Emma?" He couldn't see her anywhere.

"I'm okay, I think." A hand waved from beneath the mattress. "I'm just stuck."

The truck engine revved and a door slammed outside. Then the upper end of the trailer caved in, bearing down on them. Dante rolled to the side, letting the mattress take the bulk of the blow.

When the world quit shaking, Dante was jammed between the mattress and the wall. Metal squeaked against metal and the trailer seemed to groan.

"Dante?" Emma called out.

"I'm going to try to move this mattress." He squeezed himself against the wall and rolled the mattress back. "Can you get yourself out?"

"I'll try." Emma reached up, grabbed the edge of the sink and pulled herself out from beneath the mattress.

Dante let the mattress fall in place and hauled himself up on it, ducking low to keep from hitting his head on the crushed trailer. His stomach lurched when he saw the bumper of the truck through a crack in the wall. Whoever had driven them into the ditch had crashed the truck down on top of them. If it shifted even a little, they'd be stuck in there, trapped and possibly crushed.

Light and cold wind filtered through the broken window over the sink. Placing his head close to the opening, he listened.

"Is he gone?" Emma whispered.

A small engine roared above them. If he wasn't mistaken, Dante would guess it was a snowmobile. "I think that's him leaving now." And none too soon. The truck above them shifted and the walls sank closer to where he and Emma crouched on the mattress.

The door was crushed and mangled. They wouldn't be getting out that way. If they didn't leave soon, the truck would smash into them. "We have to get out of here."

"How?" Emma asked.

Dante lay back and kicked the rest of the glass out of the window over the sink. Then, using the pillow, he worked the jagged edges loose. "You go first," he said.

"And leave you to be crushed?" Emma shook her head. "No way. If you can get out, I can get out."

"If I get stuck, neither one of us will get out. If you go first and I'm trapped, you can go for help."

Emma worried her bottom lip between her teeth. "Okay. But you're not getting stuck." She edged her body through the tight opening and dropped to the ground. "Now you!" she called out. "And throw any blankets or coats you can salvage out with you."

Dante scavenged two blankets from the rubble and pushed them through the window. He followed them with Emma's winter jacket.

Metal shrieked against metal and the trailer's walls quaked.

"The truck's shifting!" Emma called out. "Get out now!"

Dante dove for the small window, wondering how he'd get his broad shoulders through the narrow opening. He squeezed one through and angled the other, the rim of the window tight around his ribs. Then he was pushing himself through.

Emma braced his hands on her shoulders and walked backward as he brought his hips and legs almost all the way out.

The entire structure wobbled and creaked, then folded like an accordion.

Emma dragged him the rest of the way, both of them falling onto the ground as the truck's weight crushed the remainder of the trailer walls beneath it.

Dante rolled off Emma and stood, pulling her up beside him. Together they stared at the wreckage.

She shook in the curve of his arm. "If one more minute had passed..."

His arm tightened around her. "We're out. That's all that matters."

"But who would do this?"

"I don't know, but I'm sure as hell going to find out."

EMMA COULDN'T REMEMBER the road leading into the dig site being as long as it was, until she had to walk through snow to get to a paved road. Her toes were frozen and her jacket barely kept the cold wind from chilling her body to the bone. But she couldn't complain when all Dante had on were his thermal underwear and the blankets he'd salvaged from the trailer before it had been crushed beneath her truck.

With the truck a total write-off, she'd hoped the snowmobile she'd left parked outside the night before would be usable.

Whoever had tried to kill them had stabbed a hole in the snowmobile's gas tank and ripped the wires loose. It wasn't going anywhere but a junkyard.

If they wanted to get help, they were forced to trudge through three feet of snow for almost two miles just to reach a paved road. And as the North Dakota countryside could be desolate, it could be hours or days before anyone passed by on the paved road.

Tired, hungry and cold, Emma formed a smile with her chapped lips. At least she wouldn't die a virgin. "Are you doing okay?" she asked. "We could stop and hunker down long enough for you to warm up."

"I'm fine." Enveloped in the two blankets he'd thrown from the wreckage, his thermal-clad legs were more exposed to the elements than anything else. "We should keep moving."

Emma could tell he was trying not to let his teeth chatter. She slipped her arm around him and leaned her body into his to block as much of the wind as she could. Blankets provided little protection against the icy Arctic winds. If they didn't find help soon, he'd freeze to death. How much could a man persevere after being shot down and nearly crushed?

Her gaze swept over him. The man, all muscle and strength, displayed no weakness. But as cold as she was, he had to be freezing.

Though the storm had moved on and the sun had come out, the wind hadn't let up, seeming to come directly from the North Pole.

When they reached pavement, Emma almost felt giddy with relief. With the gravel road she'd come in on buried in snow, she hadn't been completely sure they were headed in the right direction.

"Which way?" Dante asked.

Emma glanced right, then left, and back right again. "If I recall correctly, the man who owns this ranch lives in a house a couple of miles north of this turnoff."

A cold blast of wind sent a violent shiver across her body.

"Here." Dante peeled one of the blankets off his back and handed it to her.

"No way." She refused to take it. "I'm warm enough. You're the one who needs it."

"I'm used to this kind of cold. I grew up in the Badlands."

"I don't care where you grew up. If you drop from hypothermia, I can't carry you." She stood taller, stretching every bit of her five-foot-four-inch frame in an attempt to equal his over six-feet-tall height. "Put it back on."

He grinned, his lips as windburned as hers, and wrapped the blanket back around his shoulders. "Then let's get to it. The sooner we get there, the sooner I get my morning cup of coffee." Wrapping the blankets tightly around himself, he took off.

Emma had to hurry to keep up, shaking her head at his offer of a blanket when she had all the snow gear on and he had nothing but his underwear. Stubborn man.

Her heart warmed at his concern for her and the strength he demonstrated.

So many questions burned through her, but she saved them for when they made it to shelter and warmth. Emma focused all her energy on keeping up with the long-legged Native American marching through the snow to find help. With the sun shining brightly, the blindingly white snow made her eyes hurt and she ducked her head, her gaze on Dante's boot heels. She stepped in the tracks he left as much as possible to save energy, though his strides were far longer than hers.

After what felt like an eternity, cold to the bone, her teeth chattering so badly she couldn't hear herself think, Emma looked up and nearly cried.

A thin ribbon of smoke rose above the snow-covered landscape. Where there was smoke, there was fire and warmth. Fueled by hope, she picked up the pace, squinting at the snowy fields until the shape of a ranch house was discernible.

Less than a tenth of a mile from the house, Emma stumbled and fell into the snow. Too stiff to move quickly, she didn't get her arms up in time to keep from performing a face-plant in the icy crystals.

Before she could roll over and sit up, she was plucked from the snow and gathered in Dante's arms.

"P-put me down," she stammered, her teeth clattering so hard she was afraid she'd bite her tongue, but was too tired to care.

"Shush," he said and continued the last tenth of a mile to the front door of the house.

Her face stinging from the cold, all she could do was wrap her arms around Dante's neck and hold on while he banged on the door.

Footsteps sounded on the other side of the solid wood door and it swung open.

"Dear Lord." An older gentleman in a flannel shirt and blue jeans stood in sock feet, his mouth dropped open.

"Sir, we need help," Dante said.

"Olaf, don't just stand there, let them in and close the door. Can't let all that heat escape with the power out." An older woman hurried up behind Olaf. "Come in, come in."

Olaf's jaw snapped shut and he stepped aside, allowing Dante to carry Emma through the door.

Even before Olaf closed the door behind them, heat surrounded Emma and tears slid down her cheeks. "We made it." She buried her face against the cool blankets covering Dante's chest.

"Set her down here on the couch in front of the fire," the woman said, urging Dante forward. She waved a golden retriever out of the way and pointed to the couch she was referring to. "The storm knocked the power out last night and we've been camping out in the living room to stay warm by the fireplace. We have a generator, but we save that for emergencies."

Emma almost laughed. To most people, a power outage would constitute an emergency. The hardy folks of North Dakota had to be really down-and-out to consider power failure to be an emergency.

Dante set Emma on the sofa and immediately began pulling off her jacket.

"Let me," the woman said. She waved Dante away. "You go thaw out by the fire." As she tugged the zipper down on Emma's jacket, she introduced herself. "I'm Marge, and that's my husband, Olaf." The woman's white eyebrows furrowed. "Should I know you? You look familiar."

"I think we met last summer. My name's Emma." Emma forced a smile past her chapped lips. "Emma Jennings from the UND Paleontology Department. I was working at the dig up until yesterday."

"I thought the site had been shut down at the end of the summer," Olaf said.

Emma shrugged. "Since we've had such a mild fall I've been coming out on weekends. I'd hoped to get in one last weekend before the permafrost."

"And then the storm last night…" Marge shook her head. "You're lucky you didn't freeze to death."

"I c-can do this," Emma protested, trying to shrug out of her jacket on her own.

Marge continued to help. "Hon, your hands are like ice. It'll be a miracle if they aren't frostbitten." The woman clucked her tongue, casting a glance over her shoulder at Dante. "And him out in the cold in nothing but his underwear. What happened?"

Olaf took the blankets from Dante and gave him two warm, dry ones. "Did your truck get stuck in the snow?"

Emma's gaze shot to Dante. She didn't want to frighten these old people.

Dante took over. Holding out his hand to Olaf, he said, "I'm Dante Thunder Horse. I'm a pilot for the Customs and Border Protection unit out of Grand Forks. My helicopter was shot down several miles from here yesterday."

Olaf's eyes widened, his grip on Dante's hand tightening before he let go.

When Dante was done filling them in on what had happened, Olaf ran a hand through his scraggly gray hair and shook his head. "Don't know what's got into this world when you can't even be safe in North Dakota."

Emma laughed, more tears welling in her eyes. After their near-death experiences, she was weepier than normal. For a short time there, she had begun to wonder if they'd find shelter before they froze.

"Mind if I use your phone?" Dante asked. "I need to let the base know I'm alive."

Marge tucked a blanket around Emma. "Olaf, hand him the phone."

Olaf gave Dante a cordless phone. Dante tapped the numbers into the keypad and held the phone to his ear and frowned. "I'm not getting a dial tone."

"Sorry. I forget, without power, this one is useless." Olaf took the phone and replaced it in the powerless charger. "Let me check the one in the kitchen."

A minute later, he returned. "The phone lines are down. Must have been knocked out along with the electricity in the storm last night."

"I need to get back to Grand Forks. My people will have sent up a search and rescue unit."

"I can get you as far as Devil's Lake," Olaf said. "But

then I'll have to turn back to make sure I get home to Mamma before nightfall."

"Don't you worry about me. I can take care of myself," Marge insisted.

"We don't want to put you in danger," Emma said.

"No, we don't," Dante agreed. "If we could get as far as Devil's Lake, we can find someone heading to Grand Forks and catch a ride with them."

"I'd take you all the way to Grand Forks, but with the snow on the road and the wife here, keeping the house warm by burning firewood…"

"We wouldn't want you to leave her alone that long," Dante assured Olaf. "It'll be a long enough drive to Devil's Lake and back."

"I'll get my truck out of the barn." Olaf hurried into the hallway leading toward the back of the house. "Mamma, find the man some of my clothes. He can't go all the way to Grand Forks in his underwear." Olaf shot a grin back at them as he pulled on his heavy winter coat, hat and gloves.

Marge left them in the living room and headed the opposite direction of her husband. When she returned, she carried a pair of jeans, an older winter jacket and a flannel shirt. "These were my son's. He's a bit taller than Olaf. They should fit you better."

"I'll have them returned to you as soon as possible."

"Don't bother. He has more in the closet and he rarely makes it up here in the wintertime. We usually go stay with him and his family in January and February. They live in Florida." She grinned. "It's a lot nicer down there at this time of year than up here."

Dante smiled at the woman and accepted the clothing graciously.

"There's a bathroom in the hallway if you'd like to dress in there." Marge pointed the direction.

Dante disappeared and reappeared a few minutes later dressed in jeans that fit a little loose around his hips and were an inch or two short on his legs. The flannel shirt strained against his broad shoulders, but he didn't say a word.

Emma figured he was grateful to have anything more than just thermal underwear on his body.

He shrugged into the old jacket and zipped it. "I'll go help Olaf with the truck."

"Stay inside," Marge insisted. "You've been exposed to the weather enough for one day."

"I'm fine." He nodded toward Emma, his dark eyes smoldering. "I'll be back in a minute for you."

Emma's heart fluttered. She knew he didn't mean anything by the look, other than he'd be back to load her up in the truck.

Alone with Marge, Emma wished she was warm enough to go out and help, but the thought of going out in the cold so soon after nearly dying in it didn't appeal to her in the least. How did Dante do it?

"That's some man you have there," Marge said, fussing over the blankets in Emma's lap.

Emma started to tell Marge that he wasn't her man, but decided it didn't matter. The farmer and his wife had been very helpful, taking them in and providing them warmth and clothing.

"How long have you two been together?" Marge asked out of the blue.

Now that she hadn't refuted Marge's earlier statement, Emma didn't know whether she should tell her they weren't together. "Not very long" were the words she came up with. They were true in the simplest sense.

She and Dante had only been together since she'd found him in the snow beside the helicopter wreckage the day before and one other time when they'd had coffee together on campus.

Marge smiled. "You two make a nice couple. Now, do you want to take an extra jacket with you? Olaf keeps blankets and a sleeping bag in the backseat of the truck in case we get marooned out in bad weather. Make use of them. I know once you get cold, it's hard to warm up. Sometimes it takes me days for my old body to catch up."

Used to the North Dakota winters, Emma nodded. To think Dante was out in that cold wind helping the old man get the truck ready sent another shiver across Emma's skin.

"I've got my camp stove going and some water heating for coffee. If you're all right by yourself, I'll rustle up some breakfast for the two of you."

"You don't have to go to all that trouble." Emma's belly growled at the thought of food.

Marge laughed. "No trouble at all. We rarely have visitors so far north. It'll be a treat to get to fuss over someone." She left Emma on the couch.

The rattle of pans preceded the heavenly scent of bacon cooking. By the time the men came in from the cold, Emma's mouth was watering and she pushed aside the blankets to stand.

"Everything's ready," Dante said.

"Good. Then come have a seat at the table and eat breakfast while Olaf and I have our lunch. No use going off with an empty stomach." Marge set plates of hot food on the table and cups of steaming coffee.

"We really appreciate all you've done for us. Truthfully, we'd have been happy just to sit in front of the fire to thaw." Emma sat in the chair Dante pulled out for her and stared down at eggs, bacon, ham and biscuits. "Breakfast never looked so good," she exclaimed.

"You're an angel." Dante hugged the older woman and waited for her to sit in front of a sandwich and chips before he took his seat.

Marge's cheeks bloomed with color.

"My Marge can make most anything with a camp stove and a Dutch oven. And she can dress a mule deer like a side of beef."

Marge waved at her husband. "He only married me because I liked hunting."

Olaf grinned. "And she was the prettiest girl in the county."

Emma hid a smile. The pair clearly loved each other. "How long have you two been together?"

Olaf's head tipped to one side. "What's it been? Thirty years or more?"

Marge shook her head. "Going on forty."

"And you still don't look a day over twenty-nine."

"Big fibber."

Emma caught Dante's smile and joined him with one of her own. The warm food and good company went a long way toward restoring her stamina.

By the time Marge and Olaf bundled them into the truck, Emma was beginning to think all was right in a crazy world. She found it hard to believe that only that morning someone had tried to kill them.

As Olaf drove the long, snow-covered road to Devil's Lake, Emma had far too much time on her hands to think. Whoever had shot down Dante's helicopter hadn't been satisfied with him being injured. He'd come back to finish the job. The big question was, would he try again?

Chapter Five

At the truck stop at Devil's Lake, Dante was able to get a call through to headquarters. The dispatcher on duty was relieved to hear from him. They'd sent out several helicopters to circle the last known location of his helicopter. The snow had done a nice job of hiding the crash site and they'd just located it beneath three feet of powder when Dante had made contact.

Dante waited while the dispatcher connected him to his supervisor, Jim Kramer.

"T.H., where the hell have you been?"

Dante laughed. "Slogging through three feet of snow to get to someplace warm."

"You had us all worried out here when you didn't show up at quittin' time."

"Nice to know someone cares." Dante had been with the CBP long enough to be a part of the team. When a chopper went down, everyone took it personally. The loss of a teammate hit everyone hard. "Rest assured, I'm not dead, yet."

"Glad to hear it." Jim paused. "What happened?"

"I was shot down by a man with a Soviet-made RPG."

"What?"

"Look, I'm sitting at a truck stop in Devil's Lake. The storm hit this area pretty hard and a lot of electric and phone lines are down. I was about to hit up a few of the truck drivers to see if anyone could get us back to Grand Forks. When I get back, I'll fill you in on all the details."

"Fair enough. But I can do you one better. Biacowski is out searching for you. I'll send him over to pick you up."

"As long as he has room for two."

"What do you mean?"

"I had a little help getting away from the burning fuselage and then surviving the storm last night by someone who works out at the university."

"Thank him for me, will ya? You know how hard it is to find good pilots."

"Will do." Dante didn't bother to correct his supervisor on the gender of the person who'd helped him. After arranging a location to pick him up, Dante hung up and turned to find Emma hugging Olaf.

Something that felt oddly like jealousy tugged at his insides. Not that he had anything to fear from Olaf. The man was married and old enough to be Emma's father.

What bothered him was that she'd felt comfortable hugging the old guy and hadn't so much as touched Dante since they'd made it back to civilization.

When Samantha was alive, he'd been jealous of any man she'd so much as said hello to. Which was practically everyone in camp. She'd laughed and told him to get over it. Though he'd never told her, he never had. His love for her had bordered on obsessive. If he was honest with himself, he was certain had Samantha lived, he'd have driven her away. She had a mind of her own and resented when he told her what to do.

He'd only done so out of fear of losing her. And his fear had played out. Samantha had died outside the wire. Glancing across at Emma, he could see very few similarities between the two women. Where Samantha had straight, sandy-blond hair and gray-blue eyes, Emma had curly dark hair and dark brown eyes.

Being a female captain in the army meant Samantha had to have a tough exterior and confidence to command the soldiers in her company. Emma appeared to be afraid of men. But she'd shown no fear when she'd used her snowmobile to ram into the guy shooting at him. Her fear was in being alone and naked with a man.

Samantha had been hot as hell in bed and liked being on top half the time. Emma...

Her soft brown eyes met his and she smiled. Though she wasn't as sexy as Samantha, she had her own sweet serenity that made him calm and excited all at once. His heartbeat fluttered and he longed to be naked with her, buried beneath the blankets, touching her, bringing her body and senses to life.

She'd been like an exotic flower opening for the first time. And she'd given him something special, something she couldn't take back. Too bad he wasn't in the market for a relationship. Emma would be well worth the trouble.

Her cheeks grew pink.

Dante realized he must have been staring and shifted his gaze to the sky. The thumping sound of helicopter blades was music to his ears. His heart was heavy at the thought of the crashed Eurocopter AS-350 lying in a burned-out heap beneath the snow on Olaf's ranch. Helicopters weren't cheap and took time to replace. He'd gone over and over in his mind what he could have or should have done in the situation, but nothing would undo what had been done.

Biacowski set the helicopter down in a field bordering the small town of Devil's Lake.

Olaf drove the pair to the edge and let them out close enough to walk to the aircraft.

Once again, Emma hugged the older man and thanked him.

Dante stuck out his hand and shook Olaf's. "Thank you for all you and your wife have done for us."

"Thank you for your service, Dante. I hope you and your girl will come visit us again." The man grinned. "Hopefully under better circumstances next time."

Emma gave him a gentle smile. "We'd like that."

The pilot remained with the aircraft as Dante and Emma approached, hunched over to avoid being hit by the still-turning rotors. Once Dante had Emma settled in the backseat and buckled in, he handed her a headset so that she could hear the conversation up front.

Finally, Dante climbed into the copilot seat.

Dante settled the spare headset over his ears.

Biacowski glared at him. "Don't ever scare me like that again."

"Sorry to inconvenience you." Dante chuckled. "I have a feeling that if you hadn't called in sick, one or both of us would have been dead in that fire. I seriously doubt that as much as Emma helped, she could have saved both of us."

Chris glanced over his shoulder at Emma and gave her a thumbs-up. "I owe you one. Emma, is it?"

She nodded.

"Hell, the CBP owes you one. Dante's one of our best pilots."

She adjusted the mic over her mouth and spoke softly. "Glad to help."

Biacowski leaned toward Dante. "Where'd you find her? She's cute."

Dante glanced back at Emma, knowing full well she

could hear what the pilot said. "I didn't find her, she found me."

"I want the whole story when we get back."

"You got it. Just get us back before nightfall. It's already been a long day for both of us."

Dante settled back in his seat, thinking he'd close his eyes and take a short nap on the way back. A glance to the rear proved Emma had nodded off. She had to be exhausted after nearly being killed and then slogging through knee-deep snow to find shelter.

Though he closed his eyes, the rumble of the engine and the thumping of the rotors made his blood pump faster and his hands itch to take the controls. Giving up on a nap, he opened his eyes and scanned the snow-covered landscape below, half expecting to find a man on a snowmobile pointing an RPG at him.

His nerves knotted and remained stretched tight until the lights of the Grand Forks International Airport blinked up at him.

Biacowski hovered over the landing area and set the helicopter down like laying a sleeping baby in its crib.

Dante climbed into the backseat before the rotors had time to stop spinning and helped Emma out of the harness.

"I'll take you home as soon as I debrief my commander." He stared into her sleepy eyes. "Will you be okay for an hour or two?"

"I can catch a taxi back. You don't have to worry about me."

"My supervisor will want to hear your story, as well. You actually saw the man who fired on my helicopter."

"I didn't see much."

"Whatever you saw, he'll want to know about." Dante

grabbed her hand and led her toward the building. Bia-cowski followed.

Jim Kramer met them at the door to his office, showed them in and offered them coffee. "Do I need to get an ambulance to have you two taken to the hospital?" Kramer frowned, staring hard at them. "You both look like you got rolled in a fight."

Dante's gaze met Emma's and he sighed. "We did get rolled and almost lost the fight." He told his side of what had happened over the past twenty-four hours and waited while Kramer questioned Emma.

"Could you describe the man on the snowmobile?"

Emma shook her head. "Other than he had black hair, no. He was seated, so I couldn't get a feel for how tall he was and it all happened so fast, I was more worried about him running over Dante than getting a clear description of him."

Kramer came around the side of his desk and held out his hand to Emma. "Thank you for saving one of my best pilots." His lips twisted. "He's also a vital member of this team and we'd have missed him."

Dante shifted in his chair, uncomfortable with the praise when he'd allowed himself to get shot down. "Sir, whoever shot me out of the sky came back to finish the job. When he finds out he wasn't successful, he could be back. And if he thinks for a moment that Emma could identify him, he'll be after her."

Kramer leaned against his government-issued metal desk and ran his hand over his chin. "You have a point. I suppose I could assign a man to keep an eye on her."

Emma leaned forward in her chair. "I don't need anyone to keep an eye on me. I'm fully capable of taking care of myself."

Kramer shook his head. "Whoever did it has to know

it's a federal crime to shoot at a government agent. If there's any chance you can identify him, he might come after you next."

Dante leaned toward her and took her hand. "Let the boss assign an agent to you. At least until we catch the bastard."

Emma's lips pressed into a tight line, her cheeks filled with color. "No, thank you. I'm off for the next four weeks on Christmas break. I'll be vigilant and watch my back. No need to tie up resources babysitting me."

Kramer glanced at Dante. "I can't force her to accept help."

Dante's gaze met Emma's. From the stubborn look on her face he could tell she didn't like having people make decisions for her. But after all she'd done for him, he needed to be sure no one would come after her. He turned back to his boss. "I have a lot of use-or-lose vacation time on the books, right?"

"Yes, you do," Kramer confirmed.

"I'd planned on spending a little time with my family at the Thunder Horse Ranch over the holidays. If it's all right by you, I'd like to take my leave now. I'll spend part of it with Emma until we figure out who was responsible for destroying a perfectly good helicopter and then tried to kill us."

"Do I have a say in any of this?" Emma asked.

Dante's lips quirked up on the corners. "Only if it's to agree."

"Well, I won't." She pushed to a standing position. "I like my solitude and I don't need someone treating me as a charity case and guarding me as if I were a child."

Admiring her gumption, but no less determined, Dante stood beside her. "If it helps, you won't even know I'm there. I'll keep an eye on you from the comfort of my vehicle outside your apartment." He knew even before he said the words that they would get her ire up. And they did.

"Like a stalker?" She straightened.

Kramer stood, chuckling. "I'll let you two duke it out. I have a schedule to juggle. As of now, you're to report to the hospital for a quick checkup, and then you're on leave until after the first of the year. You're dismissed. And, T.H., try to stay out of the cold this time. The temperature outside is minus fifteen with a windchill of minus thirty and it's supposed to drop tonight to minus forty."

"Trust us. We don't plan on spending tonight in the elements," Dante assured his boss. "Although, it wasn't all bad."

Kramer left his office and headed down the hallway to the hangar.

When Dante turned to Emma, he noted the blush rising up Emma's neck into her cheeks.

"I won't be responsible for you missing out on family time during the holidays," she muttered.

Dante's lips twitched, but he fought the smile. She was deflecting his reference to their lovemaking and he found it endearingly cute. "I promise to spend some of my leave with my family."

"And you really don't have to spend any of it with me."

"What if I like being with you?" he quipped.

"What if I don't like being with *you?*" Twin red flags flew in her cheeks and her brown eyes flashed.

This was an Emma he liked as much as the soft, sexy one he'd made love to in the little trailer. He pulled her into an empty office and lifted both of her hands in his. "Do you really mean that?"

"You said so yourself, 'no guarantees.' Don't start feeling sorry for me."

"I don't feel sorry for you. I'm worried about you."

"Well, stop. I can take care of myself. I have for years."

"Fair enough." Rubbing his thumbs over the backs of her hands, he gazed into her eyes. "You're independent and you've taken care of yourself for a while. But have you ever had someone try to kill you before today?"

She opened her mouth to retort, but nothing came out.

"No," he answered for her. "Well, I have, and it's not fun. And it's not the right time to be on your own."

"I don't need you to be my bodyguard."

"Emma." His grip tightened on her hands. "What are you afraid of? The bad guy or me?"

She blurted out, "I'm not afraid of either." Her head dipped and she stared at her boots. "I'm afraid of me."

His heart melted at the way her bottom lip wobbled. "Why?"

Her glance shifted to the corner of the room and she didn't say anything for a full ten seconds. Then she admitted, "I've been independent for so long, I'm afraid of becoming dependent on anyone."

Dante suspected there was a lot more to her fierce independence than having been that way for a long time. Someone in her past must have hurt her. "Relying on someone else doesn't have to be a bad thing. And it's only temporary. Once we catch the bad guy, you can go back to being independent."

She didn't throw it back in his face, so he figured she was wavering. He went in for the clincher.

"Besides, you saved my life twice." He lifted one of her hands to his lips and pressed a kiss there. "I owe you. And if you don't let me pay you back by providing you a little protection in the short term, I'll always owe you my life. You can't let me go through life with such a huge obligation hanging over me, can you? It will threaten my manhood."

Her brows knitted. "You don't owe me anything. And there's nothing in this world that could possibly threaten your...er...manhood."

The way she stumbled over the last word made him think back to the trailer when her soft curves had pressed against his hard body. In an instant, he was hard all over again.

Her cheeks flamed and he could swear she was there with him.

"Please." He hooked her hand through the crook of his arm. "Let me play bodyguard for a little while. You won't regret it."

She sucked in a deep breath and let it out. "Do you really think I could be in danger? Me? I live the most boring life imaginable. How could I be a threat to anyone?"

"You saw his face."

"Surely whoever it was will assume we died in the trailer," she argued.

"When he discovers the fact that we didn't, he could come back to finish the job."

"I *barely* saw his face."

"He doesn't know that. He would only know that you and I are still alive, and we could possibly identify him."

Emma heaved another sigh. "Okay. I'll let you play bodyguard, but only for a couple of days. Surely by then they'll find out who started this whole mess."

Satisfied that he had her agreement to keep an eye on her, Dante didn't tell her that the shooter might never be found. He'd take one day at a time until his leave ran out. Maybe he was overreacting. If he did nothing and something happened to Emma, he'd never forgive himself.

THE AIRPORT WAS several miles away from the city of Grand Forks. As they stepped out into the bitter wind, Emma looked around, gathering her coat around her chin. "Are we taking a cab back to Grand Forks?"

"No." Dante guided her toward the parking lot. "I parked my Jeep out here."

A shiver shook her from the tip of her head to her toes and left her teeth chattering. "By chance does it have heated seats?"

He pulled his key fob out of his pocket and hit a button. "As a matter of fact, it does."

"Thank God," she said through chattering teeth.

"And even better, it has a remote starter and should be warming up by the time we get to it."

A dark pewter Jeep Wrangler with a hard top and raised suspension roared to life a hundred yards from where they stood.

"Yours?" Emma nodded toward the sound of the engine.

"Mine." He shrugged. "I always wanted one. I'd been saving for it since I got back from the sandbox."

Emma glanced up at him. "Sandbox?"

"Afghanistan."

She pulled her collar up around her ears to keep the wind from blowing down the back of her neck. "Were you a pilot in the war?"

He nodded, his gaze on the car ahead.

That explained his nightmare when she'd woken him in the trailer. At first she'd thought it was from having crashed in the helicopter, but it had seemed even more deep-seated. He'd said he'd been shot at before. It had to have been then.

She wondered what scars he carried from his time on

active duty. Did he have post-traumatic stress disorder? Had he watched members of his unit die?

Clouds had moved back in to cover the warming sun, and the north wind blew hard enough that Emma had to lean into it to get to the Jeep. Windchill of minus thirty was hard to take even when one wasn't tired and worn down from trudging for miles in the snow and cold. By the time they reached the Jeep, she practically fell into its warmth.

The drive into Grand Forks was conducted in silence. As Dante turned left when Emma would have turned right to go to her apartment, she remembered she hadn't given him directions. "I live in an apartment close to the university."

"And I live in an apartment on the south side of town." He shot a glance her way. "I thought we'd stop there first so that I could collect some clothes that fit and a few items I'll need."

"Need for what?"

"To stay with you."

"With me?"

"Well, yes. I thought we had this all settled. I'm your bodyguard for the next few days."

"But that doesn't mean you'll be staying with me."

"How else am I supposed to guard your body if I'm not in the same building with you?"

"But…" She bit down on her lip and stared out the window. "My apartment is really small." The thought of the hulking Native American in her apartment threatened to overwhelm her. And they weren't even in her apartment yet.

"We could stay in my apartment, but I thought you'd be more comfortable in yours."

She searched for the words she needed to set her world back to rights. Emma Jennings lived an ordered existence. Ever since a certain helicopter had crash-landed close to her dig, her life had been anything but ordered. *Chaos* was the word that best described the world she'd been thrown into.

"We'll stay in my apartment," she snapped. "But that's as far as it goes. You can sleep on the couch."

Dante sat in the driver's seat, his lips quivering on the corners.

If he smiled, she'd…she'd…ah hell, she'd probably fall all over herself and drool like a fool. The man had entirely too much charm and charisma for a lonely college professor to resist.

I'm doomed.

Dante glanced her way. "Did you say something?"

"Not at all," she squeaked and clamped her lips shut tight. Just because they'd made love once, didn't mean they'd hop right back into the sack at her apartment. He wasn't into commitment, and making love more than once would be too much like commitment to Emma. No, she couldn't take it if she made the mistake of falling for the handsome border patrol agent. No, he wasn't the kind of guy to stick around. The men in her life had a way of disappearing just about the time she started to think they might stick around.

It would be better to keep her distance from Dante and save herself the trouble of a broken heart.

She swallowed a groan. How the hell was she going to keep her distance when he would be camped out in her apartment?

Chapter Six

"I'll stay here in the Jeep while you collect your belongings," Emma offered when they pulled up outside Dante's apartment building.

"Sorry." Dante tilted his head toward her. "What kind of bodyguard would I be if I left you out here in the cold, alone? Bundle up. You're coming in with me."

Emma didn't know what she expected when she entered Dante's apartment. As good as he'd been to her since she'd defended him against the shooter, she didn't know much about him. She expected his apartment to reveal something about his life. Instead, it was as stark and impersonal as a doctor's office.

Dante went to the kitchen first and grabbed a cordless phone. "I need to check in with my family in case they got word of my crash."

Dante headed for the bedroom, speaking into the telephone as he went. Apparently he got an answering machine. "Mom, it's Dante. In case you've seen the news reports about the helicopter crash involving a border patrol agent, I'm okay. Yes, it was mine, but I'm not hurt. Call me when you get a chance. Love you."

While Dante was leaving the message and packing his bag, Emma studied what little there was in the living room and kitchen.

The furniture was plain and functional with a brown leather couch and lounge chair and a rather plain coffee table and television. On the bar that separated the kitchen from the living area were two framed photos. One was of a family of six. Four brothers and their mother and father. All the men were like Dante, swarthy, black-haired and built like brick houses.

Emma peered closer. The second man from the left had to be Dante several years ago. It was him, with a few less creases around his eyes and a happy, carefree smile.

Emma found herself wishing she'd known that happier, younger Dante before he'd been jaded by a war half a world away.

"Dante, is this picture in the kitchen of your family?"

"Yes," he called out from the bedroom.

"How old is this photo? You look so much younger."

"It was taken about four years ago, when my father was still alive."

So his father was dead. Another detail of Dante's life she was learning. "I'm sorry."

"We were, too." Dresser drawers opened and closed and a closet door was opened.

Emma set the frame on the counter and lifted the other.

The other photo was of Dante in a flight suit, standing with a couple of men and one woman in desert camouflage uniforms. Dante had his arm around the woman. She wore her hair pulled back in a tight, neat bun, her makeup-free face smiling into the camera. Sandy-blond hair and light gray-blue eyes, she was a woman men could easily fall in love with. She had one of those sweet, outgoing, girl-next-door faces with an added dose of steel. She'd have to have been tough enough to handle the ten-to-one men-to-women ratio in the desert.

Emma admired women who volunteered for armed services. She herself had tried to go into ROTC, but an injury to her shoulder as a child had kept her from passing the physical.

Emma stared down at Dante's arm draped over the woman's shoulder. In her heart she knew this woman had meant something to Dante.

"What are you doing?" Dante demanded.

Emma jumped and dropped the photo frame back on the counter. She'd been so engrossed in the two photographs she hadn't noticed Dante had returned to the living area carrying a duffel bag and wearing freshly laundered jeans and a blue chambray shirt. He was even sexier in clothes that fit.

A guilty flush burned her cheeks at being caught snooping about his private life. But she refused to ignore the picture, wanting to know more about this man she'd made love to. "Who is she?"

He started to walk by, headed for the door, but stopped beside her instead. "Someone I used to know."

Lifting the frame again, she stared across the floor at him. "She's very pretty."

Dante's gaze went to the photo, his eyes staring as if looking back in time, not at the paper picture but at the memories it inspired. "Samantha made the desert bearable."

Something in his voice made Emma's heart squeeze in her chest, but she couldn't stop herself from observing, "She has a nice smile."

He nodded. "Everyone at Bagram Airfield loved Samantha."

Emma studied Dante's face, her heart settling into the pit of her belly. "Did you love her?"

His gaze shifted from the photo to Emma. "What?"

"Did you love her?"

"Yes."

"And do you still?" Emma asked quietly.

His lips thinned, his dark green eyes unreadable. "Yes."

Emma glanced around the sterile apartment. There were no signs of the woman. Surely he wouldn't have taken Emma out to have coffee if he was still involved with her. "What happened?" she dared to ask, the question burning in her heart.

"She died in an IED explosion while visiting an Afghan orphanage outside the wire."

A heavy lump settled in the pit of Emma's gut as she stared down at the beautiful face, so happy and alive. "That's terrible."

"Yeah," he said, the word clipped and as emotionless as the room they stood in. "Ready?"

Emma nodded and set the frame on the counter. "I'm sorry for your loss. She must have been a very special woman."

"She was."

And there she had it. Samantha was a very special woman. How could Emma compete with that? No wonder he'd had coffee with her one time and walked away without calling again. Emma didn't measure up to Samantha's perfection.

Her heart fell even farther, landing somewhere around her shoes. And he'd made love to her only to find out she was a pathetic virgin. Heat burned her cheeks and she ducked her head to hide her shame. "I'm ready to leave."

She led the way through the door and stopped on the threshold. "I really wish you'd just drop me off and forget about this bodyguard gig."

Dante frowned. "Why are we arguing about it again?

I thought we'd settled this. I'm going to stay with you for a few days. I promise not to get in your way."

How could he not get in her way? Dante Thunder Horse was larger than life and had given his heart to a dead woman.

Emma had to remind herself that Dante wasn't providing her protection to get closer to her. Why should he? He'd had perfection. Making love to Emma had probably been just something that had happened to keep them warm.

Pushing all thoughts of sex with Dante to the back of her mind, Emma squared her shoulders and nodded. "You're right. It's only for a few days. Then you'll be on your way home to your family and I'll go back to my work as a professor." Spending Christmas by herself as usual. How pathetic was that?

Because her mother had died and she hadn't spoken to her father since, she had no one. Christmas was one of those holidays she dreaded each year. This year would be no different.

Dante threw his duffel bag into the back of his Jeep and opened the door for Emma. She slid past him, careful not to touch him and set off all those errant nerve endings that jumped anytime he was near. He might not see her as a potential sexual partner, but Emma's body sure couldn't forget her first time making love. The man had been amazing. Her foot slipped as she stepped up on the Jeep's running board and she crashed back into Dante.

His arms surrounded her and he crushed her to his chest.

Emma's heart thundered against her ribs. His arm crossed her chest beneath her breasts, one of his big hands covering her tummy. Even through her thick winter coat, she could feel his warmth.

In that instant, in his arm, her thoughts scrambled. For a moment, she imagined him holding her because he wanted to, not because she'd practically thrown herself at him. Accidentally, of course.

Once she had her feet under her, she tried to push out of his arms.

"Steady there," he said. "That running board can get slick in the icy weather."

Now he tells her. "I'm okay. I'll be more careful next time."

"Oh, I didn't mind. I just want to make sure you're not hurt."

"Thanks." As she scrambled into the Jeep, she felt his palm on her rear, making certain she didn't fall back this time.

Embarrassed by her clumsiness and her body's instant reaction, she settled into the leather seat and turned her face away from Dante as he climbed into the driver's seat. She gave him the directions to her apartment and sat in silence as he drove across town.

She tried not to look his way, but she couldn't help it. The man had the rugged profile of his ancestors, complete with chiseled cheekbones and a strong jaw.

Several times he glanced into the rearview mirror, his brows furrowing.

"What's wrong?" Emma finally asked as they approached the street to her apartment complex. When they passed her turn, she swiveled in her seat. "You missed my turn."

"I can't swear to it, but I think someone was following us."

Emma spun to look behind her. "In Grand Forks?"

"I know it's a small city by most standards, and there aren't that many places for people to go, but the vehicle

behind me has been on my tail since I left my apartment."
Dante relaxed. "Good, he turned off." Dante sped up and
turned at the next corner, going the long way around to
circle back to her apartment complex.

"It could be my imagination, but I'd rather be safe
than sorry." He pulled into the parking lot and parked
the Jeep on the far side of a trash bin, out of visible range
of the street.

Emma thought he was taking his job as a bodyguard
to the extreme, but didn't say anything. This was Grand
Forks, North Dakota, not Chicago or Houston.

As soon as he put the Jeep in Park, Emma unbuckled
her belt and carefully climbed out to stand on the ground.
She didn't want a repeat performance of her earlier awkward actions.

"I'm on the second floor." She led the way up the outside staircase to the entrance of her apartment and bent
to retrieve her spare key from beneath a flowerpot with
a dead plant covered in a dusting of snow.

"You really shouldn't leave a key to your apartment
out here. Anyone could get in."

"I've been living by myself for years."

"I know, but still, it's not safe."

"Well, since my purse is in my crashed truck at the
dig site, I'm glad I had a key beneath the flowerpot. It's
almost impossible to catch the apartment manager in his
office on a weekend." She unlocked the door and entered,
switching on the lights.

Nothing in her apartment had changed. After all that
had happened, it seemed both anticlimactic and reassuring at the same time. "You can set your bag by the
couch," she said. "I'm sorry, but I don't have a lot of
groceries. I had planned on stocking up when I got back
from the dig site."

"We can go to the store when you want."

"I need to call my insurance agent and deal with my truck and I guess the state police to report the accident." She turned toward him shaking her head. "I'm not even sure what I'm supposed to do."

"I'll take you down to the state police station and we can give a statement. My supervisor should already have given them a heads-up. That should get the ball rolling. They might want to bring in the Feds since it was attempted murder and an attack on federal property."

"And a federal agent," Emma reminded him. He seemed more concerned about the helicopter than his own life.

He shrugged and continued. "The National Transportation Safety Board will investigate the downed helicopter. And the Department of Homeland Security will also want to get involved as it could be considered a terrorist attack since the man used a Soviet-made RPG to shoot me down."

A tremor shook Emma. "We're in North Dakota, not Afghanistan."

Dante's face grew grim. "And the attacks on the Twin Towers and the Pentagon were here in America."

"It's hard to accept that nowhere can be considered safe anymore."

A vehicle alarm system went off in the parking lot below her apartment, making Emma jump. She laughed shakily. "Guess I'm getting punchy."

Dante strode to the window, glanced out through the blinds and shook his head. "That's my Jeep. I guess someone bumped into it accidentally. The alarm is supersensitive."

Emma joined him at the window and stared down at his SUV. The lights blinked and a siren wailed.

Digging his key fob from his jeans pocket, Dante aimed it at the vehicle. The alarm and blinking lights ceased and it grew quiet again.

Emma hadn't realized just how close she was standing next to Dante until she turned to face him at the same time as he faced her.

"Better?" he asked with a smile.

She nodded, her tongue suddenly tied, words beyond her as she stared at those lips that had kissed her senseless.

He reached out to cup her cheek. "I promise I'll do my best to protect you." Then ever so gently, he brushed his mouth across hers.

Emma exhaled on a sigh, her body leaning into his as if drawn to him of its own accord.

He slipped a hand around to the small of her back, and the one cupping her cheek rounded to the back of her neck, urging her forward as he returned for a longer, deeper kiss.

His tongue thrust between her teeth, sliding along hers in a sensuous caress that left her breathless.

The hand at her back slipped beneath her sweater, fingers splaying across her naked skin.

She wished she was completely naked, lying beside his equally naked body. Though she was unskilled in the art of making love, she'd follow his lead and they'd—

A car door slammed outside, breaking through her reverie.

Dante lifted his head and glanced out the window. "I'm sorry. I promised you wouldn't even know I was here. That kiss was uncalled for."

"That's okay." She wanted to tell him that she'd liked it, but didn't want to sound too naive or desperate. Though every ounce of her being wanted him to pull her back into his arms and kiss her again.

Dante's hands fell to his sides and he stuffed them into his pockets.

Emma couldn't move away, afraid her wobbly knees wouldn't hold her up. Instead, her gaze followed his to the parking lot below where backup lights blinked bright and a truck eased out of the parking space beside Dante's SUV.

Emma tensed. The driver was turning too sharp and his tires didn't seem to be getting enough traction to straighten the vehicle.

"He's going to hit your Jeep," Emma said, diving for the door. She flung it open and started to shout to the driver to stop.

Before she could get a word out, the world seemed to explode in front of her.

EMMA WAS BLOWN backward, hitting Dante square in the chest, knocking him onto the floor of her apartment. He fell flat on his back and Emma landed on top of him. With the wind knocked out of him and his ears ringing, he lay for a moment trying to comprehend what had just happened.

Then he was scrambling to his feet and racing down the steps to the parking lot below. His Jeep was a blackened hulk with a hole blown through the driver's side.

The truck that had been backing out of the space next to his was drifting backward across the icy surface of the pavement, the hood had been blown upright and the driver was slumped at the wheel. Smoke billowed out of the engine.

Dante ran to the truck and yanked at the door. It was locked. He banged on the window and shouted to get the driver's attention, but he wasn't waking up no matter how hard Dante banged or how loud he shouted.

The truck slid back into a car and stopped, but smoke billowed from the engine compartment and then flames sprang from the source of the smoke.

Desperate to get the man out of the truck, he glanced around for something to break the window with. The ground and the sidewalks were covered in snow from the night before and nothing jumped out that would be strong enough to break the glass.

Behind him, he heard footsteps clambering down the stairs and Emma slid to a stop beside him. "Use this," she said and slapped a hammer in his palm.

Dante gave a brief grin. Emma was smart and resourceful.

He rounded to the passenger side of the vehicle and slammed the hammer into the glass. It took several attempts before he broke all the way through and could reach his hand in to hit the automatic door-lock release.

As soon as he did, Emma pulled open the driver's door and reached inside to unbuckle the seat belt.

The flame surged, the heat making Dante's face burn. "Get back!" he shouted, racing around the other side of the truck.

Emma ignored his entreaty and tugged at the driver's arm. "We have to get him out."

Dante arrived at her side. As soon as she backed away, he grabbed the man and pulled him out, draping his limp body over his shoulder. He turned and nearly ran into Emma. "Move, move, move!"

With the burden of the man weighing him down and the ice-covered pavement slowing his steps, Dante ran after Emma, barely making it to the apartment building before the flame found the truck's gas tank. The second explosion in less than ten minutes rocked the earth beneath them and he crashed to his knees on the concrete.

Emma appeared in front of him and soon other apartment dwellers emerged from their rooms to see what all the commotion was.

Emma pointed to a woman who stood in the doorway of her apartment with her hair up in a towel and yelled, "Lisa, call 9-1-1!"

The woman's eyes widened and she spun back into her apartment and reappeared with her cell phone pressed to her ear, talking rapidly to the dispatcher on the other end.

"Here, lean on me. Let me help you up." Emma slipped one of Dante's arms over her shoulder and helped him to rise with the man in tow. Grateful for her help, he tried not to put too much weight on her as he clambered to his feet.

"We should get him inside where it's warm," Emma said, angling toward the woman on the cell phone.

She stepped back and let them enter.

Dante laid the man out on the couch and straightened.

"I need blankets," Emma said.

Lisa, still holding the phone, nodded toward the hallway. "The ambulance and fire department are on their way. The dispatcher wants me to stay on the phone until they arrive. You can find blankets in the hall closet."

"I'll get them." Emma disappeared and reappeared with two thick blankets.

Sirens wailed and soon the apartment building was surrounded by emergency vehicles, lights flashing. Firemen leaped out and quickly extinguished the blaze, but not before two other cars had sustained damage.

The emergency medical technicians brought in a backboard and loaded the driver onto it and carried him out to the ambulance.

By the time city police and the state police took their statements and the tow truck came to collect the disabled vehicles, day had turned to night. Not that the days were very long during the North Dakota winters.

Emma thanked Lisa for all her help and led the way back up to her apartment.

Dante followed her in, closed the door behind him and leaned against it.

She faced him with shadows beneath her eyes and a worried frown creasing her forehead. "If you had been in your Jeep…"

"I'd be dead. And if you'd been with me in the passenger seat, you'd be either dead or severely injured. I hope that truck driver makes it."

"Toby," she said. "His name is Toby and he's a student at UND. I hope he makes it, too. He has a promising future as an aerospace engineer." Emma ran a hand through her hair and stared across at him, her eyes glassy with unshed tears.

Dante's heart squeezed at the desperation in her tone. He opened his arms and she fell into them. Wrapping her in his embrace, he leaned his cheek against the side of her head. "It's not safe here."

"If it's not safe here, it won't be any safer at your apartment." She looked up at him with those anxious brown eyes. "We have nowhere else to go."

Dante shook his head. "Yes, we do." He turned her around and gave her backside a gentle slap. "Pack your bags. We're going to the Thunder Horse Ranch. We'll leave first thing in the morning."

Chapter Seven

Emma lay in her bed with the goose down comforter pulled up to her chin and stared at the ceiling. Exhaustion should have knocked her right out, but for the life of her, she couldn't go to sleep. Too many thoughts tumbled in her mind, too many images of the past twenty-four hours kept replaying through her head like a recurring nightmare.

The only thing that kept her from having a full-blown anxiety attack was the man lying on the couch in her living room. Dante was the one island in the murky river of her thoughts keeping her afloat.

As independent as she thought she was, she'd give anything for him to lie beside her, take her into his arms and tell her everything was going to be all right.

She'd lean her face against his naked chest and breathe in the scent of him and all would be well with her world and she'd finally be able to go to sleep.

Like hell. If he was lying naked beside her, she'd be too tempted to run her hands over his body and explore all those interesting places she'd missed when they'd made love in the cold interior of her now-destroyed camp trailer.

Achingly aware of the man in the other room and too

wound up to lay still a moment longer, Emma finally gave in, flung back the covers and sat up.

A large shadow moved and Dante appeared in the doorway. "Can't sleep, either?" He leaned against the door frame, his arms crossed and his legs crossed at the ankles.

Emma couldn't see his expression, but the faint glow through the blinds from the security light outside her living room window backlit the man, making him appear larger than life and incredibly sexy. He wore nothing but gym shorts, his swarthy, Native American skin even darker in the dim lighting.

She swallowed hard. "No. I keep thinking back over everything that's happened."

"Me, too." He crossed the room to sit on the edge of her bed. "As soon as I lay my head down, my thoughts spin."

"You could have died. Four times."

"And you could have died almost as many."

Emma harrumphed. "I feel like a big wimp." She smiled, though her lips trembled.

"Do you mind?" He moved to sit beside her and pulled her into the crook of his arm.

Emma leaned into his body, feeling immediately warmer and more secure than before he showed up in her doorway.

"As I see it, you're pretty darned brave." He held up a thumb. "First, you risked your life by nearly crashing your snowmobile into the man who shot me down. A wimp wouldn't have done that."

Emma didn't think it had been at all heroic. "I didn't think. I just reacted."

"But you reacted. Most people would have hesitated. It took someone with a backbone to charge in...without thinking." He unfolded his pointer finger. "Second, you kept your head when the trailer was caving in around us and got the hell through the window fast enough so that I could get out. Then you helped me squeeze through. I doubt very seriously I would have made it out in time without your help."

"You would have," she insisted.

He unfolded another finger. "You walked several miles in frigid cold without a single complaint, when I know you had to be hurting."

She snorted. "And fell on my face before we made it to the house."

"And gave me an opportunity to be a hero. Carrying you that last little bit was nothing, and it made me look good to Olaf and Marge." He chuckled, the vibrations sending tiny electric shocks through her.

She turned her cheek into his bare chest and closed her eyes. Daring to touch him, she laid her hand on him and felt the rise and fall of each breath he took. "Keep talking. I'm still not convinced."

Another finger unfolded as he scooted down in the bed until he was lying beside her. "When the truck was on fire and an explosion was imminent, you risked your life to help get Toby out." His arm tightened around her. "Sweetheart, you're not a wimp. You're pretty impressive if you ask me."

She wanted to ask if she was anywhere near as impressive as Samantha, but knew it wouldn't be appropriate to compare herself to a dead woman. Dragging her into the conversation would only bring Dante more pain.

Instead, she settled against his side.

"Go to sleep, Emma. If you'd like, I'll stay awake to be on the lookout until morning."

"No, we have a long trip ahead of us and I'll bet you plan on doing most of the driving."

"I'm used to long stretches of sleeplessness. I can handle it."

"You might be able to, but I can't. Surely we'll be okay if we both get some sleep. I'm a light sleeper. I'll let you know if I hear anything strange."

"I suppose it will be all right. Do you want me to go back to the couch?"

"No," she said, her hand flexing against his chest as if that alone would keep him from getting up if he wanted to. "I promise not to seduce you."

He chuckled. "Okay, but I wouldn't be opposed if you did."

Though she wanted to feel gloriously satiated like she had felt in the trailer, she also didn't want him to think she was needy. For a moment she considered making the first move, but then squelched the idea.

Dante sighed and rolled her onto her side away from him, then spooned her body with his. "Sleep. It's been a long day and tomorrow promises to be equally trying."

"Let's hope not. I could do with less drama."

"You and me both." His arm tightened around her middle and he drew her close.

For a long time, Emma lay in Dante's arms, sleep eluding her. When his breathing became more regular and deeper, she relaxed, a little disappointed that he hadn't tried anything.

Exhaustion finally claimed her and she fell asleep, cocooned in the warmth of Dante's body, her last thought being that she could get used to this far too easily.

DANTE SLIPPED BACK into another nightmare when his helicopter had been attacked in Afghanistan.

Having taken hits, he was barely able to bring his helicopter back to Bagram. But he had and set it down as smoothly as if it wasn't damaged. He was congratulating himself when one of the guys in the back said, "Giddings was hit. We need an ambulance ASAP."

As he ripped his harness loose, he gave instructions to the tower, slipped from the pilot's seat and dropped to the ground. He ran around to the other side where the gunner was being unbuckled from his harness and carried out of the craft.

Giddings had volunteered to be a gunner and had competed with others to claim the position. He'd been a damned good gunner, saving their butts on more than one occasion.

At twenty-three, he was barely out of his teens, a kid. And he had a young, pregnant wife back in the United States due to give birth in less than a month. Four weeks from redeployment back to the United States, he'd insisted on flying this mission.

Dante could kick himself for letting the kid fly. The closer they came to redeployment the more superstitious they became. It seemed that only the really good guys managed to be jinxed their last month in the sandbox.

When the ambulance arrived, Dante insisted on riding with them to the hospital and he stayed until Giddings was out of surgery and out of danger. He'd make it.

It had all happened so fast. One minute they were flying a mission, the next he was waiting for the doc to tell him the verdict on one of his crew.

It wasn't until he was on his way back to his quarters that he made the turn to swing by Samantha's room. She would be off duty by now and he really needed to see her.

She shared quarters with another personnel officer, Lieutenant Mandy Brashear. He might not get her alone, but at least he could share a hug and a kiss. After nearly losing a member of his team, he really needed the reassurance of her warm body next to his.

When he stopped outside her door, he heard the sound of someone sobbing. Without hesitating, he pushed open the door and entered. "Samantha?"

Lieutenant Brashear lifted her head from her pillow and stared up at him with tear-streaked cheeks, her eyes rounding as she recognized him. "Oh, Dante," she said, ignoring the protocol of addressing a higher-ranking officer by his rank and last name. "You haven't heard?"

Dante stiffened, his heart seizing in his chest, guessing what Mandy would say before she did. "What's wrong? Where's Sam?" He looked around the small room, although he knew she wasn't there.

"Oh, God." Mandy's tears gushed from her eyes and her words became almost incoherent as she sobbed and spoke simultaneously. "She went to the orphanage today... I...can't...believe...Oh, God." She buried her face in her hands and sobbed some more.

His hands and heart going cold, Dante gripped Lieutenant Brashear's shoulders and lifted her to her feet. "Where is Sam?"

"She was in the hospital when I left her," she blurted. "Dante, she's...she's...dead."

Dante ran all the way back to the hospital where he'd been just minutes before, outside the surgical units, waiting for Giddings to be sewn up and released. He hadn't known that in the unit beside Giddings, Samantha had taken her last breath.

He got back in time to see them zip her into the body bag. They wheeled her out on a gurney. All sealed up and final. He didn't even get to say goodbye.

"Dante," a female voice called to him.

For a moment he thought it was Samantha, but she had a gravelly voice; this was a smooth, sexy voice calling his name.

"Dante, wake up." A hand shook his shoulder this time.

Dante opened his eyes and looked up into Emma's face and blinked, for a split second wondering what she was doing in Afghanistan. Then he remembered he wasn't in the Middle East, but back in North Dakota having been attacked on multiple occasions. He rolled off the side of the bed and landed on his feet. "What's wrong?"

Emma smiled. "I'm sorry, but your cell phone is ringing. That's the third time it's rung in the past fifteen minutes."

Shaking the cobwebs from his head, he hurried into the living room and grabbed his cell phone off the coffee table where he'd left it. In the display window was the word Mom.

It was two o'clock in the morning. She wouldn't call at this hour unless it was an emergency. These thoughts whisked through his mind as he hit the talk button. "Mom, what's wrong?"

"Oh, thank goodness you answered." She took a deep breath and let it out before continuing. "Pierce and Tuck were in an accident and are in the hospital in Bismarck."

His hand tightened on the phone. The last time he'd been at the hospital in Bismarck, his father had died from injuries sustained when he'd been thrown by his horse. "What happened?"

"Yesterday, they were on their way home for the weekend when Pierce's brakes gave out. From what the police said, they had been traveling pretty fast with the roads being clear still. This was before the big storm." His mother spoke to someone in the background and returned to the story. "They had come up on an accident on the interstate. That's when the brakes must have failed. Rather than slam into the vehicles stopped on the interstate, they drove off into the ditch. The truck flipped, rolled and landed upside down." Her voice broke on a sob.

Dante's heart squeezed hard. He wished he was there to comfort his mother. The woman was a rock and if she was in this much distress, it had to be bad.

She sniffed. "I'm sorry. I can't do this." The phone clattered as if it had been dropped.

"Mom?" Dante listened and could hear female voices. "Mom!"

"Dante, this is Julia." Julia was Tuck's wife and the mother of his little girl, Lily. "Tuck was thrown twenty yards and suffered a concussion, but Pierce was trapped inside the truck until the fire department could get there from Bismarck and cut him out. They didn't get him out until the storm hit. They almost didn't make it back to Bismarck in the ambulances."

"Damn." Though he'd been away fighting in the war and then living on the opposite end of the state of North Dakota, he was still very much a part of the Thunder Horse family and he loved his brothers. To be that close to having lost one hit him hard.

"Tuck's okay," Julia continued. "It's Pierce we're all worried about. When the truck flipped he sustained a couple of broken ribs, a punctured lung and we don't know what else. He's had some internal bleeding and he's still unconscious. They've sedated him into a medically induced coma until they can figure out what else is damaged."

Dante pinched the bridge of his nose, his own crash pushed to the back of his mind. Apparently his mother hadn't heard about it and hadn't received the message on her answering machine at the ranch. He'd have to contact the ranch foreman, Sean McKendrick, and have him erase it before she got home. No use worrying her more when he was fine.

"How's Mom holding up?"

"She's doing okay, but the emotional strain is wearing on her," Julia said. "We knew you'd planned to be here next week, but with Pierce and Tuck both in the hospital and Maddox on the other side of the world in Trejikistan with Katya and not due back until next week, we thought you might want to be here."

Dante straightened. "I'm coming home."

"Thank goodness." Julia's words came out in a rush. "Roxanne is here with Pierce, and with your mother here, the foremen of the two ranches are on their own. And, Dante…" Julia's voice dropped and she paused. Footsteps sounded at her end as if she was walking down a hallway. Then she continued, "There have been some suspicious accidents happening out there. Your mother thinks it's just bad luck, but Roxanne and I think someone is sabotaging things. We're afraid if we don't have a Thunder Horse out there keeping an eye on things, there won't be a ranch to come home to. Amelia has gone so far as to hire a security firm to set up surveillance cameras."

"Why didn't she tell me?"

"She knows she can't ask you guys to come home every time something goes bump in the night. With Maddox out of the country, she wanted something to make her feel safe. Thus the security system."

The thought of his mother being scared enough to hire a security firm bothered Dante more than he could believe. "I'll stop in at the hospital on my way through. It'll take me between four and five hours to get there. I can be there around seven in the morning."

"Oh, Dante," Julia begged, "please wait until morning. The last thing we need right now is another Thunder Horse in a ditch. And I don't think your mother could worry about one more thing."

"Okay. I'll wait until closer to sunup. Expect me at noon."

"Good. Just a minute. Your mother wanted to talk to you one more time."

Dante braced himself, his eyes burning as his mother got on the phone. "Dante, your brothers are going to be okay."

"I know, Mom. I'm worried about you."

She snorted, the sound hitching with what he suspected was a sob. "I'm a tough old bird. Don't you go worrying about me. And don't you come rushing out here thinking we all need saving. Maddox will be home before you know it, and Pierce and Tuck will be up and giving him hell. Take care of yourself, son."

"I will. I love you, Mom."

"I love you, too."

When he rang off, Dante stood for a long time, with the phone in his hand, his thoughts flipping through all the chapters in his life, so many of them, including the days he'd spent riding across the Badlands on wild ponies he and his brothers had tamed. Their Lakota blood had run strong through their veins and their mother had encouraged them to embrace their father's heritage.

Wakantanka, the Great Spirit, had watched over their antics, protecting them from harm.

Dante closed his eyes and lifted his face to the sky. Where was the Great Spirit when his brothers' truck had flipped? Perhaps he'd been there. Otherwise they would both be dead.

A hand on his arm brought him back to the apartment.

"What's wrong?" Emma stood beside him in a short baby-blue filmy nightgown, her pale skin practically glowing in the darkness.

"My brothers were in an accident."

She gasped. "Are they okay?"

"So far."

"You have to go to them."

"We'll leave in the morning and stop at the hospital in Bismarck on our way to the Thunder Horse Ranch."

"I meant to ask, just where is the Thunder Horse Ranch?"

"In the Badlands north of Medora."

"Okay." She smiled. "I'll be sure to pack my snow gear. In the meantime, you need sleep. It's a long way there."

He shook his head. "I can't sleep."

"Then come lay down with me. Even if you don't sleep, you can rest." She took his hand and led him back into her bedroom, offering him comfort he gladly accepted.

When he stretched out on the bed beside her, she lay in the crook of his arm, her cheek pressed to his chest, her hand draped across his belly. He lay staring at the ceiling, thinking about his brothers and his mother and wishing his father was still alive.

"Stop thinking," Emma whispered against his skin. Her warm breath stirred him, reminding him that he wasn't alone with his thoughts.

Emma skimmed her hand over his chest and down his torso and back up in soothing circles. "Think of something else," she urged as her hand drifted lower.

He captured her wrist before she bumped into the rising tent of his shorts. "Once again, don't go there unless you mean it."

She tipped her chin and stared up at him. The little bit of light shining around the edges of the blinds gave her face a light blue glow and her eyes shone in the darkness. "I mean it."

He let go of her wrist and her hand slid lower until it skimmed across his shaft, which became instantly hard and pulsing.

He drew in a slow steadying breath. "Why are you doing this?" A sudden thought reared its ugly head and he flipped her over on her back and pinned her wrists to the mattress.

Her eyes rounded and shone white in the darkness.

"Are you doing this out of some misguided sense of pity?"

Emma shook her head. "No. Not at all."

"Then why?"

"I'm sorry. I shouldn't have been so forward." Her eyelids swept low over her eyes. "I understand if you're not interested in someone so...so..."

"So what?" he asked.

"Inexperienced," she finished, a frown settling between delicate brows.

He nudged her knees apart and settled lower between her legs, letting the hard ridge of his erection brush up against the juncture of her thighs. "Oh, I'm interested all right. But why are you? I don't need anyone's pity."

She glanced away from him and he'd bet her cheeks were flaming. "I was curious," she whispered.

"About what?"

"If the second time would be as good as the first?" She stared up at him, the limited lighting making her face glow a dusky-blue.

The tension leached out of him and he dropped low to steal a kiss. Though it wasn't stealing when she gave it freely. Emma tasted of mint and smelled like roses, the scent light and fragrant but not overpowering. Samantha had reminded him of honeysuckle growing wild and untamed. The two women were as different as night and day.

Where Sam had captured his interest with her unfettered ability to grasp life by the horns and ride, Emma was like an English rosebud, waiting for the sunlight to unfurl.

He released her hands and bent to claim her lips in a crushing kiss. Partly because of the burning desire ignited inside him and partly out of anger for making him think about Sam again. He'd tried so hard to put that chapter of his life behind him, to forget what he'd lost in her and how life had stretched before him empty without her in it.

Quiet, studious Emma had been the first woman he'd even considered dating since Samantha's death. And after having coffee with her, he'd refused to see her again, afraid that being with her meant he was dishonoring the memory of Samantha. Or that he was finally starting to forget her.

The truth was that Samantha was gone forever and Emma was lying beneath him, willing to slake the hunger in his body. If he made love to her, it would mean nothing but a physical release to him. His body recognized needs his mind had refused to let him satisfy.

Once he started, he couldn't seem to stop and Emma didn't cry out or tell him no. Part of him wished she would.

He trailed kisses from her mouth to the edge of her jaw and down the long line of her throat to the pulse beating wildly at the base.

Her fingers curled around the back of his neck and

urged him to continue his downward path to the swells of her breasts beneath the sheer fabric of her nightgown.

He grabbed the hem and ripped it up over her head and tossed it aside.

She lay beneath him, bathed in the soft, gray-blue light shining around the edges of the blinds, her breasts peaked, the nipples tight little buds.

Dante swooped down to taste first one, then the other, rolling the taut buttons between his teeth and across his tongue. When he sucked it into his mouth, she arched her back off the bed, pressing it deeper into his mouth. He gladly accepted, flicking the tip with his tongue.

Slowly, he teased his way across her ribs, slid a hand between her legs, and parted her folds to stroke the strip of flesh hiding there.

Her breath caught and held.

When he started to remove his hand, she covered it with hers and pressed it down, encouraging him to continue.

For someone who'd never had a lover, she learned quickly and wasn't too shy to let him know what she liked.

Before long, her breathing grew ragged and she dug her heels into the mattress, her bottom rising above the sheets as she called out his name. "Dante!"

Her body pulsed beneath his fingers until finally the tension subsided and she fell back to the bed, with a shuddering sigh. "Amazing."

Dante cupped her sex and leaned up to kiss her full on the lips before lying on the bed beside her.

"Wait." Emma leaned up on her elbow, her hand going to the hard line of his manhood. "What about you?"

"Watching you was enough for me."

She frowned, her fingers curling around him. "But you're still…"

"Hard?" He laughed though it took a lot for him to force it out. "I could drive nails with it right now."

"Then, please." She tugged on him, but he refused to budge.

"I don't have protection."

"We didn't have it last night."

"And that was pushing the limits. I won't risk it again. Now, if you happen to have something…?" His lips twisted. "I thought not." He tucked an arm behind his head and pulled her up against him. "I'll take a rain check in the meantime. Sleep, Emma. I have a feeling tomorrow will be another long day."

Emma settled beside him, curled against his side. Whether he wanted her there or not, she wasn't too proud to take advantage of his offer to hold her until she went to sleep.

Warm, safe and satisfied, she drifted to sleep with a smile on her face. She had to remind herself she was an independent college professor and that when all this was over, Dante would move on and possibly never see her again.

But while she had the chance, she'd take whatever scraps he was willing to throw her way. If it meant she was desperate and lonely…well, then it was true. She *was* desperate and lonely, and whatever memories she stored up during her time with Dante would have to do.

In her life history, she was destined to be alone. The men who'd come and gone in her life had been prone to have an aversion to commitment. Emma had long since convinced herself it was her or at least the magnet she seemed to carry around that attracted men who refused to commit.

Tomorrow was another day and she'd better get some sleep if she wanted to be awake when they finally made it to the Thunder Horse Ranch.

Chapter Eight

Dante glanced across at Emma as she leaned back in the seat of the SUV he had rented for the next couple of weeks. She hadn't spoken much throughout the trip and the circles beneath her eyes were more pronounced. Though she'd slept part of the night, they hadn't really had a decent night's sleep in two days.

The back of Dante's neck was stiff and he could feel some of the bruises and sore muscles he'd acquired in the helicopter and trailer crashes.

He'd insisted on a four-wheel-drive SUV for the trip, knowing the roads to the ranch could be difficult during the summer and impassible in a two-wheel-drive vehicle during the harsh North Dakota winters.

The insurance company would take their time sorting out the details of replacing the Jeep. A full investigation would have to be performed by the National Transportation Safety Board on the helicopter crash and the FBI would assist the state police with the case since it involved federal equipment and personnel.

If Pierce and Tuck were in any shape to assist, theirs was the closest FBI regional office to the crash site. Though they would not be assigned the case, Dante knew they would be involved enough to keep him informed of the progress.

So far, not a single terrorist organization or survivalist group had stepped forward to claim responsibility for shooting down his helicopter.

He'd checked in with his boss, who informed him that the police and investigation team from the state crime lab had combed over the burned out hull of the helicopter finding no more evidence or gleaning any more information than he'd already imparted. The snowstorm had covered the snowmobile tracks and more snow was predicted within the next twenty-four hours.

The winter that had held off until now had set in and wouldn't loosen its hold until late April.

Emma slept for the first hour and a half of the drive to Bismarck. The road crews had worked hard to clear the interstate highways between Grand Forks and Fargo and between Fargo and Bismarck. Other than a few slick spots, they hadn't had to slow too much, but the wind blowing in from the northwest pounded the rental, forcing them to use a lot more gasoline than if it had been calm.

By the time Dante reached the hospital in Bismarck, he was ready for the break before the additional three-hour trip to Thunder Horse Ranch. The clouds were settling in, making the sky a dark gray. If they didn't get on the road soon, they might not make it to the ranch. The weather reports on the radio were predicting whiteout conditions starting after dark.

As he pulled into the hospital parking lot, he braced himself for what he'd find. Cell phone reception had been limited between Fargo and Bismarck, with long stretches without any reception whatsoever.

When they'd neared Bismarck, he'd checked his phone. No missed calls and no text messages. He prayed that no news was good news, and climbed out of the car, stretching stiff muscles.

Before he could get around to the passenger side, Emma was already on the snowy ground, pulling the collar of her coat up around her ears.

They entered the hospital together. Emma took his hand and squeezed it. "If your brothers are anything like you, they'll be fine. Thunder Horse men seem to be pretty tough."

He returned the pressure on her hand, thankful she'd come with him. Dante remembered where the ICU was located having been there when his father was taken there. He'd died in the ICU shortly after he'd been admitted to the hospital.

The acrid scent of disinfectants and rubbing alcohol still brought back bad memories and reminded him of his loss.

It was exactly noon when he stepped out of the elevator and saw his mother, surrounded by Julia and Roxanne, talking to a man in a white lab coat.

Dante hurried forward, still holding on to Emma's hand. "What's going on? How's Pierce?" he demanded.

His mother turned, her face lighting up when she saw him. "Dante." She wrapped him in her arms and hugged him so tight he could barely breathe. And it felt good. Like coming home.

After a moment, he set her away from him and asked again, "How's Pierce?"

"Oh, Dante." His mother wiped a tear from the corner of her eye and Dante's stomach fell.

Roxanne stepped forward and draped an arm around Amelia's shoulders. "He woke up." A smile spread across her face and her eyes misted. "He woke up a while ago. Briefly. The doc says that's a good sign." She bit down on her bottom lip and a tear slid from her eye and down her cheek.

For as long as Dante had known Roxanne, she'd never cried in front of him. To see her cry now was nearly his undoing. "Is he going to be okay?"

The doctor stepped forward. "As far as we can tell, he appears to be recovering. We're going to keep him a little longer to monitor his condition. If he continues to improve, he should be able to go home."

His mother smiled through her tears. "It's a miracle." She shook her head. "The news showed pictures of his truck and it's a wonder he's still alive."

"Where's Tuck?"

"Someone looking for me?" Tuck appeared behind him, carrying two cups of steaming coffee. He walked with a limp, but he was wearing jeans and a clean flannel shirt and, other than a few bruises on his face, looked like Tuck. He started to hand the coffee to Dante. "You look like you could use this more than I can. Other than a few bruises and scrapes, I'll live. What happened to you?"

Dante had forgotten the bruise at his temple until that moment. He shrugged. "I ran into the door in my apartment."

His mother's eyes narrowed. Amelia Thunder Horse had that keen sense and woman's intuition. She always knew when he was lying. For a moment she looked like she was going to call him on it, but then she noticed the woman standing behind him and raised her brows asking politely, "Are you with Dante or are you waiting to speak with the doctor?"

Emma opened her mouth to speak, but Dante jumped in before she could. "Mom, this is Emma Jennings." Rather than burden his mother with their problems, he blurted, "Emma's my fiancée. She's come to spend Christmas with us. I hope you don't mind."

The family converged on the two, shock in everyone's expressions, especially Emma's. But she recovered quickly, wiping the surprise from her face.

His mother enveloped Emma in a bear hug, her eyes wet with unshed tears. "Wow, this is a surprise. A much-needed surprise. After all the tragedy and worry...this is wonderful."

Julia took her turn hugging Emma. "Congratulations. I'm so happy for you two. I'm Julia, Tuck's wife."

"I'm Tuck, one of Dante's brothers." Tuck hugged her, looking over the top of her head at Dante, pinning Dante with his stare. "How come we haven't heard anything about her up until now?"

Roxanne shoved him aside. "I'm Roxanne, Pierce's wife. Nice to meet you."

Emma hugged one after the other, muttering her thanks, looking flustered, her cheeks bright pink.

His mother wiped another tear from her eye and sniffed. "This is all so sudden."

Dante slipped an arm around Emma's waist and pulled her up against him. "I know. Seems like only yesterday we met. But when you know, you know. Right, Emma?" He smiled down at her, praying she'd continue to go along with his ruse.

She looked up into his eyes and nodded. "That's right. You just know." She looked out at the people surrounding her and gave a shaky smile. "I hope you don't mind my showing up unannounced."

Amelia hugged her again. "Not at all. There's plenty of room at the ranch and I'm just so happy that Dante's found someone. I've been worried about him since his return from the war."

"Mom—" Dante took his mother's hand "—I'm fine. I have a great job with the CBP and I'm still flying."

"And now you have Emma." Amelia sighed. "All my boys will be happily married and giving me grandchildren."

The elevator door pinged behind Dante, and Sheriff Yost from Billings County stepped through and strode to Amelia, taking her into his arms. "Amelia, darling. I came as soon as I could get away."

Dante's back teeth ground together at the proprietary way Yost held his mother in his arms.

Tuck stepped forward, his fists clenched. "What's he doing here?"

Amelia frowned at Tuck. "It's all right. William came when I called. He's working with the Burleigh County sheriff and the state police to determine the cause of the accident."

Dante stiffened, his arm tightening around Emma. "I thought you said Pierce's brakes went out."

Amelia shot a glance at Tuck.

Tuck faced Dante. "We had the truck hauled to the forensics lab in Bismarck. A mechanic did a preliminary look at the brakes. They'd been cut almost all the way through."

"When?"

"We don't know." Tuck rubbed the back of his neck. Scratches and bruises stretched down his arm, his elbow skinned and raw.

Yost interjected, "I spoke with the mechanic myself. Since the brake lines weren't completely severed, it took a while before all the brake fluid leaked out."

"We didn't know until it was too late to do anything about it." Tuck's gaze went to the door of a room across from the nurses' station.

A nurse stood and walked their way. "If you could,

please move your family reunion to the waiting room. We don't want to disturb the other patients."

The group moved to the waiting room.

Dante glanced around the room, his gaze going from Tuck to Julia. "Where's Lily?"

Julia smiled. "When Tuck's supervisor heard he'd been in an accident, he and his wife came to the hospital. His wife is keeping Lily right now." Julia took Tuck's hand. "We were just about to leave to go pick her up now that Tuck's released. We'd planned on going back to the ranch, but now that you're here…"

"Emma and I are headed that way."

"Then you'll want to get there before the weather," Yost said. "The reporters are predicting another twenty-four inches and whiteout conditions late this afternoon."

Tuck pulled Julia's arm through his. "If you're heading back now, I'd like to stay until Pierce comes out of it."

Dante nodded, his gaze shifting briefly to Yost and back to his brother. "I'd feel better if you stayed. I can check on things back at the ranch and over at the Carmichael Ranch, as well." The Carmichael Ranch was adjacent to the Thunder Horse Ranch. Pierce lived with Roxanne at her ranch when he wasn't on duty with the FBI in the Bismarck office. Maddox Thunder Horse usually handled the day-to-day operations of Thunder Horse Ranch while Roxanne ran the Carmichael.

"Thanks." Roxanne took his hand. "I'm not leaving here without Pierce."

Dante squeezed her hand. "I didn't expect you to."

Amelia wrapped her arms around him and hugged him. "Be careful getting there. I don't know what I'd do if another one of my boys gets hurt."

He kissed the top of her head. "I'll be fine. You guys

worry about Pierce. Emma and I will figure things out back at the ranch. I would like to visit Pierce before I leave."

"He's only allowed one visitor at a time for a few minutes only." His mother smiled apologetically at Emma. "You can stay here with us while he goes."

Dante left Emma in his mother's hands, walked across the polished tile floor to the room his mother indicated and pushed through the big swinging door.

Pierce lay on a hospital bed, his large frame stretched from the headboard to the footboard. Covered in wires and tubes, he lay still as death, his bronze skin slightly gray, cuts and bruises marring his face.

Dante had been to visit soldiers in worse shape, but seeing his brother hooked up to all the gadgets and monitors hit him hard. They'd already lost their father. This shouldn't be happening.

His own helicopter crash seemed insignificant since he'd walked away from it relatively unscathed. Pierce was strong and with the help of *Wakantanka,* the Great Spirit, he'd pull through. But a little prayer wouldn't hurt.

Dante closed his eyes and lifted his face skyward. *"Wakan tanan kici un wakina chelee,"* he spoke the words softly, feeling them in his heart and the hearts of his ancestors. May the Great Spirit bless you, Thunder Horse.

EMMA EXITED THE hospital at Dante's side, her head still spinning with the congratulatory words of Dante's family echoing in her ears. Pulling the hood of her jacket up around her ears, she waited until they got in the SUV before saying, "What was that all about?"

Dante twisted the key in the ignition and backed out of the parking space. "What was what about?"

A shot of anger burst through her. "Fiancée?" She didn't know why his lie was making her so mad. Perhaps it was because his family had welcomed her so openly and with such love...it made her mad to build up their expectations only to disappoint them.

His lips twisted and he shot a quick glance at her. "I'm sorry. It was the only thing I could think of that would keep my mother from asking too many questions about my appearance and why you were with me."

"So you told her we were engaged? I could think of a dozen other things we could have told her but that."

"It's only for the short term, just through Christmas break. Once Pierce is out of the ICU and is home and well enough, she'll quit worrying about him and we can straighten it all out."

"I don't like lying to your family." Emma glanced out the window at the bleak skyline. "Especially to your mother."

"I don't like seeing her cry," he said softly.

All the anger slid away as Emma recalled the tears in Amelia Thunder Horse's eyes and the shadows of worry over her sons' accident. If Dante had told her he'd been shot out of the sky, she might have had a heart attack or at the very least a nervous breakdown.

Emma sighed. "I guess you did the only thing you knew how. I wouldn't want to burden your mother more when your brother is in the ICU."

Dante reached across the console and squeezed Emma's hand and kept holding it for a while afterward.

She stared down at his big fingers clasped around hers, her chest tightening. "You have a nice family."

"Yeah."

"You and your brothers are close?"

"They'd do anything for me and vice versa." He turned to her. "What about you? Do you have siblings?"

"No."

"What about your folks?"

"Gone." Which was true about both. Her mother was dead and she had no idea where her father was.

"I'm sorry."

"Don't be. I'm used to being on my own."

"No one should be alone during the holidays."

She shrugged. "I don't mind." Which was another lie. She hated the holidays for just that very reason. As much as she tried to tell herself it didn't matter, watching others laughing and taking time off to spend it with their families had always been hard on her. She'd been happy to spend her weekends alone on the dig. Digging in the dirt meant she wouldn't have to spend her weekends in her empty apartment. Perhaps she'd get a cat for company.

They traveled in silence the rest of the way to the ranch. The weather held all the way up to the last turnoff leading up to the sprawling ranch house when the first snowflakes began to fall. It wasn't long before more followed, cloaking the sky. By the time Dante parked in front of the house, the wind had picked up, blasting the snow sideways.

"You can go on in," Dante shouted over the wailing Arctic blast. "I need to check on the foreman and the animals in the barn."

"I'll go with you." She zipped up her coat, pulled her hood over her ears and shoved her hands into warm gloves. The frigid wind stung her cheeks, making her blink her eyes. Snowflakes clung to her lashes in clumps.

"You should go inside. I can handle this."

"Please," she said. "I need to stretch my legs."

"In this?"

"You forget, I'm from North Dakota, too." She grinned and followed him to the barn out behind the house.

Several horses were out in a corral, their backs already covered in a thin layer of snow. They trotted along the fence as Dante and Emma approached.

Dante opened the gate and snagged the halter of a sorrel mare. "Think you can lead her into the barn?" he yelled into the wind.

Never having been around horses, Emma figured there couldn't be much to walking a horse into the barn. She reached up and slipped her gloved hand through the harness.

The mare jerked her head up, practically lifting Emma off the ground. She bit down hard on her tongue to keep from screaming and tugged on the harness, urging the horse toward the door to the barn.

Dante passed her, leading a big black horse that danced sideways, tossing its head.

Thankfully, the mare followed the black horse through the door.

Once inside, out of the wind, the horse settled into a plodding walk.

"You can let go of her, she knows which stall is hers," Dante said. "I'll get the other two."

"What can I do?"

"Fill two coffee cans with sweet feed out of that bucket." He pointed to the corner where two large trash cans stood. One had big block letters drawn on the side that spelled out SWEET FEED. The other had CORN, written in capital letters.

Taking two coffee cans from a shelf above the trash cans, Emma opened the sweet-feed bucket and filled the trash cans with the sweet mash of grain and corn and what else, she had no idea, but it smelled like molasses.

The horses already in their stalls whickered, stomping their hooves impatiently.

The barn door swung open and Dante entered leading two large horses. He took them to their stalls and came back to grab the two cans. He filled the feed troughs in two stalls and returned to fill the feed buckets with more grain for the other two horses.

"I didn't see the foreman's truck outside. I hope he gets back before the storm gets any worse." He glanced down at her. "Ready?" he asked, holding out his hand.

Emma nodded and took his hand. He had to push hard to open the door, the wind was playing hell against the barn.

Once they were outside, Dante closed the barn door and then took off at a slow jog toward the house.

The snow had thickened until she could barely see the large structure of the ranch house in front of her.

Dante led the way, holding her gloved hand. When they reached the house he twisted the doorknob on the back. It was locked. Tearing his glove off his hand, he reached into his pocket for his keys and unlocked the door, pushing Emma through first. He quickly stepped in behind her and slammed the door shut.

Emma stood in a spacious kitchen with a large table at one end and a big gas stove at the other. Red gingham curtains hung in the window over the sink, making the blustery winter weather outside look cheerful from the warmth inside. For all the beauty and hominess, something wasn't right.

As she raised her hand to push her hood off her head, she stopped and sniffed.

Dante must have sniffed it at the same time, his nose wrinkling as he unzipped his jacket.

"Gas," Emma said softly.

When Dante started to shove his jacket off, Emma's heart leaped. "Don't move!"

Immediately, his hands froze with his jacket halfway over his shoulders.

"You smell it too?" she asked. "If you take your jacket off, as dry as it is in here, it might let out a spark. My hood does it every time I push it back from my head."

"Good point." He glanced at her. "Get out."

"I'm not going without you."

"If something happens to me and you both, no one will be around to get help. Don't argue, just get out." He walked to the door, holding his arms away from his sides to keep the Gore-Tex fabric from rubbing together and potentially causing a spark.

Emma's lips pressed together. "Okay, but be careful. I'd hate for my brand-new fiancé to go up in flames before I get a ring out of it." Though her words were flippant, her voice quavered. She opened the door carefully and exited.

Dante left the door open, the wind blowing snow through the opening onto the smooth tile floor.

Emma hunched her back to the frigid cold and waited while Dante turned every knob on the stove and the one for the oven, as well. Once he'd secured the stove and checked the gas line into it, he left the kitchen, disappearing around a corner into the darkened house.

By the time he returned, Emma's teeth were chattering and her eyelids were crusted with snowflakes.

"It's safe now. I have all the exterior doors open and there's a good breeze blowing through."

Emma stepped in from the outside. Although she was out of the wind, she was still cold and shivering. The clouds had sunk low over the house, blocking out any light from the setting sun well before dusk. Darkness descended on Thunder Horse Ranch.

Dante pulled her out of the breeze blowing through the house and enveloped her in his arms. "I want to wait a few more minutes before I feel confident it's safe."

Leaning her face into the opening of his jacket, she pressed her cool cheeks to his warm flannel shirt.

He took her hands in his, unbuttoned his shirt and pushed them inside against his warm skin. He hissed at the cold but didn't remove her hands. "Warmer?" he asked.

She nodded, not certain she could talk at that point. Her teeth were still clattering like castanets.

After a good five minutes with the cold wind blowing through the house, Dante closed the back door and went around the house closing the rest, mopping the snow-drenched floor with a towel he'd grabbed out of the bathroom.

When Emma started to take off her jacket, Dante placed a hand over hers. "Wait until it warms up in here to at least sixty degrees."

Content to do as he said, Emma stuck her hands in her pockets and glanced around the kitchen. "Did you locate the source?"

His brow furrowed. "One of the stove's burners was left on."

Emma's gaze captured Dante's. The attacks on Dante's helicopter, the trailer incident, his brothers' cut brake lines and now a house filled with gas were all too close together. "Does that happen often?"

"Never. When my mother talked my dad into buying a gas stove, she promised she'd handle it with care and always turn off the burners. He didn't want a gas stove in the house, afraid one of us kids would light our hair on fire or something. Mom was cautious about the knobs. If she even suspected she might not have turned off the stove, she'd drive a hundred miles back to check."

"Could she have left it on when she rushed to the hospital after your brothers' accident?"

"Maybe, but not likely."

"Coincidence?" Emma asked, shaking her head before he answered.

"I think not." He glanced around the kitchen. "Julia had said something about Mom hiring a security team to set up surveillance around the house. She's had some incidents, as well." He nodded to the corner. "Looks like they've started the work but have yet to install the cameras.

Emma followed his gaze, noting where wires stuck out of the corners of the room.

Dante left the kitchen and strode through the rest of the house, moving from one room to another.

Emma followed. Wires stuck out of the walls in every common area and in the hallway.

"What kind of incidents were they having here?" Emma asked, trying to keep up with him, noting the homey decor and wood flooring.

"I don't know. I think she was afraid to say anything in front of my mother. I'd hoped to find out more from the foreman."

"But he's not here."

No, and Dante had a lot of questions for the man. Where the hell was he?

When Maddox had started traveling to his wife's country of Trejikistan, he and his mother had hired Sean McKendrick to manage the ranch in Maddox's absence. Amelia was capable of a lot of things, but it was a lot for a lone woman. Sean had proven himself knowledgeable about horses and cattle and a good carpenter when things needed fixing. And he seemed to have a good heart and a love for the North Dakota Badlands.

Dante stopped in the living room and glanced down at an answering machine. A light blinked three times, paused and blinked three times again.

He punched the play button and listened.

"Mom, it's Dante. In case you've seen the news reports about the helicopter crash involving a border patrol agent, I'm okay. Yes, it was mine, but I'm not hurt. Call me when you get a chance. Love you." He erased the message.

"Good thing you got home first," Emma said. "Or else the jig would be up."

The second message played. *"Amelia, Sean here. Had to go into Medora at the last minute to pick up some supplies and the Yost boy. If you get back before I do, the horses need to come into the barn before the storm hits."* Dante deleted the message and played the third.

"Amelia, Sean again. Having troubles with the truck engine. Don't think I'll make it back to the ranch before the storm. I'll get a room at the hotel for the night and be back first thing in the morning. I'm putting a call into the Carmichael Ranch to have the foreman come over and take care of the horses."

As he deleted the last message on the answering machine, the phone rang.

"This is Dante."

"Dante, I'm glad you're home. It's Jim Rausch from the Carmichael Ranch. Sean tells me he's stuck in Medora for the night and there's some horses needing put up before the storm."

"I've already taken care of them," Dante reassured the man. "How are things your way?"

"Everything's locked down. Looks like that storm's gonna last until sometime in the middle of the night. I just wanted to get everything in place so that I'm not out in the snow in my house shoes. How's Pierce doing? Your family make it back to the ranch with you?"

"No, they're staying in Bismarck, close to the hospital. Pierce is still out of it. Although he did wake briefly."

"Sorry to hear that. What about Tuck?"

"Banged up, but on his feet."

"Good," Jim said. "Glad he's okay. I saw in the news about your helicopter crash. I guess you're okay if you're at the ranch."

"I am. I left a message on Mom's answering machine about it, but since she hasn't been home, and she hasn't seen the news, I didn't bother telling her. She's got enough to worry about."

Jim snorted. "And then some."

"Tell me about it." If anything were happening at the Thunder Horse Ranch, news would have made it to the Carmichael Ranch. Though Pierce spent his weeks in Bismarck, he commuted to the Carmichael Ranch where his wife, Roxanne lived.

"There's been one accident after another. First the barn door fell off its hinges and nearly crushed your brother Maddox the day before he left with Katya. Three days later, the hay caught fire in the barn. Sean was able to put out the fire before it did any damage, but it was close."

"What do you know about the security system Mom's having installed?"

"Sheriff Yost's son has a security business. He's doing the work. From what Roxanne said, he's not finished."

"No, not even close."

"Roxanne tells me Maddox is cutting short his stay in his wife's country to come home early because of all that's been happening. Your mother tried to convince him she's fine, but none of us like what's happening. And now this crash with your brothers. It's enough to push a sane woman over the edge."

Exactly Dante's worry. "Thanks for the update."

"Glad you're there to take care of things. Let me know if you need any help."

"Thanks, Jim."

Dante hung up the telephone and stared across the floor at Emma. "I'm sorry to say, but I think by saving my life, you've walked into a bigger can of worms than we originally thought."

Chapter Nine

Emma insisted on spending the night on the couch in the living room. Being alone in the big house with Dante made her uncomfortable. After being in the presence of his family and extended family, she found herself wishing she really did belong and that was a dangerous thing to do.

She had bad luck with families. Her father had left when she was a little girl. As a single parent, her mother had left her alone since the age of twelve so that she could save money on babysitting.

To survive, she'd learned to cook and do her own laundry and that of her mother's or it wouldn't have gotten done. Her mother worked her day job and a night job to keep her in a private school.

A month after Emma graduated from high school, her mother caught a staph infection at the nursing home where she cleaned rooms. Within two weeks, she'd died.

Completely alone at eighteen, Emma had depended on herself since. Too many times when the world seemed too harsh or the tasks too hard, she'd gone back to her rented room and cried herself to sleep. She'd have given her right arm to have someone hug her and tell her everything would be all right.

She'd completed her undergraduate degree working nights washing dishes at a local restaurant. Then she worked her way through her master's degree as a teacher's assistant. She'd captured the attention of the department head and was offered a teaching position when she completed her master's and went on to get her doctorate, determined that no matter what, she would always be able to support herself without working two jobs like her mother had.

All in all, she'd had a limited family experience, whereas Dante's family was almost storybook perfect. Lucky man.

Dante had gotten up before dawn, dressed and went out to tend to the animals, leaving Emma to dress and scrounge in the kitchen for breakfast. The refrigerator was well stocked with enough food to feed an army. A freezer in the pantry was full of what looked like a half a cow's worth of packaged beef, frozen homegrown vegetables and loaves of bread.

She supposed they had to buy in bulk when they could only get to the major grocery stores once every other month and maybe not at all during the fierce winters.

Whipping up a half a dozen eggs, she chopped onions, tomatoes and black olives and tossed them in a skillet, pouring half the eggs over the top to make an omelet.

When she had two plates loaded, the back door opened and a frigid blast of air slammed into her. "Holy smokes." She danced out of the draft and grabbed the pot of coffee she'd made and poured a cup full. "Sit. I have breakfast ready."

"Thanks." Dante stomped his feet on the mat to get the snow off his boots and sniffed the air. "Smells better than gas." He winked and shrugged out of his jacket, scarf, gloves and an insulated cap. "You don't have to wait on me, you know. My mother taught us boys to cook and clean dishes."

"I know. But I was up and it gave me something to do. Besides, it's just as easy to cook for two as it is for one."

"Thanks." He pulled out her chair and waited for her to sit, before claiming one for himself. Then he wrapped his hands around the mug of coffee and let the steam warm his face. "Heaven."

His appreciation of her efforts warmed her. "Have you heard anything about your brother?"

"As a matter of fact, my mother called late last night after you were already asleep."

Emma held her breath, praying for good news after all the bad.

"Seems Pierce woke up late last night demanding dinner." Dante smiled. "He'll be okay if he's already bellowing for food."

Emma let go of the breath she'd held, a weight of dread lifting from her shoulders. She'd never met Dante's brother, but she understood how horrible it was to lose a family member and she didn't wish that kind of loss on anyone. "Thank God."

"They hope the doc will declare him fit and cut him loose today."

"That soon?"

"He's already been up and they've moved him from the ICU. It's only a matter of time before they throw him out."

"That's good news."

"I got ahold of Tuck and told him what happened to us."

Her head jerked up. "Does he know we're not really engaged?"

"No, I didn't tell him that part. I figured it would be

hard enough to keep Mom from knowing about our crash without disappointing her about seeing her last son settling down."

"Now that your brother is going to be okay, shouldn't we tell her the truth?" The thought made her belly tighten and she set down her fork, no longer hungry. Amelia had been so happy at her son's announcement.

"No. Let her enjoy her Christmas. After the holidays, when everything settles down and we've figured out what the hell's going on, we can break it to her. She'd be better prepared to handle it then. Maddox will be back with his wife, Katya. Maybe they'll have a baby or something to keep Mom from worrying about me."

"Are they expecting?"

Dante laughed. "I wouldn't be surprised. And in the meantime, Tuck works for the FBI. He's going to put feelers out on the crash, the trailer demolition that almost included us and the explosives that took care of my Jeep."

Emma's lips quirked upward. "Must be handy having a brother in the FBI."

"Even handier to have two," Dante corrected. "Pierce is also in the FBI."

"Two FBI agents and a CBP agent. Don't you have one more brother? Is he in the FBI, as well?"

"No, he's the only one who stayed to be a full-time rancher."

Emma glanced around. "Then where is he?"

"He married Katya Ivanov, a princess from Trejikistan." He raised his hand. "It's a long story, which I'm sure they'd love to tell you all about over the holiday. They're visiting her brother in her home country and should be back soon."

"You have a very interesting family. How do you keep up with them?"

"Through Mom." Dante smiled. "She's the glue that holds us all together."

Having met Amelia Thunder Horse, she could see how. The woman was open, loving and cared deeply about her boys and wanted them to be happy. And she seemed to include their wives in her circle of love.

An ache built in the center of her chest and her eyes stung. To change the subject before she actually started crying, she swallowed hard and asked, "How much snow did we get?"

"It wasn't as bad as the weatherman predicted. We only got about a foot. We should be able to make it to town and collect the foreman and whatever supplies we might need."

"I think your mother's pantry and freezer are stocked for the apocalypse."

He laughed out loud. "Just wait. You haven't seen how much the Thunder Horse men can eat."

"If they're all as big as you, I can imagine."

Dante helped her clean the kitchen, proving his mother had taught him well. If he bumped into her more than he should have and reached over her, pinning her against the counter, it was only to get to the cabinet above.

Emma didn't read anything more into it than she dared. Dante Thunder Horse was a very handsome helicopter pilot, and he could do a lot better than dating a mousey college professor like Emma Jennings.

By the time they'd finished the dishes, she was flushed and her body oversensitized to his every touch.

"I'll be ready to go as soon as I brush my teeth." Emma hurried away to lock herself in the bathroom. The woman staring back at her in the mirror was a stranger. Her cheeks were full of color and her brown eyes sparkled. Even her dark brown hair was shinier. What had gotten into her? This was all make-believe and would end when the holiday was over.

The devil on her shoulder prodded her. So what did it hurt to live the dream for a few short days?

"A lot. It could hurt a lot," she whispered to the woman in the mirror.

Herself.

And Dante's mother when they finally told her the truth. But she'd support Dante in any decision he made, as any good mother would. She'd see that Emma wasn't the right woman for Dante and accept that it was a mistake.

The warmth of the woman's arms around her still resonated with Emma, and she missed her mother all over again.

She asked herself again, what would it hurt to pretend she was a part of this family, if only for the holiday? It would help Amelia get through it without more undue stress, Emma would have Dante and his family around her for protection and she wouldn't spend Christmas alone.

She ran a toothbrush over her teeth and made a solemn vow to herself not to lose her heart to a man that was still in love with a dead woman.

Splashing her face with water and then drying it on a towel, Emma squared her shoulders, hurried out of the bathroom and slammed against a solid wall of muscle.

Dante's arms came up around her to steady her on her feet. "Are you okay?"

Her breath lodged in her throat, her body tingling everywhere he touched it from her thighs to her breasts. "Yes." Emma's fingers curled into the fabric stretched across his chest. "Yes, I'm fine." Her pulse thumping hard in her veins, she straightened and stepped back.

"I was just about to knock and see if you were going to be ready anytime soon."

"I'm ready. All I have to do is grab my coat." *And pull myself together.*

"Wear your snow pants. It's extremely cold and windy out there."

"Okay." She hurried to the living room, jammed her legs into her snow pants and dragged them up to her waist, zipping and snapping them in place. Her boots went on next and finally her jacket. So much for being sexy in the morning with Dante. Dressed up like the Michelin Man, she looked like any other guy gearing up for the North Dakota weather. Puffy and shapeless.

"I'm ready." She crossed to stand in front of him, feeling lumpy and ugly.

A smile slid across Dante's face and he cupped her chin. "Anyone ever tell you that you're cute when you're all bundled up like the kid in *A Christmas Story?*"

She stared up at him, not sure if he was serious or just pulling her leg, surprised by the gleam in his eye and even more surprised when he bent to kiss her and whispered, "I missed you last night."

Before she had time to digest his comment, he turned and walked out the door into the cold, biting wind, stopping long enough to hold the door for her.

She walked through, still wondering why he'd kissed her and what he'd meant by his words.

THE DRIVE INTO Medora took twice as long as usual with the fresh snow and the unfamiliar vehicle. Dante didn't know the full extent of the little SUV's limits and wasn't willing to test them any more than he had to. He needed to get to town, pick up the foreman and do some asking around about what was going on in the area.

Maybe someone had information that would shed light on the happenings out at the Thunder Horse Ranch. He might also find out if the accidents were limited to the Thunder Horse family or if others in the area were having similar issues.

In Medora, Dante stopped at the diner, figuring Sean would probably hang out there with nowhere else to go until the truck was running.

He parked the vehicle on the main road running through town and helped Emma down. They entered the diner together. As he suspected, Sean was seated at one of the tables with a cup of coffee, a plate with a half-eaten biscuit and one of the biggest gossips in town sitting across from him. The local feed-store owner, Hank Barkley, knew as much, if not more, about everybody's business than Florence Metzger, the owner of the diner.

Sean stood when he spotted Dante and held out his hand. "Good to see you in one piece. I heard Pierce is feeling better."

Dante almost laughed out loud at the news.

Hank rose to his feet and shook Dante's hand. "Heard he was hollering for breakfast. He had us all worried." The man's inquisitive gaze fell on Emma and he asked, "Who do you have with you?"

"Emma Jennings." He introduced the men to her and asked, "Got room for two more?"

"Sure," Hank said. "We were just killin' time."

"Yeah, looks like we have until spring." Sean glanced out the window. "I don't think this batch of snow is going to melt until April."

Emma slipped out of her jacket and took one of the seats at the table. Dante sat in the chair beside her, his leg touching hers. Even through the thick snow pants and his insulated coveralls, he got a jolt. Something about Emma made his blood hum and his libido kick into overdrive. It had been a long night alone in his bed. Between getting up to check on her and lying in his bed awake but dreaming about making love to her, he'd slept little. A twinge of guilt accompanied these feelings. Memories of Sam were fading, which caused him more pain.

"Everything holding up out at the ranch?" Sean's words broke into his thoughts.

Dante nodded. "I took care of the animals before I left for town."

Sean and Hank sat across the table from Dante and Emma, each lifting his cup of coffee.

"Mack said he'd have to order a water pump for the truck and it would take a day or two for it to get in," Sean said.

"Then it's a good thing I came to get you." Dante glanced up at Florence when she stopped at the booth.

"Dante Thunder Horse, if you aren't a sight for sore eyes." The diner owner hugged him and looked over at Emma with open curiosity. "Is this the little filly you're engaged to?"

Emma's eyes widened.

Dante pressed a hand to her leg, his lips twitching. "Who'd you hear that from?"

Florence propped a fist on her ample hip. "I have a cousin working at the hospital in Bismarck."

Sean smiled. "I got the news from Hank."

Hank's chest puffed out, proudly. "Heard from Deputy Small, who got it from Sheriff Yost."

"I suppose the whole town knows by now?" Dante sat back and glanced at Emma.

Her face was pale and she gnawed on her bottom lip.

She hated lying to people and the more folks who knew, the more she'd probably consider she was lying to.

He draped an arm over her shoulders and leaned over to kiss her cheek. "The answer to Florence's question is *yes*. This is Emma Jennings from Grand Forks. My fiancée."

Sean, Hank and Florence all congratulated them at once, shaking Dante's hand and coming around the table to hug Emma, before resuming their original positions.

"That's just wonderful." Florence clapped her hands, her eyes shining. "Young love is so beautiful. But seriously, let me see the ring. You know it's all about the ring. It tells a lot about the man giving it."

Emma's face blanched even more, and then turned a bright red.

Dante hadn't even thought about a ring until that moment and he could see how uncomfortable Emma was with all the attention the lie had brought. "Shh, Florence, you'll spoil the surprise." He gave her a conspiratorial wink.

Florence frowned at first and then slapped a hand over her mouth. "Oh, yeah. Christmas is right around the corner."

Disaster averted, Dante took Emma's hand and held it in his like a newly engaged man would. Her fingers were stiff and cold. "But enough about us." Dante leaned his other elbow on the table. "What's going on around here?"

Hank and Florence were more than willing to fill him in on all the happenings of the small community. Frank and Eliza Miller had another baby. That would make five. Jess Blount and Emily Sanders got married a couple of months ago and were already expecting. Old Vena Bradley passed in her sleep last week, and her daughters aren't talking to each other because they can't agree on who gets what of the deceased's Depression-era glass collection.

Dante listened, bearing with the litany of social gossip, recognizing most of the names.

A customer at another table waved at Florence.

"I gotta get back to work. Yell if you need anything." She hurried off to pour coffee and deliver orders for the customers.

Turning to Hank, Dante asked, "How are things in town? Any new businesses or old ones that closed? Any new people you've seen around?"

"The Taylors finally sold their hardware store to a couple from Fargo. The old sawmill closed just before Halloween, and that abandoned hotel building sold to an investor from Minneapolis, and he's been renovating it." Hank paused to breathe, then launched into more. "I think it's because of the oil speculators who've been here off and on for the past six months, trying to buy up land."

"Same oil speculators that were here last summer?" Dante asked.

"Yes, and some new ones," Hank said.

Sean's brows furrowed. "Your mother didn't tell you about them? They've been out to the ranch several times, one in particular, that Langley fellow. He's bad about showing up whenever he likes. No matter how many times she tells him she's not selling the ranch or mineral rights, he keeps coming back. It's part of the reason she's having the security cameras and an alarm system installed."

Dante leaned forward. "What about the accidents out at the ranch? Do you think the speculators are responsible? Could they be trying to scare my mother into selling?"

Sean crossed his arms. "It would take a lot more than that to scare your mother into selling. She's feisty and doesn't let much slow her down." He chuckled. "That woman has more spunk than most eighteen-year-olds."

"But the ranch is a big responsibility for a lone woman, with Maddox gone a great deal of time," Dante observed.

Sean bristled. "I'm out there as much as I can be. I guess I could insist on her coming to town with me when I go for feed and supplies. I wouldn't mind the company. And those accidents could be just that—accidents. The barn door could have been working its way loose. You know how bad the winds are out here. And the hay was green when we put it in the barn. It could have caught fire due to spontaneous combustion."

Dante knew green hay could catch fire. That's why they usually were careful to let it dry before baling. He understood the hay had to be baled sooner because, after they'd cut the hay, a rainstorm had been predicted and they had to get it baled before the rain. "But to have two accidents like that in one week…" Dante shook his head.

The foreman shrugged. "The sheriff didn't find any evidence of tampering that could account for the door or the hay. We were just lucky no one was hurt."

"No footprints or fingerprints?"

"It rained late the night before the door fell. If someone loosened the hinges, it was before the rain. All footprints would have been washed away."

"What about the fire? Anyone out at the ranch that shouldn't have been?"

Sean's lips tightened. "Your mother was out on a date, and I was on my way back from the feed store when it started."

"Whoa, whoa, whoa." Dante held up his hand. "My mother was out on a date?"

Sean didn't respond.

But Hank did. "Sheriff Yost has been courtin' your mother. I've heard him say on more than one occasion that he wants to marry her. He told Florence he's been in love with Amelia since before she married your father, back when she sang in the *Medora Musical* in the summer."

"I didn't think she was that serious about the man."

"He's persistent," Hank said. "I'll give him that."

Sean scowled. "I don't know what she sees in him. She deserves better than that."

Dante studied the foreman. Something in his tone made him sound almost jealous.

Emma, who had been sitting quietly during the entire conversation, sat forward. "Are the oil speculators still in town?"

"Yeah. Some of them have rooms in the part of the hotel that's been newly renovated."

"What do you know about the security system Mom's having installed?" Dante asked.

"All I know is that Ryan, Sheriff Yost's son, started putting it in a couple of weeks ago, but he's waiting for some cameras that were back-ordered."

"I didn't know Ryan was back in this area. Didn't his mother take him to live on the Rosebud Reservation way back when she divorced Yost?"

Hank rubbed his hands together like a man staring at a particularly tasty meal. "I spoke with Ryan myself. He left the rez when he was eighteen, spent four years enlisted in the army, deployed to Afghanistan, got out and went to work as a security guard contracted to construction teams in Afghanistan for a couple of years. When he came back to North Dakota, he went to work for a man who installed security systems. About a year ago, his boss retired. Ryan took over this region for the security company. His territory is pretty much everything from Bismarck west. I think he's even got Minot."

"Is he based out of Medora?"

"For now. But he's on the road a lot. He even bought an old plane he uses to get back and forth faster. Got his pilot license so he can fly it himself."

"That boy seems to be doing something with his life," Sean said. "Not all of the boys from the rez are equally successful."

Dante knew that. His great-grandfather had moved off the reservation when he was old enough to leave. Though his heart remained with the Lakota people, he knew he had to get away to make a life for himself and his family.

"The boy doesn't look much like Sheriff Yost. Got more of his mother in him. Some of us wondered if he really was Yost's son. When his wife left him to return to the reservation, she didn't want anything to do with Yost, and Ryan never visited his father."

"Where is Ryan now?"

"I heard he had a job in Bismarck," Hank said. "Should be back later today. He's staying at the hotel they're converting. I think that's where the oil speculator is staying, as well."

Dante sat back, digesting all the information he'd been given. "Anything else going on around here that should raise some red flags?"

Sean grinned. "We'd like to hear more about what happened to you. We saw pictures of the crashed helicopter. You know it's only a matter of time before your mother finds out about it."

"Hopefully, by being here, she won't get upset. She'll see that I'm all right and let it go."

Sean grinned. "Don't bet on it. Amelia will be calling your boss to tell him you can't fly anymore."

Dante could imagine his mother doing that. Almost. She had never been happy about the danger her sons faced in their chosen career fields, but she respected their decisions and was as proud as any mother over her sons' accomplishments.

Pushing back his chair, Dante stood and held out a hand to Emma. "I have a few errands to run before I head back."

"Anything I can do for you?" Sean rose to his feet, as well.

"If you need feed, you might want to load some in the back of the SUV I rented. Emma and I will be back shortly and we can get back to the ranch."

"We could use more feed for the horses."

Dante tossed the keys to the foreman and helped Emma into her jacket. "Good to see you, Hank."

Florence passed by and he stopped her to give her a hug. "Good to see you, too, Florence. You're as beautiful as ever."

"Oh, now, Dante, you know how to make an old woman swoon." Her cheeks were flushed and she hugged him back.

Grabbing Emma's gloved hand, he made his way through the tables to the door.

Before Dante stepped out of the diner, his cell phone rang. The caller ID screen had Mom in bright letters. He answered, "Hi, Mom. How's Pierce?"

"The doctor's already discharged him. Can you believe it? I tried to get him to keep him for another day, but he said he was too disruptive to the hospital staff and that he'd be better off recuperating at home. We're already on the interstate and should be home in less than three hours, if the Great Spirit is willing and the roads stay clear."

"Who's driving?" he asked, knowing Pierce would hate letting someone else do the driving.

"Roxanne." His mother chuckled. "Pierce wanted to, but she told him to be quiet and lie down."

"What about Tuck?"

"He's headed home as well, but later this afternoon. He had some things he wanted to check on at his office. Then he, Julia and Lily will be on their way home for the holidays."

"What are you coming in?"

"We rented a four-wheel-drive vehicle for two weeks, or until the insurance company can make heads or tails out of what happened to Pierce's truck."

"Did you test the brakes?"

His mother snorted. "Tuck got under the hood, then under the car itself to check the brakes. He reported that everything looked serviceable. No leaking fluid or broken lines."

"Good. I'd like to have all of my family home for Christmas."

"Yes, and won't it be wonderful with everyone there. And now that you have Emma, our little family is complete and growing."

Dante's teeth ground together, but he held his tongue. Why ruin his mother's Christmas? She seemed thrilled that he'd found a woman to share his life.

His gaze shot to Emma walking beside him, her collar pulled up, her long brown curls whipping around her face. He was certain she didn't have a clue how beautiful she was.

She turned her head, catching him staring at her and she stumbled on the sidewalk. "What?" she asked.

"Nothing," he said. "I was just thinking how glad I am you decided to come with me. I hope you enjoy my family as much as they're sure to enjoy you."

Emma blinked up at him, long strands of rich chocolate hair dancing around her face. "You think they will?"

"Positive." He took her gloved hand in his and pulled her into the curve of his arm.

They walked the rest of the way to the little hotel which exterior looked brand-new. Once they entered the lobby area, Emma realized it still had a lot of work to go on the interior.

"May I help you?" a bored young woman asked.

"Can you tell me if Ryan Yost is in his room?"

"No." The woman smacked her gum, gave Dante a sweeping glance and smiled up at him. "I have empty rooms. Need one?"

Dante gave her his most charming smile. "Maybe."

Chapter Ten

The young lady's face flushed with pleasure and she batted her eyes.

Emma's own knees weakened when Dante turned up the wattage on his smile. Normally dark and intense, when he smiled it changed his entire appearance.

In his photo with Samantha, he'd smiled like this. Emma found herself wishing she could bring back the happiness he'd felt before he'd lost the love of his life. What would it be like to be loved so completely by a man like Dante?

Dante leaned over the counter toward the blushing girl. "Nicole? Is that your name?"

She nodded. "Yes."

"Such a pretty name for a pretty girl."

Nicole pressed one hand to her chest and brushed her long blond hair back behind her ear. "Thank you."

"I'm—"

Nicole raised her hand. "Don't tell me. You're a Thunder Horse. I can tell by your features. You look a lot like Maddox."

Dante inclined his head. "That's right, Maddox is my brother. I'm Dante." He turned toward Emma. "And this is Emma. We're Ryan's friends," Dante said, twisting the pen on the counter between his long, dark fingers.

"It's been a long time since we've seen him and we just wanted to say hello."

"Oh, is that all?" Her lips spread in a smile and she played with the ends of her hair. "He's been living here since they got room 207 finished. But he's not there right now. When he left this morning, he said he wouldn't be back until around noon."

"That's all we needed to know." Dante straightened and winked at the girl. "If you have a pen and a little piece of paper, I could leave a note on his door to contact us when he gets back in."

Nicole immediately dug beneath the counter and surfaced a pad of sticky notes and an extra pen, scribbling something on the top note. "Will this do?" She slid the pad and pen across the counter.

She'd written her phone number on the top page and the words *call me* beneath.

"Perfectly." Dante winked again, gathered the items and looked around.

"The stairs are behind the potted plant." Nicole pointed to a fake ficus tree in the corner of the lobby. "First floor up, second door on the right."

"Thank you." He turned to Emma. "Do you mind waiting here, sweetheart? I'll only be a minute."

Her heart skipped a couple of beats at the endearment before she remembered it was all part of the ruse. "I'll wait here." Emma darted a glance at the blonde.

Nicole watched Dante disappear around the corner before she turned her attention back to Emma. The young lady's brows rose and her lip curled in a little sneer. "Dante's from here. I'd recognize the Thunder Horse name and those beautiful cheekbones anywhere." Her gaze slid over Emma. "But you must be new around here."

Emma nodded. "I live in Grand Forks. I'm…" She didn't know whether or not to announce that she was Dante's fiancée. The lie didn't come easily to her lips. "I'm here visiting the Thunder Horse family."

Her brows furrowing, Nicole tilted her head. "Is Dante the Thunder Horse brother that just got engaged?" Her eyes narrowed as she surveyed Emma anew. "Are you the fiancée?"

Damn, word spread like wildfire in the small town. "Y-yes," Emma acknowledged. Then she straightened her shoulders and spoke with more conviction. "It was so sudden. He surprised me yesterday with his proposal. I'm still getting used to the idea." Forcing a smile to her lips, she pretended to be the giddy bride. Okay, so he hadn't proposed, but had gone directly to announcing their engagement. But she had been surprised. "I was so shocked, I barely knew what to say."

Nicole snorted. "Obviously you said yes." Her gaze shifted to Emma's hand. "What? No ring? What a shame."

Emma's cheeks heated and she stuffed her hand in her pocket. "Not yet." She leaned forward, her voice dropping to a whisper as she used Florence's supposition. "Could be what he's planning for Christmas." There, it wasn't a complete lie. By the time the holidays were over, the engagement would be broken.

But for now, she could pretend, and Nicole could back off her flirting with Emma's pretend fiancé.

Two workmen entered the lobby carrying a heavy roll of carpet.

Nicole left her position and hurried down the hallway to open a door for them.

Two more men entered the lobby, both wearing suits

and expensive-looking trench coats. When they spotted Emma, the first man smiled.

"Well, what have we here?" The man stuck out his hand. "I'm Monty Langley, my partner here is Theron Price. And you are?"

Emma ignored the outstretched hand still encased in black leather gloves. "I'm Emma."

"Emma, Emma, Emma." The man leaned on the counter, his gaze traveling from the tip of her head to the snow boots on her feet. Glad she wore several layers of clothes, she raised her brows.

"Are you checking in to the hotel?" Monty asked.

"No."

"No? Well, would you care to have a drink with me later? I'm sure we can find a bar around here somewhere."

"No, thank you." She hoped he'd get the hint.

"Well darn, and here I thought things were looking up in this godforsaken little hellhole."

"I guess you were wrong." She smiled and turned away, watching his movements through her peripheral vision.

The man's eyes narrowed and he glanced at his partner. "Come on, Theron. I have a bottle of whiskey in my room." As he walked down the first floor corridor, he shot back over his shoulder. "And they say the people are friendly in North Dakota."

"To friendly people, not jackasses," Emma muttered.

"I heard that," Langley said.

Once the two men disappeared into a room down the hall, Emma took the opportunity to escape up the stairs to room 207.

Dante wasn't anywhere in sight, and the door to room 207 was slightly ajar.

She pushed through and entered. "Dante?" she whispered. The room was dark, the drapes pulled over the window. Clothes were strewn across the floor and bed, and the trash can was overflowing with empty food containers. She couldn't make out Dante's form in the shadowy interior.

A hand clamped over her mouth from behind and she was pulled back against a hard chest.

Emma's pulse leaped and she drew her arm forward to slam into her attacker's gut. Before she could, warm breath caressed her ear.

"Shh," Dante whispered, his lips brushing the skin beneath her earlobe. He dropped his hand to her shoulder and squeezed. "I'm almost done here."

"What are you doing?" she whispered.

"Looking around."

Was he crazy? "Isn't that breaking and entering?"

"Only if you get caught." Dante shrugged. "Besides, the door wasn't locked."

"Still, Nicole could come up and find you. Or worse, what if Ryan Yost were to walk in?"

"He hasn't, has he?"

"Yet. Langley and Price, the two oil speculators, showed up downstairs."

"Really? Maybe we should talk to them."

"I have no desire to. Langley hit on me."

Dante tipped her chin. "The man has good taste."

"We should leave now."

"And we will." He checked out the door, then dragged her out behind him. He closed the door and attached a sticky note to the outside.

Dante barely gave her time to read the note before he was tugging her down the hallway and the staircase.

Langley and Price hadn't come out of their room and

Nicole was still down the hallway with the workmen when Dante and Emma headed for the exit.

A dark-skinned man with a military haircut and piercing dark eyes pushed through the door before they could escape. His eyes narrowed for such a brief moment Emma almost didn't notice.

He stopped in front of them, blocking their exit. "You're one of the Thunder Horse brothers, right?" He held out his hand. "Ryan Yost."

Emma's heart dropped into her belly. It had been this man's room they'd been in. Had he arrived a minute earlier, he'd have caught them.

Dante gripped the man's hand and gave him a cool, calm smile. How could he act so nonchalant when Emma had to clench her hands into fists to keep them from shaking?

"Last time I saw you, you were a skinny little kid in the fifth grade," Dante said.

Ryan nodded, his lips curling into a smirk. "Yeah, that would have been right before my mother divorced the sheriff and we moved to the rez. Are you back in Medora for good?"

Dante shook his head. "No, I'm only here to visit family."

"Of course." Ryan glanced around. "Were you looking for me?"

"As a matter of fact, I was. My mother wanted to know when you might be back out to finish installing her security system."

"Right. I've been waiting for the cameras I ordered to come in. I expected them today, but apparently they were delayed. I should be out there tomorrow to install them."

"That's great. I'll let her know."

"I was surprised she wanted a system installed," Ryan noted. "Most folks around here leave their doors unlocked."

"Times have changed," Dante said.

"Yes, they have. It's been good for my business, anyway."

"I suppose so." Dante glanced toward the exit. "I better let you get back to what you were doing. We'll see you at the ranch tomorrow."

Ryan stepped aside, allowing them to pass. "You can count on it."

Back outside in the cold, Emma pulled her collar up around her neck. "What the hell was that all about?"

Dante's lips firmed. "Someone's trying to hurt the Thunder Horse family. I want to know who."

"You think Ryan Yost is the man behind it?"

"I don't know at this point. That's why I wanted to talk to him. Since he wasn't around and the door was unlocked, I thought I'd check out his living quarters and get a feel for the guy."

"I thought you knew him."

"He's a year younger than me. I knew him vaguely when we were in grade school, but, like he said, his mother divorced Sheriff Yost and took him to the reservation before he left the fifth grade. I haven't seen him since."

Dante grabbed her hand and headed back toward the SUV parked in front of the diner.

Sean was waiting inside and stepped out when Dante approached. "Ready?"

"Yup." Holding up his hand, Dante said, "I'll drive."

Sean tossed the keys and Dante caught them, hit the unlock button on the fob, then helped Emma into the passenger seat before going around to the driver's side. Sean slid into the backseat.

On the drive back to the ranch, Sean filled Dante in on other information about the happenings at the ranch.

"The wild horses have moved into the canyon. I spotted a mare with a limp. I think it was the one your brother calls Sweet Jessie. I'd like to get out there and check on her sometime today if possible and bring her back if she needs doctoring."

"She had a foal last spring, didn't she?"

"Yes. He's doing good on his own, but I'm worried about her."

"Perhaps I can help out." He turned to Emma. "Have you ever ridden a horse?"

Emma shook her head. "Sorry." Life on a ranch was so far out of her league. "Isn't it kind of cold to be out riding?"

Dante's lips twisted into a wry smile. "North Dakota ranchers don't get any breaks. The animals always come first."

"You're right." Nevertheless, a chill slithered down Emma's spine. "I'd like to go. Is it hard to ride a horse if you've never done it?"

Sean laughed from the backseat and Dante smiled. "The dead of winter might not be the best time to learn. If you want to go out with us, I could take a snowmobile. Sean will need to ride a horse in order to lead Sweet Jessie back if she needs tending."

Feeling inadequate, Emma felt the heat rise in her cheeks. "I don't want to slow you down."

"Not at all. If anything, we can get out to Sweet Jessie sooner than Sean and assess the situation. By the time Sean gets there, we'll have her roped and ready for him to lead her back, if need be."

Mollified, Emma nodded. "Okay. I would like very much to go, as long as I'm not in the way."

By the time they reached the ranch, Emma was feeling more relaxed around Sean and Dante, listening to their plans for what needed done before the next big storm rolled in.

When they drove up the driveway to the ranch house, Dante said, "Oh, good. The family made it."

Three vehicles stood out front—a shiny new SUV, a big ranch truck with knobby tires and a white SUV with the markings of Billings County Sheriff written in bold letters on the side.

Once again, her nerves got the better of her and she took her time climbing out of the vehicle.

"Looks like the sheriff arrived with them." Sean headed for the house ahead of them.

"What's he doing here?" Dante muttered as he climbed out. He walked around the side of the SUV, his face tight, and hooked Emma's elbow, leaning close. "Don't worry. My family doesn't bite…much."

"I'm not worried about teeth marks. I just don't like leading them on."

"As far as they're concerned, we're engaged. I don't see any need to tell them different."

"But it's a lie."

Dante stopped and faced her, holding her gloved hands in his, smiling. "If it makes you feel any better, I'll tell them we decided to hold off on the engagement so we can spend more time getting to know each other."

Emma sighed. "I would feel a lot better. Thanks."

Dante pulled her arm through his and walked with her toward the house.

Sheriff Yost emerged from the house as they walked up the steps.

The older man stuck out his hand. "Dante, glad you could make it home."

"Sheriff." Dante shook the man's hand. "I'm glad to be home."

"I just stopped by to see that your mother made it home all right." The sheriff plunked his hat on his head. "Well, I better get back to work."

Dante stepped aside, allowing the sheriff to leave.

Emma could sense the animosity from Dante. He didn't like the sheriff and didn't want him dating his mother. She understood. He probably felt it was a betrayal to his dead father.

The sheriff climbed into his SUV and backed out of the yard, turning down the drive to the gate.

"I just don't trust that man."

"Why?"

"I don't know. Gut feel, instinct. Something." He shrugged. "Come on, let's face the gauntlet."

Before Dante could grasp the door handle, his brother Tuck threw it open. "Dante, you sly devil, get in here." Tuck embraced Dante. "I was still out of it yesterday when you made your announcement. I didn't congratulate you properly." He hugged Dante again. "Julia and I are so happy for you."

"About that—"

Julia hooked Emma's arm and drew her into the living room. "Tuck's mother was so happy, she was beside herself. I think it was the only thing that got her through the day and into the night. She'd been so worried about Pierce, I think she was on the verge of a nervous breakdown. And then you and Dante arrive with your wonderful news and it perked her right up."

Emma bit her bottom lip, wanting to say something but at a loss for what words to use.

"Speaking of Mom and Pierce, where are they? Emma and I had something to say." Dante glanced around the room.

Roxanne emerged from the hallway, her face tired but happy. "Mom was so excited to have her brood home, I had a hard time convincing her that we could feed ourselves and that she needed to rest. She tucked Pierce into his bed and crawled into her own, too tired to argue."

"You should have been there last night," Julia gushed. "She had a dozen questions about your engagement. All the possibilities kept her mind busy so that she didn't have time to dwell on Pierce. And when Pierce woke up and found out you'd gotten yourself engaged, he almost left the hospital right then and there to come shoot you for not telling us all sooner."

Emma's heart had settled like a lump in the pit of her belly. With Amelia and Pierce exhausted from their ordeal and beyond their limits, Emma couldn't break it to them that her and Dante's engagement was a sham.

"About the engagement. It's not what you think…" Dante started again.

Julia, Tuck and Roxanne all turned toward him, smiling.

Emma took Dante's hand. "What Dante is trying to say is that it was all pretty sudden and we haven't even had time to get a ring."

"No ring?" Roxanne crossed her arms over her chest. "Isn't that how you ask a woman to marry you, by offering her an engagement ring?"

Dante glanced down at Emma, his gaze questioning.

"Tell them how you proposed, Dante." Emma smiled at him, giving him a subtle wink.

Julia clasped her hands together. "This is all so romantic."

Dante's eyes widened and then narrowed slightly. He faced his brother and two sisters-in-law. "Well, we haven't known each other very long, but I knew as soon as I met her that Emma was someone special."

Emma almost snorted. He'd had coffee with her and then run like a scalded cat, never to call her later. Feeling a little guilty, but somewhat vindicated, she waited with her brows raised to see what story he'd spin about asking her to marry him.

"Go on," Tuck said, smirking. "Tell us all how it's done."

"There really wasn't much to it. One minute we were just friends and the next minute I asked her to marry me."

"Seriously?" Roxanne crossed her arms. "Did you at least get down on one knee?"

Dante tugged at the collar of his shirt. "No. I just—"

"Blurted it out," Emma finished and took his hand. "It was so spontaneous and unrehearsed." Her pulse beating hard, she raised his hand to her cheek. "I can't imagine anything more romantic." And she couldn't, because she could never imagine anyone, especially Dante Thunder Horse, asking her to marry him. And he never would, for real.

"True love." Julia sighed. "Straight from the heart."

"That's right." Dante bent and kissed Emma's cheek.

"Come on, Dante, give her a real kiss," Tuck urged.

"Yeah, Dante, show us what got her to say yes."

Dante's jaw tightened.

Emma's cheeks burned. "Really, we're not that demonstrative in public," she insisted.

"The hell we aren't." Dante swept her into his arms and kissed her long and hard.

At first she was stiff and nonresponsive, too shocked by his move to think. But as his lips softened and moved over hers, she melted against his body. He traced the seam of her lips until she opened her mouth and his tongue speared through, caressing the length of hers.

Emma rose up on her toes, lacing her fingers around his neck. The world fell away and it was only him and her, alone.

"Ahem." Tuck cleared his throat. "You've made your point."

"What a kiss." Julia wrapped her arms around Tuck's waist and leaned into him.

Dante broke the kiss and leaned his forehead against Emma's for a moment. "Are you okay?" he asked.

She nodded, her tongue still tingling from the sweet torture of his.

Finally, Dante moved away and clapped his hands together. "Now, if you'll excuse us, Emma, Sean and I were headed out to check on Sweet Jessie."

"I'm coming," Tuck said.

"You were just in a car wreck," Dante said. "Give yourself at least another day to recuperate."

Tuck's brows rose. "I would think you'd need the recuperation time more than me."

"That's right," Julia said, lowering her voice to a whisper. "We saw the news clip on your helicopter crash."

Roxanne tilted her chin, staring closely at Dante. "We also saw an article in the morning paper about an explosion in Grand Forks that put one man in the hospital. Were you part of that, as well?"

Emma's cheeks heated. If they knew about the crash and explosion, how long would it take for them to figure out that she and Dante weren't really engaged?

Roxanne's eyes widened. "You were there!" She clapped a hand over her mouth. "That was your Jeep, wasn't it? That's why you're driving a rental."

Dante raised a hand. "It was an accident and neither Emma nor I were hurt in it."

"But you could have been," Tuck reminded him.

"I'd prefer Mom didn't know about the crash or the explosion," Dante said. "She's had more than enough drama for a lifetime."

Julia pursed her lips. "It's only a matter of time before she finds out. Nothing much gets by Amelia and she's tougher than you think."

"Look—" Tuck stepped into the fray "—we've all agreed not to say anything to Mom. But if she asks, we won't deny it."

Dante inhaled and let it out. "Fair enough."

"Now, do you want me to help you with the horses?" Roxanne offered.

"I'd go," Julia said. "But I'm not much good wrangling horses, and Lily's down for her nap with your mother. I hate to leave her."

"No." Dante held up his hand. "The three of us can handle this." He nodded to Roxanne. "And I'm sure Pierce will be looking for you when he wakes."

"It's supposed to drop down to minus twenty tonight," Tuck said. "Don't stay out past four-thirty when the sun sets."

As he headed for the door, Emma's hand in his, Dante called over his shoulder, "If we're gone any longer, send out a search party."

"Will do."

Dante stopped in the kitchen to swipe a handful of baby carrots from the refrigerator and stuffed them into the pocket of his snow pants.

While Sean hurried ahead to the barn, Dante hung back in the mudroom, making certain Emma had the right winter-weather gear on to ride on the back of the snowmobile. "Standing out in that wind is bad enough, riding on the back of the snowmobile is even colder."

"I'm tougher than I look," she assured him. Emma appreciated the extra care he gave her ensuring she would be warm enough, arming her with a warm wool scarf and heavy-duty insulated gloves and an insulated helmet.

When they reached the barn, Dante went in. An engine revved and he emerged minutes later on a sleek red snowmobile. Scooting forward, he jerked his head, motioning for her to climb on the back.

Glad she didn't have to stay at the house and lie to people she barely knew, Emma climbed aboard and wrapped her arms around Dante's middle. She liked being with him, even out in the frigid cold. And when they were alone together, she could be herself. No lies. She wished they could keep going.

Chapter Eleven

Dante sped out of the yard as Sean led his horse out of the barn. Already past noon, clouds had accumulated in the western sky. The weatherman had predicted more snow that night. If nothing else, at least it would keep the saboteur from sneaking up on them and causing trouble. And if he did try something at night, he prayed the snow wouldn't hide his tracks.

Flying across the snow-covered prairie of the Badlands, he let go of the strain and pressure of the past couple of days. Out here, it was him, the sky and the incredible woman holding on to his waist. He could almost forget his life in the army, Sam and the other men of his unit.

He pushed aside the guilt of letting go. The cold reminded him of what was important—paying attention to the terrain and the time. If they were stranded out in the cold, especially near dusk, they might not be found until morning. Once the night got as cold as it would get, they wouldn't last until morning.

It took thirty minutes of steady riding to make it all the way out to the canyon. Without the added protection of foot and hand warmers, Emma's extremities would be getting pretty cold. He slowed the snowmobile and shifted her hands under his jacket, the cold gloves touching his bare skin made him jump. Unable to help her feet, he prayed the boots would keep her toes warm enough to ward off frostbite. He would have left her back at the house, but he wanted to keep a close eye on her. Not that he didn't trust his family, but they had their hands full and he figured she would have insisted on coming anyway.

When he finally made it to the edge of the canyon, he drove along the rim until he found the path leading down and stopped the snowmobile, shutting off the engine. "We walk from here."

Emma swung her leg over the back and swayed, holding on to the seat of the machine.

Dante got off and stood beside her. "How are your feet?"

"Cold. But not too bad now that we've stopped."

"I'll let you drive on the way back. There are hand and feet warmers for the driver."

"Now you tell me." She smiled. "No, really, I'm okay." She pulled off the helmet, laid it on the back of the snowmobile and secured her jacket's hood over her head. "What now?"

"We go down into the canyon and find the horses." He glanced down the path and back at her. "I should have warned you there would be hiking involved. If you're not up to it, you can stay here and wait for Sean."

"I told you, I'm tougher than I look. Lead the way."

He liked her spunky attitude and willingness to pitch in. For a college professor, she was a lot more apt and able than he'd originally given her credit. Still, it was a steep climb down into the canyon and even more difficult coming out on the snow and ice. If he saw that she was having any trouble, he'd turn back and get her out of the canyon.

They made it to the bottom with little trouble and the

sound of the snowmobile engine had alerted the wild ponies. They'd come to see if he had brought them treats.

Sweet Jessie, the tamest of the herd, led the way, favoring her right front leg with a decided limp, but no less determined to get to them ahead of the herd. She loved carrots and would follow him anywhere for the tasty treat. Especially in the dead of winter when food was scarce.

Her foal followed, his coat thick and fuzzy.

Emma's eyes widened. "They're so beautiful. Are they yours?"

"No, they're the wild ponies of the Badlands. They don't belong to anyone."

"Then why are you out here?"

"My family has always taken care of them, looking out for them and providing the Bureau of Land Management with an accurate annual count. When one is sick, we help if we can."

Dante pulled off his glove and fished in his pocket for the carrots. Already the cold wind bit at his fingers. When he had the carrots in hand, he gave half of them to Emma. "Hold these out in your hand."

"She won't bite me?"

"She might nibble a little, just keep your hand flat and she won't hurt you."

Emma held out her hand as he'd instructed, the carrots in the palm of her glove.

Dante slid his glove back on and kept his carrots out of sight.

Sweet Jessie trotted to within twenty feet of them and stopped.

"Why did she stop?" Emma whispered.

"She doesn't know you." Dante spoke softly to keep

from startling the other horses. "Give her time to learn you aren't a threat to her."

"She's so much bigger than I am. How could I be a threat?"

"You'd be surprised how threatening humans can be to the wild horses."

Sweet Jessie inched forward a little at a time, her neck stretching, her nostrils flaring, steam rising from her nose with each breath. When she was within three feet of Emma, she lifted her chin and nuzzled the carrots out of Emma's gloved hand.

Emma let out a soft gasp, a smile spreading across her face as she glanced up at Dante.

In that moment, the sun broke through the clouds and shone down on her face. Her dark hair framed her cheeks, the cool air making them rosy. But it was the flash of teeth and the excited gleam in her eyes that hit Dante like a punch to the gut.

Emma Jennings was a beautiful woman. So full of life, so innocent in many ways and strong and daring in others. This was the woman who'd ridden her snowmobile straight into danger to save him and then had given her virginity to him in the middle of a blizzard.

He reached for her, without realizing that was what he was doing.

Her smile slipped from her lips and her eyelids drifted halfway closed, her lips puckering slightly to receive his kiss.

In the frigid cold of the North Dakota Badlands, Dante Thunder Horse found himself on the slippery slope of possibly falling for a woman he'd only been around for a grand total of four days.

He pressed his lips to hers, taking them slowly at first. But as he deepened the kiss, his hunger grew and he crushed her to his body, frustrated by the amount of clothes standing between them.

Emma lurched, knocking into him and the moment was lost.

Sweet Jessie, impatient with their kissing, had sniffed out his other stash in the palm of his hand. The one fisted and holding Emma close.

The mare nudged him again, pushing Emma against Dante.

He laughed and set Emma to the side, offering the carrots up to the horse.

While Jessie's lips snuffled for the treat, Dante reached up and wrapped his hand around her frayed halter.

When the last of the carrots were gone, Sweet Jessie tossed her head, trying to loosen Dante's hold on her.

"You might want to step back," he told Emma.

She slipped from his arms and pressed a gloved hand to her swollen lips, her eyes bright and shimmering in the fleeting sunlight.

Dante held tight to Sweet Jessie, refusing to let loose.

After several attempts to shake him off, Jessie nuzzled his jacket, looking for more carrots.

Dante smoothed a hand over Jessie's nose and spoke softly. "Emma, could you hand me the lead rope?"

Emma scooped the rope from the ground and laid it across his open palm.

He snapped the lead on one of the metal rings in the halter. "Come on, Sweet Jessie. Let's see what's going on." He edged closer and pressed his shoulder to hers, then eased down to the leg she'd favored as she'd trotted up to them.

At first, she refused to let him lift the hoof. As he leaned harder against her, she shifted her weight to the other foot and he was able to raise the injured one.

As he'd suspected, the tender pad of her foot had been cut, and was infected and swollen with pus. She needed it drained and to have a poultice applied. And she needed to be kept in a clean, dry environment until the injury was well on its way to healing.

"Is it bad?" Emma asked.

"If we leave it alone, it might heal on its own."

Emma frowned. "And if it doesn't?"

"The infection could spread and she might die."

"Are we going to take her back to the barn?"

"That's what Sean will do when he gets here." Dante straightened and glanced up at the path. "You should go first. I'm going to lead Sweet Jessie out. I don't want you to be in danger if she spooks and tries to break away."

"Okay." Emma turned toward the path and started up the hill, climbing with quick, measured steps, pacing herself for the steep ascent out of the canyon. Every few steps she glanced over her shoulder to make sure Dante was still behind her.

Holding the halter in one hand and the lead in another, Dante led the horse up the narrow trail.

Every time rocks skittered down the slope, Emma's pulse leaped and she swung around, only to see the man and horse steadily climbing behind her.

Halfway up the hill, Emma was breathing hard, but confident she wouldn't have to stop before she made it to the top.

Head down, eyes forward, she took another step.

A loud blast cracked the frigid air and the earth beneath her feet shifted; gravel slid over the edge of the path and tumbled down the hill.

When she glanced up, the entire hillside seemed to be sliding downward toward her. "Landslide!" she cried out and turned back.

Sweet Jessie reared and nearly knocked Dante over the side of the trail. He let go of the lead and dropped to his knees.

The horse spun, lost her foot and slipped a hoof over the edge before she got her balance and raced back down the hill.

Higher up and closer to the source of the landslide, Emma knew she wouldn't get out of the way fast enough. When the wave of sliding rock and gravel hit, her feet were swept out from under her and she slid down the side of the steep slope, bumping and slamming against every rock, boulder and stump along the way. Pain ripped through her arms and head as she rode the wave of earth to the bottom of the steep precipice and slid thirty feet along the base of the canyon before the world stopped moving.

Gravel and small rocks continued to pelt her as she lay still, counting her fingers and toes and flexing her arms and legs. Everything seemed to be working okay, so she sat up.

"Emma!"

Emma shifted her head and glanced up.

Thankfully Dante had been farther to the north of the source of the landslide, the trail he'd been walking on had been spared. But if he didn't slow down in his race to the floor of the canyon, he'd end up causing a land-slide of his own.

"I'm okay," Emma called out, the sound barely making it past her lips. Had she not been so bundled in snow pants and thick clothing, she might have more cuts and broken bones.

She rolled to her side, starting to feel the bumps and bruises she'd acquired in her pell-mell slide down the canyon wall.

"Don't move," Dante yelled. "You could have a spinal cord injury."

Ignoring him, Emma pushed to her hands and knees and stood. Her ankle hurt and she'd be a mass of bruises, but she was alive.

Dante arrived at her side, his dark face pale, his eyes wild. "You shouldn't have moved." He pulled her into his arms and held her. "Thank the spirits, you're alive." He continued to crush her to his chest, his arms so tight around her she could barely breathe without pain knifing through her.

"Careful there, Dante, I think one of my ribs is broken."

"Is that all?" He laughed, pushed her to arm's length and smiled down at her, running his hands through her hair, brushing the dirt off her face. He cupped her cheeks in his palms and bent to touch her lips with his. "You scared me."

"I scared you?" She chuckled, wincing with the effort. "I was pretty scared myself." She glanced around. "Where's Sweet Jessie?"

"Probably halfway to Fargo." He hugged her again, more gently this time, and then frowned, his gaze shooting back to where the trail had been. "What I want to know is how that landslide started in the first place."

Dante scanned the rim of the canyon above, searching for movement. Nothing but a few pieces of loose gravel moved between him and the top. Based on the loud crack he'd heard before the ground shifted, someone had set off a small explosion that started the landslide that almost killed Emma.

His jaw tight, anger rippling through him, Dante slipped an arm around Emma's waist and draped hers over his shoulder. He moved her to a safe location in the shadow of a huge overhang of solid rock.

"I'm going up to get the snowmobile."

"I didn't think you could get it down the trail."

"Not that trail, and definitely not now. But there's a wider one farther along the top of the canyon. I didn't want to bring it down here and have the noise frighten the horses."

"But that's already happened with the noise and the falling rock."

"Will you be all right staying here for a few minutes by yourself?"

She nodded, a shiver shaking her frame.

Dante needed to get her back to the ranch. Even though she hadn't had any major breaks, with a fall as frightening as that and all the bruises she'd probably acquired, she could go into shock. He hated leaving her, but it would take longer for him to carry her out of the canyon than to climb out and come back for her on the snowmobile.

"Go. I'll be okay." She wrapped her arms around herself and pulled her hood close around her face and smiled.

Dante ran across the rocks, headed north to the trail he knew was farther along the steep sides of the canyon walls. Hidden by a huge boulder, it was hard to spot until he passed it.

Soon he was on his way up the wider trail, breathing hard and worried about leaving Emma in the canyon.

What seemed like an hour later, he emerged on the rim of the canyon and glanced around for the person responsible for causing the landslide.

Nothing stood out on the flat landscape except the snowmobile he'd arrived on. He hurried toward it, praying whoever had set off the landslide hadn't damaged the snowmobile or wired it for explosives.

Desperate to get back to Emma before she went into shock, he shifted to sling his leg over the top and stopped short. Something stuck out from beneath the hood of the engine compartment. It looked like a strip of black electrical tape. Careful not to apply undue pressure, he lifted the hood and stared down at what looked like a lump of clay with a mechanical device stuck in the middle. A wire led from the device to the vehicle's starter switch.

He'd seen C-4 explosives before, but not on a snowmobile. The way he saw it, he had two choices. He could walk away and leave the snowmobile out there and wait for Sean to arrive on horseback. That would mean putting Emma on the back of the horse to transport her to the ranch at a very slow pace while one of them stayed out in the cold until help could return. It would be dark soon and the temperature would drop rapidly.

Or he could take his chances, disarm the bomb and be on his way. He studied the mechanism and the wire leading to the starter. It looked like the electrical charge from the starter would be the catalyst to detonate the bomb. If he pulled the wire off the starter wire, it should disarm the bomb.

Then again, he wasn't a bomb expert and he could blow himself up if he wasn't careful.

Dante stared out across the land and there was no sign of Sean. He sent a prayer to *Wakantanka,* reached in, gripped the wire and pulled it loose. Blessed silence met him and he released the breath he'd been holding.

Carefully, so as not to bump the C-4 and the device, he lifted it off the engine and walked a hundred yards away from the snowmobile and set the explosives on the ground. When he returned to the snowmobile, he checked the ground for tracks.

Another snowmobile had been there, one with a

chipped track. There was also a dark spot on the snow. He touched it with his finger and lifted it to his nose. Oil. The machine had been leaking oil.

Too worried about Emma to look further, he hurried back to his vehicle and went over it one more time with a very critical eye. Confident he hadn't missed another cache of explosives, he climbed on, grit his teeth and hit the starter switch. The engine roared to life. Shifting into forward, he drove the vehicle along the rim of the canyon to the wider trail leading down to the bottom.

Emma was hunched over at the base of the overhang where he'd left her. Her cheeks were pale and her lips were turning blue. "Come on, sweetheart." He helped her onto the seat and climbed in front of her. "Can you hold on?"

"I'll do my b-best," she said, her teeth chattering so hard it shook her entire body.

Slowly, he climbed the trail out of the canyon, holding on to her arm with one hand, steering the snowmobile with the other. When they reached the top, he realized Sweet Jessie had followed.

Dante left Emma on the snowmobile and tied the lead rope to the back of the vehicle. Moving slowly enough the horse could keep up on her sore hoof, he limped toward the ranch, a little at a time.

Fifteen minutes into their long trek back, snow began to fall. Out of the snow and clouds, Sean appeared on horseback.

Dante gave him a brief rundown of what had happened, speaking quietly enough so that Emma couldn't overhear him. Then he passed Sweet Jessie's lead rope to Sean and climbed onboard the snowmobile.

Emma leaned into him, her arms not nearly as tight, her face frighteningly pale. Dante drove as fast as he could without losing Emma off the back and pulled up in front of the house.

Rather than beep the little horn and upset his mother or brother, Dante dismounted, gathered Emma in his arms and carried her into the house.

Tuck met him at the door. "I thought I heard the snowmobile." When he saw Dante was carrying Emma, he moved back. "What happened?"

"Trouble," Dante said. "I'll tell you all about it once I get her warm and dry. Is Mom awake?"

"Dante?" His mother appeared behind Tuck. "Oh, dear. What's happened to Emma? Did she fall off the back of the snowmobile?"

Dante's teeth ground together. "No, she slid into the canyon on a landslide. Someone call the sheriff."

Chapter Twelve

She must have passed out on the way back to the ranch house. Once inside, the warmth surrounded her and she swam to the surface, nestled in Dante's arms, a crowd of his family gathered around. Immediately embarrassed at being the center of attention, she struggled weakly against Dante's hold.

"I can stand on my own," she insisted. "Please, put me down."

"Not happening," Dante responded.

"Want to lay her on the couch?" his mother asked.

"No, she's been through too much, riding a landslide all the way to the floor of the canyon."

"Wow, and no broken bones?" Tuck shook his head. "She's tough. Emma, you'll fit right in around here."

"Thanks," she said, her heart warming along with her cheeks.

"Yeah, well, I can't tell if anything is broken until we get her out of these clothes," Dante said.

"Nothing's broken," Emma maintained. "Put me down. I can take care of myself."

Dante's mother clucked her tongue. "Now, Emma, sweetie, you're practically family and you've been hurt. Let us fuss."

"You've already had more than your share of injured

family. You don't need to worry about me. Pierce needs you more."

"Someone call my name?" Pierce Thunder Horse appeared in the hallway holding an ice bag to his forehead.

"Pierce, what are you doing out of bed?" Roxanne hurried toward him, grabbed his arm and tried to steer him back down the hallway.

"I'm just fine, except for this knot on my head." He removed the ice bag to display a goose egg–size lump on his forehead along with several other cuts and bruises and a black eye.

Emma felt like *he* looked and she almost laughed, but couldn't because her ribs hurt and her lip was split. "If you'll put me down, I'll crawl into a shower and bed."

"Dante, honey, carry her to the bathroom. I can help her out of that snowsuit and into a nice warm bath."

At that moment, a warm bath sounded like heaven. Emma almost cried.

"I'll take care of her," Dante said.

"I'll get her some hot cocoa, painkillers and warm a blanket." Amelia whirled away.

The remaining members of his family and extended family stepped aside to allow Dante down the hallway. Too exhausted to argue, Emma leaned her cheek on his chest and closed her eyes.

"I'm going to set you on your feet. Think you can stand?" Dante asked.

Emma opened her eyes to discover they were in a bathroom with marble counters and a big mirror. One look at her wild, tangled hair and she groaned. "I'm a mess."

A chuckle rose up his chest and shook against her body. "How are you supposed to look after falling off a cliff?"

She sighed, tilting her head toward the mirror. "Better than this."

"I happen to think you look great. Here, let me have your coat." He unzipped the insulated jacket and eased it off her arms. "Okay so far?"

She smiled. "So far so good." Reaching for the waistband of her snow pants she tried to unzip them, her fingers fumbling with the zipper.

"Let me." He took over, sliding the zipper down and then shoving the pants off her legs, leaving her standing in jeans with her thermal underwear beneath.

Emma closed her eyes again and laughed. "Nothing says sexy like nine layers of clothing and thermal underwear."

Dante removed the jeans, slipping them down over her long johns "I happen to find women in thermal underwear very sexy." As if to prove it, he skimmed a hand along the side of her legs from her calves all the way up the outside of her thighs as he rose from helping her out of her jeans. When he straightened, he rested his hands on her hips. "Ready to take off the rest?"

Exhaustion disappeared as a blast of adrenaline-powered lust ripped through her, making her pulse race and her blood burn through her body.

"Shower or bath?" he asked, his hand on the hem of her shirt.

The tub was barely big enough for one person to stretch out, but plenty big enough if they stood. "Shower."

She lifted her arms, grimacing at the twinge of pain in her ribs. Her shirt and undershirt slid up over her head and then was dropped to the floor.

Dante turned to switch the water on in the shower and adjusted the temperature. Then he helped her out of her thermal underwear. When she finally stood in nothing but her bra and panties, Dante's gaze swept over her from head to toe.

"Oh, baby, you really did get beat up."

It wasn't what she wanted to hear. His words only meant she looked like hell.

But he bent to kiss a bruise on her shoulder that was already turning a deep shade of purple. He shifted to kiss another bruise on her arm, and across to press a kiss to the swell of her right breast where a strawberry mark indicated yet another.

"They don't hurt," she assured him.

When he straightened and stared down at her, Emma's heart sank.

"Much as I'd love to kiss you all over, you need your rest."

"I'm okay, really." Afraid she might sound too needy, she tried to reach behind her to unhook her bra and winced.

Dante turned her around and flipped the hooks open.

Her breasts spilled free and she let the straps slide down her arms. "Join me," she whispered.

His hand slid up her arms and cupped her cheeks. "Not tonight. I couldn't bear it if I hurt you more. I really think we should take you to Bismarck to the hospital and have them look you over."

Emma shook her head. "I'm only bruised."

He stared hard at her, his eyes narrowed. Finally he sighed. "You're very tempting, do you know that?"

She shook her head.

"But you've been through hell." He backed toward the door, his lips firming into a straight line. "Get in there and get your shower while I find something for you to wear."

Emma slid out of her underwear in front of him. Still,

he didn't take her up on the invitation. Instead, he turned and walked out, closing the door firmly behind him.

Disgruntled and too tired to do anything about it, Emma stepped behind the shower curtain, washed and rinsed her hair and ran a soapy washcloth over her entire body until she had all the grit washed away.

When she stepped out of the shower to dry off, a flannel pajama top lay on the counter. The top was big enough to fit several of her in it. She lifted it to her nose and sniffed. It smelled like Dante. Quickly slipping into it, she discovered why there were no pants to go with it. The shirt hung down past her buttocks and halfway down her thighs. A pair of her panties and her brush lay beside the shirt. Soon, she had brushed the tangles out of her hair and was dressed enough to leave the bathroom and step out into the hallway.

Several doors lined the wall. Dressed in nothing more than a big shirt, she didn't feel up to facing the family, but she didn't know where else to go but the living room where she'd slept the night before.

"Oh, good, you're out." Amelia appeared at the end of the hallway. She hurried to Emma's side and wrapped an arm around her waist. "Come on, let's get you into bed. I'm sure you're past exhausted."

Hustled to the second door on the right, Emma went with the woman, thankful she didn't have to face the rest of the family. All she wanted was a big painkiller and a really soft bed.

And if she had all her wishes…Dante lying beside her, holding her.

Amelia flung open the door and ushered her into the room. The bed was a big four-poster with a goose down comforter and a handmade quilt folded at the foot of the bed. The blankets were pulled back and crisp white sheets beckoned to her.

"Climb in, sweetie. There's a glass of water on the nightstand and a couple of pain pills to ease your discomfort."

"Thank you." Emma crawled into the bed and lay back on the pillows.

Amelia tucked the blanket around her and smoothed her damp hair back from her face. "You poor thing. What a way to start your visit on the ranch. Don't be too put off. It's not always so crazy around here. We go for years without any excitement."

Emma touched the woman's hand, a wave of longing washing over her. She missed having a mother and being taken care of. If she wasn't careful, it would be too easy to get used to it. "I'm sure it's lovely."

"There now, get some rest."

"Mrs. Thunder Horse?"

"Please, call me Amelia. All my daughters-in-law call me that."

A guilty twinge lodged in her throat. Emma swallowed hard. "Where's Dante?"

"Sean got back with Sweet Jessie. He and Tuck are helping doctor her hoof."

"Oh, good."

"He'll be in as soon as they have her settled." Amelia turned out the overhead light, leaving the lamp lit on the nightstand. "If you need anything, just yell."

"Thank you, Mrs. Thunder Horse."

She smiled. "Amelia. Please, call me Amelia. 'Mrs. Thunder Horse' is a mouthful."

"Amelia," Emma complied, liking the woman's open friendliness.

When Dante's mother left her alone, she took the pain

pills and washed them down with water, then lay back, wishing she felt good enough to go out to the barn and watch as they helped the injured horse.

She assumed she was in Dante's room. The sheets smelled like him and the decor was subtle shades of blues and browns. Very masculine, yet homey.

Several pictures lined the walls of Dante and his brothers at various ages. One was of all four boys holding up fishing poles and their catches. Another was of Dante, rifle in hand, kneeling on one knee next to what appeared to be a mule deer he'd bagged. He had a serious look on his face, but she could see the happiness and triumph in his eyes.

The last picture was of Dante wearing army dress blues, his back straight, shoulders squared, hair short and an American flag in the background. He looked proud, and so handsome Emma's heart pounded.

As the time passed, her pulse slowed, her eyelids drifted closed and she wondered where Dante would be sleeping when he finally came in.

DANTE DRAGGED HIMSELF into the house well after ten o'clock. The sheriff had come and Dante gave his statement about the explosion, the landslide and the explosives he found in his snowmobile. Once Yost left, Dante, Sean and Tuck had spent the next couple of hours working in the barn with the injured mare.

Sweet Jessie had been spooked about being herded into a stall when she'd been used to roaming the plains free. They had finally given her a mild sedative so that he and Sean could work on her sore hoof pad while Tuck held her head. Once they'd drained the abscess, they applied a poultice, gave her feed and water, and watched for a while to ensure she didn't kick the poultice loose.

All the while he'd been concentrating on healing the horse, Dante pushed what had happened that day in the canyon to the back of his mind.

Now that he was done and on his way back to the house, memories of the day flooded him. The one that stood out most in his mind was of Emma tumbling down the very steep wall of the canyon all the way to the bottom.

He hurried into the house.

His mother met him in the kitchen with a plate of food and a mug of coffee. "She's in your bed, asleep. You might as well eat and shower."

Tuck and Sean joined him at the table and he gave them the more detailed description of what had happened, and about the explosives still sitting out on the plains. By the time the sheriff had arrived at the ranch house, darkness had settled in and the snow was falling in earnest. He'd determined it was too dangerous to go hunting for explosives that could be buried under the snow by now. Especially in the dark. He'd call the state police and ask for the assistance of a bomb-sniffing dog. Hopefully, they'd get out there the next day and retrieve the explosive device before anyone else was hurt.

"Want me to call in the FBI bomb squad?" Tuck asked.

Dante considered his offer. "It might not be a bad idea. Is there any way to trace the C-4?"

"Not if they pulled all the packaging off it before deploying it."

Dante shook his head. "It was all clay."

"Maybe we can pull fingerprints from the clay, the detonation device or your snowmobile."

"Did you run the names I gave you by your guys at the bureau?" Dante asked.

"They're conducting a background check on Monty

Langley and Theron Price, the two speculators Hank mentioned, I'm having them run a check on Ryan Yost, the sheriff's son. I haven't heard anything yet."

"Yost has a plane. Have them run a check on flight plans in and out of Grand Forks." Dante's hand tightened around his coffee mug. "We have to find who's doing this before someone gets killed." Especially if that someone was Emma. "I think it's pretty apparent that whoever's doing this is targeting the Thunder Horses."

Tuck nodded. "Unfortunately, Emma was collateral damage."

That's what had Dante worried. "Who else is going to be caught in the cross fire until we resolve this situation?"

"I don't know, but I'm as afraid for Julia and Lily as you are for Emma. I keep wondering if I should send them away until all this dies down."

"What about your mother?" Sean added. "She's liable to get hurt, too."

Amelia entered the room. "Who's liable to get hurt?"

Sean leaped to his feet and offered her his chair. "Please, sit."

"Thank you." She smiled up at him as she took the seat. "You're such a gentleman."

Sean winked at her. "I only offer my seat to beautiful women."

Dante was stunned to see his mother's face flush a pretty pink. It made her appear twenty years younger.

She jumped right into their conversation with "Are you three talking about all that's been happening?"

"Yes, we have," Tuck said. "We think you and the ladies should leave the ranch until this situation is resolved."

She glared at the men. "I'll do no such thing. This is my home. I won't be run out of it."

"Amelia, we don't want you hurt," Sean said. "We think the boys are being targeted for some reason. The women might get caught in between."

"Well, I think it's up to us to decide what we want to do about it." Dante's mother lifted her chin and challenged the others with a pointed stare. "I've lived more than half my life here on this ranch. I won't be bought out, sold out or forced off by anyone. This little piece of heaven is my sons' heritage. Their father and I held on to it for them."

"Nothing's worth losing you, Mom," Dante said. "Or losing Emma."

"Or Julia and Lily," Tuck said.

"Or Roxanne," Sean added.

"I'm not going anywhere," Amelia stated. "So what are we going to do about this?"

Dante chuckled. "We got our pride from our father, but we got our fierce determination from you, Mom."

"Darn right you did." Her stern expression dissolved into a worried frown. "I hate seeing my boys injured. We have to put a stop to this. If only we knew who was doing it."

"And why." Dante pushed away from the table and stood. "Right now, I'm going to get a shower and then I'm going to check on Emma. Do you think we should take shifts through the night?"

Sean nodded. "I'll take the first one. You've been through a lot these past couple of days. Get some sleep."

Dante shot a glance at his mother to see if she reacted to Sean's statement.

Amelia crossed her arms over her chest. "If you're wondering whether or not I know about your helicopter crash, rest assured. I do. I've known since shortly after you visited Pierce in the hospital. You know a thing like that can't be kept a secret."

"I'd hate to know what other so-called secrets you know."

"I know more than you think. I might be getting older, but I know when my sons are keeping things from me." She gave him a grim smile. "It comes from years of practice. Anything you want to tell me?" She pinned him with her stare.

Dante almost blurted out that his engagement to Emma was a sham, but he bit down hard on his tongue to keep at least that little tidbit from her. The only two people who knew the truth were himself and Emma. No gossip would be able to pass it along to his mother. "No, Mother, I don't have anything else to tell you."

She snorted, her eyes narrowing slightly. "Well, get some sleep. I'll stay up with Sean for a while. I'm too wound up to sleep, anyway."

Dante ducked his head into his room. Emma was curled on her side, sound asleep, looking so small and fragile in his big bed. She didn't deserve to be hurt like she had. The fall could have broken every bone in her body or killed her.

She slept with her hand tucked beneath her cheek. She'd rolled up the sleeves of the big pajama shirt he never wore and looked even sexier in it than in a bikini.

Desire stirred inside him. Knowing he would do nothing to quench it that night, Dante slipped into the bathroom, stripped off his smelly clothes and turned on the cool water. After a quick scrub, he wrapped a towel around his waist, crossed the hallway and entered his room.

Normally he slept in the buff. To spare Emma some embarrassment, he slipped into the pajama bottoms that matched the top that she wore. He bent over her to check her breathing.

Emma rolled to her back and her eyes blinked open, two beautiful brown eyes that stared up at him sleepily. "Are you coming to bed?"

"I'll sleep on the couch."

"Please." She reached up and wrapped her arms around his neck, her lips soft and enticing.

He bent to brush his against them.

"Stay," she entreated, tightening her hold.

Knowing it would be difficult to lie in bed beside her and not touch her or make love to her, Dante heard himself agreeing before he'd thought it all the way through. "Okay, but just until you go back to sleep."

"No. All night." She scooted over, making room for his big body.

When he lay down beside her, she snuggled close, resting her head in the crook of his arm.

With a soft sigh, she closed her eyes and her breathing deepened.

Dante lay still for a long time, studying Emma in the light from the lamp on the nightstand.

Her dark hair lay in soft waves around her face, emphasizing her pale skin and the angry bruises.

She'd saved his life, only to put her own in danger. She didn't deserve it. Tomorrow, he'd get her out of there. Maybe the FBI had a safe house he could send her to until the trouble blew over.

And when they found the saboteur, he could resume his life as a CBP officer and maybe he'd look her up for a cup of coffee. If she dared see him again.

After all that had happened, he hadn't thought as much about Sam or the war that had taken her life. All his focus had gradually shifted to Emma.

Maybe it was time to let go of Sam and get on with his life.

Emma moaned in her sleep, her brow furrowing as if she were caught in a nightmare.

Dante gathered her close and pressed his lips to an uninjured spot. "It's okay," he whispered against her hair. "You're safe."

She settled against him and grew still, a smile tilting the corners of her lips.

Dante fell asleep with Emma in his arms, praying to the Great Spirit for her protection. He wasn't absolutely certain she was safe and that had him very concerned.

Chapter Thirteen

Emma woke the next morning to sunlight pouring in through the window onto the bed, warming the blankets. Even before she opened her eyes, she reached out for the warm body beside her.

The spot next to her was empty, the sheets still warm. Dante hadn't been up long. The sheets still carried his scent and heat.

Emma rolled over onto her back and winced. Yes, she had some bumps and bruises, but it could have been so much worse.

Throwing back the covers, she eased out of the bed, her muscles sore and stiff. Someone had brought her bag into the room the night before. She rummaged for something to wear and unearthed a pretty red sweater and jeans.

Dressing quickly, she ran her brush through her hair and pulled it back, securing it with an elastic band. A quick peek out in the hallway and she padded across to the bathroom to relieve herself, wash her face and brush her teeth.

She left the bathroom and followed the sounds of voices down the hallway to the big kitchen where the Thunder Horse men sat around the table with their spouses.

Amelia stood by the stove, stirring fluffy yellow

scrambled eggs. "Sit, Emma. We were just talking about what happened yesterday and what the boys think we should do today. You might want to weigh in."

Roxanne sat beside Pierce, her dark red hair curling down around her shoulders, her arms crossed over her chest, green eyes flashing. "I'm not leaving. So you can get that thought right out of your mind, right now."

"Me, neither," Julia agreed. Lily ate slices of banana beside her in her high chair.

"Who's leaving?" Emma asked.

"Not us!" Amelia, Julia and Roxanne said as one.

Emma smiled. "I'm sorry, but I don't have a clue what you're talking about."

Dante stood and offered her his chair.

Pierce spoke up. "We were saying that it would be best for all the ladies to pack up and leave until we figure out who has been trying to hurt the Thunder Horse brothers." He tried to frown but winced for the effort.

Amelia scooped scrambled eggs onto a plate and set it on the table in front of Emma. "The men, bless their hearts, think they'd be doing us a favor by sending us off to the cities to shop until they can get to the bottom of the attacks on all of them."

Emma stared up at Dante. "Is that true?"

Dante's brows furrowed. "No. At least not the part about the shopping. However, we discussed it. After all that has happened, it's not safe for the women to be here."

Emma's eyes widened. "So you think we'll just pack up and leave because you men think that's the best thing for us?"

Dante's frown deepened. "Well, yes."

Emma fought the smile threatening to curl her lips. She liked seeing the consternation clearly written on

Dante's face and mirrored in Tuck's and Pierce's expressions. "Without giving any of us a choice?"

"It's the only way to keep you all safe," Dante said.

"Since I'm a guest here, I'll do whatever you say. But if I'm going to be booted out of the house, you should at least know my opinion of the ruling." She spoke quietly but with conviction that had the men listening. Heat rose up her cheeks as all gazes fixed on her. She crossed her arms and tilted her chin up. "I think it stinks."

The women all clapped their hands.

Roxanne took up the cause. "As Emma, the college professor, so eloquently put it, your idea stinks. So, get used to it. We're staying put until this storm blows over."

"And what if one of you gets hurt?" Pierce demanded. "Had that truck landed any other way, I'd be a dead man."

"We'll take our chances," Amelia said. "It's not for any one of you to make that decision for us. I can shoot just as well as any one of you boys. I know how to defend what is mine."

Emma let go of the smile that had been creeping up around the corners of her lips. She could just picture Amelia Thunder Horse wielding a rifle, loaded for bear. Her smile faded and she glanced up at Dante. "Again, I'm just a guest here. If you ask me to leave, I'll go back to my apartment in Grand Forks."

Dante's lips firmed. "No. Whoever shot down my helicopter knows you saw him. He might come after you in Grand Forks to eliminate any witnesses."

"That's the only other place I'd go."

"I'm still the head of this household." Amelia stood with her shoulders squared, holding her spatula like a scepter. "If Emma wants to stay, she can stay."

Emma smiled at the older woman, knowing that if Dante told her he wanted her to leave, she would. She was there because of him. As much as she appreciated Amelia's invitation, she wouldn't feel right staying if Dante wanted her gone.

The telephone hanging on the wall beside Tuck rang. He turned and answered it, walking out of the room with the cordless handset.

Dante pulled up a chair beside her. "You should eat. You missed dinner last night."

Emma lifted her fork, amazed at how hungry she was. She had a forkful of steaming eggs halfway to her mouth when Dante asked, "How are you feeling today?"

"I'm fine. A bit stiff and sore, but I'll live." She popped the eggs in her mouth and chewed.

"I wish you would let me take you to see the local doctor."

Emma swallowed. "Really, I'm okay." Then to end the argument, she shoved more eggs into her mouth. She wanted to be mad at his insistence on seeing a doctor, but it was nice for a change that someone was concerned about her health after her fall. Living so long on her own, she'd had to weather her illnesses alone.

Tuck returned to the kitchen and replaced the phone in its charger. "That was my buddy at the FBI. He ran that background check on Langley, Price and Ryan Yost." Tuck paused, frowning, his gaze going to his mother. "Price is clean of any criminal record. Langley had an assault on his record from a couple of years ago, but the woman who filed the complaint retracted it."

"The two of them showed up together on the property two weeks ago," Amelia said. "I told them then that I wasn't interested in discussing the sale of the land or the mineral rights."

"And they left?" Tuck asked.

"Yes." Amelia's brows dipped. "Then Monty Langley

came back the next day to ask if I'd consider leasing the mineral rights. He said he had some big oil company wanting to tap into the oil reserves beneath our property."

Roxanne nodded. "They hit me up for it, as well. I did some reading. As you're all aware, the oil industry is booming in North Dakota since they discovered the Bakken formation stretches from Canada all the way to Bismarck. This isn't the first time speculators have been to the ranch."

"Maddox handled them last summer," Amelia said. "Since Maddox has been gone, they might think they can coerce me into signing something."

Julia laughed. "They obviously don't know anything about you."

Amelia smiled, then said, "I need to talk to the lawyer and have each of my sons added as co-owners of the property. That way no one person—namely me—can sell without the permission of the other."

"I don't think any of us want the property sold or split up," Dante said. "This is our home. It wouldn't be right to break it up."

His mother pressed a hand to his shoulder. "Exactly."

Tuck cleared his throat. "Mom, you know how all of us brothers feel about Sheriff Yost."

"I know that you don't care for him." Her eyes narrowed. "Why?"

"It might be none of our business, but what is your relationship with the man?"

She looked away. "You know I've been going out to dinner with him. He's been a perfect gentleman with me."

Emma studied the looks on the Thunder Horse brothers' faces. Apparently they didn't trust the sheriff and found it troublesome that their mother did.

Amelia continued, "Though you're right, it's none of

your business who I date, I'm still young enough to appreciate being treated like a woman, not just someone's mother or grandmother." She smiled at Lily, who was happily smearing banana on her face.

When the men all stared at her as if she'd lost her marbles, Emma almost laughed. They only saw their mother.

Amelia Thunder Horse was still a beautiful woman with needs and desires of her own.

"Of course you're a woman," Tuck said. "And I have no problem with you dating. Dad's been gone for nearly three years now. You should get out and have some fun. Our concern is Yost. I had my buddy at the bureau run a check on Ryan Yost."

"He's the boy installing the security system in and around the house," she confirmed.

Tuck stared at his mother. "Do you trust him?"

Their mother's brows drew together. "I trust his father."

Pierce snorted a rude word beneath his breath.

Tuck continued, "Ryan had some scuffles with the law before he became of legal age and joined the military. After he served his time, he went back to Afghanistan as a civilian contractor for a couple of years."

"I know all that. He comes highly recommended by the security firm he works for." Amelia rested her hands on her hips. "I didn't hire him because he was William's son."

Tuck raised his hands. "Okay. I just want you to be cautious about the people you allow inside the house."

"I am. No one knows better than I do that a lone woman on a ranch out in the middle of nowhere is an easy target. Especially when Maddox is out of the country. That's why Maddox hired Sean. Having him here has been a godsend."

Sean nodded. "It's a pleasure to be here as protection for a beautiful woman who is nowhere past her prime."

All the Thunder Horse family stared at Sean in shock.

Sean held up his hands. "Just telling it like I see it. I'll shut up now." He leaned his back against the wall, a ruddy blush sneaking up beneath the tan on his cheeks.

Amelia's eyes flared and she glanced down, her lips curling. "Did you find anything else about Ryan Yost I should be concerned about?"

Tuck shook his head, almost as if he was disappointed. "Not yet."

Amelia lifted her head and stared at Tuck. "Then leave the boy alone. I want that system installed sometime in the near future." She folded a dishtowel over the handle of the oven and smoothed her blouse. "Now if you'll excuse me, I'd like to steal the ladies away from you." She raised her hand. "Not to take them on a shopping trip to the cities, but to help me sort through some things I want to box up and give to charity."

Emma finished her breakfast, washed her plate in the sink and left it to dry on the rack. She followed the sound of female voices to the last doorway at the end of the hallway. It opened into a large room with a massive bed positioned at the center of one wall and a fireplace in the corner with a cheery fire burning.

"We're in here," Julia called out.

Feeling like an outsider, Emma paused at the doorway into a large walk-in closet.

Amelia sat cross-legged on the floor in front of an old trunk filled with letters, photographs and scrapbooks. If not for the strands of gray hair among the darker ones, she could have been a woman half her age.

"You have to see these pictures." Julia patted the floor

beside her. "Look at Dante at five years old. Wasn't he a cutie?"

She handed Emma a picture of a little boy with dark hair hanging down to his shoulders.

"I let them wear their hair long during the summer. The boys liked pretending they were wild Indians in the Old West." Amelia chuckled. "They'd spend the summers shirtless and mostly barefoot, riding horses and helping their father as much as they could." She handed a photo to Julia. "This is Tuck when he was ten. All legs and skinny as a rail."

Julia laughed. "He was so thin."

Amelia reached for another stack of photos. "I couldn't keep meat on their bones. They ran it all off." She leafed through the pictures and handed them over to Roxanne. "There are so many of the boys hunting and fishing. We spent a lot of the summer camping out in the canyon. We'd count the wild ponies during the days and pick out the constellations in the stars at night."

Emma enjoyed hearing stories about the boys growing up on a ranch, spending their summers running around in the sun. She loved the outdoors. As a paleontologist she spent much of her time outside digging in the dirt. At night she'd lay out under the stars, dreaming about other people who'd lived long ago, staring up at the stars, just like she was.

Roxanne held out a photo. "Is this Pierce's father when he was young? Pierce looks just like him."

Emma leaned over at the same time as Julia and Amelia. The man in the picture looked much like Pierce, but he was standing with his arm around a young woman with midnight black hair, dark eyes and the high cheekbones of the Lakota.

"Yes, that's my John, before we met. He dated a young

woman from the reservation up until a week before we met. They had just broken up when he met me. I guess I caught him on the rebound." She tapped her finger to the picture. "She ended up marrying William Yost within a month of breaking up with John. She's Ryan Yost's mother. I believe her name was Mika, the Lakota name for *raccoon*."

Emma stared down at the woman with the dark eyes and sultry look. "She was pretty."

"I know." Amelia laughed. "I don't know what John saw in me."

"A beautiful woman with a big heart." Julia leaned over and hugged her mother-in-law. "I'm so glad I married into such a wonderful family."

Amelia kissed Julia's cheeks. "I love my sons, and I always wanted daughters. I couldn't have picked better ones than all of you."

Roxanne reached out to clasp Amelia's hand. "We love you."

Having just met the woman, Emma sat silent. She didn't feel as though she had the right to say anything, even if deep in her heart she knew the woman was genuinely good and loving. So she sat staring at the photo of the woman and Amelia's dead husband who looked very much like Dante.

How different would the family have been had John Thunder Horse married Mika?

And now Amelia had Mika's son working for her.

Amelia sighed. "How much of this stuff should I get rid of?"

Julia clasped the pile of photos to her chest. "None of the pictures."

"No, none of the photos." Amelia glanced at the clothing hanging above her head and stood. "I should give his clothes away. It isn't as if he'll need them anymore." She ran her hands along the rows of jeans and flannel shirts neatly hung by type and color. "He could wear overalls and look so handsome. I will always love John. But now that he's been gone for three years, it's time to let go of some of him to make room for the rest of my life."

"You're still so young. You deserve to find happiness." Julia stood and put her arm around Amelia.

"Is it wrong for me to think that way? Is it possible to find the love of your life twice in one lifetime?" Amelia laughed, her hand shifting to the opposite side of the closet. "For that matter, I should toss half of my clothes, as well. They remind me too much of my life with John. If I'm going to make a fresh start, I should start with a fresh wardrobe."

"That's the spirit." Roxanne fished a dress out off the rail. "Stay or throw?"

Amelia smiled. "I wore that the day John took me to Minneapolis to see *Cats* at the theater." She chuckled. "He hated sitting through all that singing, but he knew how much I loved it."

Roxanne's brows rose. "Does it stay or go?"

Amelia sucked in a deep breath and tilted her head sharply. "Go." She selected several more dresses and passed them to Julia, who set them on a chair outside the closet. Amelia made her way to the back of the closet and stopped, her hand freezing on a white garment bag hidden behind some old coats.

Roxanne reached over her head. "Let me." She unhooked the hanger from the rail and carried the garment bag out of the closet and laid it on the bed.

Emma followed her, wondering what was in the bag.

"With all my sons married or getting married, it brings back memories of my wedding to their father." Amelia emerged from the closet carrying a white hatbox slightly yellowed with age.

Julia perched on the edge of the bed beside the garment bag and made room for the hatbox. "How long did you know Tuck's father before you married?"

Amelia smiled. "Two weeks. He found me the last week of the *Medora Musical* in the Burning Hills Amphitheatre. I was one of the singers in the show. He stayed until all the guests had left and the cast was cleaning the theater afterward."

"I can't imagine John Thunder Horse sitting through the entire show." Roxanne's lips quirked upward. "I don't think I ever saw him when he wasn't riding a horse. He was always all about his horses and the ranch."

"Not that week. He asked me to marry him at the end of our first week together when I was supposed to head back to Bismarck where I was to start college that fall. I never went back to Bismarck to college. We eloped to Vegas a week later. He bought me this dress for our wedding in a little chapel on the strip." She unzipped the garment bag.

Inside was a timeless wedding dress made of soft, pearl-white satin. The V-shaped neckline was simple with a few lace and pearl embellishments. The back dropped low in an elegant scooped neckline. Understated and formfitting, the dress was perfect.

Emma's heart squeezed tight in her chest.

"I love this dress," Julia sighed. "I so wished it would have fit me when I married Tuck for the second time."

"I bet you were a beautiful bride." Roxanne ran her hand over the satin. "It's a gorgeous dress."

Amelia smiled at the gown. "I had hoped that one day my daughter would be able to wear my gown for her own wedding." The older woman chuckled.

"But you had four sons," Emma added, her own eyes misting. "Speaking as an only child, they were very lucky to have each other."

"Yes. My boys have had their differences, but for the most part, they would do anything for each other." Amelia lifted the dress out of the garment bag and held it up to Emma. "You and I are about the same height, and I was once about the same size as you, though you would never guess it now." She smiled up at Emma, her eyes shimmering with moisture. "I would be honored if you'd wear it for your wedding to Dante."

Emma held up her hands, horrified that this woman would offer this lovely dress to her when their engagement was fake. "I couldn't."

Amelia pulled the dress back. "Of course, you might have something altogether different in mind for your wedding. I'm sorry, I'm just a sentimental old fool."

Amelia looked anything but old, and Emma couldn't bear to break her heart. "No, I think the dress is absolutely perfect in every way. It's just…" What could she say? That she'd lied all along, that she never intended to marry her son? "It's just that I hadn't even thought that far ahead." She gave Dante's mother a weak smile. "But when I do marry, that dress would be exactly the kind of dress I'd always dreamed of."

"Try it on," Julia insisted. "We want to see you in it, don't we, Roxanne?"

"You bet." Roxanne sat on the edge of the bed. "Go on. If you're embarrassed about changing in front of us, you can go into the closet and close the door. It's big enough for an army to change in."

Before she could protest, Amelia laid the dress across her arms and turned her toward the closet door. "Do you need help getting into it?"

"No, I can manage." Emma needed help getting out of the big fat lie she'd told. With the three women waiting in the bedroom for her to come out in the wedding dress, Emma had no choice. She stripped out of her jeans and the sweater she'd put on that morning, unhooked her bra and stepped into the gown.

The satin slipped across her skin, light and smooth, gliding over her hips so easily it felt like air. She reached behind her and zipped the back, a little apprehensive about how low the neckline dipped down her back, almost to her waist.

The dress could have been tailored for her; it fit perfectly, hugging her hips and breasts like a second skin. The skirt fell in an A-line, pooling at her feet, the train stretching out three feet behind her. A full-length mirror hung on the back of the door. When Emma looked up and caught a glimpse of her reflection, she gasped and froze, tears welling in her eyes.

It was absolutely exquisite.

"Come out, we want to see!" Julia called.

Hating herself for the lie she was perpetuating, Emma opened the door and stepped out of the closet.

The women had been talking, but when they spotted her standing there, the room grew so silent Emma could hear the crackle of the fire in the fireplace.

Amelia covered her mouth with her hands and tears slipped down her cheeks. "Emma," she said, her voice cracking.

"You're beautiful," Julia said, her voice barely a whisper.

"Wait." Amelia opened the hatbox and pulled out a bridal veil, unfolding the lengths of lace-trimmed tulle. She pressed the comb into Emma's hair and turned her toward a full-length mirror.

The woman staring back at her was a stranger. Dressed as a bride, her hair around her shoulders, the veil framing her pale face, she wanted to cry.

"I'm no expert, but I think you found your dress," Roxanne announced, clapping her hands together. "It couldn't be more perfect if you'd had it designed for you."

Amelia reached for Emma and hugged her. "Dante is a very lucky man to have found you."

What could Emma say to that? Nothing. He hadn't actually found her. She'd found him dragging himself out of his burning aircraft.

"Do you like it?" Amelia held her at arm's length, her gaze searching Emma's face. "You can tell me if you don't. I won't be offended."

Emma glanced down at the satin dress and nodded. "I love it." Feeling more of a heel by the minute, Emma backed out of Amelia's arms. "I'm sorry. But I think the fall yesterday took its toll on me. If you don't mind, I need to go lie down."

Amelia's eyes widened. "Of course, dear. How inconsiderate of me. I should have known better than to keep you rummaging through my closets. Here, let me unzip you." She helped unzip the dress and Emma ran for the closet where she removed the veil, stripped out of the beautiful dress and put her own clothes back on.

When she was finished, she emerged from the closet. The women were busy folding the clothes that would go to charity. Emma laid the veil and dress on the bed, her fingers skimming across the smooth satin fabric, regret tugging at her.

"Please excuse me," she said and hurried from the room.

She ran for the bedroom she and Dante had slept in the night before and crawled up in the bed, pulling the blanket around her. It still smelled of Dante. As she lay there, she thought of Dante helping her out of the collapsing trailer first, when it meant he might not make it out at all. She thought of how he'd helped an injured horse out of the canyon in the frigid cold, of how he'd risked his life rather than leave her in the canyon any longer than he had to.

She still tingled all over when she thought of the way it felt when Dante wrapped her in his arms, and how gentle he'd been when they'd made love for her first time, and then again in her apartment. She remembered their first kiss and the way it felt to lie in bed beside him.

Then she thought of how beautiful she felt in his mother's wedding dress and of the lies she'd told these good people. Of how they'd hate her when they learned the truth.

Tears slid down her cheeks as she realized what had happened in the short amount of time she'd been with Dante. No matter how much she'd told herself not to get involved, she'd done it. She'd fallen head over heels in love with the big Lakota man.

And no matter how much she might love him, Dante was in love with a dead woman and had told her up front he wasn't looking for a relationship. He wasn't ready.

Her chest hollow, Emma curled into a ball, buried her face in the pillow and cried.

When she could cry no more, she promised herself to leave at the first opportunity. She couldn't stay there, in love with Dante and his family, when it would all end. The sooner she severed the ties, the sooner she could start getting over him.

Chapter Fourteen

Dante, Pierce, Tuck and Sean fed the horses and worked with Sweet Jessie's sore foot. The swelling was down and the horse was impatient to be outside. They all agreed it would be better to keep her in the warm, dry barn until the wound had scabbed over a bit.

Dante gave the horse sweet feed and water and ran a currycomb over her fuzzy coat.

When he and his brothers stepped out of the barn, they noticed a vehicle pulling up in front of the house. After all that had happened, Dante wasn't comfortable with anyone driving up to the ranch house that didn't have an appointment or who hadn't called first. He hurried to the house, bursting through the kitchen door.

Following the voices, he found his mother, Roxanne and Julia in the front foyer, talking to a young man with jet-black hair and dark skin, about Dante's own age.

Julia turned to Dante. "You remember Ryan Yost, don't you?"

Dante nodded. "We spoke yesterday."

Ryan shifted the box he carried from one hand to the other and held out his hand. "Dante."

Dante shook his hand. "Ryan."

The other man held up a box. "Those cameras came in like I thought they would."

Amelia waved him inside. "Let me know if you need anything."

"Thank you, ma'am. I think I have all that I need, except a ladder."

"I'll get it," Sean offered and headed for the back door. Moments later, he came in dusting snow off his jacket and carrying a ladder.

Dante watched as Ryan set the ladder up in the living room, attach a camera to the wires in the corner and screw the mount into the wall.

Tuck joined Dante at the edge of the room. "I think Sean and Pierce can handle things here. Why don't you and I go to Medora and question the oil speculators?"

Dante nodded. "Let me check in on Emma."

His mother stopped him in the hallway. "Don't forget tonight is the kickoff of the Cowboy Christmas events in Medora. It's a tradition for the family to attend. I'd like to take Emma, as well."

"She'd like that." Dante smiled. "Tuck and I can meet you in town so you don't have to wait on us."

His mother nodded. "That's a good idea."

Dante stepped into the room where Emma lay sleeping, the blankets pulled up around her. He tiptoed to the bed and stared down at her face. Her dark hair splayed across the white pillowcase and her cheeks appeared to be streaked with tears.

Why would she be crying? Were her injuries more than she was letting on? Did she miss her home in Grand Forks?

His chest tightened. He found himself wanting to take away her pain. Dante brushed the hair from her face and bent to kiss her cheek.

Emma turned her face at the last minute and their lips

brushed together. Her arm slid up around his neck, dragging him closer.

"I'm heading to town to question the speculators. Will you meet me at the diner later when the family comes to town for the festival?"

"Mmm."

He kissed her again, this time, deepening the kiss, his tongue sliding between her teeth to caress hers.

She returned the pressure, her response stronger this time.

When he reluctantly broke away, she looked up at him with dark brown eyes, the shadows beneath them making her appear sad. "Be careful," she said.

"You, too." He brushed his knuckles against the softness of her face. "I'll see you later."

"Goodbye," she whispered.

Dante left the room, feeling as though he should stay and spend the afternoon holding Emma. He hadn't thought much about Sam since Emma had come into his life. Even the guilt he'd experienced at first was fading. He finally realized Sam would have wanted him to get on with his life.

With Emma he could see a future.

His mother followed him to the front door where he dressed for the outdoors and waited for his brother to appear.

"You know she's special, don't you?" his mother said as she held his coat for him while he slipped his arms into the sleeves.

"Who, Emma?" He chuckled. "Yeah. I know."

"Then don't let her get away."

He paused and stared down at his mother. "Why would I?"

She snorted softly, holding on to his gloves. "How

many times have you successfully lied to me, Dante Thunder Horse?" she demanded.

He thought back over the years and his lips twisted. "Never."

"That's right." She handed the gloves over. "I knew when you made the announcement at the hospital that you were lying."

"I'm sorry, Mom. I shouldn't have. But I didn't want to worry you more with Pierce lying in ICU."

"Actually, I'm glad you did. It gave *you* time to get to know her better and to see how much you really care about her."

"Mom, I've only known her a few days. That's not enough to base a lifetime of marriage on."

His mother shook her head. "That's all it took for me and your father. We knew within the first hour of talking. He proposed after a week and we were married for thirty years before he passed."

"I didn't think I could love again."

"Sam was a different chapter in your life. Emma is a fresh beginning."

"I'll always love Sam."

"Son, that's the beauty of the human heart. You don't have to stop loving Sam, just like I'll never stop loving your father. But there is someone else out there you could love, as well. And I'm hoping that there might be someone out there for me. I'm not too old to want someone else in my life. I have you boys, but you have your own families."

He squeezed her hand gently. "And you deserve to love again."

"As do you."

Dante pulled his mother into his arms and hugged her. "Please tell me you're not considering Sheriff Yost."

She laughed. "I had, but I'm not so sure anymore. I think I'll keep my options open."

Sean appeared from the direction of the kitchen. "I put a pot of coffee on, care to join me?"

Amelia smiled up at Dante. "I do have options, you know."

Dante grinned as his mother left him to join Sean for that cup of coffee in the kitchen.

"Ready?" Tuck asked as he pushed past him to exit out the front door. "We're going in my truck. And we'd better hurry if we want to talk to the oil speculators before the town gets crowded for the Cowboy Christmas kickoff."

Dante almost told Tuck he'd question the men tomorrow. He wanted to go back into the room with Emma, pull her into his arms and tell her...

Tell her what?

That he could be well on his way to falling in love with her and would she give him a chance to find out?

With the idea too new to him, he decided he'd be better off waiting until later that night to hold her in his arms and make it right.

EMMA MUST HAVE fallen back asleep after Dante left. She didn't wake until Amelia poked her head in the doorway a couple of hours later.

"Emma, it's time to get ready. We're all heading into Medora for the kickoff of the annual Cowboy Christmas festivities. We leave in thirty minutes."

"I'm awake," she assured the woman. She sat up, feeling every bruise and bump and stiff muscle in her body, along with the deep sadness of knowing she'd be leaving. On the nightstand beside a glass of water, lay the keys to the SUV Dante had rented in Grand Forks.

If she really was leaving, now would be the best time

to do it. With Dante in town, the rest of the members of his household leaving for Medora, she could sneak away. She slipped into her snow gear and pulled on her boots.

Stuffing her toothbrush, hairbrush and a change of clothes in her purse, she left the rest of the contents of her bag in the bedroom and stepped out in the hallway.

"Look at you, all ready to go," Julia said, hurrying to one of the bedrooms. "We'll be a few more minutes. We had to wait for Ryan to leave before we could begin getting ready."

"He was here?"

"While you were asleep. Got half of the cameras wired. He's supposed to be back tomorrow to finish the job."

"I didn't even hear him working," Emma said.

"We had him work on the installation of the cameras at the other end of the house so that he wouldn't disturb you and Lily while you both napped." A tiny cry came from down the hallway. "That's my cue. All I have to do is get Lily dressed and I'll be ready."

Amelia emerged from her bedroom, wearing a bright red Christmas sweater. "I had a call from Maddox while you were sleeping. He and Katya flew into Bismarck over an hour ago. They're on their way and should be to Medora in time for the festivities. Isn't that wonderful?" The older woman beamed. "All my children home for Christmas." She wrapped her arms around Emma and hugged her tight. "I'm so glad you're here with us."

Guilt tugged at Emma as she returned the hug. "Thank you for all you've done for me," she said, fighting back tears. "I'm supposed to meet Dante at the diner. Do you mind if I leave a little early? I have a few things I want to pick up at the store before it closes."

Amelia's brows furrowed. "Is that a good idea to go off on your own with all that's happened?"

Emma forced a smile to her stiff lips. "I'll be fine. If I have any trouble on the road, all of you will be behind me shortly. I'll just wait until you come along."

"I could be ready to go in five minutes," Amelia assured her. "Just let me touch up my makeup and grab my purse."

"No hurry. I really can manage this on my own." Emma hugged Amelia one more time. "Goodbye." Before Amelia could come up with another argument to keep her there or go with her, Emma hurried out the door to the SUV and climbed in.

The vehicle started right up, of course. It couldn't be cranky and die to keep her from making her break from the Thunder Horses. Deep down, she wanted to stay and become a part of this family. But she couldn't make Dante love her and she wouldn't stay knowing he didn't and never would.

The stolen kisses and making love had only been a passing fancy to him. His heart would always belong to Sam.

Shifting into Reverse, she backed up, turned and drove down the long driveway toward the highway. She took one last glance in her rearview mirror before the ranch house blended into the snow and all she could see was the thin wisp of smoke from the fireplace.

She turned onto the highway headed toward Medora and the interstate highway that would take her back east. She could stop in Bismarck and stay the night or push through and arrive in Grand Forks around midnight.

Snow fell in big, fluffy flakes, thickening the farther she drove from the Thunder Horse Ranch, making it difficult to see the road in front of her. As she came to a crossroad with a stop sign, she pressed her foot to the brake.

The tires skidded and she started sliding toward the ditch.

Heart pumping, she turned into the skid and righted the vehicle, just in time to see the form of a man walking alongside the road ahead, headed toward her.

As her lights caught him in their beams, he lifted his head and waved her down.

Carefully applying her breaks, she slowed and rolled down the passenger window.

"Thank goodness you stopped." Ryan Yost poked his head through the window. "I thought I'd have to walk all the way back to the ranch house."

"What happened to your truck?" Emma asked.

"It slid into the ditch about half a mile ahead. The roads are pretty tricky."

"Are you headed back to the ranch or to town?"

"To Medora, if you don't mind."

She popped the locks on the SUV and the man climbed into the passenger seat.

"Where is the rest of the Thunder Horse clan?"

"They should be right behind me."

"In that case, turn here," Ryan said.

"What?" Emma glanced at the dirt track leading off the road. "Why?"

"Because I said so." Ryan grabbed the steering wheel and yanked it to the right.

Emma held on as the SUV bumped off the road onto the narrow strip of dirt lightly covered in snow. Pulse pounding, she fought to right the vehicle. When she had the SUV under control, she braked to a stop and shot an angry glance at Ryan. "What the hell are you doing?"

That's when she saw the dark, hard form of the gun

in his hand pointed at her head, and a rush of icy-cold dread washed over her.

"I'm taking what should have been mine."

Knowing she could be a victim or she could try to escape, Emma chose to try rather than go along with whatever Ryan had in mind. "Why do you say that? What should have been yours? Surely not me." She spoke calmly while her left hand inched toward the door handle.

Ryan laughed. "It's not you, but I've learned that to get to them, you have to go through the ones they love."

"Are you talking about the Thunder Horses?" she asked.

"Of course I'm talking about the Thunder Horses. Keep driving," he commanded. "Far enough off the road they won't see you when they drive by."

Emma eased her foot off the brake but didn't apply her foot to the accelerator. The vehicle inched forward along the bumpy road.

"Faster!" Ryan yelled and leaned across to slam his own foot down on hers. The vehicle leaped forward.

At that moment, Emma flung the door open, elbowed the man in the face and threw herself out of the vehicle. She hit the rocky ground hard and rolled out of the way of the tires.

Pain shot through the arm she'd landed on, but she scrambled to her feet and ran as fast as she could in the snow and her clunky boots.

A car door slammed and gravel crunched behind her.

By the time she reached the paved road, her lungs burned from breathing the frigid air and her muscles were screaming, but she pushed forward. Her foot hit the icy surface and she skidded and slammed onto the pavement flat on her back, the wind knocked out of her lungs.

Lights blinked far down the road toward the ranch

house. If only she could get up and keep running. They'd find her.

Emma sucked in a breath, rolled over onto her hands and knees and tried to get up.

Ryan hit her like a linebacker, plowing into her and knocking her into the ditch on the other side of the road. He landed on top of her and covered her with his body, pressing her face into the snow and ice.

She struggled, but he weighed more than she did and he had her arms and legs pinned beneath his.

The muffled sound of a vehicle engine came and went. Though she tried to scream out, she knew she wouldn't be heard. Even if she was, he might still have his gun on him. What would happen if they stopped? Would he shoot Amelia, Julia or Lily before the men took him down?

Emma wouldn't be able to live with herself if he did, so she lay quietly, no longer fighting to free herself. Once the vehicle drove by, she'd come up with another plan. If she lived long enough.

Chapter Fifteen

Dante and Tuck stopped at the hotel where the oil speculators were staying. Nicole was on duty, looking as bored as usual. "Ah, the Thunder Horse brothers. Here to see Ryan, again?"

"We're not here to see Ryan. We'd like to talk with Monty Langley and Theron Price."

"Sorry, unless you have an appointment, they've asked not to be disturbed."

Tuck pulled out his FBI credentials. "What room are they in?"

Nicole stared at the big *F-B-I* letters and nodded. "Impressive." She jerked her head toward the hallway. "They have rooms 109 and 110."

As Tuck and Dante took off in that direction, she called out, "But they aren't there."

"Any idea where they are?"

"Why do you want to know?"

"I can't answer that."

"They just got back from a ride on their snowmobiles." She snorted. "They usually have dinner at the diner around this time every day, like clockwork. I'd check there."

"They own snowmobiles?" Dante asked.

"Yeah, they keep them out back in the storage shed."

"How do we get inside the shed?"

Nicole shrugged. "Open it. We don't lock it."

Dante left the hotel and ran around the outside to the back where a weathered storage shed stood in the corner of the lot. He pushed the door open and stepped inside. The light from the doorway splashed across two fairly new snowmobiles.

"So, they own snowmobiles," Tuck said. "So do most of the people in this area."

"The one that was out by the canyon had a broken track and was leaking oil." He studied the one closest to him while Tuck dropped to his haunches beside the other.

After a moment, Tuck straightened. "This one doesn't have a broken track or an oil leakage."

The lighting wasn't the best, so Dante skimmed his hand along the top of the vehicle closest to him, feeling the tracks for any inconsistencies. One of the tracks had a notch chipped out of it. Ducking his head, Dante saw something shiny on the ground beneath the engine. He reached his hand beneath it and felt warm, sticky oil.

"A lot of snowmobiles have chinks out of their tracks and leak oil."

"Yeah, but I don't believe in coincidence." Dante left the storage shed.

"Where to?" Tuck asked.

"The diner, to find us some oil speculators."

He and Tuck climbed in the truck and drove the block to the diner, parking in front.

Through the windows Dante could see Hank and Florence at the bar counter. At a table on the south side of the diner, two men sat drinking coffee.

Dante was first out of the truck and into the diner. He marched up to the two men. "Monty Langley and Theron Price?"

The younger one with sandy-blond hair raised his eyebrows. "I'm Monty, he's Theron. What can we do for you?"

"Where were you two yesterday around three o'clock in the afternoon?"

"Why?" Monty asked.

Tuck stepped up beside Dante and flashed his FBI badge. "Just answer the question."

Monty raised his hands. "We were here in the diner with Mr. Plessinger for most of the afternoon. About have him ready to lease his mineral rights." He dropped his arms and smiled. "Are you two ready to talk money?"

"Hell no," Dante responded.

Theron frowned. "Then what's this all about?"

"Someone tried to kill me and my fiancée yesterday out at the canyon. He used C-4 explosives. The kind people might have access to if connected with an oil drilling operation."

Monty stood, his hands raised. "Whoa there, cowboy. I'm a lover, not a killer. The closest I get to the oil is when I take my car in for an oil change."

Florence stepped into the conversation. "I can vouch for the two of them. They worked over poor ol' Fred Plessinger all afternoon, drank two pots of coffee between them and ate an entire coconut cream pie."

Tuck's cell phone buzzed and he stepped away from the group to answer it.

"Where were you two four days ago? Were you anywhere near Grand Forks?"

"We've been here in Medora the entire week," Price said. "We're not scheduled to head back to Minneapolis until the end of the month."

"Do you have proof?" Dante asked.

Monty pulled a pocket-size day planner out of his

jacket and handed it to Dante. "Look at my schedule. Any one of these people I've had appointments with can vouch for my whereabouts."

Dante glanced at the names on the man's minicalendar. He recognized many of them. The men seemed slimy but legit in their alibis. He handed the planner to Monty. "I'm sorry to have bothered you."

"Sounds like someone is out to get the Thunder Horse clan. What with your brothers' brakes going out, your helicopter going down and now the explosives. Do you all have good insurance policies?" Monty held out a card. "I have a friend who sells life insurance."

Dante walked away and joined Tuck near the door.

"Are you sure?" Tuck ran a hand through his hair, his face pale. "Thanks. I'm on it." As soon as Tuck hung up, he pushed through the door. "Come on, we have to go."

"What's wrong?"

Tuck climbed into his truck and started the engine as Dante slid into the passenger seat. "I had my contact at the FBI run a check on flight plans for Grand Forks and Bismarck to see if Ryan Yost's name or plane came up. They had a couple of hits. He flew into Bismarck two days before your crash and out the next day, landing in Grand Forks the day before your crash. Then he flew out of Grand Forks a couple of days after your crash."

Dante's blood ran cold. "It adds up all too well. He could have cut your brakes and left them to bleed out, hopped in his plane to Grand Forks to target me. Now he's out at the house with the family."

"Pierce and Sean are there," Tuck said, pulling out of the diner parking lot onto the highway.

"But they're not suspecting anything." Dante hit the speed-dial number for home and pressed his cell phone to his ear. It rang five times before he gave up. "No answer."

"They could be on their way to town for Cowboy Christmas." Tuck glanced ahead as they approached the edge of town. "As a matter of fact, isn't that Pierce's SUV?"

The SUV pulled up beside them, the window rolled down and Pierce stuck his head out. "You're headed the wrong way."

"Where's Ryan Yost?"

"He left thirty minutes before us. I figure he's back at his hotel," Pierce said. "Why?"

"Do you have everyone with you?"

His mother answered, "Yes, we do. Except Emma. She was on her way to meet you at the diner." She unbuckled her seat belt and leaned over Pierce's shoulder. "Emma's not with you? She left ten minutes before we did."

Dante's heart fell down around his knees. Emma was missing and Ryan Yost might be the one responsible. Where would he take her? And why?

His cell phone buzzed in his hand and he glanced down. A text message came through with a number he didn't recognize in the display screen.

If you want to see Emma alive, come to the ranch. Alone.

Dante's hand shook as he held out the phone to Tuck.

Tuck read the message and glanced over at Pierce. "We have a problem."

Pierce pulled off the road, climbed out of the SUV and walked over to Tuck's truck. The three brothers read the message again.

"He's at the ranch with Emma," Dante said. "I have to go."

"Who's at the ranch with Emma?" Pierce asked.

"Ryan Yost."

"Where's Emma?" Dante's mother pushed her way through her sons. "And why are you concerned about Ryan?"

Dante debated telling her something to pacify her, but the look on her face was enough. "We think Ryan Yost has her. I just got this text." He showed his mother the cell phone.

"Oh, dear Lord. I knew I should have insisted she ride with us."

"If she had, you all might be the ones he's holding hostage."

Amelia stared up at her sons. "But why?"

"Good question. Only Ryan can answer that. For now, I have to go." Dante held out his hands to his brother Tuck. "Give me the keys."

"You're not going alone."

"I have to. If I don't, he might kill Emma."

"He might kill her anyway. Why not let us come with you? We're the ones trained for this."

"You forget I fought in the war."

"Yeah, but you have no training in hostage negotiation."

"I can't risk it." Dante climbed into the truck and stuck the key in the ignition.

"We're coming with you." Pierce opened the back door and got in the crew cab.

Tuck climbed into the passenger seat. "What he doesn't know won't hurt. We have your back."

"What about me?" Amelia asked.

"Maddox is supposed to arrive about now. Send him out when he does. And, Mom, I need you to stay in town and keep Lily and Julia safe," Tuck said. "Promise me."

Amelia nodded. "And promise me that you three won't do anything stupid and get yourselves shot."

"We promise," they said as one.

"Want me to notify the sheriff's department?" she asked.

"No!" they said in unison. "If it's his son, he might take sides. The wrong side."

"Got it." Amelia stepped away from the truck and raised her hand. *"Wakan tanan kici un wakina chelee."*

Dante drove toward the ranch, his foot heavy on the accelerator. He appreciated his mother's prayer to the Great Spirit, but he wasn't the one who needed it.

Emma was.

Chapter Sixteen

Emma came to and blinked at the lights shining from the lamps on end tables above her. For a moment she was disoriented, her vision blurred and pain throbbed at her temple.

The last thing she remembered was fighting to stand after the SUV full of the Thunder Horse family had passed by. One moment she'd gotten a good kick at his shins, the next moment she was awake in the living room of the Thunder Horse ranch house.

"Looks like you'll be around for the fireworks after all," a voice said.

She turned her head, a flash of pain making her close her eyes until it passed. When she opened them again, she could see Ryan Yost standing beside the window, peering through a crack in the blinds.

"Someone's coming. Let's hope it's the people I specifically requested and not any more." He clapped his hands together. "Today, I finally get my revenge on the people I hate the most."

Emma struggled to push to a sitting position, realizing that her hands were secured behind her back by something that felt like duct tape. Using her elbow, she pushed up and drew her legs under her, sitting up. Thankfully, he hadn't tied her feet together. She glanced around for something sharp to rub the tape on. Every edge seemed to be soft or rounded. "Why are you doing this?"

"I'll tell you why. For years, my father hated me, hated my mother and hated everything about our lives together. When my mother couldn't take it any longer, she jerked me out of my school here in Medora and hauled me back to the reservation where I would have rotted in hell."

Emma's head ached, but she had to keep the man talking. Maybe she could reason with him. "And what does that have to do with the Thunder Horses?"

"On one of her normal drunken binges, she let slip a secret she'd kept from me and from my father. A secret that made everything perfectly clear. William Yost was in love with the woman who married John Thunder Horse, not my mother."

"So?"

"And my mother was in love with John Thunder Horse and they'd been dating up until John met Amelia and dumped my mother. My pregnant mother."

Emma's mind cleared and focused on what the man had just said. "Are you saying John Thunder Horse was your father?"

"Damn right he was. He left my mother when she was pregnant. She was forced to marry Yost and had me eight months later."

Ryan slapped a hand to his chest. "I should have grown up on the Thunder Horse Ranch, not that hellhole of a reservation. I should have had the best of everything they had."

"Are you certain? Have you done a DNA test?"

"I look like a Thunder Horse, damn it!" He jerked Emma up by her arm and glared into her face. "I've never looked anything like William Yost."

"Because you look like your mother." Sheriff Yost

stepped into the house, gun drawn, closing the door behind him. "Ryan, what are you doing?"

"Daddy." Ryan practically spit the word out. "So glad you could come to your *son's* coming out party. Pull up a seat. We're waiting for the other main player to arrive."

Footsteps pounded on the porch outside and a voice shouted, "Emma!"

"Dante, don't come in!" Emma cried.

Ryan looped his arm around her neck and yanked her up by the throat. "Shut up."

Dante flung the door open and entered, his eyes blazing. "Leave her out of this, Ryan."

"Oh, no. I wouldn't dream of it. I've worked too hard setting this all up to end it here."

"What do you want? The ranch? Money? You name it." Dante stepped closer.

"Stop right there." Ryan pointed his gun at Emma's temple. "Another step closer and I'll shoot her."

"Why are you doing this, son?"

"Because I'm not your son."

"What are you talking about?"

"My mother told me her secret. A secret I suspect you always knew. She had an affair with John Thunder Horse before she married you, and before *he* married Amelia. She was pregnant when you married her. That's why I was born eight months after your wedding."

Sheriff Yost raised a hand. "Whoa, son, where did you hear such an idiotic story?"

"From my mother. The woman you kicked out of your house and sent back to live on the reservation. If I had been your son, you wouldn't have let her take me." Ryan's lip curled back, baring his teeth. "It all made sense when she told me I was John Thunder Horse's son. You hated me, and you hated my mother for what she did."

Ryan's arm tightened around Emma's neck. She struggled, unable to get air past her vocal cords to utter a protest.

"Let go of Emma," Dante pleaded. Emma's face was beet-red and starting to turn blue. "She had nothing to do with what happened between your father and mother."

"No way. While you and your brothers lived the life *I* should have, I wallowed in a broken-down trailer while my mother drank herself into oblivion every night. When she wasn't slapping me around, she was telling me what a failure I was compared to the four of you."

"Ryan, I don't know what your mother told you, but it was a pack of lies. I tried to get you back, but the court didn't want to go up against the tribal council. Your mother told them she wanted you to grow up knowing the way of your ancestors. They wouldn't listen to me. I loved you. I wanted you to live with me."

"Then why did you kick us out?"

"I didn't." Yost stepped closer. "You have to believe me. Your mother had problems. She was delusional. I think her breakup with John was the last straw. I didn't see it until we'd already married. And with you on the way, I couldn't divorce her."

"Lies!" Ryan dragged Emma back toward the hallway. "You threw us out."

"She told you that, didn't she?" William said quietly. "The truth was that she left me and took you with her to punish me."

"No. That's not how it was. You hated me and ruined my life. Now I'm going to ruin yours." Ryan's hand shook as he held it to Emma's head. "If you don't shoot Dante right now, I'll put a bullet through Emma's head."

"What will shooting Dante gain for you?"

"It'll be one Thunder Horse down and you will have

killed him. Amelia will never love you after you've killed her precious son." Ryan's face turned red, his eyes bulging. "Shoot him now or I swear the woman dies!"

Dante turned to the sheriff. "Do it. Shoot me if that's what it'll take to free Emma. She'll die anyway if he doesn't loosen his hold soon."

"I can't shoot you." The sheriff held his gun to the side. "I won't."

"I've never trusted you. Never thought you were man enough to fill my father's shoes or deserve to be with my mother. If ever there's a time to prove me wrong, now is it. Shoot me." Dante held his arms out to his sides, glancing over at Emma's face turning purple. "Now!" He prayed Yost would do it, but that he'd graze him, not hit him in a place that would be fatal. If Ryan thought him dead, he might let go of Emma long enough for her to breathe, buying time.

Sheriff Yost raised his 9 mm pistol and aimed. "God have mercy on my soul." He pulled the trigger.

The bullet's impact jerked Dante's arm back and he was flung to the side, angling toward Ryan Yost.

As Dante crashed to the floor, Ryan loosened his hold on Emma's neck.

Her knees buckled and she slipped to the floor.

Ryan raised his gun, pointing it at Sheriff Yost. "Now I'll be the hero for shooting the man who killed Amelia's son, and you will be blamed for setting off the explosives I have positioned around the house." Before he could pull the trigger, Dante swung his leg, sweeping Ryan's feet out from under him. His shot hit the ceiling and he landed hard on his back, his gun skidding across the hardwood floor out of his reach.

Emma, having caught her breath, spun around on her hip and kicked the gun farther away from him.

"No! You'll ruin everything." Ryan grabbed her hair and yanked hard.

Dante, his arm bleeding and his vision getting gray and fuzzy around the edges, flung himself on top of Ryan, pinning him down with his good hand, keeping him from digging the detonator out of his pocket.

Then everything seemed to happen at once. Tuck and Pierce stormed into the house, followed by Maddox and the rest of the family.

Tuck pulled Dante off Ryan.

"Don't let him get his hands in his pockets. He has a detonator in it and he says he has the house rigged to explode."

Tuck rolled Ryan onto his belly and slapped a zip tie around his wrists, then carefully dug the detonation device from his pocket and set it aside for the bomb squad. "You have the right to remain silent…"

As Tuck read Ryan his Miranda rights, Dante crawled over to where Emma was struggling to get up with her wrists still bound behind her back with duct tape.

Maddox leaned over Dante. "Let me get her." He pulled a pocketknife out of his pocket and sliced through the tape, freeing her wrists.

As soon as she was free, Emma flung her arms around Dante's shoulders. "I thought you were dead. Why the hell did you tell the sheriff to shoot you?"

"Sweetheart, you were turning a pretty shade of blueberry. Another minute and you wouldn't have made it." He winced, pain slicing through him where she hugged his injured arm. "I'm getting blood on your clothes."

"Oh, my God. Lie down. Someone call an ambulance."

Pierce handed her a towel. "Apply pressure to the wound to slow the bleeding."

Tuck placed a call to 9-1-1, requesting an ambulance and bomb-sniffing dogs.

While Maddox helped Dante out of his jacket, Emma folded the hand towel into a wad. Once Dante was out of the jacket, the wound bled freely. Emma eased Dante onto his back and applied pressure to the wound.

"Emma." Dante grasped the wrist holding the towel in place.

"Am I hurting you?"

"More than you'll ever know."

"I'm sorry, but if I let up, you'll start bleeding again."

He chuckled. "Not the arm." He laid his other hand over her chest. "Here. You're hurting my heart."

"I don't understand."

"You made me feel again." He lifted her empty hand and pressed it to his chest. "You made me ache so bad I thought I was going to die."

Her eyes misted. "I'm sorry, I don't want to cause you any pain. I know how much you loved Sam. I was leaving to go back to Grand Forks so that I wouldn't make you feel like you had to choose."

"That's the point. I didn't want to love anyone else. I didn't want to choose between you and her. But then you ran your snowmobile into a man who tried to kill me not once but three times.

"I'd have done it for anyone."

"I know. That's what I love about you. You're selfless, endearing and beautiful in so many ways."

"No, I'm just me. A college professor with very few social skills."

"You have all the skills I need, and you're the most beautiful woman I know. Because you're beautiful inside and out. You showed me that I didn't have to choose. That I could love you both."

Emma laughed, the sound catching on a sob. "You've been talking to your mother, haven't you?"

"She's smarter than I ever gave her credit for." Dante pressed her hand to his lips kissing her knuckles. "I'll never underestimate her again. Nor you."

As Tuck dragged Ryan to his feet and shoved him toward the door, the rest of the Thunder Horse family arrived with the ambulance, a state policeman and the only other deputy on duty in Billings County. Rather than risk anyone else being hurt, the party was moved out of the house.

Ryan was bundled into the state police car and carted off to Bismarck where he would face a multitude of charges.

Sheriff Yost hung around to make sure no one went inside the house his son had rigged with explosives.

Dante let the medics bandage his wound but refused to go with them to the hospital in Dickinson. "I want to make sure my fiancée doesn't run out on me." He held on to Emma's hand as he sat on the gurney, his legs dangling over the side.

Emma smiled sadly. "But don't you see? It's over. You don't have to protect me anymore. I can go back to Grand Forks."

"Is that what you want?" he asked.

Her head dipped and she stared at her feet, which were up to her ankles in snow. "You said no guarantees."

"Yeah, well, I was wrong."

His mother walked up to him where he sat and laid a hand on his shoulder. "Dante."

"Just a minute, Mother."

"No, really, if you want to do this right, take this." She removed the glove from his hand and one of hers. Then she slipped the diamond engagement ring off her finger.

The ring his father had given her when he'd asked her to marry him over thirty years ago. She pressed it into his bare palm. "Now do it right."

Dante glanced down at the ring, a flood of emotions rising up his throat. When he turned to Emma, he knew what he had to do.

Emma stared at the ring in his hand, her eyes wet with tears, her head shaking back and forth. "Don't. I don't need your pity."

"Pity? You think I'd get down on my knees in the snow because I pity you?" Dante slid off the gurney and dropped to one knee. "Emma Jennings, in the short time we've been together, we've been through a lot. You've saved my life more than once and you've shown me that I have so much more life to look forward to and I can't think of anyone I'd rather spend it with. Will you marry me?"

Emma's knees buckled and she dropped to the ground beside him. "Are you sure this is what you want?"

"I've never been more sure." He took her hand in his and removed her glove. "Marry me."

Tears slipped down her cheek even as snowflakes clung to her eyelashes and she nodded. He slipped the ring on her finger, feeling happiness bubble up inside him. He rose to his feet and lifted her up in his arms. "Mom, Pierce, Tuck, Maddox, meet my fiancée, the beautiful Emma Jennings. We're getting married."

"I thought you were already engaged," Pierce said.

Dante grinned and hugged Emma close. "Brother, in case you didn't know it already, it's all about the ring."

Chapter Seventeen

Emma's pulse pounded and her hands shook as she stood in the hallway of the ranch house, wearing Amelia's beautiful wedding dress, awaiting her cue. When the strains of Mendelssohn's "Wedding March" blared over the sound system, she stepped forward.

Maddox, dressed in a black tuxedo, offered her his arm and walked her into the living room toward the big stone fireplace at the center, where Dante stood with his brothers on the left and his brothers' wives on the right, and the justice of the peace they'd brought in from Medora in the center.

Christmas morning was bright with sunshine and it promised to be the best day of Emma's life. Her heart was so full, she could barely breathe. It had all happened so fast. The entire Thunder Horse clan had pulled together to make the wedding happen in an incredibly short amount of time.

This was it. She was about to become Mrs. Thunder Horse.

Dante stood tall, his gunshot wound bandaged and hidden beneath the sleeve of his tuxedo. He'd combed his dark hair back and his green eyes flashed when she'd appeared.

Amelia sat in a front row chair with Sean sitting to

her right and what seemed like half of the Medora citizens seated in the other chairs filling the room. A huge Christmas tree stood in the corner, lights shining and a bright star crowning the top.

Through the window she could see fat white snowflakes falling and frost making pretty designs on the glass. The day couldn't have been more beautiful and the man she was about to marry more perfect.

Emma walked toward him wondering if this was all a dream and she'd wake up in her apartment cold and alone. But when Dante smiled, his green eyes shiny, she knew it was real.

He held out his hand and she took it, knowing he'd always be there for her.

"Emma Jennings, do you take Dante to be your husband? To love, honor and cherish so long as you both shall live?"

Emma spoke in clear voice, never more certain in her life of her answer, "I do."

"And, Dante, do you take Emma to be your wife—"

Dante lifted her hands and held them tight. "I do, to love honor and cherish so long as we both shall live. Can we wrap this up? I want to kiss my wife."

Laughter rose from the crowd as Dante did just that, kissing Emma in front of everyone. When he finally let her up for air, her cheeks were warm and she couldn't stop smiling.

The justice of the peace shrugged. "They said yes. Folks, meet Mr. and Mrs. Dante Thunder Horse. May the Great Spirit bless you both."

"You heard the man, the last Thunder Horse brother is hitched," Tuck said. "Our family is growing."

"Yeah, and it's about to get even bigger." Maddox slid an arm around Katya and grinned. "Katya's pregnant."

Tuck whooped. "I don't know how you found time, gallivanting all over the globe. And don't that just beat all?" He lifted his Lily in his arms and held her up. "Lily's going to be a sister. Julia and I are expecting our second."

"Uh—" Pierce raised a hand "—I was saving it until after the wedding, but Roxy and I are expecting, too."

Amelia clapped her hands to her mouth, her eyes alight. "All those grandbabies. I am truly blessed."

Everyone turned to Emma and Dante.

Tuck spoke. "Well? What are you two waiting for? Get busy so our kids can all grow up together."

"You heard them, Wife. Let's get crackin'." Dante swung Emma up in his arms and marched her out of the room.

Her heart swelled with the love she felt for this man and his entire family. Being married to a Thunder Horse was going to be everything she ever dreamed of and more. The Great Spirit had truly blessed them.

* * * * *

COMING SOON!

We really hope you enjoyed reading this book. If you're looking for more romance, be sure to head to the shops when new books are available on

Thursday 13th December

To see which titles are coming soon, please visit **millsandboon.co.uk**

MILLS & BOON

LET'S TALK

Romance

For exclusive extracts, competitions
and special offers, find us online:

- f facebook.com/millsandboon
- 🐦 @MillsandBoon
- 📷 @MillsandBoonUK

Get in touch on 01413 063232

For all the latest titles coming soon, visit
millsandboon.co.uk/nextmonth